The Club Series book six

THE REVELATION

Josh and Kat Part II

Lauren Rowe

Chapter 1
Kat

The door to Jonas and Sarah's suite closes behind Josh's back and I look down at Josh's laptop, holding my breath with excitement. This is it. I can't believe I'm finally gonna read Josh's application to The Club, after all this build-up. My chest is tight. My stomach is in knots. What on earth did that man write that's made him so skittish about revealing it to me? Well, I guess there's only one way to find out:

Name?

"Joshua William Faraday," he writes. Oh, I didn't know Josh's middle name is William. For some reason, seeing his full name makes my heart flutter.

With this application, you will be required to submit three separate forms of identification. The Club maintains a strict "No Aliases Policy" for admission. You may, however, use aliases during interactions with other Club members, at your discretion.

"OK," he writes.

Age?

"29," he writes.

I stop and think. Josh is thirty. I wonder when he had his birthday? I'd love to know his zodiac sign. Damn, it sure would suck donkey balls if it turned out we were cosmically incompatible.

Provide a brief physical description of yourself.

"I'm 6'1, 190 lbs. I've got brown hair and blue eyes and tattoos on my torso and arms. I prefer not to talk about the meanings of my tattoos at length, so please tell whoever gets assigned to me not to ask about them.

"I work pretty hard at keeping fit," he continues. "I'm a big believer that a man only gets one chance at a first impression, so I try to make mine count, every time. Just to be clear: I'm not applying for membership to The Club because I have some sort of inferiority complex about my appearance (I don't) or because I can't attract women on my own (I can)."

I can't help but smile. Even when Josh is being kind of douche-y, he's sexy as hell to me.

With this application, you will be required to submit three recent photographs of yourself to your intake agent. Please include the following: one headshot, one full-body shot revealing your physique, and one shot wearing something you'd typically wear out in a public location. These photographs shall be maintained under the strictest confidentiality.

Oh, this I gotta see. I scroll down, assuming Josh's photos will be attached to the end of his application, but they're not there. I scan the top of the document, looking for some indication of where I can find his pictures—but, nope. There's nothing. Goddammit! I grab my phone.

Josh answers my call immediately. "Wow, that was fast," he says. "I'm only just now walking into the casino."

"Where are your photos?"

"My photos?"

"Yeah, the three photos you submitted with your application."

"Oh, my *photos*." He pauses. "Why do you want them? You already know exactly what I look like."

"I just want to see them."

"But you've already seen every inch of me—you've seen my YOLO'd ass, for Chrissakes." He snickers. "Not to mention my balls."

I join him in snickering. "Up close and personal."

He snickers again.

"But I still wanna see your photos."

He sighs. "How 'bout this? I'll come back up there and let you take three photos of me any which way you want. We'll have a photo shoot, just you and me, baby."

"Ooh, sounds fun—I'll definitely take a rain check on that offer. But I still wanna see the photos."

He grumbles. "But *why*?"

"Because I wanna see what photos you thought would best represent yourself to perverts in a sex club."

There's a long pause. "You're such a fucking pain in the ass, you know that? A terrorist and a colossal pain in the ass."

"I told you—I'm a *Scorpio*. We're extremely focused and we also have a disproportionate sense of entitlement. Plus, I gave you my three photos—a deal's a deal."

He laughs. "Oh my God, those photos, Kat."

"You liked them?"

"I *loved* them. The one of you in your undies was so hot—and then I practically pissed myself laughing at the one of you pretending to barf over the toilet. You're so funny."

"Thank you. You're pretty funny yourself—but funny ain't gonna get you off the hook, dude. Those photos are part of your application, which means they're part of your promise."

He grunts. "*Fine.* Are you familiar with Macs?"

"Yeah, I've got one—from your brother, actually."

"My brother gave you a Mac?"

"Yeah. To replace the one The Club stole from me."

"That was awfully nice of him—I didn't know Jonas knew how to be nice."

"Yeah. He's been super nice to me. Okay, quit stalling. Where are the photos?"

He groans. "*Fine.* Go to 'Finder' and click on 'Pictures' on the left side of the screen."

"Yep. Okay."

"And now do you see the folder..." Josh says, but I don't hear the rest of his sentence because something has caught my attention on Josh's laptop screen: a folder labeled "Sick Fuck." Well, jeez, with a name like that, the folder might as well be named "Open me, Kat!"

"Do you see it?" Josh says.

"Mmm hmm," I say, clicking on the "Sick Fuck" folder.

Oh my God. I'm looking at a bunch of photos of naked women—lots and lots of naked women—all of them blonde, all of them gorgeous, and all of them striking poses like porn stars.

"Kat? Are you still there?"

"Yeah, I'm here," I say, scrolling through the photos. There's probably close to twenty different women here. "Josh, who are all the blondes?"

"What?" he asks, his voice suddenly tight.

"The porn stars in the folder labeled 'Sick Fuck'?"

"Jesus Fucking Christ! Get out of there, Kat! That's personal!"

3

"Who are they?"

"I didn't give you permission to look through my private stuff. *Get the fuck out of there right now.* Jesus!"

"Oh, waah, waah. So you like porn—you're such a pervert." I laugh, but he doesn't join me. "Come on. Just tell me who they are. It's no big whoop."

"This is a total breach of trust. Absolutely inexcusable."

I ignore his outrage. It's an extremely effective tactic I've learned from observing my brothers over the years: remain calm in the face of indignation and then deny, deny, deny any and all wrongdoing until the person angry with you simply forgets what they're mad about.

"Are these photos off the Internet, or are they women you actually know?" I ask calmly.

There's a long silence. "This is total bullshit," he grumbles, but it's clear his outrage is already beginning to soften. "I want to lodge a formal complaint," he says.

I laugh. "With whom?"

"With... the Common Decency Police."

"Okay. Duly noted. Complaint lodged."

"Because you *suck*."

"Yes, I do, actually, as we both know very well. And if you ever want me to do it again, then answer my question."

Out of nowhere, his fury roars back to life. "Oh, fuck no," he bellows. "Let me set you straight about something right here and now: I do *not* tolerate any form of sexual extortion in a relationship. That's an absolute deal-breaker with me. You wanna suck my dick? Great; then suck it. You don't wanna suck it? Then don't. But don't use sex as a weapon to manipulate me. I fucking *hate* that."

My heart lurches into my throat—and not because Josh is chastising me—I don't care about that—but because Josh just said he doesn't tolerate any form of sexual extortion *in a relationship*. Are Josh and I *in a relationship*?

"Jeez," I manage to say. "Overreact much?"

"I'm not *overreacting*," Josh replies. "I absolutely *hate* that shit."

"Okay, okay. Jeez-*us*. I'm sorry. I'll never again say, 'If you want me to suck your dick, then fill-in-the-blank.' Happy?"

"Yes. Thank you. I hate that shit."

"Fine. Got it. But I must say I find your whole speech awfully

4

ironic considering I used sexual extortion to get you to give me your application in the first place."

He pauses. "Hey, wait a minute—you *did*, didn't you? Well, that was kinda shitty of you."

"Hey, whatever works."

There's a long beat during which I'm smiling from ear to ear.

"So," I say. "You still haven't answered my question, Playboy: Who are all the blonde playmates?"

He makes a sound of frustration. "I was hoping you'd forgotten about that."

"No chance. I'm a Scorpio. We hold grudges. So who are they?"

"You don't have permission to be snooping around in that folder, Kat. Click out."

I don't reply to him—I'm too busy looking through the folder.

"Hello? Madame Terrorist? Did you hear me? Exit the folder. You're trespassing."

"Yeah, I heard you. And I would totally follow your instruction, I really would—but the thing is, I'm having somewhat of a *conundrum*."

"And what is that?"

"It's kind of like a dilemma."

"Have I done something to give you the impression I've got the vocabulary of a sixth-grader? I know what a *conundrum* is—I'm asking what is *your* conundrum, specifically?"

I seriously can't wipe the smile off my face. "Well, on the one hand," I say, "I really want to respect your request. I *really, really* do, because I'm actually a fairly nice person, despite the way I tend to behave around you, and also because I think you're probably right: it was very, very naughty of me to go through your personal stuff without permission."

"Thank you. And on the other hand?"

"Well, on the other hand, I really, really like being *naughty*."

Josh makes a sexy sound. "*Oh*. Well, that *is* quite a *conundrum*. What on earth are you gonna do about it?"

"I dunno—I haven't decided yet. Maybe I'll just look through your pervy blonde-porn-star folder while I figure it out." I scroll through the photos again, my smile hurting my cheeks. "These women all look the same, Josh," I say, still going through the photos. "Looks like you've got a *type,* huh?"

5

He audibly shrugs. "I like what I like."

"Who are they?"

He pauses briefly and then exhales. "They're just women I've met."

"*Met*? I'm guessing you've done more than *meet* these girls."

He doesn't reply.

"Have you *slept* with all of these women?"

"So now you're slut-shaming me?"

"No. I'm the last person in the world who would ever slut-shame anyone."

"You do realize the whole point of your application to me was to make me feel safe enough to reveal my inner-most perverted thoughts to you? You're supposed to be luring me into *emotional intimacy*, Kat."

"Oh crap. That's right. Shoot. I should have warned you: I suck at emotional intimacy. I'm working on it, though, I swear."

"You're never gonna break down my walls now," Josh says playfully.

"Damn. Oh well." I audibly shrug and he laughs. "So who took all these photos? Was it you?"

"Nope."

"No? Oh, I thought you were gonna say yes. Did you take *some* of them?"

"So we're playing a game of Perverted Twenty Questions, are we?"

"Yeah. Isn't it *fun*?"

"No."

"Come on. I've still got nineteen questions to go."

"Nineteen? Ha! More like ten. And that's generous."

"Okay ten. Did you personally take *any* of these photos?"

He exhales loudly. "Just one."

"Oh, now that's an interesting answer. Not what I expected. I thought it'd be all or nothing." I suddenly remember Sarah saying Oksana photographs every girl in The Club. "By George, I think I've got it," I say. "Are these the women you slept with in The Club?"

Josh sighs loudly. "Correct. All but two of them."

"Well, now I'm confused again. You mean all but two of these women were in The Club—or there are two Clubbers missing from this folder?"

"Your mind is a scary place, Kat. You're like Henn but in a totally different context. You're a man-hacker."

I laugh. "Thank you. Now answer the question, please."

He exhales audibly. "Every woman from The Club is there—*plus* there are two non-Clubbers in the folder, too."

"Ah. Interesting. Two bonus-women from real life. This just gets more and more intriguing. Which ones are the non-Clubbers and why'd you put them in the folder with all the Clubbers?"

"Aren't you out of questions yet?"

"Nope." I pause. "I've still got eight to go."

He scoffs.

"You personally took *one* of the non-Clubbers' photos—not *both* of them?"

"Correct."

"Hmm. So that means one of the non-Clubbers *sent* you her photo?"

"Correct. You're now officially out of questions."

"No way. I've still got at least eight left."

"Eight? You started with ten and you've asked like fifty."

"I've been asking *sub*-questions to questions, Josh—sub-questions don't count as full questions."

He grumbles.

"So, come on, which one of these pretty ladies was the one non-Clubber you personally photographed? And why'd you put her in the Sick Fuck folder with all the others?"

He pauses. "No comment."

"Aw, come on."

"You've got my application. That's what I promised you—nothing more. Perverted Twenty Questions is now officially over."

"Aw. Not fair."

"It's totally fair—and if not, then too bad. Life isn't fair."

"Just tell me why you have all these photos and then I'll drop it. I promise."

Josh exhales. "Okay, Madame Terrorist. Fine." He mutters something to himself under his breath. "I requested a specific type of girl in my application, and so The Club emailed me photos of women they'd selected for me to make sure they were exactly what I wanted. And at the end of my membership-month, I didn't know what the fuck to do with all the photos so I put them into a folder."

"And labeled it 'Sick Fuck.'"

He doesn't reply.

"And you didn't have any inkling these women were hookers before Jonas told you?"

Josh pauses. "I was pretty specific about what I wanted in my application, so I figured The Club likely made some kind of special arrangement to deliver on my wishes—but I didn't know for sure. Just because a woman is willing to meet a rich guy in a hotel room and fulfill his sick-fuck-fantasies doesn't necessarily make her a hooker, does it?"

I consider that bit of logic. "No," I finally say. "Not necessarily. Especially when he looks like you."

"Thank you. But, honestly, I really didn't care one way or the other if the women were being paid on the side—I just didn't wanna know about it. All I was trying to do was escape reality for a month—I wasn't looking for some sort of deep soul connection."

"So you asked for blondes?"

"Kat," he says softly. "You've got my application. Just read it. No more questions."

The earnest tone of his voice has thrown me. I thought we were bantering, and now, suddenly, he seems totally sincere. "Okay. I'm sorry."

"It's okay."

I wait a beat. "But can I ask one more teeny tiny itty bitty question? In the name of emotional intimacy?"

He chuckles despite himself. "What?" he asks.

"Thank you. Wow, we're *killing* the emotional intimacy thing, Josh. We're emotionally intimate beasts."

He chuckles again. "This isn't emotional intimacy, Kat—this is just plain torture."

"I'm almost positive they're one and the same thing," I say. "Though I can't be sure."

He laughs a full laugh, which I take as a good sign. "Okay, Madame Interrogator, what's your last question?"

"Do you typically only sleep with blondes—or just in The Club? And is it sex with *blondes* that makes you a sick fuck?"

He pauses for a moment. "That's two questions."

"Sorry. Couldn't help myself."

"Okay. Here's the deal: I'm gonna tell you the answer to these two questions and then this interrogation is officially done."

"Okay."

"I don't *only* sleep with blondes. I've been with women of all shapes, sizes, colors, ethnicities, and hair colors, and I've enjoyed them all. In fact, I've enjoyed them all *immensely.*"

"Thanks. Little more info than I needed."

"And, no, I don't have some bizarre complex whereby I think sleeping with a beautiful blonde woman somehow transforms me into a sick fuck. Yes, I specifically requested *blondes* in The Club because The Club was about fantasy-fulfillment and escape from reality, and, call me unimaginative or trite, but when I shop at the fantasy store, at least for purposes of fulfilling the fantasies I specifically asked for in The Club, that's what I want—a classic blonde. Why? I don't know. It's just the way I'm wired—I definitely have a *type.*" He makes a sound that emphatically signals he's done talking.

"Thank you," I say smoothly, scrolling through the photos again. "Yep, I'd agree you definitely have a type." I snort. "Actually, they all look just like..." I abruptly stop speaking. Holy shit.

There's a long beat.

"Yeah, Kat," Josh finally says. He lets out a loud puff of air. "They look just like *you.*"

He's read my mind. I swallow hard.

"Less attractive versions of you, of course," he continues softly. "They're all wannabe-Kats. You're what my brother refers to as the 'divine original.'"

I'm tingling all over. "The '*divine original*'?" I breathe. "What's that?"

He lets out a long groan. "I can't believe I just said that. It's this Plato-thing Jonas is always babbling about. Forget I ever said it—I wanna gouge my eyes out every time my brother mentions it and now it's me who's saying it. Gah."

I press my phone into my ear, my breathing shallow. "What does it mean, Josh?" I ask softly. "Whatever it means, it's making me tingle all over."

"It just means you're the original template and everyone else is a knock-off." He lets out a long sigh. "Like, you know, you're the authentic Gucci bag and everyone else is one of those counterfeits they sell on the sidewalk in New York."

I pause, letting that sink in. I've never been to New York,

actually, but his metaphor is still perfectly understandable to me. "So does that mean I make you a sick fuck more than anyone else?"

He growls with exasperation. "You don't make me a sick fuck— *no one* makes me a sick fuck. Someone I cared about once *called* me a sick fuck and I was pissed as hell about it when I named that folder, that's all. I was, you know, flipping that person the bird when I named that folder."

While Josh has been talking, I've been leafing through the photos. There's one girl I keep going back to again and again. She's not working the lens or *trying* to be sexy like the others—in fact, the woman is clearly put off by posing for the photo—and her shyness about the whole thing makes her all the more alluring. Suddenly, there's no doubt in my mind this shy girl is the non-Clubber Josh photographed himself—and, if my Scooby Doo senses are right, she's also the one who pissed him off by calling him a "sick fuck."

"What about the shy one?" I ask.

"The shy one?"

"The one who looks mortified to be posing for a naked photo? She looks pretty divine-original-ish to me. Is she the one you photographed yourself?" I swallow hard. "Is she your ex-girlfriend?"

He doesn't reply.

"Did she call you a sick fuck?"

"Click out of there, Kat," he says softly, a stiffness overtaking his tone. "Interrogation over."

My skin erupts in goose bumps. He's not kidding around. Shoot. He sounds genuinely upset.

"Okay, I'm out," I say, exiting the folder.

"I'm gonna go," he says evenly. "Happy reading."

"No, *wait*. Please, Josh. *Wait*." The angry edge in his voice has made my chest tighten. Clearly, I've pushed too hard. "I'm sorry, Josh. Sometimes I take things too far. It's a major flaw of mine."

Josh chuckles despite himself.

I bite my lip, smiling into the phone. "I'm sorry—I didn't mean any harm."

"Says the woman with a bomb strapped to her chest." He lets out a long exhale. "Just read my goddamned application, okay? I can't take it anymore. The anticipation's killing me. Just read it and make your decision already."

"My *decision*?"

He pauses. "Whether to sleep with me or not," he finally says.

"Oh yeah, that's right," I say. "Well, a girl's gotta know if she's gonna wake up chained to a goat."

"No, a *donkey.*"

"Oh yeah. That's right. A girl's gotta know these things."

"You never know what might happen with me. I'm kind of a sick fuck."

"According to whom?"

He doesn't reply.

"The Shy Girl?"

He pauses. "Yeah."

"That's Emma?"

"Yup."

"Well, Josh, I haven't even read your application yet, and I can already tell you Emma was full of shit."

He lets out a yelp of surprise.

I clear my throat. "So back to the reason I called in the first place," I say. "Where are the three photos you submitted with your application?"

"Well, strangely enough, Kat, they're in a folder marked 'Club Application Photos.' Imagine that."

"Oh. Well, gosh. That makes a whole lot more sense than putting them into a folder called 'Sick Fuck.'"

Josh sighs. "Hey, can I just come up there? I thought I wanted to stay as far away as possible while you were reading my application, but all of a sudden I'd rather just sit next to you while you read it and watch your facial expressions."

My heart leaps. "Are you by any chance planning to *distract* me again, Joshua William Faraday?"

"Maybe."

I smile broadly into the phone. "Yeah, I think that's a great idea," I say. "Get your YOLO'd-ass up here, Playboy. We'll read the damned thing together, line by perverted line—and *maybe,* if you're extra nice to me, I'll let you distract me again."

I can hear his smile again.

"I'll be right there," he says.

11

Chapter 2
Kat

The minute Josh and I hang up from our call, I scroll through his blonde-girl "Sick Fuck" folder again, this time more slowly than before. These are some spectacularly gorgeous women here—and he thinks I'm some sort of 'ideal form' of all of them? Surely, he's just flattering me. I mean, come on.

I stop scrolling.

Holy crap.

I recognize one of the women in the folder. I think she's a well-known model—like, literally on Victoria's Secret ads and the covers of fashion magazines. Yep, I'm sure of it. Her name is Bridgette something. Is she the 'bisexual supermodel' Josh said he turned down? She's gotta be the second non-Clubber in the folder.

I look at my watch. Gah. Josh should be here any minute. I click out of the "Sick Fuck" folder, intending to take a quick peek at his three photos before he arrives, but on a sudden impulse, I find myself dragging the entire "Sick Fuck" folder into the trashcan and pressing "Empty trash." Oops. My finger must have slipped.

And now back to my actual mission. I click into the folder marked "Club Application Photos" and open the first of three images. It's a headshot. Josh is smiling and looking as charismatic and confident as ever. Oh man, those eyes. I could sit and stare at them all day long. He's gorgeous.

I click on the next photo. It's classic Josh Faraday. He's in a perfectly tailored, blue designer suit, looking like an ad for Hugo Boss or cologne. Yummy.

I click on the third photo and... *ka-boom*. My ovaries explode like two little nuclear bombs. Josh is completely nude in this third shot, every inch of his ripped and muscled—*and erect*—body on full display—and, oh my fuck, the shit-eating grin on his face is so unapologetic, it instantly makes my blood boil with desire. Holy crappola, as Sarah would say, I'm short-circuiting at the sight of him.

Without even thinking about it, I click into Josh's email account, address an email to myself attaching Josh's smoking-hot-bad-boy-with-a-gigantic-boner-selfie, and press send. Zowie, as Sarah also likes to say, that sucker's definitely gonna inspire countless future orgasms.

Hey, as long as I'm sending myself stuff from Josh's computer, I figure I might as well send myself his application, too, right? That way, if he distracts me again when he gets up here, I'll be able to read it later from the comfort of my own bed.

Just as I press "send" on my second email to myself, a notification message flashes across the upper right corner of Josh's screen: he's got an email from someone named "Jennifer LeMonde" with the subject line "Hey, Cutie!"

My stomach clenches.

My lip snarls involuntarily.

Jen.

Oh, God, I shouldn't do it—I know I shouldn't. But show me a woman in my exact shoes who wouldn't read that goddamned email and I'll show you a woman with no pulse or vagina—or, at the very least, no balls.

I open the email.

"Josh!" Jennifer LeMonde writes. "OMFG! I'm so bummed you didn't come to NYC with me. My mom's show was amaaaaaaaaaazing. You would have loooooooooooved it. Critics are saying she's a shoo-in for a Tony. And the party afterwards was REDONK. You should have seen the A-listers who showed up! I've attached a pic of Mom and me at the after-party. (Mom says hi, btw—she totally remembers you from that time we all stayed at our house in Aspen.)

"I wanted to send you a quick note to thank you for calling me after Reed's party. I was pretty bummed at how everything went down that night, to be honest. I'm really glad we had a chance to talk so you could clear everything up for me.

"I've been thinking about what you said and I totally understand where you're coming from. I feel the exact same way. So if you're ready to chill with someone who's not gonna explode like a fricking grenade all over you like The Jealous Bitch (can you say drama?? OMG!), then let's hang out again. I'm totally up for what you suggested. We'll just hang out and have some fun and see where it leads. No pressure. Nothing serious.

"So, anyway, next weekend is my birthday (the big 2-9!) and my mom's letting me use our house in the Hamptons to celebrate. I'm gonna invite a bunch of friends and I really want you to come. No drama. Just FUN FUN FUN! It would be the best birthday present EVER if you'd come and hang out (and hopefully make me scream again!! Heehee!).

"I know how much you like my 'pretty titties' (LOL!) so I'm attaching a special pic just for you. It's just a little something to tide you over 'til you can come see them in person (and motorboat them again if you want! LMFAO!). Thanks again for explaining everything to me when we talked. We're defo on the same page. No relationship. Nothing serious. I'm totally down with that plan. XOXOXOXO Jen."

I have never felt this capable of murder in my entire life.

Holy I Wanna Beat the Living Shit Out of Her, Batman.

And Then I Wanna Cut Off His Balls and Roast Them Over the Burning Embers of His Fucking House, Batman. And Then I Want To Eat Them In Between Two Graham Crackers.

I'm gritting my teeth so hard, they're about to crumble like shards of bleu cheese in my mouth. I'm 'The Jealous Bitch,' huh? Did Jen coin that cute little nickname for me, or did Josh help her come up with it—perhaps during their after-party phone conversation? Was that phone conversation when Josh "suggested" they get together again so he could "motorboat" Jen's "pretty titties" *again*?

Why the hell did Josh call Jen after Reed's party? He told me he wasn't the least bit interested in her. Did he rush back to his room for a little phone sex after washing the barf off his shoes and my hair and putting me to bed?

I should click out of this email, I really should—that would be the self-preserving thing to do—but instead I torture myself and click on the first photo attached to Jen's email.

I shriek.

What the holy hell? Jen's mom is *Gabrielle LeMonde*? I blink rapidly, my brain overloading. Gabrielle LeMonde is a national treasure—an icon! I've seen every one of her frickin' movies—and not just the comedies, either!—the really boring ones in which she spoke in a spot-on British accent, too! What. The. *Hell*?

Well, this sure sheds light on why Josh hooked up with Jen in the first place. If I were a twenty-three-year-old guy with a huge dick, I'd have fucked Gabrielle LeMonde's daughter too, just to be able to say I did—especially if she had a body like Jen's. And Jesus, now it makes total sense that Jen pals around with movie stars like Isabel Randolph. Good lord, Jen's entire contacts list must be a who's-who of Hollywood's young elite.

My head is spinning. I feel like I'm gonna barf. It's suddenly hitting me like a ton of bricks that Josh is literally one of the world's most eligible bachelors—like *literally*. Holy shit. Before this moment, Josh was Sarah's boyfriend's brother—his gorgeous and rich brother—his hilarious and well-dressed brother—his smoking hot and sexy brother—his brother who arranged for me to stay in Vegas *and* keep my job, too—his brother who fucked me so brilliantly, I blacked out there for a minute—but, still, just a human-brother-dude who presumably puts his pants on one leg at a time (and who presumably stows his donkey-dick in one of those pant legs before zipping up).

But now, out of nowhere, it turns out Josh is some quasi-celebrity-god among men who lives in an alternate universe populated by world-famous actresses and their spawn? And Victoria's Secret supermodels? Oh, and freaking Red Card Riot, too? What the heck? Who is this Most Interesting Man in the World who could hop a cross-country flight on a whim for no other reason than to attend the birthday party of a fuck-buddy who happens to be the daughter of Gabrielle LeMonde? Gah! Insanity.

My stomach flips over.

I'm usually a confident girl—probably more so than the average Jane, if I'm being honest—but how could I ever be so cocky as to think a guy like that would ever pick *me* out of literally *anyone* on the planet to choose from? I roll my eyes even though I'm sitting here alone. I've always had a pretty high opinion of myself, truthfully (which isn't something I usually admit out loud), but all of a sudden, in comparison to the women who populate Josh's rarified world, I feel shockingly average. Not to mention, quite possibly, really *gullible*, too. Has Josh just been selling me a line of bullshit? Does he make *every* girl feel special the way I've been feeling with him? Have I been a fool?

Oh, jeez, my eyes are filling with tears. Why do I suddenly feel like I'm standing at Garrett Bennett's door all over again, about to get annihilated? I take a deep breath to steady myself.

The healthy choice would be to click out of Jen's email right now. It's making me doubt Josh and I don't want to do that. He's been nothing but incredible toward me. Generous. Attentive. Affectionate. Passionate. I'm acting crazy right now. So what if Jen's mom is Gabrielle LeMonde? That doesn't change anything. Why is that sending me into a tailspin? I should shut Josh's laptop and stop this right now.

But I don't.

In fact, I do the opposite: I open the second picture attached to Jen's email.

Holy Oh-No-She-Didn't, Batman.

If I felt sick after seeing the picture of Jen with her movie-star mom, then I feel terminally ill after seeing this second photo.

It's a naked selfie of Jen. She's smiling broadly and pushing her "pretty titties" up toward the camera—obviously inviting Josh to "motorboat" them "again."

My eyes prick with tears. Is Jen a pathetically desperate girl who's pursuing a hot guy after he's clearly told her to get lost? Or, to the contrary, is she a girl who's merely going after a guy who slept with her and then continued *encouraging* her? Josh told me he's not interested in Jen—and yet he called her after Reed's party. Why'd he do that? And what did he "suggest" to her when they spoke? Suddenly, I don't know what's what anymore.

My heart is racing. I wipe my eyes. I never cry and I'm not gonna start now. Hell no. It's so unlike me to feel this jealous and insecure. God, I hate myself right now. I'm acting like a freak and a puss and a lunatic. I need to detach. I need to stop caring. Josh Faraday isn't my boyfriend (though I admit I want him to be), and I'm not his girlfriend. I've got no right to feel this way. The man can do what he wants.

No, he can't. He's mine, goddammit. Mine.

I slam Josh's laptop shut and set it on the table. I've got to get the hell out of here. Josh will be here any minute to "distract" me from his application and I need to pull my shit together before then—because right now I feel like I'm going to fly completely off the handle and say a million things I'm gonna regret.

I stand to leave—just as the door of the suite bursts open.

Josh bounds into the room. "Hey, Party Girl with a Hyphen," he says, holding up a condom packet playfully. "Can I interest you in a little *distraction* from your reading?"

I stalk straight past Josh toward the front door, my eyes burning and my mouth clamped shut.

"Kat?"

I march to the door and fling it open like I'm trying to take the damned thing off its hinges.

"Oh shit," Josh says. "You read my application without me?" His voice is pure anguish. "Goddammit, Kat. Lemme explain. This is exactly why I didn't want you to read that stupid thing in the first place."

Chapter 3
Josh

"Kat, come on!" I shout at her back, but she keeps marching down the hallway toward the penthouse's private elevator, her arms swinging wildly. *Déjà fucking vu.* How many times am I gonna have to chase this goddamned terrorist down a fucking hallway? "Oh, come on, Kat. It wasn't *that* bad."

But she just keeps on marching. She pounds on the call button for the private elevator and crosses her arms, her back to me.

"You can't possibly be *this* upset. What the hell?"

She whirls around and I'm shocked to see hot tears streaming down her cheeks.

Panic floods me. My application made her *cry*? Shit. I've obviously grossly miscalculated the situation. I'm floored. "Kat," I blurt, my chest tightening. "I know everything I wrote in that application came off as douche-y and angry and fucked-up, but the truth is I was just heartbroken when I wrote all that shit." Oh God, the words are tumbling out of my mouth. "I'd just gotten out of a three-year relationship that didn't end well," I ramble, "and I won't go into detail about everything that happened, but trust me, I had some shit to work out." I take a deep breath. "I was devastated, to be perfectly honest—I felt like there was something deeply wrong with me, and..." My heart is racing. I swallow hard. "For reasons I don't wanna go into, there was no way for me to do any of that stuff I wrote about with my girlfriend. And that was okay, *of course*, because I never would have pushed her to do anything she wasn't comfortable with—*never*—but when we broke up—well, actually, when she *cheated* on me instead of doing me the courtesy of actually breaking up with me—I figured, 'Well, fuck it. YOLO. Life throws you lemons, make lemonade.' So I joined The Club and rode a month's worth of Mickey Mouse roller coasters so I could pull my shit together and move on. And I don't regret any of it because it actually worked—I totally moved on and now I'm perfectly fine." Shit. I'm rambling. I'm incoherent. I'm out of breath. Fuck. I force myself to stop talking.

Kat's tears have dried up. She's stone-faced and looking at me like I've got fingers growing out of my head.

"To be perfectly honest," I continue, even though I know I should shut the fuck up, "I didn't expect you to be so upset by what I wrote. I admit I didn't wanna give you my application, but it wasn't because I was *ashamed* of what I asked for, it was because I didn't wanna have to explain all this shit about Emma to you. I'm not ashamed about The Club, Kat. I was *single*. It was one month of my life. No one was hurt—far from it." I shift my weight. Shit, I think I'm digging myself an even deeper hole. "Frankly," I continue, deciding the best defense is a good offense, "I'm shocked you're so upset. Now that I've gotten to know you—or at least I *thought* I'd gotten to know you—I actually thought you'd be pretty understanding about everything I wrote—or, at least, about most of it." My voice cracks, despite my best efforts to sound calm and collected. I rub my forehead. "I honestly thought you'd maybe even get off on some of it."

Her eyes are wide.

The bell dings on the private elevator behind Kat's back. The doors open and then close—but, thankfully, Kat doesn't move from her spot in the hallway.

What the fuck happened to the woman who wrote me that awesome 'application' to the 'Josh Faraday Club'? The woman who felt crushed when some asshole called her a slut and said she wasn't 'marriage material'? Where's the girl who admitted she has a shitload of crazy-elaborate sexual fantasies, for fuck's sake? I thought my perverted shit would be right up her alley, I really did. And where the fuck is the incredible girl who rode a Sybian 'til she squirted and literally passed out? Because I can't imagine *that* girl reacting to my application with *tears*. I run my hand through my hair. Shit. I feel like I'm reliving that last, horrible, blindsiding conversation with Emma all over again.

"Just please tell me why you're crying," I say, trying to keep my voice from sounding panicked. "I truly thought you'd understand about my application."

"Josh," Kat begins, but then she pauses.

My stomach twists with anticipation. Here it comes. I brace myself.

"I haven't read your application," she says softly. "You've misunderstood me."

I close my eyes. Oh, how I wish I could stuff every word I just said back into my stupid goddamned mouth. I open my eyes. Shit.

"I started reading it, yes," she continues. "But then I called you when I got to the part about your three photos, and then I saw your 'Sick Fuck' folder and—oh, yeah, bee tee dubs, I permanently deleted that folder, sorry, I can be kind of impulsive sometimes." She takes a deep breath. "And then I went into your email account to send myself that naked photo of you with the gigantic boner—oh, and I also sent myself your application, too, by the way—sorry if that pisses you off, but, whatever, I am what I am—and, anyway, while I was in your email account, you got an incoming email." Her lip curls with unbridled disgust. "And *that's* what I'm crying about, Josh: the freaking *email.*"

I can barely breathe. "What email?"

Her eyes water and she wipes them. "An email from Jen—your blast from the past."

The hair on my neck stands on end.

"And let me just say this," Kat says, her voice edged with barely contained rage. "If a woman is totally into you and you keep stringing her along, even though you're not into her, then at some point you're not a *playboy*, you're just a flat-out *prick.*"

"*What?*"

"Unless, of course, you *are* into her and you've been peddling me a line of total bullshit this whole time—in which case, you're not just a *prick*, you're also a flat-out *liar.*"

"What the *fuck* are you talking about, Kat?" I ask, dumbfounded. "What did Jen say in her email?" I pull my phone out from my pocket and frantically scroll through my inbox. And there it is—an email from Jen. I quickly read it, doing my best to see Jen's message through Kat's (batshit-crazy) eyes. "Oh, Jesus," I stammer. "No, no, no, Jen *completely* misunderstood me," I blurt. "I called to tell her I'm not interested in her—I swear to God—that's what I told her."

"Well, Jen sure seems to think you called to 'suggest' something along the lines of you 'motorboating' her 'pretty titties'—*again.*" Her nostrils flare. Her face is bright red. She looks like a fucking fire-breathing dragon right now.

Shit. I look at Jen's email again, my heart racing. "Kat, no. I didn't suggest a fucking thing. I told Jen I wasn't interested in her. I said I'm not in the market for a relationship."

"Maybe you *think* that's what you said to her, but clearly you didn't. Because she clearly thinks there's still a chance for *something* with you, Josh, and when it comes to you, she'll obviously take any little crumb she can get, no matter how small and pitiful."

"Well, shit. Hang on. Lemme read it again."

"It makes me wonder if you're ever completely honest when it comes to women. Do you ever just tell it like it is? Or do you always spin things to avoid hurt feelings—or maybe to keep your motorboating-options open?"

"Hang the fuck on, Kat. Jesus fucking Christ, you demon-woman, lemme fucking look at it."

Kat presses her lips together and crosses her arms over her chest, her eyes blazing. "I don't mind a manwhore if he's honest about it—I really don't—I mean, as long as he's not running around collecting baby-mommas or STD's—*but I absolutely cannot stomach a goddamned liar.*"

"Fuck, Kat. Would you shut the fuck up for a minute? Jesus, you're a fucking lunatic." I look down at my phone and read again while Kat silently fumes. "Okay, clearly there's been a huge misunderstanding," I say when I'm done reading.

"Don't forget to take a peek at the photos she sent you, too," Kat says. "They're super-duper awesome."

I'd be a fool to open those photos with Kat standing right here, I know—but I do it, anyway. Why? Because, apparently, I'm every bit the suicide-bomber she is.

I open the first photo. It's Jen and her famous mom, their cheeks pressed together.

"Yeah, so what?" I say. "Who cares if Jen's mom is—"

"Open the second photo, Josh."

I roll my eyes and open the second photo. Oh. Wow. Hello, Jen's beautiful tits. Yeah, that woman's got some gorgeous tits, I

21

must say. But so what? I look up at Kat, ready to tell her she needs to take a chill-pill, and she's absolutely seething with jealousy. If she were a cartoon character, her skin would be green and steam would be shooting out her ears.

I stifle a grin, remembering Kat's sexy little speech about how she never, ever gets jealous. The girl is all talk. I open my mouth to speak, but before I can say a goddamned word, Kat launches into me again.

"Do you always just tell women what they want to hear, Josh? That's what I wanna know. Which leads me to the million-dollar question: Have you just been telling *me* what I wanna hear?"

My urge to smile vanishes. I throw up my hands, suddenly enraged. "Gimme a break, Kat. I've been one hundred percent honest with you and you know it."

"I'm not so sure. You keep telling me I'm 'the most beautiful woman you've ever been with' and then I see you've been with a freaking Victoria's Secret 'Angel.'"

"So?" I ask.

"So, then I know for a fact you're just blowing smoke up my butt."

"Oh my God. You're *pissed* I said you're more beautiful than a Victoria's Secret supermodel?" I take a deep breath, trying to control my rising anger. "Why are you doing this? I haven't given you shit about Cameron Schulz or any of the guys you've slept with—and it sounds like there's plenty to choose from."

Oh shit, I shouldn't have added that last bit. Ooph. The top of her head just popped off.

"Well, maybe you'd react differently if Cameron emailed me a photo of his balls and asked me to 'motorboat' them!" Her eyes bug out. "*Again!*" she shrieks.

I stifle the urge to laugh. She's pretty funny right now.

Kat's still fuming. "And you wanna know the reason *why* Cameron's not sending me goddamned dick-and-ball-pics?" she continues. "*Because I was honest and clear with him about my lack of interest.*"

"Oh, okay, sure, Kat—you're so fucking *honest* all the time. Let's talk about that cute little speech of pure fiction you made about how you never, ever get jealous unless you're in a committed relationship. Hmm? What about that?" I scoff. "So, okay, maybe I didn't get my words exactly right when I talked to Jen. But that was because I was trying to let her down easy. At least I was trying to be *nice*."

She clenches her jaw. "What does that mean? You don't think I'm nice?"

I pause. "No, I... I think you're nice—really nice. It's just that..." Why do I keep feeling like I'm digging myself a deeper hole? "It's just that, you know, you're a Scorpio," I say.

She looks at me blankly.

"God wouldn't have designed you with a stinger on your tail if he didn't want you to use it on occasion, right?"

Her mouth is hanging open.

"But that's okay. I like your stinger." Oh boy. I'm really not doing myself any favors here. Okay. Once again, the best defense is a good offense. "Jesus Christ, Kat," I say. "You're just like my fucking brother—physically perfect and you don't even know it. And you're needy just like him, too." I shake my head. "Kat, you're absolutely beautiful. I told you. I couldn't have designed you better myself. But you're also insane, apparently. You're seriously driving me crazy."

Her cheeks flush.

There's a long beat.

"I'm not usually this crazy," she says softly. She twists her mouth. "Something happens to me when I get around you." She throws up her hands. "Look, I'm being an asshole—okay? I realize that. I'm sorry." She exhales and flaps her lips together. "I tell you what. I'm gonna go downstairs and meet up with Henn and do the photo thing for my Oksana passport, okay? And while I do that, why don't you stay here and write a reply to Jen. Whatever's the truth, just tell her, once and for all, as clearly as possible."

"I'm not interested in her, Kat, like I keep saying."

She bares her teeth. "Glad to hear it. And after I do the photo thing with Henn," she says, "I'm gonna sit my butt down at a Blackjack table, drink some whiskey, and get control of myself. I'm sorry I lost it—that email just really threw me for a loop."

"Why?" I ask. "I already told you I fucked Jen. And, yeah, okay, I buried my face in her tits when I did it. So sue me." I grin. "She's got some really nice tits."

Kat presses her lips together.

"Kat, she means nothing to me, like I said. I only called her because I told her I would when I ran back into the party and practically ran her over trying to get your shoes and purse."

There's a long beat.

"I don't get why you're reacting this way," I say.

Kat looks up at the ceiling and then back at me, her face suddenly awash in emotion. "Just tell me right here and now, once and for all: are you Garrett Bennetting me?" she blurts. Tears suddenly flood her eyes and she wipes them.

"*That's* what this is all about?"

She nods.

I roll my eyes. "*No*," I say emphatically. "Of course not. I shouldn't even have to tell you that."

She wipes her eyes again. "All those women, Josh." She looks up at the ceiling like she's trying to keep tears from spilling out of her eyes. "I don't care if you're a manwhore. It's just... you can have any woman you want—anyone at all. The daughter of Gabrielle LeMonde—"

I scoff loudly, shutting her up.

"A Victoria's Secret Angel."

"A devil-woman with battery acid in her heart."

Kat bites her lip, obviously trying to suppress a smile. "Emma."

"A woman who called me a sick fuck and then promptly ran off with a dude who owns polo ponies and wears a fucking *ascot*."

There's a long beat. Kat's eyes are unreadable to me.

"I'm obviously way out of line here—just a total head case," she says. "I'm sorry." She exhales loudly. "I'm gonna go get a drink and play blackjack while you reply to Jen's email. She's a twat and a half, don't get me wrong, but even twats have feelings, too, and she deserves an honest response. Lemme just go downstairs and pull myself together for a bit, okay? I'm really sorry I'm acting so crazy."

She turns around to pound the elevator call-button, her shoulders slumped.

Fuck this shit. I'm not in the mood to write an email to *Jen* right now. There's only one thing I want to do: kiss my smokin' hot Party Girl with a Hyphen.

I bound down the hallway to Kat, my cheeks on fire, a massive lump in my throat, my dick rock hard. I grab her shoulders, whirl her around to face me, and kiss the shit out of her. "I'm not Garrett Bennetting you, Kat," I mumble into her lips. "I promise."

Chapter 4
Kat

My kiss with Josh has ramped up to full-throttle-I-wanna-fuck-your-brains-out within seconds. Josh breaks away from me, his blue eyes darkening with heat, slams my body roughly into the wall, yanks my mini-skirt up, and pulls my panties down.

I throw my head back, shaking with my arousal, and it bangs sharply against the wall of the hallway. But even the pain of whacking my head feels fucking awesome right now. I'm absolutely hyperventilating with anticipation. "Josh," I breathe, shoving my hand into his open pants and grasping his erection. "I'm sorry. I'm batshit crazy."

"You really are."

I laugh.

"I'm not like him, Kat," he breathes. "I'd never do that to you."

"I know. I don't know why I'm so crazy," I say. "I'm sorry."

"It's okay—apparently, I get off on crazy."

He shoves his hand into his pocket frantically but comes up with nothing but the key card to Jonas and Sarah's suite. He tries his other pocket and again comes up with nothing. "*Fuck*," he says. "I must have left the condom on the table in the suite."

"We don't need it," I gasp, grasping his erection with authority. "I'm on the pill. I'm clean. Just fuck me." I'm writhing against the wall, crazed by my arousal.

Without another word, he slams me against the wall like he's mugging me and plunges himself into me with shocking ferocity.

"You feel so fucking good," he says, moving his hips exactly the way he did on the dance floor the other night.

I groan and shudder with pleasure and relief.

25

"I love feeling your pussy against my cock with nothing between us." He bites my neck. "You've got a magic pussy, Kat."

Oh, God, I love that he's a dirty-talker.

After a few minutes of Josh's deep thrusting and heated whispers into my ear, I make my patented just-burned-my-hand-on-the-stove sound and he growls his reply, his hips moving relentlessly.

"You're always so wet for me. Oh shit. You're so fucking *wet*."

"I start dripping the minute you step within twenty feet of me," I growl.

He lets out a long, low moan that's so sexy, I convulse with excitement.

"I can't get enough of you. I've never been addicted like this."

My skin pricks all over with a sudden chill. "Oh, God," I say. "Here it comes." For an instant, I feel exactly like I'm gonna throw up. My insides are beginning to warp and twist. "Oh, shit."

"Come on, baby." He kisses my ear and gropes my breast. "Come on."

"Oh shit!" I claw at his chest and pull at his hair and devour his lips as my body explodes with painful pleasure. Oh my God, I can't get enough of this sensation. *I can't get enough of this man.*

"You're amazing," he says, his voice gruff, his thrusts turning brutal. "You feel so good."

I feel swept away. I can't even remember where I am. It's like Josh and I are flying, weightless, swirling together. I'm high on him. On his hard shaft moving in and out of me. On his scent, the taste of his voracious lips, the sound of his sensuous growls in my ear. He's completely overwhelming me in every way.

Except, wait, I think I just heard something besides Josh's growls in my ear.

"You feel so fucking good," Josh says, his hips gyrating forcefully. "So wet. So tight. Oh, fuck."

Hang on. Was that a little dinging noise? Almost like a bell?

Before my brain can answer that question with the phrase, "Yes, you dumbshit—that was the freakin' elevator," Henn's strangled voice echoes into the hallway: "Oh my fuck. Gah!"

I freeze, instantly mortified at the sound of Henn's horrified voice, but Josh doesn't stop. To the contrary, he impales me with monster-truck force into the wall and lets out a strangled sound that quite plainly signals he's in the midst of an extremely pleasurable orgasm.

I hold my breath and close my eyes, letting the dual sensations of Josh's climax and my own wretched embarrassment about Henn stumbling upon us undulate simultaneously through me.

I hear the sound of the elevator doors closing followed by nothing but Josh panting in my ear. I open one eye and cautiously peek at Josh. He's staring at me, his face beaded with sweat, his eyes smoldering. I glance over his shoulder toward the elevator, my heart racing, my clit rippling with an aftershock. The elevator doors are closed. Josh and I are alone in the hallway. Henn's nowhere to be found.

I look at Josh again, my cheeks blazing with a strange mixture of embarrassment and arousal, my heart racing. We stare at each other for a long, silent beat, our chests heaving in synchronicity. After a moment, one side of Josh's mouth hitches up, ever so slightly, into a smirk.

"Well, that was embarrassing," he says.

And that's all it takes—we both burst into hysterical laughter.

Chapter 5
Kat

"I'd love to rinse off real quick," I mumble, pulling up my G-string. "Jeez, Josh. That was a lot."

He laughs. "Sorry, not sorry." He pulls out his phone. "Lemme just text Henn and tell him we'll be down in a few. I'm sure he came up here wanting to take your passport photo."

"I'm so embarrassed."

Josh scoffs. "Eh, he'll get over it." He looks at his phone. "Oh, I've actually got a text from ol' Henny. Imagine that."

I wince. "What does it say?"

"It says, 'Where the fuck are you guys? Text me where to find you.'" Josh snickers. "Well, I guess he got his answer, huh?"

Josh taps out a reply, laughing to himself as he does.

"What are you saying to him?"

"Just that we'll be down in a few."

"Oh, good. I was worried you were—"

"*And,* that I missed his text because you and I were busy taking ol' one-eye to the optometrist."

"You did not!"

He shows me his phone. He did. In those exact words.

"*Josh!*"

He laughs. "Hey, nothing smooths out an awkward situation better than humor. Trust me, I should know. I've been smoothing out awkward situations my whole fucking life."

"Ugh. *Josh.*" I put my hands over my face.

"Kat, the man saw me fucking the shit out of you. I don't think my text will come as a huge surprise." When I don't join Josh's laughter, he nuzzles his nose into my ear. "Aw, don't worry, babe.

28

He'll recover. Henn's got a whopper of a crush on you, for sure, but he's a big boy." He moves my hair behind my shoulder and kisses my neck. "Maybe seeing us together will help Henn move past his little crush." Josh's phone pings in his hand and he looks at it. "Henn says, 'Meet me in an hour. An eye exam should never be rushed.'" Josh laughs heartily. "See? What did I tell you? Little Henny's already bounced back."

"You're not embarrassed Henn saw us screwing the crap out of each other?"

"Well, yeah, of course, I'm embarrassed. Fucking in front of Henn isn't high on my list of things to do. But I'm not gonna lose any sleep over it. At least I was fucking an insanely gorgeous woman and not a goat. Well, not this time, anyway."

"Ha, ha. Don't make bestiality jokes, Josh—I still haven't read your perverted application. Speaking of which, how have I *still* not read your perverted application?"

"Hey, I gave it to you. I've met my obligation. If you haven't read it by now that's on you."

"How do you keep distracting me? Are you some sort of evil genius?"

"Yes, I am—the world's dumbest evil genius."

"I just realized something," I say, having a genuine epiphany. "You've been diabolically controlling me this whole time, haven't you? Controlling me while letting me think *I'm* controlling *you*."

He shrugs. "I'm wise and powerful, babe; I warned you right from the start." He shoots me a megawatt smile. "What's the rush on reading that damned thing, anyway? You said you emailed it to yourself, right?—so now you can read it whenever."

I smile. I can't believe how relaxed and easygoing Josh has become about his application—what a turnaround since we first started sparring over it.

Josh looks at his watch. "Jonas and Sarah should be landing in D.C. in about an hour—Jonas said they'd be landing around seven Washington time. So let's take a nice, long shower, let you rinse out your cooch and maybe scrub off some of that batshit-crazy you've got all over you—and then we'll meet Henn for the photo thing. By then it'll be time to touch base with Jonas and Sarah to see if they have any news about today's meeting with the feds." He pulls me to him close. "And *then* we'll grab a few hours of sleep together in my room, just me and you." He kisses my neck. "Sound good, my crazy little Party Girl with a Hyphen?"

I think my heart's gonna burst right out of my chest. "That all sounds perfect, Playboy."

Chapter 6
Kat

Up 'til now, all of my naked interactions with Josh have been fast and furious. But now, in this steaming hot, post-hallway-fuckery shower, I'm finally getting the chance to slowly touch and appreciate every inch of Josh's muscled, tattooed body. And appreciate it, I do. Holy hot damn. He's gorgeous.

I squirt shower gel into my palm and eagerly run my hand over his "Grace" tattoo on his chest and then down the ruts and ridges of his abs and across his pelvis, skimming my palm between the "V" cuts in his waist and over the word "OVERCOME."

And, glory be, as I touch Josh, he returns the favor, slowly exploring every curve and crevice of my wet body with his palms and fingertips.

"You're beautiful," Josh says softly in my ear, kissing my neck. "Gorgeous."

My fingertips slide to the tattoo on the right side of his torso, behind his ribcage. Before now, I haven't paid much attention to this one. But now that I'm studying it, I'm noticing it's an intricate scene of a fish swimming in a river, shaded by an overhanging tree on a nearby riverbank.

"What's the story on this one?" I ask, touching the fish with my fingertip.

He runs his hand across my right nipple and down my side, over the curve of my hip, and down my ass cheek. "I'll give you my standard answer first," he says softly, his lips grazing my ear. "And then, I'll tell you the whole truth."

"Okay," I whisper, just before his lips find mine.

We kiss for a long time, letting the hot water pelt us as we do, our hands exploring each other as our lips and tongues intertwine.

31

Finally, Josh pulls away from my mouth and licks my jawline.

I shudder with pleasure. Oh, God, I can't get enough of him. I'm absolutely intoxicated with him.

"Your tattoo?" I breathe.

"Sorry, I got distracted," he says. He smiles and his eyes sparkle. "My standard answer is it's a fish because I'm a Pisces," he says, his hands skimming over my ass. "Which is true."

"You're a *Pisces*?" I say, pulling away from him in surprise.

"What? Is that bad?"

"Oh, no. It's just... " I trail off. There's no way I'm gonna explain that Pisces is the astrological sign most compatible with Scorpio. "You just seem like such a classic Pisces, that's all," I say smoothly.

"Yeah? What are the characteristics of a classic Pisces?"

I think briefly. "Compassionate, adaptable, accepting, devoted, and imaginative."

He puts his forehead on mine. "Wow, I *rock*."

I laugh. "Don't get too enamored with yourself. That was just the *good* Pisces stuff. You're also indecisive, self-pitying, lazy, and escapist."

"Oh shit." He grins. "I *suck*."

We both laugh.

He kisses me again.

"What about you, Miss Scorpio? What's the rap on you?"

"I'm loyal, passionate, resourceful, and dynamic."

He laughs and pinches my ass. "Dead-on accurate." His hands migrate up my back. "Now what's the shitty Scorpio stuff?"

I frown. "Well, *supposedly*, I'm obsessive, suspicious, manipulative, unyielding, and... *jealous*. But I think that's all a load of crap."

We both burst out laughing.

"Oh my God, that's hilarious," he says. "Maybe there's something to this astrology stuff, after all."

"It's amazing how spot-on it can be."

"So you're pretty into it?" he asks.

I shrug. "I don't manage my life based on astrology—I told you, I'm not one to think everything's fated—I'm a firm believer in kicking ass—but I do think it's crazy how accurate astrology can be regarding people's personalities and compatibility."

"When's your birthday?" he asks.

"November sixteenth. When's yours?"

"March ninth—and Jonas', too, obviously."

"Aw, that's right. I forgot Jonas is a Pisces, too. Sarah's also a Pisces." I smile wistfully. "They're Pisces-Pisces-sittin'-in-a-tree. That's so sweet."

"Two Pisces is good?"

"It's amazing. Pisces-Pisces is one of the top love compatibilities on the Zodiac. When two Pisces join together, it's a deep spiritual connection. They're both water signs, so two Pisces *meld* together completely, intertwining and becoming inseparable. They bring out the spiritual side in each other."

"What about Pisces-Scorpio?"

I can't believe Josh just asked me about our astrological love compatibility. My heart is racing. "Pisces and Scorpio are highly compatible, too—also both water signs," I say, my skin pricking with goose bumps even under the pounding hot water. "But a Scorpio-Pisces union is especially notable for its intensity and off-the-charts passion. When Pisces and Scorpio get together, it's like *ka-boom*."

His eyes flicker. "Hmm. I think maybe I'm becoming a believer in astrology."

He presses himself into me and I feel the unmistakable sensation of a hard-on jutting into my hip. I look down. *Oh, hello.* Josh has apparently fully recovered from our tryst in the hallway and he's ready to go again. Holy hell, Joshua William Faraday is a virile motherfucker.

Josh smirks and slides his fingers between my legs. "I think I'm officially addicted to making you come," he says softly. "You're my new favorite game."

I never thought I'd see the day, but I actually think I've had my limit of body-twisting orgasms for one day. But, damn, this man's definitely got a gigantic boner. Looks like there's only one thing for a girl to do: without saying a word, I kneel and take Josh's hard-on into my mouth.

I rarely give head, actually—a guy's gotta be pretty damned special to me to exert that kind of effort—but when I *do* give it, then by God, I do it right. And this time is no exception.

Technically, I already gave Josh a blowjob while I rode the

Sybian, but if I'm being honest, that really wasn't my best work—I certainly didn't deliver the Katherine Morgan Ultimate Blowjob Experience the way I'd normally do, that's for sure. Of course, under the circumstances, my lackluster oral performance couldn't be helped—I defy any woman to supply a mind-blowing blowjob while having an orgasm-induced seizure on a jet engine—but now, suddenly, I feel an urgent desire to show Josh exactly what my mouth can do.

Why? Because I want him. I want him *bad.* And in my experience, there's no weapon more lethal in a woman's arsenal than giving a man the best blowjob of his life. If she can do this, she can have anything or anyone she desires. Harsh, perhaps, to state the fact so starkly. But true nonetheless.

I begin licking and sucking on Josh's shaft, and he immediately makes it clear he's an ardent fan of my work. But I'm just getting started. Because a blowjob worthy of being called a Katherine Morgan Ultimate Blowjob Experience can't be good. It can't even be great. No, a blowjob worthy of this lofty title must be nothing short of mind-blowing.

Of course, every mind-blowing blowjob starts at its inception with a can-do attitude—a girl's *really* gotta want to suck that dick—or else she truly shouldn't even bother.

To get myself in the right frame of mind to deliver oral epicness, I engage in a little *role-play,* if you will, a little mental trick that turns me on and inspires me to reach for greatness every time: I simply imagine I'm a high-priced call girl who charges a million bucks per blowjob and my only mission is to make my client say, "You're worth every fucking penny, baby." Oh man, it gets me going every time. (And if I'm turned on, I'm motivated to turn *him* on, too.)

But while a good attitude is an essential ingredient to giving a man the most intense oral experience of his life, it can only take a girl so far if she doesn't also have fantastic technique.

Through trial and tribulation, I've surmised that the most effective oral techniques ascend a "ladder of pleasure," if you will, that goes a little something like this:

Rung One. If a girl aims to give a man at least a *pleasurable* blowjob (which should be a baseline goal, or else why is she putting a cock into her mouth, for crying out loud?), then she's gotta lick and suck that guy's dick like she's got heatstroke and it's a popsicle on a summer day.

Rung Two. If a girl wants to give a man a pleasurable and highly memorable blowjob (which, again, should be every girl's goal—because sucking a man's dick and then being forgotten is definitely not something to aspire to in life), then she's gotta lick and suck that man's dick *plus* his balls *and* she's gotta do it all like she's been bitten by a rattlesnake and his dick and balls contain the antidote to the venom.

Based on conversations with friends and articles I've read in *Cosmo,* I'd venture to guess that's where most girls stop climbing the ladder of pleasure—at Rung Two.

But I'm not most girls. In fact, I'm exactly what Josh accused me of being: I'm a frickin' terrorist. If I'm gonna give head, then by God, I'm gonna make the owner of that dick and balls fall head over heels in love with me.

Which brings me to Rung Three. At rung three, a girl's gotta do all of the above, *plus* fondle every freakin' inch of his jewels and back forty and taint, including massaging his asshole (and fingering it if he seems into it); *plus* she's gotta grip his shaft like it's a life preserver and she's a woman-overboard in stormy seas. But she can't stop there. Hell no. She's also gotta suck on his tip like it's liquid chocolate. Take his balls into her mouth while pumping his shaft and swirling her tongue on his tip and licking and sucking his little hole like she's high on meth and she thinks that hole is spurting more juice.

I've just reached the third rung of the ladder on Josh.

He moans like a dying buffalo.

Clearly, he's thoroughly enjoying his Katherine Morgan Ultimate Blowjob Experience.

And, holy hell, so am I. Oh my, yes. *So am I.* In fact, I'm getting off on doing this for Josh almost as much as if he were doing the same for me between my legs. This is new. I've never felt quite this turned on before while giving head. Oh my God. I think I'm gonna come.

Oh my hell. I think it's time to identify a fourth rung on the ladder of pleasure: doing all of the above things in a hot, steamy shower with the sexiest man alive, Joshua William Faraday.

Josh releases into my mouth with a grizzly bear growl and I'm surprised to realize I'm coming too, right along with him. Wow, that's a first. A truly delectable first.

When I'm done, and Josh's hard-on has stopped jerking and rippling in my mouth, I stand up and get a long mouthful of hot water from the showerhead, loosen my jaw, and turn back to him.

His eyes are on fire. He kisses me greedily, shaking with an aftershock. "Oh my God, Kat. That was... *Thank you.*" He kisses my nipple and begins to kneel, obviously intending to return the favor.

"Hang on," I say, touching his shoulder. "I'm good."

He looks up at me, surprised.

"We've got to get downstairs to meet Henn," I say.

"But I wanna get you off, too," he says, grinning. "It's only fair."

"Oh, I came. Like a freight train. While I was swallowing."

His face ignites. "Are you serious?"

I smile and nod.

"Oh my God. You're amazing." He straightens up. "You're a unicorn, Kat. You're... oh my God." He's in a frenzy. "What planet are you from? You're amazing."

"Hey, I'll certainly take a rain check, though," I say. "When we have more time, maybe you can try to beat me at my own game." I wink. "A little competition never hurt anyone."

He smiles lasciviously. "Oh, Party Girl. You're on. I look forward to it."

Chapter 7
Kat

Josh turns off the water and we step out of the shower together.

"So what's the second half of the story of your fish tattoo?" I ask.

He hands me a towel and I begin drying myself.

"Oh, yeah. Sorry. I got distracted. *Again.*" He laughs and towels himself off. "You seem to have that effect on me." He takes a deep breath. "The tattoo represents something my mom always used to say to Jonas and me." He grabs his pants off the floor of the bathroom and begins dressing. "I don't actually have a ton of coherent memories about my mom—we were pretty little when she died—but one thing I remember really clearly is she always called Jonas and me her 'little fishies'—because, you know, we're Pisces." He flashes me a huge smile. "My dad said she loved astrology. Just like you."

My heart leaps. "Oh, cool," I say, but on the inside, I'm kind of freaking out to share this similarity with his mother.

"Yeah, so my mom always said, 'Everybody's a genius, but if you judge a fishy by its ability to climb a tree, it'll live its whole life believing it's stupid.'"

"Ah," I say, scrutinizing his tattoo. "That's a pretty wise and powerful thing to say."

"She didn't make it up—I looked it up—it's a quote from Einstein. But she loved it and said it all the time."

"So your fishy is swimming along happily in the river, rather than climbing the nearby tree?"

"Wouldn't want the poor guy spending his whole life believing he's stupid."

"Of course not, especially since he's wise and powerful."

Josh finishes buckling his belt. "So tell me something, PG. Another round of the honesty-game."

"Sure."

"Did a little piece of you get turned on when Henn saw us fucking?"

"What?" I blurt, utterly appalled. "Of course not. I was absolutely mortified."

Josh silently buttons his shirt.

"Why?" I ask. "Were *you* turned on?" I zip up my miniskirt and reach for my shirt.

"No. Not at all." He finishes buttoning his shirt. "I was just curious, based on something you wrote in your application."

"Josh, it was *Henn,*" I say. "I'm gonna have horrible nightmares about him stumbling upon us 'til the day I die."

We're both fully dressed. Josh grabs my hand and leads me out of the bathroom, toward the main room of the suite. "Yeah, I know. Me, too. But..." he begins tentatively. "Does the idea of *someone* watching you turn you on? Someone who's not Henn?"

My pulse has begun pounding in my ears. "Like, *who*?"

"I dunno. When you had your little lesbo-encounter in college wasn't the other girl's boyfriend watching?"

My cheeks flush. I nod.

"And did you like it?"

I've never talked about this with anyone. I clear my throat. "Yeah."

"You liked him watching?"

I nod. "The fact that her boyfriend was watching was the hottest thing about the whole thing."

Josh's face lights up.

"Well, that and, you know, the whole excitement of doing something taboo. But the actual making-out part—you know, what my friend physically did to me, what I did to her—that wasn't the real turn-on. If we'd been in private, just the two of us, it never would have happened."

"Interesting." Josh leads me to the table in the middle of the suite and sits me down. He leans over me, his hands on the arms of my chair. "And did the boyfriend join in with you two girls at some point?"

I've never told anyone about that night. My heart is racing. I nod.

"And did you like it when he did?" He leans forward slightly, leveling his blue eyes with mine.

"Um. It was just okay, to be honest. The guy was *really* into his girlfriend. So once things got going, I pretty quickly started feeling like a third wheel, and I didn't like that feeling."

He chuckles.

"At all."

He grins. "Why doesn't that surprise me?"

"I've come to realize I need to be the center of attention."

"No shit?" He flashes a cocky grin.

I try to look offended at that comment, but it's impossible. I join him in laughing.

He glides to the bar. "How about a quick drink before we meet Henn?" He looks at his watch. "We've got about twenty minutes."

"Just some water. I'm pretty wiped out."

"Water it is. So was that your only threesome, Party Girl?" he asks, busying himself behind the bar.

"Yeah. I never had the desire to do it again after that. I realized I was more turned on when her boyfriend was watching than when he actually joined in."

"Interesting," he says, mixing a drink behind the bar. "So you said in your application you have lots of fantasies. Is that one of your fantasies—someone watching you with another person?"

My cheeks are on fire. "Um, no, not really. I haven't given it much thought since then. But I guess it could be kind of fun to experience the whole thing the way my friend did—being the center of attention instead of the third wheel. I was just window dressing during the whole thing, but I suppose it might be fun to be the *window.*"

He brings me my water, his eyes blazing. "Here you go," he says. He places my water on the table in front of me and sits down next to me. He places his hand on my thigh.

"What about you?" I ask, my heart thumping in my chest. "Would you be interested in... watching?"

"Just tell me where and when."

Oh shit. He misunderstood me. I was speaking hypothetically—

asking him whether he has the general fantasy of watching a *hypothetical* woman he's attracted to getting it on with another woman. I wasn't specifically asking him if he wants to watch *me* with another woman.

There's a long beat as I try to figure out how best to clarify my question.

Josh takes a long sip of his drink. "But only if you were totally comfortable with it," he adds, his eyes burning.

"Is that a martini?" I ask.

"Yeah, you want one?"

"Maybe just a sip of yours."

I'm expecting him to slide his drink toward me, but, instead, he takes a long gulp of his drink, grabs my face, leans into me, and kisses me deeply, letting the delicious fluid in his mouth gush into mine.

"Holy shitballs," I say when he pulls away from my lips. "That was so freakin' hot." I laugh.

He licks his lips. "So do you think you'd be up for letting me watch you with a woman? I'd really enjoy it."

I pause. "I'm not bisexual."

He shrugs. "You don't need to be. You wouldn't have to do much to make me very happy. You could do as little or as much as you'd want. What you do isn't really the point of it for me."

He slides his martini to me, reading my mind, and I take a long sip.

"You wouldn't have to do anything that makes you even remotely uncomfortable. You'd be surprised how little it takes to make me a very happy boy."

My pulse is pounding in my ears. "I think it would depend," I say. I put down the drink.

"On what?"

"On who the other woman was."

He smiles broadly.

"In college, my friend and I were both totally weirded out afterwards and we never got back to normal," I say. "The experience pretty much ruined our friendship."

He leans forward, his eyes locked onto mine, and cups my jawline in his palm. "What if you could pick the woman? And do as little or as much as you pleased with her?"

I swallow hard. My heart is beating wildly. "It... would... be totally up to me?" I stammer.

He leans back and drops his hand from my face, his eyes ablaze. "The question wouldn't be whether the woman turns *me* on—the only question would be whether she turns *you* on. If so, that would do wonders for me."

My head is spinning. "Would you ultimately join in and have sex with both of us—or just with me?"

"What would you prefer?"

"Just with me."

"Then that's what I'd do."

"You'd have to swear not to lose control and start fucking the other woman."

He scoffs. "Kat, I'm not an animal. I don't 'lose control' and start fucking people like a dog humping a leg. I'm not some sort of sex offender."

I think my heart is medically palpitating. "Because if you started having any kind of sexual contact with the other woman, then I'd get crazy-jealous."

Josh shoots me a look that says "no shit" but he doesn't say anything.

"If we did it, it wouldn't be all about making me jealous, right? It'd be about turning me on—and, therefore, you?"

"Correct."

"Making me jealous wouldn't be some sort of secret, ulterior motive?" I feel like my heart's gonna hurtle right out of my chest. "You wouldn't tell me one thing beforehand, just to get me to do it, and then blindside me later, right?"

His face melts into total sincerity. He puts both hands on my cheeks this time and leans his forehead against mine. "Kat, I'd *never* blindside you, in any context. Sexual or otherwise."

My heart is racing so fast, I'm practically yelping for air. "Because I'd only do it if the other woman was gonna be the third wheel, not me." I can't believe I'm negotiating the terms of this. How did this conversation go from hypotheticals to actual negotiation so quickly?

"I'd respect that," he says. "One hundred percent. It'd be all about you. I wouldn't lay a finger on the other woman if you didn't want me to. Not even a pinky."

I'm having a hard time pushing air into my lungs. "That's what I'd want," I say. "Not a finger. Absolutely no contact between you and the other woman. It'd be all about me and you."

"Done." His eyes are like lit torches.

"And you'd sit and watch?"

"I would."

"Would you jack off?"

"If that's something you'd be okay with."

"Yes."

"Then, yes."

"But you wouldn't come. I'd want you to be able to fuck me. Really hard."

He shudders. "When I got to the point I couldn't stand it anymore, I'd pull you aside and tell the other woman to leave and I'd fuck the shit out of you."

I'm breathless. My skin is bursting with heat. I slide from my chair to sit on his lap and he wraps his arms around me. "Or, who knows," I purr, "maybe you'd tell her to stay and watch—see what she's missing out on?" I can't believe I just said that. This man brings out a whole new level of naughty in me.

Clearly, Josh can't believe I just said that, either. "If that's what you'd want, absolutely," he says. "Totally up to you."

I can barely breathe. "And she wouldn't be anyone either of us knows?" I say softly. "Nobody you know?"

"It'd be whoever you pick, babe. Anyone at all, as long as she tests clean. I don't give a fuck who she is. It's all about you."

My clit is throbbing so hard, it hurts. "But what if I wind up picking someone you're more attracted to than me? I'd be able to tell, and I wouldn't like it," I say.

He places his fingertip in the cleft in my chin. "That's literally impossible."

Holy fucking shit. I seriously can't breathe right now. I'm trembling. I swallow hard. "We'd do it and never see her again? Because I wouldn't want this kind of fantasy-thing to follow us into our real life."

He chuckles.

"What?"

"You just perfectly articulated why I joined The Club."

I make a face that says, "I see your point" and he smiles broadly.

"You're amazing, Kat," he says. He puts his hand under my chin and kisses me. "I think you might be perfect." He kisses me again. And then again. "You're kinda freaking me out, actually."

My head is spinning. I can't focus. I lean into him and bite his lower lip, totally aroused, and he makes a noise of surprise.

I suck on his lower lip and then pull away. "How would we find her?" I whisper, licking my lips from our kiss.

"It'd be easy to do if we set our minds to it, I'm sure."

"We'd have to be one hundred percent sure we'd never see her again. I wouldn't want some horny blonde bitch stalking you afterwards." I jerk back.

"What?" He looks concerned.

"*Jen.*"

The aroused expression on Josh's face instantly vanishes. "No, Kat. Fuck no. Anyone but Jen."

"No." I roll my eyes. "Not *Jen*. Her email, Josh—I want you to reply to Jen's email. I want you to tell her you're not interested in her. Right now. Show me."

He shakes his head and exhales, letting his lips flap together in exasperation as he does. "Way to lick me and punch me in the balls *again*, PG. Jesus Fucking Christ. Madame Terrorist returns."

"Open your laptop, Josh," I say, punching him in his shoulder. "We're gonna send that bitch an email right now and put her out of her freakin' misery—and therefore put me out of mine."

Chapter 8
Josh

"Hey, Jen," I say, enunciating the words as I type them onto the screen of my laptop. Kat's sitting on my lap, her arm around my shoulder, the side of her head against mine, staring at my screen as I type. "Thanks for your invitation to your birthday weekend," I write. I stop and look at Kat. "That okay so far, boss?"

"So far, so good," she says. "Continue."

"Why don't *you* just write it? Something tells me you're gonna rewrite the whole damned thing anyway, no matter what I say."

She laughs. "Nope. This is all you."

I roll my eyes. "Remind me why I'm doing this?"

"You mean why are you replying to Jen at all? Or why are you doing it with me looking over your shoulder?"

"Both."

"Well, you're replying to Jen because you're not a total douche and she deserves a reply. She invited you to her twenty-ninth birthday party, after all. The polite thing to do is RSVP."

I purse my lips, annoyed.

"*And* you're doing it with me looking over your shoulder because this email reply is gonna give me near-orgasmic pleasure. And you like giving me pleasure, right, baby?"

I grumble.

"Aw, poor Josh has to put on his big-boy pants. Come on. Just hit her with some compassionate honesty. The more you do it, the easier it gets. Trust me."

"I just don't like hurting people's feelings."

She scoffs. "And letting her twist in the wind is gonna hurt her feelings less than an honest email? I've been in her shoes with guys,

44

and believe me, a girl feels like a piece of shit when a guy doesn't even give her the courtesy of a reply."

"There's a man alive who didn't give you the courtesy of a reply?"

"Mmm hmm."

"I don't believe it."

"Turned out the guy was married."

"Ooph."

"And I had absolutely no idea."

"God, men are such pricks."

She laughs. "Come on. Quit stalling. You're so damned good at distracting me."

"I already told her twice. Once in New York and then again on the phone after Reed's party. She's just deaf or dumb, I guess."

"No, you *think* you told her, but you must not have." She shrugs. "First rule of PR, Josh: failure to communicate is on the speaker, not the listener."

I let out a loud puff of air. "I was pretty damned clear both times, Kat."

"Obviously not," Kat says. "She's really into you, Josh—which means she's hearing what she wants to hear and telling you what she thinks you want to hear. You need to shut the door and turn the frickin' lock." She pauses pointedly. "Unless you don't *want* to shut the door?"

"Gimme a fucking break."

She motions to the screen. "Then, type."

I begin typing again. "I hope you have a great birthday," I write, saying the words out loud as I do. "I won't be able to join you. I'm..." I stop typing. "You're gonna rewrite all of this, aren't you?"

"Just keep going."

"Well, shit. *You* write it, for fuck's sake. What am I gonna say to the girl, 'I'm not into you? I used you for sex? I was thinking of Kat when I fucked you'?"

Kat's face lights up like the Fourth of July. "Oh, I like that." She motions to the screen. "Write that."

"I'm not gonna write *that*."

"Is it the truth?"

"Well, yeah."

"All of it?"

45

"Yeah."

"Even the part about you thinking of me while fucking her?"

"Of course. I already told you that."

"No, you didn't."

"Yes, I did."

"No, you didn't."

"I sure as hell did."

"No."

"Well, if I didn't, lemme tell you now. I couldn't stop thinking about you, fantasizing about you, jacking off while thinking about you—and you wouldn't leave your date with Cameron Fucking Schulz for me and I was pissed and frustrated as hell."

"Oh, well, that's something different than thinking about me while having sex with Jen."

"What? What are you talking about?"

"Saying you worked yourself up into sexual frustration by jacking off and thinking about me and *then* fucked Jen to relieve your frustration is quite different from saying you fucked her *and thought of me while doing it*. See the difference?"

I put my hand on my forehead like she's giving me a splitting headache.

"Do you see the difference?"

"Yes. I see the difference."

"Likewise, whatever you said to Jen in New York and on the phone after Reed's party wasn't the same thing as, 'I am not remotely interested in you in any way, shape or form, so leave me the hell alone.' Whatever you said to her, she interpreted to mean, 'I am not interested in a *serious relationship* with you, but I will quite happily continue to casually fuck you.'"

I close my eyes, trying to escape the torture.

"You're hilarious."

I open my eyes. "Why?"

"Because you're this big, strong, gorgeous guy with all the swagger and confidence in the world—but secretly you're kind of a puss."

"No, I'm not. Absolutely not."

"Yes, you are. You're scared of female emotion. You're scared of making a girl cry. Waaaah."

I exhale loudly. "Can we please just write the email? Seriously. I've already spent way too much of my time on this."

"This isn't about Jen. This is about you learning a *life lesson,* Playboy. Clearly, growing up without a mom, there was no one to teach you how to understand and communicate with women. You need some tutoring."

I feel instantly defensive—but quickly realize she's got a point. "You might be right about that," I say. "I've never thought about it that way."

"Of course, I'm right. I've got four brothers and a dad to teach me how to talk and think like a dude. But who do you have to teach you how to talk and think like a chick?"

I purse my lips, considering. "My personal assistant?"

"Doesn't count."

"Then no one."

"Well, don't you worry, honey. I'm here to save the day. So let's try this again." She motions to the computer screen. "Say what you really mean. Say it kindly, but say it clearly."

I grumble, but I put my hands on my keyboard. "I'm sorry if I gave you the wrong impression when we spoke the other day," I type. "I'm not interested in pursuing a relationship of any kind with you." I stop, waiting for Kat's reaction, but she's stone-faced. I continue typing again. "In New York, I truly thought we were both up for the same thing: a meaningless one-night stand. That was probably a stupid assumption by me, given our history. In fact, I was probably being insensitive by making that assumption. I should have known your feelings might be involved. But mine weren't." I pause and look at Kat. "Okay?"

She touches my cheek and assesses me with earnest eyes. "You're doing great."

I'm floored by her sudden show of tenderness. I swallow hard and turn back to my screen. But I can't think. My heart is suddenly pounding wildly.

"Go on," she says. "Just tell the truth, whatever it is."

I take a deep breath. "The truth is," I type, "I'm interested in someone else." Oh shit, my heart is racing. "Really, really interested. I don't know where things might lead with her, or if she's interested in me in return, but I'd like to find out. And that means I can't fuck it up by being a total douche and continuing to pursue something with you."

47

I look at Kat. Her mouth is hanging open.

She puts her hand on her heart.

"And, yeah," I continue typing, "if you think I'm talking about The Jealous Bitch, you're right. She might be a grenade that unpredictably explodes all over me, but that's what I like about her."

I'm practically panting. Holy motherfucking shit.

Before I've even turned my head to get a read on Kat's reaction, her lips are on mine and her tongue is in my mouth and my hands are on her cheeks and her arms are around my neck and we're kissing the hell out of each other. She presses herself into me and I wrap my arms around her, pulling her close, grasping at her for dear life, whispering her name into her lips.

After several minutes, my phone pings on the table and we begrudgingly pull away from each other, our faces on fire. I look at my phone. It's a text from Henn:

"Hey, dipshit. I can understand you wanting an especially thorough eye exam, considering who your optometrist is," Henn writes. "But you and Kat need to get your asses down here ASAP. Meet me on the casino floor near the elevator bank in five."

Chapter 9
Kat

I crawl into bed with my laptop and sigh with happiness. Yeehaw, I'm finally gonna read Josh's application, without even the possibility of an interruption.

After Henn took my photo downstairs (after we'd finally located a simple white wall to use as a backdrop), the three of us briefly talked to Jonas, who told us the meeting with the feds is going down later today at one o'clock Washington time.

"You three need to be ready to transfer the money as early as one thirty Washington time," Jonas warned during our call. "I doubt we'll be asked to do it that quickly—I'm guessing the meeting with the feds will take hours—but you have to be at the ready, just in case."

"Sure thing, bro," Josh said. "No *problemo*."

After we hung up from our call with Jonas, I suddenly felt like I was gonna melt onto the floor with exhaustion. "I'm gonna get into my jammies, get nice and cozy in my bed, and do some *reading* before I drift off to sleep," I told Josh and Henn. "Nighty-night, boys."

"Okay, Kitty Kat," Henn said. "I've got everything I need now. See you in the morning." And off he went.

"How 'bout I come to your room with you?" Josh offered, pulling me into him.

"Nope," I said. "I'm going in alone. It's finally time for me to find out what kind of perverted-sick-fuck-goat-fucker you really are, Joshua William Faraday. No distractions."

Josh pressed himself into me. "Aw, come on, PG. I'll lie next to you in bed while you read. That way I can answer any questions you might have."

49

"No way, Playboy," I replied.

"I'll massage your feet while you read."

I paused, considering. I really love a good foot massage. "No," I finally said. "No more distractions. Nighty-night."

And now, here I am. Finally. Sitting in bed in my tank top and undies with my computer on my lap, a huge smile on my face and an Avicii song blaring through my speakers ("Addicted to You," featuring vocals by my new obsession, Audra Mae).

I quickly check my phone. I've been horrible about replying to texts and emails since coming to Sin City. This whole trip has been like entering some sort of Twilight-Zone-alternate-dimension. I scroll through my texts. I've got a text from my mom, asking me to call her so she can "hear my voice." No rush there. And a text from my oldest brother, Colby, (addressing me as Kumquat), asking me if I've gambled away next month's rent yet and telling me to call Mom so she can "hear my voice."

There's a text from my baby brother, Dax, (addressing me as Jizz), informing me he used the extra key to my apartment to "hang out" in my place for a few days and, oh yeah, by the way, oops, he ate all my food.

I've got a text from Hannah at work, telling me she misses her lunch buddy and asking me to call her whenever. I wince. Hannah's really picked up my slack at work while I've been gone. I owe her big-time.

I've got a text from Sarah from an hour ago, telling me she and Jonas landed in Washington D.C. and are set to meet at FBI headquarters later this afternoon. "Oh muh guh," Sarah wrote. "I'm crapping my pants. But Jonas is cool as a cucumber about the whole thing so he's keeping me sane."

I smile at that last sentence. Jonas is keeping *Sarah* sane? Gotta love those two.

"Go get 'em, girl," I reply to Sarah's text. "You're gonna blow all those fancy G-men away. The Vegas branch of our crew is standing by."

And, finally, there's a text from Josh from five minutes ago: "Hey, PG. Do me a favor and text me the minute you're done reading my application," he writes. "You don't have to tell me what you think about it. Just tell me when you've read it or else I won't be able to fall asleep."

"Will do," I reply. "I'm about to start reading now."

His reply is instantaneous. "Just keep an open mind," he writes. "Just remember when I wrote that thing, I was really upset."

"Yeah, yeah. I know. Don't sweat it, PB. How bad can it be?"

"Um... " he writes.

I've got a pit in my stomach. "I'll text you when I'm done," I write.

"Promise?"

"Promise."

I grab my laptop, find the email with Josh's application attached, snuggle into my soft, white pillows, happily listening to Avicii and Audra Mae serenade me, and begin reading:

Name?

"Joshua William Faraday," he writes. And, yet again, the sight of his full name sends a shiver down my spine. "Sexy man," I say out loud in my empty hotel room.

With this application, you will be required to submit three separate forms of identification. The Club maintains a strict "No Aliases Policy" for admission. You may, however, use aliases during interactions with other Club members, at your discretion.

"OK," he writes.

Age?

"29," he writes.

Provide a brief physical description of yourself.

I scan his full response to this question again. But this time reading Josh's words, my heart races and leaps: "I prefer not to talk about the meanings of my tattoos at length, so please tell whoever gets assigned to me not to ask about them."

A wave of excitement washes through me. If that's how Josh felt when he wrote those words, he certainly doesn't seem to feel that way now—or, at least, not when it comes to me.

With this application, you will be required to submit three recent photographs of yourself to your intake agent. Please include the following: one headshot, one full-body shot revealing your physique, and one shot wearing something you'd typically wear out in a public location. These photographs shall be maintained under the strictest confidentiality.

Just for the heck of it, I click onto Josh's naked-bad-boy-photo and stare at it for a moment. This man sends my pulse racing and my blood boiling in a way I've never felt before. Damn, boy—just like Audra Mae is singing in my ear right now—I'm absolutely addicted to him.

Please sign the enclosed waiver describing the requisite background check, medical physical, and blood test, which you must complete as a condition of membership.

"Done," he writes.

Sexual orientation? Please choose from the following options: Straight, homosexual, bisexual, pansexual, other?

"Straight," he writes.

Do any of your sexual fantasies include violence of any nature?

"Yes," he writes.

Whoa. Holy shitballs. Not what I expected. I move quickly to the next section.

If so, please describe in detail. Please note that your inclination toward or fantasies about sexual violence, if any, will not, standing alone, preclude membership. Indeed, we provide highly particularized services for members with a wide variety of proclivities. In the interest of serving your needs to the fullest extent possible, please describe any and all sexual fantasies involving violence of any nature whatsoever.

"I have a sexual fantasy in which I come to the rescue of a woman who's been bound and raped."

Whoa again.

Are you a current practitioner of BDSM and/or does BDSM interest you? If so, describe in explicit detail.

"BDSM interests me insofar as it relates to fulfilling the fantasy described above."

Payment and Membership Terms. Please choose from the following options: One Year Membership, $250,000 USD; Monthly Membership, $30,000 USD. All payments are non-refundable. No exceptions. Once you've made your selection regarding your membership plan, information for wiring the funds into an escrow account will be immediately forthcoming under separate cover. Membership fees shall be transferred automatically out of escrow to The Club upon approval of your membership.

"I'm interested in a one-month membership, administered

according to my exact specifications, described below. If additional payment beyond your usual monthly fee is required for you to deliver exactly what I've asked for (below), I'm open to further negotiation of your fee. Please advise."

Oh my effing God. My heart is pounding forcefully in my ears. I can't read Josh's words fast enough.

Please provide a detailed explanation about what compelled you to seek membership in The Club.

"It's pretty simple, actually: I'm joining The Club because I'm a sick fuck. Or so I've been recently told by someone I loved and trusted with all my fucking heart. Well, I might be a sick fuck, but at least I'm not a heartless liar. I'm not the one who begged me to open up, pleaded with me to tell her the truth about my deepest desires and told me it was safe and she wouldn't judge me, and then when I finally broke down and told her everything, called me a 'sick fuck' and said there's something 'deeply wrong with me' and then cheated on me with a douchebag who wears a fucking ascot and says 'bloody hell' and rides polo ponies for fuck's sake. Motherfucking bastard asshole. After three years she couldn't give me the courtesy of breaking up with me? I had to hear she'd run off with that douche from a friend? Ha! And this was all because of shit I merely *fantasized* about doing—I hadn't even done any of it yet—and she ran away screaming (and right into that fucktard's arms)?

"For three years, I tried my damnedest to *fix* her and love her and protect her as best I could. But it turns out she was too broken to be fixed and loved and protected—or at least too broken to be fixed by a 'sick fuck' like me. Well, if I'm gonna lose the only girl I've ever loved for simply *fantasizing* about doing some crazy shit, then I might as well fucking do all of it, huh? Especially now that she's gone for good, riding off into the sunset on a fucking polo pony. Why should I suffer all the consequences of being a sick fuck without reaping all the rewards, too? So let's do this shit, motherfuckers. I'm ready, baby—as ready as a sick fuck can possibly be."

I look up from my screen, overwhelmed. Holy effing shit. My heart is beating so hard, I feel like it's going to crack me wide open from the inside-out. I take a deep breath, look back down at the screen, and continue reading.

Please provide a detailed statement regarding your sexual

preferences. To maximize your experience in The Club, please be as explicit, detailed, and honest as possible. Please do not self-censor, in any fashion.

"If you were a woman telling me to be as explicit, detailed, and honest as possible and not self-censor myself in any fashion, I'd laugh in your face. But since you're some mysterious 'intake agent' at an underground sex club, and since I've got literally nothing to lose at this point, I'll do it. But here's the deal: I want absolute assurance you're gonna give me precisely what I ask for, to the letter. If after reading this you determine you can't give me exactly what I want, every fucking time, then don't approve my membership. Because, just to be clear, I don't need this club to get laid—I can do that just fine on my own with some of the world's most beautiful women. The only reason I'm applying to this club is to fulfill my 'sick fuck' fantasies, *exactly as described.* Because I don't want this shit to taint my real life.

"Before I describe what I want you to give me, let's first talk logistics—because I don't have the time or attention span to do things your usual way. The way this club was described to me by a buddy, it's my understanding you typically assign each new member a color-coded bracelet so he can hook up with like-minded women with similarly coded bracelets at bars or wherever. Well, that's not gonna work for me. I'm too busy and what I want is too specific. So what I want is for you to read this application, go through your database, and then curate compatible women for me, no color-coded bracelets or check-ins required.

"I've recently learned I'll be traveling around the country for about a month in the near future, appraising certain investment opportunities for my company. (I anticipate visiting about twelve cities over the course of one month—my exact itinerary to be finalized.) In each city of my month-long 'tour,' on each designated date (by four o' clock in the afternoon), I'll leave a room key under the name 'Emma' at the front desk of a designated five-star hotel. At precisely eight o'clock, I'll enter the reserved room to find one of two scenarios awaiting me, exactly as described below:

"Scenario One. Two willing women curated by you will be in the room, awaiting my arrival, preferably already naked. The women should expect to have sex with me and/or each other, depending on my mood and the level of my attraction to each woman. At the very least, they'll definitely perform sexual acts with each other while I watch.

"Scenario Two. When I enter the room, a blindfolded and naked woman, tied to the bed, will already be there. I will not be the one who tied the woman up—she'll already be in the required state when I arrive—which means someone besides the woman will initially need to accompany her to the room to help her get into position. By the time I arrive, that third party participant absolutely must be gone. Please note I will arrive at the room promptly at eight o'clock sharp, no earlier or later, to allow the woman and whoever's assisting her to plan the set-up accordingly.

"After I've entered the room, the woman should expect to engage in some form of sexual activity with me while she remains bound and blindfolded. The sex will be pleasurable and nonviolent. But please note we will be enacting a role-play in which the sex is nonconsensual.

"At the end of the blindfolded portion of our activities (which shall last no more than one hour at the outside), I will remove the woman's blindfold. When I do so, this will signal for purposes of our mutual role-play that I am someone entirely new, specifically someone who has newly entered the room to rescue her from the "attack" she's just endured (which, I repeat, will be pleasurable and nonviolent). I'll proceed to untie the woman and further sexual contact will likely occur at that time, at my discretion.

"A few important caveats and requirements: First, condoms will be used at all times, no exceptions. Second, there will be absolutely no violence of any nature, no exceptions. Any suggestion of violence during the rape-bondage role-play scenario will be purely theatrical and intended to enhance the role-play. Please note that words like "no" and "stop," etc. during the bondage scenario will not be heeded. If the woman feels uncomfortable or scared in any way, she must use the safe word "Sick Fuck." If she uses that phrase, I will immediately stop whatever I'm doing and take explicit instruction from her, whatever that is, including stopping, slowing down, and/or untying and releasing her.

"Third, all participating women must be extremely fit and natural blondes. This is non-negotiable.

"Fourth, at least three hours in advance of each date, each woman will leave a signed nondisclosure agreement and consent form for me at the hotel front desk (templates of both forms will be forwarded to you under separate cover once my membership is approved). The consent form shall detail the woman's understanding of and agreement to participate in all activities detailed above, especially the nonconsensual role-play, plus her understanding of the safe word and its function, and her consent to participate in all activities, without limitation. In addition, I'll also require a copy of each woman's medical testing, dated no earlier than two days before our meeting, establishing she's tested negative for pregnancy and all sexually transmitted diseases. Again, if these requirements necessitate payment beyond your usual monthly membership fee, please contact me to negotiate the increased fee. I do realize I'm asking you for services above and beyond your typical matching services, and I'm amenable to paying a premium for your individualized attention.

"Finally, if room service and/or an in-room massage is desired by my date (or dates) before I arrive at eight o'clock sharp, she/they should feel free to charge any desired expenses to the room. My primary concern is her (their) comfort and enjoyment.

"As far as which of the two scenarios is scheduled in each city on my itinerary, surprise me. As long as each scenario is represented equally over the course of the month, I'll be more than satisfied.

"So there you go. These are my sick-fuck fantasies. I wound up losing the only woman I've ever loved over them—and I hadn't even acted on any of them yet. So fuck it. Let's do this. If my fantasies are gonna ruin my life, then I should at least get to do them, don't you think?

"I look forward to hearing from you. Thank you."

I can't stop staring at my laptop screen.

I turn off the music. I need silence. I'm overwhelmed.

Holy Not What I Was Expecting, Batman.

This is a lot to take in. I feel like my brain is short-circuiting.

My head hurts.

And so does my heart.

That Emma girl really did a number on Josh, didn't she? Wow. What a bitch.

I read the entire application again, my heart racing.

Wow. It's no less overwhelming to me the second time around.

I sit and stare at the wall for ten minutes, a thousand emotions bombarding me.

My eyelids are drooping. God, I'm so damned tired, I can't think clearly. And I certainly can't formulate what I wanna say about all this to Josh just yet.

Now I understand why Josh didn't want me to read his damned application. For him, our tug-of-war over his application wasn't a game—not the way it was for me, anyway. For him, it was an act of emotional self-preservation.

No wonder he called me a terrorist.

He must have hated me for how hard I pushed.

Shit. I should have let the man have his privacy. I should have left him alone.

I grab my phone off the bed next to me and tap out a text to Josh. "I've read it," I type. "Gonna sleep now—about to keel over. Let's talk later, after I wake up."

Josh's reply is instantaneous. "Is it worse than being chained to a donkey?"

I roll my eyes. "You said I didn't have to tell you my thoughts right away—you said I only had to text that I've read it."

"Yeah, yeah, I know I said that," he writes. "And I totally meant it. But just tell me one thing now, just so I can fall asleep: What are all your thoughts about my application?"

I grin. He's so cute. "Too many thoughts all at once. I'm too sleep deprived to think. Just let me catch a couple hours of sleep and then we'll talk." I press send.

Josh's application has made me feel a thousand different emotions, all at once, but mostly, I feel a horrible pang in my heart for the rejection Josh endured at the hands of someone he loved and trusted.

I sigh. Oh, Josh. I really can't let him twist in the wind for hours while I sleep. *I* know his application doesn't change a goddamned thing between us, but *he* doesn't know that. I don't want to talk about all this in detail just yet, but I certainly don't want him to feel anxiety, either.

I pick up my phone and call him.

"Hi," Josh says, picking up my call after one ring.

57

"Hi."

There's a long beat as Josh waits for me to say whatever I'm calling to say. I can hear him holding his breath on his end of the line.

"All I wanna do is sleep," I say evenly. "That's all."

He still doesn't say anything.

"I don't wanna talk just yet. I really need to process exactly what I wanna say to you. Okay?"

"Okay," he says softly.

"But... I was thinking... will you come to my room and sleep with me tonight? I don't wanna be alone—I want to be with you."

He lets out a loud puff of air. "Hell yeah. I'll be right there."

Chapter 10
Josh

I'm jolted awake by a banging at the door. My eyes spring open.

I'm tangled up with Kat in her bed, in my briefs, and I've got a gigantic woody. I was having an awesome dream—a totally awesome dream about Kat. It was so blatantly symbolic, so *obvious*, I feel like slapping my subconscious for being so lacking in imagination. In my dream, Kat was giving me an incredible blowjob and Emma walked into the room. But rather than jerk out of Kat's mouth and rush to smooth things over with Emma, I just said, "Oh, hey, Emma. I'm kinda busy right now." And then I looked down at Kat, at her blue eyes looking up at me, and I smiled.

There's another loud bang at the door. "Hey, are you guys in there?"

Kat lifts her head, bleary-eyed. She looks at the clock and rubs her eyes. "Oh crap. My alarm didn't go off."

I leap out of bed and bound to the door. "Yeah, we're here," I call out.

I open the door to find Henn standing there. His eyes immediately train on my gigantic boner. "Well, good morning," Henn says cheerily, staring at my crotch. His eyes snap up to my face. "Dude," he says. "We've gotta be on-call to save the world today, remember?"

"Sorry," I mumble. "Our alarm didn't go off."

He motions to my dick. "Mmm hmm. Time to get your other head in the game, Faraday." He peeks past me into the room. "Kat?"

"Yep," she calls from inside the room. "Come on in, Henny."

I open the door wide and Henn strolls past me. He's definitely got his swagger on today—which makes sense: I suppose Henn's playing in some sort of Hacker Super Bowl today.

"Hey, Kitty Kat," Henn says. "Sorry to intrude on your optometry appointment *again*, but Jonas texted ten minutes ago, asking me to confirm all the money's still in place and we're ready to move at his signal. I told him we're good to go any time, boss, of course—and then I ran around like a chicken with my head cut off looking for you two losers. Jesus, guys. You're gonna give me gray hair, and I'm much too young and pretty for gray hair."

"Sorry," Kat and I say in unison.

"I know you guys are busy falling in love and all—"

My eyes instantly dart to Kat's face, my cheeks bursting with color, and she looks like Henn just stuck her finger into an electrical socket.

"—but we've gotta keep our eye on the job," Henn continues. "Jonas and Sarah went into their meeting with the feds a few hours ago and we've got to be ready, just in case. Once we've delivered the money, then you two can go off and do whatever the hell kind of eye exam you want, all night and day, but right now I need both of you to keep your eyes on the prize and your heads in the game."

I look down. This is exactly why I've stayed friends with Henn for so long: he's one of the few people in my life that calls me on my shit. He's right. I've been letting myself get hopelessly distracted from what we're here in Las Vegas to do.

"To be honest, the odds are low we'll be asked to make the transfers today," Henn continues, his tone much softer, "so I'm sure we're okay—Jonas is ninety-nine percent sure his meeting's gonna go 'til the end of the banking day today—but he wants us to stand by just in case. No room for error."

"You're totally right, Henn," Kat says. "We'll stop acting like complete idiots."

"Not you, Kitty Kat. Just *him*," Henn says, winking at her. "You can do no wrong, pretty lady."

Kat grins at Henn. "Hear that, Josh? You're a terrible influence on me." She laughs. "Do I have time to take a quick shower, Henny?" She sits up and the bed sheet slides off her torso—clearly revealing the outline of her nipples under her thin, white tank top.

Oh shit. I don't think she's ever looked sexier than she does right now.

"I think you'd better just throw on your clothes and be ready in five, just in case," Henn says, averting his eyes from Kat's skimpy tank top. He looks at his watch. "The minute banking hours are over here in Vegas, then we'll be off the hook 'til tomorrow morning and you can shower and all that. But, in theory, Jonas could call literally any time now so we've got to be ready to move on a dime."

"Okay," Kat says, rubbing her face. "Sorry, Henny. We'll pull our shit together and get our heads in the game from now on. Right, Josh?"

"Absolutely," I say. *Holy fuck, Kat's nipples look amazing in that tank top.* I look away, my cock tingling.

Kat picks up her phone. "Oh, I've got a text from Sarah. She says one of the guys in the meeting looks like he could stuff her into the trunk of his car and she'd never be heard from again." Kat chuckles to herself. "Oh, shoot, I've got another missed call from my friend Hannah. I should give her a quick call. She's probably got a question on this big account she's handling for me at work. Do I have time to make a quick call? Super-duper quick?" She bats her eyelashes.

Henn nods. "Yeah, really quick. But you might have to get off if Jonas calls and gives us the signal."

"Okay. Like lightning."

I can't peel my eyes off her. I've never seen her first thing in the morning before. She's turning me on. Especially after what happened last night: after reading my application, she opened her door, wordlessly hugged me, and led me to her bed; then, without a word, the two of us lay down together, our bodies pressed close, our arms wrapped around each other, and quickly drifted off to sleep.

It was such a simple interaction, but I have no idea how to put into words how much it meant to me. The woman had just read my sick-fuck fantasies and she serenely fell asleep in my arms. Whatever she plans to say to me about that application at some point in the future will be icing. The way she fell asleep in my arms last night? That was the cake.

Kat dials Hannah's number and presses the phone to her ear.

Her eyes drift to me as she waits for Hannah to pick up.

"How'd you sleep, babe?" she asks softly, the phone pressed to her ear.

My entire body buzzes. Has Kat called me 'babe' before? I don't think so. But if so, she's never said it quite like that.

61

"Good," I say, my skin electrifying. "You?"

"Good." She beams a smile at me. "Really, really good."

Holy shit. I feel high. With one brief and seemingly innocuous exchange, the woman just confirmed exactly what's going on inside her head: she doesn't think I'm a sick fuck.

Kat's attention is drawn to her phone. "Hi, Hannah Banana Montana Milliken," she says. "So what's up?" She listens for a minute. "Oh, no worries. Just tell them we'll do a Twitter campaign instead—that's their demographic, anyway. We'll make lemonade out of lemons. No problem. We can set up a live chat with a hashtag." She pauses. "Oh, I dunno, how 'bout hashtag-I've-got-your-pulled-pork-right-here?" She winks at me. "And then we'll select a winner," she continues. "I'd say a gift card. Yeah. That sounds good. But I can talk to them if you prefer—I'll probably be free later today to chat." She laughs. "Aw, anytime. Thanks for picking up all the slack while I've been gone."

Henn and I look at each other. The woman's a PR badass; there's no doubt about it. I love seeing her like this, kicking ass and taking names.

"Yeah, I am, as a matter of fact," Kat says into the phone, her eyes drifting to me. "Mmm hmm. Actually, yeah, he *is*." She beams a huge smile at me.

Henn rolls his eyes and shoots me a smirk.

"Funny you should ask that, Banana," Kat says, her eyes leaving me and landing on Henn. "He *does*. And he's the coolest guy you'll ever meet. Actually, he's a *fucking genius*."

Henn shifts his weight.

Kat suddenly extends her phone toward Henn. "Henn, my adorable and funny friend Hannah Millikin wants very much to say hello to you."

"To *me*?" Henn asks, his face turning red.

Kat laughs. "Yup. Come on, Henn. *YOLO*." She holds out the phone again, insisting he take it. "Hannah's the coolest girl you'll ever talk to, I promise. A total goofball. Loyal. Smart. Cute. Funny. The list goes on and on. Nothing to lose by just saying hi."

Henn waffles.

"Oh, and did I mention?" Kat says. "She got brown hair and glasses." She winks.

Henn takes the phone, his cheeks rising with color. "Well, this isn't awks or anything," he says into the phone. "Hello, Hannah Millikin. I'm Peter Hennessey—but everyone just calls me Henn." He pauses to let Hannah talk and then chuckles. "Yeah, she *did* kinda make it sound like your idea, actually." He laughs again. "She's a sneaky one, for sure." He pauses. "Um, you know, just working... I'm a computer specialist—a freelance programmer." He clears his throat and listens for a moment. "L.A., New York, Toronto, Denver—I go wherever the job takes me, and I can work from anywhere, so I travel a lot, but I mostly live in L.A. in a crappy-ass apartment. Where are you? Oh, yeah, duh. Kat just said she works with you. Yeah, sure, I get up there sometimes—I love it there. Good salmon." He pauses. "Me, too," he finally says. "Indubitably." He grins broadly at something Hannah's saying. "Yeah, I hope so. Thanks." He blushes and hands the phone back to Kat. "Here you go."

"Not so awks after all, huh?" Kat says playfully.

Henn flashes a shy smile. "Not nearly as awks as it could have been," he agrees. "She made it easy."

Kat grins and grabs the phone. "Hey, girl. Isn't he the cutest? I know, right? Sure, I'll send you a picture." She lowers her voice. "Word on the street is he's a *phenomenal* kisser, too." She beams a smile at Henn and giggles. "Yeah, I will. Okay, bye, Banana. Thanks again."

Kat puts her phone down, grins devilishly, and steeples her fingers like a cartoon villain. "Oh, my darling Henny, I have a *feeling*."

"About what?"

"About *you* and my dear friend Hannah Banana Montana Millikin. What's your sign?"

"My *sign*? Sagittarius."

Kat's face lights up. "Ah, the explorer. Well, that makes perfect sense. And super-duper perfect with Leo."

"Hannah's a Leo?" I ask.

Kat nods. "And Sag-Leo is a fabulous combo. Maybe when we're done saving the world all four of us can go out to dinner some time?"

"I'd be up for that," I say.

Henn shrugs and makes a face like he's got nothing to lose. "Um. Sure."

Kat scrolls through the photos on her phone for a moment. When she finds what she's looking for, she hands her phone to Henn. "That's Hannah," she says.

Henn looks at the phone. "Wow. She's super cute." He blushes. "Yeah, I'd totally be up for dinner. Sounds great."

"Awesome." Kat's eyes are positively sparkling. She plops her phone onto the bed next to her. "Okay, boys. I'm gonna brush my teeth and wash my face and then, *voila,* I'll be Oksana Belenko for as long needed."

With that, she hops out of bed in her itty-bitty G-string and barely-there tank top and sashays to the bathroom on her long, toned legs, her blonde hair falling down her back—completely unaware of, or not giving a shit about, the male shrapnel she's leaving behind in her glorious wake.

Chapter 11
Kat

I'm practically peeing myself with laughter.

Josh, Henn, and Reed are telling the story of how Josh wound up with "YOLO" inked onto his ass, and Will, Carmen, and I are laughing so hard, we can barely keep ourselves upright at the table.

As it turned out, Josh, Henn and I weren't called upon to make the money transfers today. At around four o' clock our time, Sarah and Jonas called to tell us we were free until eight tomorrow morning, at which time they wanted us to station ourselves outside the first bank on our agenda, ready to go at their signal. Which meant that after Josh, Henn, and I did a little shopping for clothes befitting the wealthy pimpstress Oksana Belenko, we decided to let off a little steam and have a great meal together.

"Let's call Reed," Josh suggested. "Get the band back together."

As it turned out, Reed was on his way to the airport with Will and Carmen when Josh called, but at his friend's invitation to dinner, he turned his car around. And now Josh, Henn, Reed, Will, Carmen and I are sitting together in a five-star restaurant, half-way through our amazing meal, laughing 'til tears pour down our faces.

"You *knew* I had the quote wrong the whole time?" Josh shouts at Reed, incredulous. "After ten years, this is the first time I'm hearing this part of the story."

Reed is laughing so hard, he's crying. "Of course, I knew. You were dead in the water, bro. Everyone knew it. It wasn't even close."

"Then why the hell did you goad me on like that?"

"And miss watching you to get 'YOLO' tattooed onto your ass?"

Josh can't believe his ears. "For all these years, I thought you didn't know. I thought you were being fair and impartial."

65

Reed shakes his head, laughing. "Hell no. I was Team Henn all the way. It served you right, bro. You were being a total dick about it."

Henn is howling with laughter. "You're demented, Reed."

"Hey, all in good fun."

"Fun for *you*, maybe," Josh says. "You're not the one with YOLO tattooed on his ass."

"Aw, bad tattoos happen to the best of us," Will says, slapping Josh on the shoulder. "Look at this." Will rolls up his sleeve and shows Josh a tattoo on his forearm—and I immediately slap my hand over my mouth at the sight of it. Oh my God, no. Will's got a *dragon* on his arm—one of the tattoos on my so-called list of no-no's.

"Oh, look, a *dragon*," Josh says, smiling, his facial expression morphing into one of pure glee. "Do you see that, Kitty Kat?"

My cheeks burst into flames. Holy crap. Why the heck did I name dragon tattoos as one of the items on my "social suicide" list? I was talking out my butt—pulling it out of thin air. Why the heck did I say that?

Josh looks at me and smirks wickedly and I shoot him a look that begs him for mercy.

"I got the heart first," Will says, oblivious to the nonverbal exchange happening between Josh and me. Will points to a prominent heart on his dragon's chest. "My ex-girlfriend and I got matching hearts."

Josh's face lights up at Will's use of the word "ex-girlfriend."

Oh no. *No.* This can't be happening.

"Oh, so you got the heart with your *girlfriend,* did you?" Josh asks Will. "Who's now your *ex*-girlfriend?"

"Yeah, I was sure we'd be together forever. But then she slept with my best friend, so I had to get the dragon to camouflage it."

The smile on Josh's face is positively merciless. "Hey, Kat. Did you catch that? Will's got *both* a dragon tattoo *and* an ex-girlfriend tattoo." Josh can barely contain his giddiness. "Imagine that."

My cheeks are on fire. Why, oh why, did I say all that stuff to Josh about prohibited tattoos? I was just being snarky. I had no idea what I was saying.

"What's so funny?" Will asks, looking confused. "Why do I feel like I'm missing the joke?"

Oh, God, please, no. This can't be happening. I cover my face with my hands.

"Are you feeling like crawling into a hole about now, PG?" Josh asks.

I nod from behind my hands and Josh hoots with laughter.

"Well, Will," Josh begins like he's teaching a lesson to a grade-schooler. "Kat here's got a very specific list of tattoos that she's decided in her infinite wisdom are *cliché* and stupid and therefore tantamount to committing 'social suicide,' as she so colorfully puts it."

"And dragons and hearts are both on Kat's list?" Will asks.

"No, not hearts, surprisingly. Just dragon and *girlfriend* tattoos." Josh chuckles happily. "Social suicide, both of them, Will, I'm sorry to inform you—but they're simply not allowed. I guess you'll have to get that shit lasered, huh?"

"Oh, shit," Will says. "Yeah, this is a catastrophe. I've got *two* prohibited tattoos? Damn that Stubborn Kat. She won't do anything you want her to do *and* she thinks your tattoos are stupid."

I'm dying. I'm physically dying. "No, Will, I..." I begin, but I can't speak. I've never been so frickin' mortified in my life.

"And guess what *else* is on Stubborn Kat's list?" Josh continues, beaming.

Will shrugs. "I dunno. Flowers? I've got flowers for my momma, too."

Josh shakes his head. "Nope. Flowers are allowed. Guess again. I'll give you a hint: it's on my ass."

The entire table erupts with laughter.

"Well, I can't blame Stubborn Kat for that one," Will says.

"Neither can I," Reed says. "She probably took one look at your ass and added it to the list."

"Oh no," Josh says, laughing. "That's the best part. Stubborn Kat came up with this list *before* she'd seen a single one of my tattoos."

The table erupts again. Everyone but me is laughing so hard, they can't breathe.

"Before?" Will says. "Oh shit. And you hadn't even *told* her about any of 'em?"

Josh is laughing too hard to speak, so he simply shakes his head.

I look at Henn, desperate for an ally, and he flashes me a sympathetic frownie-face. "Hang in there, Kitty Kat," he says above the fray.

Josh places his forehead down on the table, apparently spent from laughing so hard.

"Hey, at least you've only got *one* tattoo on the prohibited list," Will says. "I'm the loser with *two*."

I open my mouth to apologize profusely, but nothing comes out. This is the most embarrassing moment of my life.

"Oh shit, hang on," Josh says, trying to catch his breath from laughing. He raises his head from the table, and with great flourish, rolls up his sleeve to display the dragon tattoo on his beautiful, bulging bicep.

The whole table loses it again.

And I want to die. I truly want to die.

"YOLO *and* a dragon," Will says. "Tsk, tsk."

Josh wipes his eyes.

"And she said all that shit before she knew any of your tattoos? Aw, come on someone must have told her. She was just fucking with you." Will looks at me. "Please tell me you were just fucking with him, Stubborn Kat."

I shake my head, an apologetic look on my face. "I was just talking out my butt, being a total smart-ass."

Will hits his forehead with his palm. "Truth is stranger than fiction, man. This is the best story, ever."

Josh nods. "I seriously couldn't believe it. We were texting and I just stared at my screen, like 'oh my fucking God, I've hit the mother lode.'"

"Gosh darn it, Stubborn Kat," Will says, putting on his cartoon voice. "She sniffs out your stupid tattoos and nails you to the wall with 'em."

"Kinda the way some cats curl up with dying people at a nursing home," Reed says, and everyone laughs. "Why didn't you just tell her, man?" Reed asks Josh.

"No fucking way I was gonna tell her," Josh says. "I figured I'd let her find out the good old fashioned way—by seeing my ass." He winks and Reed and Will clink their glasses against Josh's.

"Atta boy," Reed says.

I'm peeking at the group from behind my hands, afraid to come out. My eyes drift to Henn again and he makes a face that tells me he feels my pain.

"Hey, Stubborn Kat," Josh says. "Why don't you tell the group *all* of your amazing rules. Enlighten us. Amaze us with what a hip whippersnapper you are."

"I believe a hip whippersnapper's actually called a '*hippersnapper*,'" Will says.

Everyone at the table (except for me) laughs. I can't stop hiding behind my hands. This is sheer pain right here.

"Aw, come on, babe. 'You don't make The Rules, you just enforce 'em.' Remember?"

I shake my head. "There's no way I'm making any declarations about what's cool and what's not in this crowd. Every man at this table could tattoo Bert and Ernie onto his forehead and make it look cool," I say.

Will picks up his napkin and rubs it forcefully against his forehead. "Well, I guess now would be the time to remove this makeup on my forehead and show you..."

Everyone laughs, yet again.

"You're not gonna enlighten us about all The Rules for Being Cool, Stubborn Kat?" Josh asks.

I shake my head.

"She's normally not so shy, I swear," he says.

"Come on, Stubborn Kat," Will says. "What else is on the list? We've got dragons, YOLO, girlfriends that didn't work out, and what? I've got two so far—I'm hoping to rack up some more points before the night is over."

I put my head on the table and bury my head with my arms. "Make it stop," I mumble.

Will laughs.

"Come on, guys," Henn says. "Make fun of me for a while, as usual. How 'bout I dance for you?"

"Oh, yeah. Let's make Henny dance—my favorite thing!" Reed says, suddenly giddy. He bangs on the table. "Dance puppet-boy, dance!"

Henn grumbles.

"We'll definitely have to hit my club after dinner."

Everyone agrees.

"But back to Kat's list," Will says. "Come on. What else is on it, Stubborn Kat? I bet I've got at least some of the stuff on the list, whatever it is."

Josh grabs my hand and kisses it. "You're not gonna tell him?"

I shake my head. "I'm never gonna say anything about anyone's tattoos ever again, as long as I live."

Josh grins and looks at Will. "Barbed wire on your bicep—or a tribal band, unless you're an Islander. Stubborn Kat was very specific about that. You got either of those, man?"

"Fuck no. I agree with Stubborn Kat on both. And yet, right now, I wish so bad I had both so I could pull up my sleeve and see the look on her face."

Everyone laughs at the thought, even me.

"Me, too," Josh says, squeezing my hand. "I never thought I'd be bummed *not* to have barbed wire."

"Hey, it's never too late, Faraday," Reed says, laughing. "We're in Vegas, after all."

"There you go again, Reed," Josh says. "Trying to get me inked with something stupid." He sips his drink. "Well, lucky for me, I'm not gonna get drunk tonight, or I'd probably do it."

"No, you wouldn't," Henn says. "Barbed wire would be too stupid even for you, Josh."

"Bite your tongue," Josh says. "There's no such thing as a tattoo that's 'too stupid' for Josh Faraday—not if you ply me with enough alcohol and double-dare me, anyway."

"Oh, we know, Mr. 'Welcome to the Gun Show,'" Reed says.

Josh, Henn, and Reed burst out laughing.

"'I double-dare you,'" Reed says, apparently re-enacting something—and all three guys laugh again, shaking their heads.

"You're a Neanderthal, Josh," Henn says.

Josh sips his drink happily. "I really am."

"I take it you've got a tattoo that says 'Welcome to the Gun Show'?" Will asks, incredulous.

Josh nods.

"On your arms, presumably?"

Josh nods again.

"Oh shit. *Horrible*. That's gotta be on Kat's list, too, right? Please tell me it is. That's gotta be double points."

Josh shakes his head. "Surprisingly, not on the list. Too horrible to even mention, I suppose. Right, Kat? Some tattoos are too stupid to make the list?"

My face is hot. "Please make it stop," I say.

Josh squeezes my hand and kisses the side of my head. "All in good fun, baby," he whispers to me. "This is how we show we like you." He squeezes my hand again.

"Well, dude, aren't you gonna show me?" Will says.

"Show him," Reed says.

Josh shrugs, unbuttons his shirt, and pulls it down off his shoulders, revealing his muscled, tattooed chest and the tops of his gorgeous arms—and the sight of him makes my crotch instantly start filling with blood.

Josh bends his arms behind his head and flexes and everyone at the table bursts into laughter at the sight of the tattoos on the undersides of his biceps.

"Welcome to... the Gun Show," Reed says, pointing out Josh's tattoos like he's Vanna White on *Wheel of Fortune*. "That was the night I learned Josh Faraday will do literally *anything* to get a laugh."

I've gone back into hiding behind my hands, partly because the sight of Josh baring his body in this restaurant is making me want to jump his bones and partly because I feel like I'm gonna barf.

"Hell yeah, I will. Life's too short. Hey, Kat. Are you gonna come out from hiding any time soon?" Josh asks. "Come on, babe, join the party. We're all friends here. Nobody's mad at you. It's all in good fun. It's just what friends *do* with friends—they torture them."

I slowly come out from under my arms like a turtle. "You guys, when I said all that stuff about prohibited tattoos and social suicide, I was just being a total and complete smart-ass. I just pulled that stuff out of thin air. I take it all back."

"Ha! Don't backtrack now, PG. Go big or go home, babe."

"No, I was totally wrong. Please, God, just let me reverse time and take it all back." I take a huge gulp of my martini.

"Come on, Stubborn Kat," Reed says. "Don't let Josh bully you into backing down from your closely held beliefs. Stay true to yourself."

I shake my head. "He's not bullying me. I don't believe any of what I said." I move my arm like I'm blessing them all. "You're all supremely cool. Forget I ever said any of it."

71

"How the hell did you survive with four brothers, Kat?" Josh says, spearing a vegetable on his plate. "A little bit of teasing and you back down? I expected so much more from Stubborn Kat."

"You have *four* brothers?" Will asks.

"And no sisters," Josh adds.

"Wow. That must have been fun growing up," Will says.

I nod. "Fun and hell, simultaneously—kind of like right now. Two older, two younger. They taught me to have a thick skin, for sure."

"The girl might as well have grown up in a frat house," Josh says. "She's an honorary dude. Well, usually. She's definitely acting like a girl right now." He takes a huge bite of food and grins.

I smile thinly at him.

Josh grabs my hand and kisses it again. "Well, young lady, let this be a lesson to you. I'm not only wise and powerful, I'm super cool, too—right down to my stupid tattoos." He addresses the group. "See, the thing Kat doesn't realize, is that it's the 'stupid' tattoos that are the best ones. Because mistakes, big and small, are what teach us to learn and grow."

"*Exactly*," Will says emphatically. "Even the stupid tattoos wind up being profound if you think about them like that."

"I was just being a smart-ass, Will. Please don't be offended," I offer.

"I'm not offended at all," Will says gently. "My dragon tattoo *is* kinda stupid—but the cool thing is that it's camouflage for a huge mistake." He smiles broadly at me. "That's why I love it. Every time I look at the damned thing, I'm reminded I got my heart broken into a million pieces and came out the other side a dragon." He takes a bite of his food.

Josh throws up his hands, totally enthralled. "Now see, that's what I'm talking about, bro. Every tattoo, even if it's a mistake, is a reminder of who you *were* versus who you are now. A map of your evolution as a man." He swigs his drink.

"Amen," Will says. "The body is a living canvas. It's all there: victory, failure, mistakes, lessons learned—all there for the world to see."

"You know what we should do?" Josh says to Will, slamming down his fork with sudden excitement. "We should both complete our lame-ass trifectas tonight. Together."

"Fuck yeah. Barbed wire, it is, baby," Will says. They clink drinks.

"Oh God, no, Will," Carmen says, putting her hand on Will's forearm. "Honey, no. Please."

Will laughs and takes another bite of his food. "Don't worry, Car. I'll just get it on my ass, like my boy here. A little barbed wire on my ass for you and no one else." He laughs.

"There you go," Josh says, laughing. "Genius. It's just skin, right?" He takes a bite of his steak.

"Fuck yeah," Will agrees. "I'm totally gonna do it. We're all a pile of skin and bones sooner or later. That's what gets me going every fucking day, knowing I'm running out of time."

"Amen," Josh says. "Hey, maybe I'll join you—add a little barbed wire to my dragon's neck, maybe?"

"Hey, great idea," Will says. "I'll totally add barbed wire to my dragon."

"Jesus Christ," Reed says. "Will, stop listening to Josh Faraday of all people about tattoos. Listen to him about everything else, because the guy's a fucking genius, just not about tattoos."

"Shut the fuck up," Josh says. "I'm wise and powerful about *all* things, including tattoos."

"Don't do it," Reed says to Will.

"Dude, Reed's using reverse psychology on you," Henn warns Will. "He's being the puppet master."

"No, I'm not. I'm sincerely telling *Will* not to do it," Reed says. "Although *you* should absolutely do it, Faraday. Add yet another stupid tattoo to your stupid collection."

"My collection isn't stupid," Josh says. "Didn't you hear a damned thing Will and I were just saying? Even the stupid ones are *profound,* man. We're *living canvases,* Reed. Duh. We're *artists* and *art,* all at the same time."

"Yeah, Reed. We're *living canvases,*" Will agrees with solemnity. "We're artists and art, all at the same time. We're living performance art and our tattoos are our way of flipping the bird to *mortality.*"

"That's right," Josh says emphatically. "Getting barbed wire would be like saying, 'Mortality, fuck you. You might be gunning for me, but you'll have to get through my barbed wire to get *me,* motherfucker. Raaaaah.'"

Reed rolls his eyes.

"So lemme get this straight, boss," Henn says, pursing his lips like he's considering something very serious. "You got YOLO stamped on your *ass* because you were flipping the bird to *mortality?*"

Josh laughs. "Absolutely. Now, when the Grim Reaper comes for my ass, maybe he'll see it and stop and say, 'Never mind.'"

Everyone laughs.

Carmen leans into me. "Josh is hilarious," she whispers.

I nod and bite my lip. "He sure is."

Josh swigs his drink happily. Man, he's having fun tonight.

"Okay, okay, I cannot tell a lie," Josh is saying. "I must admit, I wasn't thinking deep and profound thoughts about my mortality when I got YOLO stamped on my ass. I wasn't thinking much of anything, actually. I was just a twenty-year-old asswipe who thought he knew everything."

"Aw, don't be too hard on yourself," Reed says. "All twenty-year-old dudes are asswipes who think they know everything. I know I was."

"How old are you, Will?" I ask.

"Twenty-three," he replies. "And I don't think I know everything."

"Well, I thought I knew everything when I was twenty-three," Reed says, shaking his head. "Turns out I sure had a whole lot to learn between twenty and thirty."

"Ditto," Henn agrees. "Jesus, has it really been ten years since Josh got his stupid YOLO tat? Oh my shit, we're getting old."

"Remember when thirty sounded so old?" Reed says, looking wistful.

Josh nods. "I never thought I'd make it to thirty."

"Really?" I ask, the hair on my arms standing up. "Doesn't everyone think they're gonna live to a hundred and three?"

Josh shrugs and takes a bite of his food but doesn't reply.

I look at Josh for a long beat. When I opened my door to him last night and wordlessly took him into my arms, the look on his face was so vulnerable, it took my breath away—and, just now, that exact same expression flashed across his handsome face.

"Jeez, before we know it," Henn says. "We'll be *forty* and in the middle of our mandatory midlife crisis."

"Jesus. Who knows what fucked up shit Faraday will do then?" Reed says. "He'll probably get himself a midlife-crisis car like a fucking Lamborghini or some shit like that. Oh, whoops. Already did that."

"He's got a *Lamborghini*?" Carmen whispers to me, her eyes wide.

I nod and she mouths, "Wow."

"Hey, might as well have the douche-car to match the douche-tattoos," Josh says, clearly not the least bit offended by Reed's jab. "Like I always say, 'Go big or go home.' Right, Kat?"

I lean into Josh and put my head on his shoulder. "I'm sorry," I whisper. "I feel like an idiot."

He kisses the top of my head. "We're just teasing you, babe," he whispers back. "It's what we do if we like you. No worries—never worry in this crowd. We're just playing."

"So how about forty, big guy?" Henn asks Josh. "Can you imagine that?"

Josh shrugs but doesn't reply. He takes a bite of his food.

"Well, I can picture all of us at forty," Henn says. "We're all exactly the same as we are now—strikingly handsome, fucking geniuses—only difference is we're married and driving minivans full of screaming kids."

Reed makes a scoffing noise. "I think your crystal ball's got a loose wire, bro—at least relating to me." He swigs his drink.

"No 'married with children' for you?" I ask Reed. But, really, I'm indirectly asking Josh—hoping maybe he'll join in the conversation. Why has he gone suddenly mute?

Reed shakes his head emphatically. "No, thanks. I'm gonna be like George Clooney. That dude's got the right idea."

"Oh, I bet even George Clooney will get married one day," Carmen says. "When he meets the right woman."

"I think so, too," I agree.

"No way," Reed says. "Not George. He'll be the last man standing."

"I'm with the girls on that one," Henn says. "When George finds the right woman, he won't wanna let her go. I'd bet anything on it."

"Oh, you'd bet *anything* on it?" Reed asks slowly, rubbing his hands together.

75

"Just a figure of speech," Henn says. "Don't even try your Jedi mind tricks on me."

Josh laughs.

"Hey, Carmen. Why do you say that about George?" Reed asks. "What do you see that I don't?"

Carmen shrugs. "Oh, I dunno. I don't know the guy. He just seems like a passionate person. And passionate people are always the ones who fall the hardest." She looks at Will lovingly.

Will's face is absolutely adorable right now. He leans in and kisses Carmen on the cheek.

"I agree with Carmen," Henn says. "When a man finds the right woman, it's a game-changer." He shrugs. "So I hear."

"Aw, it sounds like you're a diehard romantic, Henn," Carmen says.

"Maybe I am. All I know is I'd love to be married one day to the right girl and maybe even have a little baby. A little daughter maybe. I think that'd be really nice."

"Really?" I say. "That's so sweet, Henny." I feel myself blushing. I sneak a peek at Josh—he's sipping his drink, not saying a word—and my cheeks blaze even hotter.

"What about you two?" Henn asks, and my stomach seizes—but when I glance at Henn, ready to deflect his question, he's looking straight at Will and Carmen, not at Josh and me.

Will and Carmen look at each other for a beat. "Um," Carmen finally says. "Well, I'd love a family one day. But I think that's a loooooong way off."

Will laughs. "Good answer." He wipes his brow comically. "Phew."

I can't bring myself to look at Josh right now and I'm not sure why. My skin feels electrified. "So what about you, Will? What does your future hold, ya think?" I ask, trying to deflect attention from my hot cheeks.

"Oh, I can answer that," Reed says. "Will's gonna be a mega-superstar." He holds up his drink and everyone follows suit. "A toast. To 2Real—the next big superstar."

"Hear, hear," everyone says, clinking glasses.

Carmen leans over and kisses Will on his cheek and he smiles.

"My boy 2Real's gonna be a household name, mark my words," Reed continues.

"Thanks, Reed."

"No need to thank me, man. I'm just telling it like it is. You're a fucking genius." Reed addresses the group. "After my party the other night, Will and Dean sat down with an acoustic guitar and started messing around, and within an hour, they'd written the bones for the most badass song you've ever heard in your life. The thing's gonna be a smash hit." He snaps his fingers. "And they wrote it just like that."

"It's totally awesome," Carmen agrees. "I can't get it out of my head."

Will's eyes are sparkling with sudden animation. "Dean and I totally hit it off—brothers from another mother. We're planning to record it in L.A. next month after Red Card Riot's tour ends."

"I bet we'll wind up making it the lead single off your album," Reed says. "It's just that good."

"What's it called?" I ask. "When I hear it on the radio a year from now, I wanna remember this conversation and say, 'I knew him when.'"

"We'll probably call it 'Crash,'" Will says. "It's pretty dope, if I do say so myself. Best song I've ever written. I can't wait to get into the studio and get it down—I've got a million ideas for the instrumentation. I'm gonna do something really unexpected with it."

Reed rubs his hands together. "I smell a hit."

The waiter arrives to clear dishes and bring refills on drinks.

"What about you, Party Girl with a Hyphen?" Josh asks, breaking his long silence. "What do you see in your future?"

"Um..." I say. Josh didn't answer this question earlier, I noticed, so I'll be damned if I will. Although, if I were being honest, I'd tell him I'm beginning to see a future that includes him. "Well, I'd really like to own my own PR firm one day," I say, opting for a safe but true answer to the question.

Josh looks completely floored by my answer. "Wow," he says. "Really? That's awesome. I had no idea. 'Party Girl PR.'"

"Hey, I like it," I say.

"Well, fingers crossed, maybe you'll come into a million bucks one day soon and you can make that happen sooner than you ever imagined." He winks.

I grin broadly. Crazy as it sounds, I'd actually forgotten about the million bucks Jonas and Josh promised me if we're actually successful in transferring The Club's money tomorrow.

"Oh yeah, speaking of PR," Reed says, "thanks for all your hard work on the campaign for my club, Kat." He laughs. "Impeccable work so far."

"Thanks for being my client," I say. "Was it you who called my boss and charmed her pants off?"

"Yeah, I called her," Reed replies. "And I couldn't have been more insistent we had to have you personally. But I just picked up the phone. It was Josh who paid the bill—he's really the one to thank, not me." He winks at Josh.

I flash a huge smile at Josh. "Well, thank you both. I'm really grateful I've been able to hang out here all this time without losing my job."

"Anything for Josh," Reed says. "I can't even count all the favors this dude has done for me over the years. Josh Faraday might have douche-y tattoos and a midlife crisis car, and he might think he's one hundred percent right about *Happy Gilmore* when he's dead wrong, and he might—"

"*Okay*," Josh says emphatically. "I think she gets the point, Reed. I'm an idiot and a douche. Move on to the good stuff."

"*But*," Reed continues. "Josh Faraday is the best friend a guy could ask for and one of the best humans you'll ever meet."

"I'm not sure if I should kiss you or bitch slap you," Josh says.

Reed puckers and Josh laughs.

Quickly, Josh, Reed, and Henn launch into another snarky conversation about something or other—but I've stopped listening to them. I'm suddenly too busy gazing at Josh and thinking about how cute he is when he laughs with his friends. I'm thinking about how beautiful his blue eyes are, especially set off by the blue jacket he's wearing and in the flickering candlelight of this swanky restaurant. I'm remembering the vulnerable look on Josh's face when I opened my door to him last night, and how he melted into my arms without saying a word besides, "Kat." I'm wondering how a man can suffer so much heartbreak in his life—his mom's murder, his dad's suicide, his brother being institutionalized, his heart getting broken—and yet still manage to laugh and joke around with his friends the way he's doing right now, like he doesn't have a care in the world.

I'm thinking all these thoughts and a whole lot more as I stare at Josh in the candlelight and hold his hand in mine.

I lean my head against his muscled shoulder and take a sip of my drink with my free hand and let out a long, relaxed, happy exhale.

Yes, I'm thinking a thousand thoughts right now—and all of them about Joshua William Faraday.

The table erupts in laughter again at something Henn just said. But I'm not listening to the conversation. I turn my face and take a long whiff of Josh's cologne, and my crotch tingles.

At my movement, Josh kisses the side of my head, even as he's still engaged in conversation with the table, and my heart skips a beat.

Holy shit.

I want him.

And with each passing day, each passing minute, I seem to want Josh more and more. I want to take him home to meet my family and watch football on the couch and eat my mom's famous chili and watch my brothers make fun of him relentlessly for one thing or another. I want to make love to him in my apartment, slowly, for hours, and then drift off to sleep, and not wonder whether he'll be there when I wake up in the morning. I want to see where he lives in L.A. and sit in the passenger seat of his car, whether it's a Lamborghini or Hyundai, while he drives me to his favorite bar— whether it's a dive bar or some hot spot—and I don't want any other woman—any other *blonde*—to sit in that seat besides me.

I squeeze Josh's hand and he squeezes back.

But feeling this way about any man, especially the world's most eligible bachelor—a playboy who dates supermodels and celebrities (and who, by the way, clearly has a pervy-streak a mile long)—sure seems like an extremely precarious thing to do.

Chapter 12
Josh

"Go, Henny! Go, Henny!" Kat chants, shaking her ass, and I laugh.

As we make our way down the hallway to my room, Kat's re-enacting the way Henn danced tonight on the dance floor at Reed's club, and she's doing an uncannily accurate impression.

I join her in doing "The Henn" and she practically falls over, laughing.

"Man, that white boy can dance," she says.

"Well, he *thinks* he can, anyway," I say.

"When it comes to dancing, isn't that all that matters?" she counters.

"No." I laugh. "Not at all."

She laughs.

"It's Reed's personal mission to get Henn to dance every time he sees him," I say. "Reed says watching Henn dance is his own personal happy place."

"Well, yeah. Reed made that pretty clear," Kat retorts. "'Dance, puppet-boy, dance,'" she says, imitating what Reed said to Henn all night long. She giggles. "You three together are just like my brothers—I felt right at home. And Will sure fit right in with you guys as the fourth musketeer, didn't he?"

"Love that guy."

"He reminds me of my little brother Dax."

"I'd like to meet your brothers," I say, and the minute I do, I want to stuff the words back into my mouth. Who just said that? Was that *me*? Dude. Saying you want to meet a girl's family is not a casual thing. "Maybe some day," I add.

She bites her lip. "Sure. Some day."

We've arrived at my room. I swipe the key card and motion to her to enter first. Shit. My heart is racing. I've got to watch myself. Slow my shit down. It's one thing to be feeling like this in Las Vegas, but her family's in Seattle—in real life. Who knows what the future holds when we leave the bubble of this place?

"Where should I put this?" she asks, holding up the duffel bag with her toothbrush and change of clothes we picked up from her room before coming to mine.

"Well, in the bedroom, of course," I say, grinning and she smiles broadly at me. I put her bag in my bedroom and come back out to the sitting area.

"Something to drink, Party Girl?" I ask, moving to the bar.

"Just water. I know I'm not living up to my nickname, but you're absolutely killing me."

"Water it is," I say, moving to the bar. "Your liver just sent you a thank you note."

"*Gracias, señor.*" She flops down on the couch in the sitting area. "So what were you and Will talking about on the way to Reed's club—something about you helping Will's dad with something?"

"Oh, nothing major. I'm just gonna see if I can do Will's dad a favor, make a few calls," I say, grabbing water bottles from the minibar.

"About what?"

"It's no big deal. He's worried his dad is making some bad investments with a buddy—maybe even getting conned by someone he trusts. I'm gonna snoop around and see what I can find out for him."

"Wow. That's nice of you. You seem to do a lot of favors for people," she says.

I push her blonde hair behind her shoulder. "Only for people I like a lot." I bite her shoulder and she giggles in response.

"Is that why Will got that ass-tattoo tonight—as payment for the favor you're gonna do for his dad?"

I laugh. "Hell no. He was just *inspired* by our deep and profound conversation at dinner to get the stupidest tattoo I've ever seen in my entire life, bar none."

She giggles again. "Why didn't you join him? I thought Josh

Faraday's never seen a stupid tattoo he didn't like. What happened to the barbed wire you were gonna get to complete your 'social suicide' trifecta?"

"I chickened out. I guess even I've got my limits." I shrug. "Or maybe I just wasn't drunk enough."

"I swear I've never laughed so hard as when Will dropped his drawers right in front of all of us and got that ridiculous thing. He took the drunken tattoo to a whole new level tonight."

"Yeah, if getting a stupid tattoo is actually deep in a twisted sort of way, then 2Real is one incredibly profound motherfucker." I chuckle. "I should sic Jonas on the guy and watch what happens."

Kat laughs. "I'm sure they'd totally hit it off."

"No, Jonas would quote Plato to Will all night long and poor Will would be like, 'Um, can you bring back the dumb Faraday now? He was a lot more fun.'"

"You're not the dumb Faraday."

"Compared to Jonas, I sure as hell am. My brother is ridiculously brilliant—a whiz with numbers, amazing at solving puzzles, always thinking about something deep and meaningful, unlike me. And the boy's got *vision*. My mom always called him magic."

Kat bites her lip. "You're magic, too, Josh."

I blush. "Not like Jonas. Now, don't get me started on what a complete and total dumbshit Jonas is about people and life in general," I continue, "and especially about relationships—that's a whole other story. The boy's a fucking tool. But, man, Jonas—now there's a magical beast of a dumbshit of a man."

She's listening to me intently. Damn, she's so fucking beautiful. I could sit and look at her all day, every day, and never get tired of her face. I put my fingertip over the slight cleft in her chin and she smiles shyly.

"So enough about my idiot-genius brother," I say softly. "Are you ever gonna tell me what you thought of my application? We haven't been alone for two minutes since Henn woke us up and I've been dying to hear what you think."

She presses her lips together. "You wanna hear what I think, huh?"

I nod, my stomach clenching.

"Well, first off..." She looks up at the ceiling, apparently gathering her thoughts. "Well, first, let's just get this out of the way: I don't think you're a sick fuck." She smiles. "But if you are, then I don't care."

I'm tingling all over. I thought she'd say that, based on the way she fell asleep in my arms after reading it last night, but it sure feels good to hear her say it out loud.

"Well, okay, maybe you're a teeny-tiny bit of a sick fuck," she amends, "but I *like* that about you."

My cock stretches its arms and yawns inside my pants.

"Secondly, I think that, whatever you did to those women in The Club for a month?" She levels me with her sparkling blue eyes. "I want you to do it to me, too—*exactly* the way you did it to them."

Oh shit. My cock just sat upright in bed and yelled, 'Do I smell coffee?'"

There's a long beat as I process what she just said.

She grins broadly. "I also think... as long as you're gonna show me your fantasies, without holding back, then, maybe, if you're willing... " She takes a deep breath. "Maybe I could show you mine?" Again, she bites her lip. "Because I'm actually a bit of a sick fuck myself."

My cock is now doing jumping jacks on the floor next to its bed. "I'd love that," I say, trying to keep my voice steady. "What are your fantasies? In your 'application', you mentioned a bodyguard fantasy and some sort of captive fantasy?"

She nods. "Yeah. Actually, I think the captive fantasy might be pretty consistent with your saving-the-raped-girl fantasy. We might be able to do a two-for-one there."

I shift in my seat, trying to relieve the pressure on my cock. "Just tell me what you want and I'll do it," I say.

She takes a deep breath. "Really? You want the whole thing?"

I nod. "Of course. Tell me the whole damned thing."

She beams a smile at me that stops my heart. "Okay, well, um, let's start with my captive fantasy." She looks giddy. "Well, I'm held captive by a horribly dangerous man who captured me in order to make me his sex slave. But then, after taking me—sensuously, *not* violently, by the way—he winds up falling desperately in love with me—and then after a while another bad guy comes to kidnap me, also intending to make me his sex slave, of course, and my original captor fends him off in a sword fight—"

"A *sword* fight?"

"Yeah, my fantasy kind of toggles between present day and a kind of historical-fiction-locked-in-a-dungeon kind of thing."

"Interesting."

"Anyway, when the second bad guy is finally dead, my original captor unties me and says I can go, because now he cares about me too much to keep me as his prisoner. It's like if you love something, set it free, you know? But I don't want to go—in fact, all I want to do is stay and fuck him for hours and hours—so that's what we do, only this time, without the bondage, because now it's my *choice* to stay and that's what makes it so sexy."

I'm in a daze listening to her, completely shocked.

There's a beat.

I suddenly realize she's not talking anymore.

"So, that's it," she declares, filling the silence.

"Wow," I say. "That was quite a bit more... detailed than I was expecting."

She shrugs. "I fantasize in Technicolor—what can I say?"

I laugh. "It's like a mini-porno."

"*Exactly*. Yes. A mini-porno starring *me*."

"And you've got more of these mini-pornos bouncing around in your head?"

"Tons."

"And who are the guys who play opposite you in these pornos?"

"Well, depending on the mini-porno-fantasy, it could be any number of fantasy-guys—Channing Tatum gets cast a lot; Charlie Hunman makes appearances quite frequently; this hot married guy who works at the bank." She blushes. "But that was all before I saw you standing in that hallway in your wet briefs. Lately, there's only one star of all my imaginary-mini-pornos: Joshua William Faraday."

I smile and so does she.

"So you think my captor-fantasy would work with your saving-the-girl fantasy?" she asks. "Or is it too weird to mix and match?"

"I think that would work just fine." I shift again. My cock is throbbing in my pants. "And what about the bodyguard fantasy? Is it pretty detailed, too?"

She smiles from ear-to-ear, clearly excited by what she's about to say. "Okay, so in *this* one, I'm a world-famous singer and my life is in serious danger because some stalker is after me. So a gorgeous bodyguard has been hired to protect me—a really serious, no-nonsense kind of guy, like a former Secret Service agent. And, one night, I'm performing a concert in a beautiful, sparkly outfit, like a kind of space-age-y-looking thing? Or maybe I've got a beautiful headscarf around my head and I'm looking really somber, sitting on a chair. It just depends what song I'm performing. But either way my bodyguard gets spooked by something he sees in the crowd and he rushes onstage and swoops me up to protect me from an assassin and he literally carries me away from harm, and even though we're not supposed to do it—because my bodyguard's a true professional and takes his job really seriously—we just can't resist our off-the-charts attraction and we totally get it on."

There's a long beat before I'm able to speak without laughing. "So you're saying you've got a porno-version of *The Bodyguard* that plays inside your head?" I say evenly, trying my damnedest not to laugh.

She makes a face. "You're making fun of me? I'm telling you my deepest, darkest, hottest fantasies and you're *laughing* at me?"

I can't contain myself anymore. I burst out laughing. "No, I'm not making fun of you, I swear. I'm sorry, babe. Continue. I'm loving this."

"I've seen *The Bodyguard* like twenty times, okay? And I've always wanted to be Whitney. Stop laughing at me."

I bite my lip, trying to stop laughing. "It sounds amazing. What else?"

"Well, I'm not gonna tell you now." She crosses her arms over her chest in a huff. "You're supposed to be making me feel safe enough to disclose my innermost thoughts, Josh—you know, luring me into some kind of *emotional intimacy*—not making me feel like a complete *weirdo.*"

I laugh. "I should have warned you—I suck at emotional intimacy."

"*Obviously,*" she says. But there's a gleam in her eye.

I touch her chin again. "I'm sorry, PG. Please forgive me. I'm a dick."

She pouts.

"Tell me more, babe. Tell me every last thing that turns you on. I wanna know. Don't hold back."

"No. You're just gonna laugh at me." She sticks out her lower lip.

"Never. Well, okay, I might laugh. But that doesn't mean anything. I laugh at everything. That's just who I am. I love hearing your fantasies, I swear."

"I have a lot of 'em, you know," she sniffs. "*A lot.*"

"Are they all as elaborate as the ones you just told me about?"

She considers. "Yeah, pretty much. I have an extremely active imagination."

"Come on, babe. Tell me everything. I might laugh, but only because I think you're so fucking adorable."

"I'll tell you if you answer one honesty-game question for me."

"Okay. Shoot."

"Why did Emma call you a sick fuck?"

My stomach instantly clenches.

"I don't get it," Kat continues. "Did you ask her to do something beyond what you wrote in your application? Because the stuff you wrote is kinky, sure, but not enough to make a girl call you names and run off with a guy wearing an ascot."

I exhale. "It's complicated."

There's a long beat.

"What's complicated about it?" she finally asks.

"I'd really rather talk about you and your mini-pornos. I've totally moved on from Emma. I really have."

"But I want to understand. Just answer this and I won't beat a dead horse, I promise. Did you ask her for something beyond what you wrote about in your application? Is there something else you fantasize about that you didn't write about—something you haven't told me yet? Because I want to know it all."

I shake my head. "What I put in my application is pretty much it. And it's what I told her about—well, actually, just the savior thing. I never even told her about the threesome thing. I'd planned to tell her that, too, but once I'd told her about the bondage-savior fantasy, it became clear there was no point in telling her anything else."

She twists her mouth. "But why? I don't understand. Was she really conservative or something? Was she a virgin?"

86

I take a long time, figuring out what to say. I breathe deeply and finally decide there's no way, other than to just say it. "Emma's sexuality was complicated." I exhale. "Everything about Emma was complicated, actually. She'd been brutally raped as a teenager and she was deeply traumatized by the experience." My stomach is turning over. "Understandably. So she needed a lot of extra tenderness... I mean, sex was just really tricky for her because she was really... you know, like I said, traumatized. So... yeah." I exhale. "I was always really patient and gentle with her and... we were together a really long time, and I wanted to try to help her, and then I just started to... you know... the reality was I started to have needs and she wasn't meeting them. And I felt really guilty about that, considering what she'd been through... But she kept pushing me to be honest with her... accusing me of wanting more than she could give me... and when I finally decided to open up and tell her everything about my past, and my mother, and about my fantasies, and I finally told her what I wanted to try, just to see if maybe the experience would maybe somehow quiet the raging voices in my head. Well, that shit didn't fly with her. In fact, nothing about me worked for her in the end. *Nothing.*" I run my hands through my hair. "I've thought about it a lot—why I was so attracted to her when we were obviously such a mismatch. Being with her was like banging my head into a brick wall, day after day. But I just wanted so badly to take care of her." I pause, thinking. "I sometimes sit and think about why the fuck I get turned on by certain things other guys probably don't. And when I analyze myself, I realize, yeah, I really *am* a sick fuck. I mean, getting off on the shit I do, when you think about what happened to my mom, it's pretty demented." I stop myself. My face is hot. I put my hands over my face, collecting myself. *Fuck.*

There's a long beat.

"I really am a sick fuck, Kat," I say simply. "I know I am. After what happened to my mom, I have no business incorporating bondage into my sexual fantasies. That's just sick. Emma was right. There's something deeply wrong with me. And telling a girl who'd been raped about it and asking her to try it with me to help me was also deeply fucked up. But what she didn't get was I was all about *saving* the girl, you understand? That's what gets me off. I just want to be the savior." I've got a lump in my throat. "Just once."

Kat nods.

87

I exhale. There's a goddamned lump in my throat that won't go away. "It's still sick, though," I say, pushing through my emotion. "Not to mention obvious and stupid." I swallow hard and the lump recedes. "It's some sort of twisted... I dunno. I guess I don't have the best imagination." I take a deep breath. "And, shit, I guess I should tell you something else, as long as I'm telling you the whole truth." I exhale and roll my eyes. "You might as well know just how obvious and stupid and deeply disturbed I really am."

Kat's sitting on the edge of her seat, her blue eyes fixed on me without blinking.

"My mom was blonde," I say. "Just like you. Just like Emma. Just like all the girls in my Sick Fuck folder. And she was gorgeous, too. Everyone always said she looked just like Grace Kelly."

Kat grabs my hand. "I figured."

"You did?"

She nods. "What did your dad look like?"

"Like me, pretty much. I have his dark hair." I squeeze her hand, grateful for her reassuring touch. "I look like my dad and Jonas looks like my mom."

Kat chuckles. "But you and your brother look so much alike, other than your hair."

"No, Jonas is the one who looks like my mom, and I'm the one who looks like my dad. My dad always said so. Maybe that's why my dad could never even stand to look at Jonas."

She blanches.

There's a long beat.

"If Jonas looks like your mom, then you do, too, Josh," she says softly. "Just with darker hair. You two look so much alike."

I shrug.

Kat strokes my arm with her free hand. "So. Okay. Fine. You're a sick fuck, Josh. Your mom made an indelible impression on you. You're obviously deeply traumatized by what happened to her. And you probably feel all kinds of guilt—totally misplaced, by the way—that Jonas was there and you weren't."

"But, Kat. It's pretty fucked up that all I wanna do is fuck beautiful blondes and my mom was a beautiful blonde. Emma thought that was really sick."

"Fuck Emma. You were *seven* when she died. Where else were

you gonna get your idea of female beauty other than from your mom—especially if she happened to look like Grace Kelly? Growing up, that standard of beauty must have gotten reinforced for you everywhere you looked. Magazines, movies. It's everywhere."

I stare at her for a long minute, not saying anything. I'm too blown away to speak. I've never had a conversation even resembling this one before. Not even with my childhood therapists.

"Josh, the bottom line for me is that the stuff you wrote in your application turned me on." She squeezes my hand. "Look, I totally get what you're saying—and I agree you've obviously got some deep-seated issues that have influenced your sexual fantasies—you've definitely got some sort of complex relating to what happened to your mom and you're searching for some sort of therapeutic release, some sort of... what's that word?" She snaps her fingers and scrunches her face.

"Catharsis?" I offer.

"*Yes*. Catharsis. Exactly. As an adult, you're using sex as some sort of *catharsis* or redemption or whatever. Okay, I get it. But so what? We're all perverts in one way or another, if we're being honest—it's just that people are so rarely honest when it comes to what they like behind closed doors. Well, I say let the doctors figure out your diagnosis if ever you're in danger of harming someone or yourself—but until then, who cares? All I know is that you make me soak my panties every time I'm near you and when I read your application, I started dripping down my thighs."

My breath catches in my throat. "Oh," I manage to say, but it's all I can muster.

The subtlest of smirks dances on her lips. "All I know is that whatever you did to those women in The Club, I'm turned on by the idea of you doing it to me, too, exactly the way you did it to them." The smirk she's been suppressing takes over her mouth. "I want you to pretend I'm one of the women in The Club and show me exactly what you like, without treating me any differently than you treated them." She lowers her voice to barely above a whisper. "I want you to treat me like your high-priced whore."

I'm rock hard right now.

Her eyes are blazing. "Actually, that happens to be one of my top fantasies."

My heart is absolutely racing. I swallow hard. "Well, but..." I sputter. "Kat, as it turns out, the women in The Club actually were paid *hookers*. I didn't know it at the time, of course, but in retrospect, there's a very good reason they were all so 'uncannily compatible' with me and eager to please."

She makes a face like I'm saying something nonsensical.

"So," I say, feeling the need to explain myself further, "unlike them, you might have, you know... *limits*."

Her eyes darken. "Don't piss on me. Don't crap on me. Don't hurt me. That's it."

She's taken my breath away. "I have no interest in doing any of those things," I say.

"Other than those three things, do whatever you want to me," she says. "Literally." Her eyes flicker. "In fact, I want you to."

I have never been more attracted to a woman than I am right this very minute. I clear my throat. "Please tell me you're not fucking with me right now."

"I'm not fucking with you," she says, heat rising in her cheeks. "I often fantasize I'm a high-end call-girl. It's what I imagined when I gave you that blowjob in the shower." She licks her lips. "I can't begin to tell you how much that turns me on."

My dick physically hurts, it's so hard.

"That's why I came when you did—because I was fantasizing I'd just given you your money's worth."

"Oh."

"So I guess I'm a sick fuck, too," she says. "Is that okay with you?"

I nod. "That's very okay with me."

"Good. Then let's just agree once and for all we don't give a shit if we're sick fucks. If we are, then so what. Fuck Emma. She's a bitch." Her eyes blaze. "Yeah, I said it. *Fuck her*. And fuck anyone else who has a problem with what turns us on. We're not screwing goats, right? We're gonna screw each other—and maybe one woman-to-be-named later, too." She snickers. "Fuck anyone who makes you feel ashamed of what you like, Josh, including Emma the Bitch."

I feel like I've entered an alternate universe. A fucking awesome alternate universe.

Kat smiles broadly and touches my face gently. "We'll fulfill each other's fantasies, right down the line. It'll be the honesty-game, sexual edition." She skims her fingertip over my lips. "Are you in?"

"I'm so fucking in."

She drops her hands from my face. "I should warn you, though, most of my sexual fantasies are gonna require you to role-play. You're gonna have to be all-in—assume your part."

"No problem."

"And if we're really gonna do this, then I wanna go big or go home."

"That's my motto."

"I thought YOLO was your motto."

"I have several."

"It's not the particular sex act that gets me going, it's the *scene*—the scenario. I don't care what you wanna do to me, as long as you set the right scene for me and let me lose myself."

My heart is racing. "Good to know. Name it, we'll do it. I'll make it happen for you exactly like you want it."

"But, wait. Think about it before you commit. Getting the scene the way I fantasize about it might take some planning on your part—and I can't be the one who arranges stuff. It has to happen *to* me, you know?—as if it's real. That's what's gonna let me lose myself completely. It's like *The Wizard of Oz.* I wanna see the giant, talking head of Oz the whole time—I don't wanna see the man behind the curtain."

I grin. "Babe, I've got this. Tell me all your fantasies, in detail, just like you told me the others, and I'll make 'em all come true, to the letter. I'll be your own personal Make-A-Wish Foundation."

She smiles broadly. "My own personal *Josh Faraday Club*," she corrects.

I wink at her. "Yours truly."

"Oh my God, I'm so excited." She wiggles in her seat. "When would we do this fantasy-exchange thing?"

"As soon as humanly possible," I say, my cock straining.

Her eyes are absolutely smoldering. "I wish we could start right now."

"Well, yeah, but unfortunately we gotta save the world first."

She snaps her fingers. "Damn it. Saving the world always gets in the way of acting out mini-pornos."

I laugh. "I tell you what. Right after we're done saving the world, we'll get started on our fantasy-fulfillment extravaganza that very night—right here in Vegas. We'll take a couple days to decompress, just you and me, before we have to return to our real lives for a bit. How 'bout we do my fantasies first here in Vegas and then we'll conquer yours the first chance we get in L.A.—because it sounds like yours are gonna take some advance planning."

"Sounds good," she says. "Better than good."

I breathe deeply, my body electrified. This woman's a dream come true.

"So let's talk about the whole watching-me-with-another-woman fantasy," she says. "Who's she gonna be? How are we gonna find her?"

"She can be anyone you want, as long as she's clean. Look in my sick fuck folder if you want. I'm sure Henn could track any of those ladies down."

She makes a face. "I deleted that folder."

"Oh, baby, my computer backs up daily. It's in The Cloud."

She rolls her eyes.

I laugh.

"No wonder you didn't get mad at me. And here I thought you were so Zen." She shrugs. "Well, I don't wanna do it with one of those girls. I want someone new."

"That's fine."

She looks on edge.

I cup her face in my hand. "Hey, if you're not into it, we don't have to do that one. I mean, if this were real life, I never would have told you about that whole thing in the first place."

"What do you mean 'if this were real life'? This isn't real life?"

I'm stumped. Of course, this isn't real life. This is Las Vegas. This is saving the world. This is fantasy-fulfillment. "I meant, if we were, you know, dating like usual. If you hadn't read my application. Due to the circumstances, you know stuff about me no other woman ever has."

There's an awkward silence.

"We don't have to do the thing with another woman. Seriously," I say.

She sighs. "Josh, I *want* to do it. I wanna pretend I'm just a girl in The Club and that you've paid to do whatever you did with all those girls, exactly the way you did it." She pauses. "Wait, no. Not exactly. I don't want you to touch the other woman. Not a pinky."

"I know. We already agreed to that. I wouldn't even want to touch the other girl, honestly. Not if I was with you. That'd be like macking down on canned Spaghetti O's when I've got a plate of homemade pasta right in front of me." I touch the slight cleft in her chin. "A pretty dumb thing to do."

Her cheeks flush. "But it's still gonna turn you on? Even though you've already done it with all those girls?"

"Honestly, I was pretty done with the whole thing after my month in The Club—it gets kinda old after you've done it a couple times, especially when you don't give a shit about either woman. But the thought of doing it with *you.*" I shudder with arousal at the very thought. I stroke her hair for a moment. "I've never gotten to do it with someone I'm..." I stop myself from saying anything more. I bite my lip and drop my hand from her hair. Shit.

"Someone you're what?" she asks, her interest obviously piqued. She tilts her head.

"Someone I'm..." I stop again. Nope. I really shouldn't say that to her.

"What?"

There's a long beat.

"What were you gonna say, Josh?" she asks. She weaves her fingers into mine. "Tell me."

I clear my throat. "I've never gotten to do it with someone I'm really attracted to beyond the physical," I say softly.

She smirks. "That's really sweet. Thank you. But it's not what you were about to say."

I pause. I can't say what I was gonna say. It's too much too soon.

"Someone what?" she prompts. "Come on. We're still playing the honesty-game, aren't we?"

"I've never gotten to do it with someone I'm in a relationship with," I say evenly.

There's a long silence.

Shit.

Fuck.

She's just staring at me, not saying anything, her hand interwoven in mine.

What am I doing? What am I saying? Why isn't she saying anything?

I pull my hand out of hers and run it through my hair. Goddammit. I should have just said "someone I'm dating." That would have been a safer bet. But are Kat and I even dating? I don't know what the fuck we're doing. This whole time in Vegas together has been so bizarre and concentrated and amazing—I can't make heads or tails of what we'd call what we're doing in real life.

Kat sighs and sets her jaw, apparently coming to some sort of decision.

"I think we should be exclusive," she says definitively.

My heart physically stops beating for a second. Holy fucking shit.

"At least during this fantasy-exchange thing," she adds quickly.

My stomach bursts with butterflies. My cheeks burst into flames. "Yeah, good idea," I say quickly. "I think so, too."

Her face is on fire. "Because I like not using condoms with you," she continues. "I like feeling you inside me with nothing between us. But I'm only willing to continue that way if we're exclusive."

"I agree." Now my heart is racing. Holy shit. My chest physically hurts. "Shit, I don't wanna go back to condoms, ever, as long as I live." Oh shit. What am I saying? What did I just imply?

"Good." Her cheeks flush. "Condoms are hereby banished. Gone." She clears her throat. "For as long as you want." She takes a deep breath. "You know, at least during the time while we're"—she takes another deep gulp of air—"doing our fantasy thing." She makes a weird face.

I nod, my heart still racing like a runaway train. "Agreed."

"Good," she says. "Yep. Done. Exclusive."

"Yep. We're officially exclusive as of right now. You and me."

She grins. "Okay. Good."

"Great."

"I'm all yours."

My entire body jolts at the sound of those three words. *I'm all yours,* she just said to me. Holy hot fucking damn, I've got to sit down.

"Okay," she says, almost to herself. She exhales loudly. "Cool."

"Cool," I say.

We sit and stare at each other, smiling, neither of us speaking.

I feel like my IQ just went down fifty points. My brain isn't functioning.

What exactly did we just agree to? She suggested being exclusive just for purposes of our little fantasy-fulfillment exchange. Does that mean we're not in an actual relationship—that we're some kind of exclusive fuck buddies? Because it sure feels like this girl's a helluva lot more than my fuck buddy. Fuck, I should ask her for clarification. But I'm not sure I wanna hear her answer.

I clear my throat. "So when are you gonna have your period? We should plan your trip to L.A. around that."

She grins. "I'm not. I take extended birth control pills. No period. I've got a year's worth of pills and I'm only two months in."

I smile broadly. "Excellent."

"So no break in our perverted activities will be required for the foreseeable future. Well, at least not on account of my period, anyway. Stuff like work and life will surely get in the way—and the fact that we don't live in the same city ought to throw a wrench in things, for sure."

"Why? It's less than a two-hour flight from Seattle to L.A. I can get a hard-on at ten and, if I charter a flight for you, you'll be at my house, sucking it by twelve thirty."

She bursts out laughing. "You're so gross."

"That's not gross. That's *romantic*."

She laughs. "You'd charter a flight just to get a blowjob?"

"I can't think of a better reason to charter a flight. Especially if the blowjob was gonna be from you. *Damn*."

She laughs again. "Well, okay, but what about work? Don't you have a company to run or something? Now that I think about it, how come you never seem to have to work?"

"Well, actually, I'm kinda between jobs at the moment. Not officially, but..." I lean in close to her and touch her golden hair. "Jonas and I are about to start a new business together. We haven't made a public announcement yet, so this is actually confidential, but we're both leaving Faraday & Sons to start something new."

"Wow. Really? Congratulations. What is it?"

95

"I can't tell you—not because I don't trust you—I do. But I promised my brother I wouldn't tell anyone about our new business before we've told our Uncle William in person—he runs Faraday & Sons with us—and I never break a promise to Jonas. Well, not to anyone—but especially not to Jonas."

Her face melts into an expression much like the one she had when she opened her hotel room door to me last night. "I can't wait to hear all about it whenever you're allowed to tell me," she says softly.

"I can't wait to tell you. If Jonas and I can pull it off the way we envision it, it's gonna be epic—well, the way *Jonas* envisions it—my brother's always the one with the big ideas—I'm just along for the ride, doing what I can to make myself useful."

She smiles and her blue eyes twinkle. "I'm sure it's gonna be amazing, whatever it is, Josh."

I pause. I was about to say something, but I suddenly forgot what it was. She's so fucking beautiful; occasionally, I lose my concentration when I look at her.

"So, hey," I say, looking at my watch. "We're meeting Henn in the lobby in about seven hours, so I think we'd better get some sleep. We'd better have our wits about us while we're saving the world tomorrow."

"Yeah, you're right. I'm a freakin' zombie right now. At some point, I'm definitely gonna need a full eight hours of sleep—you're killing me, smalls."

"Eh, we can sleep when we're dead, PG. Speaking of which, how 'bout *before* we sleep, you get that hot little body of yours into my bed and let me make good on that rain check from our shower?"

"Aren't you the one who just said we need to get some sleep for tomorrow?"

I wave my hand. "I meant we need sleep *after* I give you the best orgasm of your life."

Her eyes light up. "You sure you're up to it? That rain check was for you to go for the gold."

I lean in and kiss her slowly, taking my sweet time, grasping the back of her neck firmly as I do, and she ignites under my touch. When I pull away from her, there's no mistaking the heat in her eyes.

"I'm positive," I say, leering at her. "There's no point in doing it if I don't do it phenomenally, right?"

"I couldn't agree more."

Chapter 13
Kat

Josh, Henn and I are sitting in a dive bar in Henderson, Nevada, just down the street from the fifth and final bank of this morning's money-stealing tour. As far as we know, every single money-transfer went off without a hitch, exactly according to plan—but all we can do now is sit and wait to hear from Jonas to find out whether or not the feds were able to access the money.

"Just say as little as possible," Henn coached me this morning as we stood across the street from the first bank on our agenda. "Be pleasant and polite but completely *unmemorable*," he added—but then he looked me up and down and rolled his eyes. "Which is like telling LeBron James or an Oompah-Loompah not to be memorable."

"Henn, *come on*," I whined, trembling. "I'm freaking out. Just tell me exactly what to do."

"Don't freak out, Kat," Josh said, putting his muscled arm around my shoulders and giving me a squeeze. "You've got this."

"Indubitably," Henn agreed.

I rubbed my face. "Just tell me exactly what to do," I said, my voice wobbling. "Because I'd rather not go to prison for robbing a bank today."

"Well, you wouldn't go to prison for 'robbing a bank,'" Henn corrected. "You'd go to prison for multiple counts of bank fraud, grand theft larceny, identity theft, and conspiracy, probably." He snorted with laughter, but neither Josh nor I joined him.

"*Dude*," Josh said.

"Not at all funny," I added, gritting my teeth.

"Sorry," Henn said, stifling his grin. "Hacker humor. Gotta keep things light and bright or else you go a little cuckoo. But, okay, listen up. When you go in there, just think, 'I'm filthy rich and this is *my* money and I'll do whatever the fuck I want with it.' It's all in the attitude. You gotta have swagger."

"Just like baggin' a babe," Josh added, winking.

"Exactly—except, for God's sake, don't 'dick it up.'" Henn cast a snarky look at Josh. "That might work in a bar, dude, but we're in my house now."

Even through my anxiety, I couldn't help but grin.

Henn grinned. "And *never* flirt. You'll be too nervous and it'll come off as weird. Just open with a simple pleasantry to get your nerves out—maybe like, 'how's your morning going?'—and then, *boom*, launch into instructing the teller about the transfer in a clear, calm voice. Don't explain *why* you want the transfer or act apologetic—they're not doing you a favor here—it's *your* money."

"Jesus," I mumbled, putting my hands over my face. "You guys really think I can pull this off?"

"Of course," Henn said. "The trick is to *be* Oksana Belenko—not *pretend* to be Oksana Belenko."

"Wax on, wax off, Kat," Josh added reverently.

I laughed. "I know, right? Henn's totally Mr. Miyagi-ing me right now."

Henn rolled his eyes and forged ahead. "You already *look* the part—thanks to Josh's impeccable sense of style—now all you have to do is *be* the part."

I looked down at my ridiculously priced designer outfit—Prada dress, Louboutin heels, and Gucci bag—all supplied by Josh the day before during a whirlwind shopping spree. "Oksana Belenko wouldn't be caught dead in anything less than Prada," he'd insisted.

"I have to admit, being dressed like a *mill-i-on-aire* definitely makes me feel more Oksana-Belenko-ish," I said, staring at the bank across the street. I tried to smile breezily, but I couldn't do it.

Josh assessed my ashen face for a long beat. "Henn, give us a minute," he said, and without waiting for Henn's reply, he cupped my entire head in his palms like a bowling ball and kissed me full on the mouth. When he pulled away from kissing me, still holding my head firmly, he leveled me with his sapphire-blue eyes. "You've got this, Katherine Ulla Morgan," he said quietly, gazing with intensity into my eyes—and then he did the thing that's rapidly becoming my Achilles' heel: he gently touched the slight indentation in my chin.

And, just like that, my stomach stopped turning over and my jaw set.

I nodded. "Okay," I said. "Freak-out officially over."

Josh kissed my forehead. "There's my girl. Okay, Henn," he called over his shoulder. "Oksana's ready to rob a bank now."

"Yeehaw," Henn replied. "Oksanta Claus is coming to town, bitches. Let's do this."

And now here we are, an hour and a half later, all transfers completed, drinking beers and Patron shots in a seedy bar, waiting to hear from Jonas.

Just like Henn promised, the whole thing went off without a hitch (or so it seems thus far). Each and every bank believed, without a doubt, that I was the one and only *mill-i-on-aire* (many times over) Oksana Belenko—and therefore entitled to do whatever I pleased with *my* millions of dollars. Of course, I crapped my Stella McCartney panties (another gift from Josh*)* every single time I waltzed into yet another new bank and informed the teller of my desire to close my account—especially when a teller went to get his or her manager for "standard approvals." But, each and every time, my panty-crapping turned out to be completely wasted energy because no matter the approvals or security clearances or identification required at any particular bank, thanks to Henn, I always checked out as Oksana Belenko.

Indubitably.

Josh throws his head back, laughing at something Henn just said.

I sip my beer, still trying to get the shakes out.

"'Oksanta Claus is coming to town'?" Josh says, laughing. "Where do you come up with the shit you say, Henn?"

Henn shrugs. "I just get divine inspiration, what can I say?"

The waitress passes our table and Josh flags her. "Another round, please." He holds up an empty shot glass and shoots her a panty-melting smile.

The waitress visibly swoons. "You got it, sugar."

I bring my beer to my lips again, and my hand visibly shakes.

"You okay, Kat?" Josh asks.

"Yeah." But the truth is, I feel like I'm gonna barf—and not from the Patron. Today was insane. It's one thing to want to do something outrageously scary to help your best friend, and it's quite

99

another to physically force yourself to actually do it while crapping your pretty undies the entire time. As I found out today, thinking about doing something brave (or tremendously stupid) and doing it are two very different things.

"Do you need—" Josh begins, but his phone rings and we all jump.

"Here we go," Henn says, rubbing his hands together.

Josh puts his phone to his ear, his eyes bugging out. "Jonas," he says evenly, and then he listens. "Oh, thank God." He addresses Henn and me. "We did it, guys. They got it all."

Henn fist-pumps the air, but all I can do is lean back in my chair, my body melting with outrageous relief.

"We're in a bar in Henderson," Josh says. He looks around and his eyes fall on a television behind the bar. "Yeah, they've got one, but it's not on." He listens for a moment and rolls his eyes. "Really? We've been sitting here wondering this whole fucking time, shitting our pants, and you didn't—" He listens again and smiles wickedly. "*Oh.* Well, then I forgive you." He snickers. "I'm sure you were. Okay, we'll turn on the TV and check it out. I'll call you right back." Josh flags the waitress. "Hey, could you turn on the TV—put it on the news?"

"Sure, sweetie." She walks over to the bartender, says something, and the TV comes on—and, literally, instantly, there's no doubt our crafty little *Oceans' Eleven* crew has hit a grand slam homerun.

"Just keep it here," Josh calls to the bartender.

On the screen, a female reporter is talking into the camera while a banner declaring "Terrorist Threat Foiled in Las Vegas" scrolls beneath her. Behind the reporter, law enforcement officers in Kevlar vests are marching in and out of a cement building, carrying boxes.

"Hey, could you turn up the sound, man?" Josh calls to the bartender.

"... being told by federal authorities the terrorist plot was 'sophisticated, imminent and massive,'" the reporter is saying.

I'm confused. They're calling The Club *terrorists*? Maybe I don't fully understand the implications of that word. The Club was plotting *terrorism*?

"... and that the terrorist organization has ties to the Russian government."

Henn chuckles. "Dude, it's like I'm a fucking ventriloquist."

"Straight from your puppeteering mouth into the reporter's," Josh replies, his eyes fixed on the screen.

I'm totally confused. What the hell are Josh and Henn talking about?

An older woman with dyed blonde hair appears on-screen being escorted into a dark sedan.

"... in this footage from earlier, we see one of the alleged terrorists being taken into custody," the reporter says.

"Is that Oksana?" I ask.

Henn nods. "Yup."

"She's a *terrorist*?" I ask dumbly.

The look that passes between Henn and Josh in reaction to my question makes me feel like I must be having a total blonde moment. What the heck am I missing here?

The reporter continues: "... the names of the two alleged terrorists killed during the raid have now been confirmed by authorities—"

"*Henn*," Josh says insistently, yanking on Henn's sleeve.

"Yeah, I know," Henn says, batting Josh's hand away like he's swatting at a fly.

"... the two men killed in a shoot-out with federal authorities at the scene were Mak-sim Be-len-ko and Yu-ri Na-vol-ska," the reporter says slowly, clearly doing her mighty best not to screw up the pronunciations of the names.

"Oh shit," Josh says, beaming, and Henn high-fives him.

"Both," Henn says.

"Fan-fucking-tastic."

What are they talking about? My brain is struggling to process. The Maksim guy who got killed is obviously that creepy Max guy who ordered the hit on Sarah and demanded a freebie from her. Well, good riddance to that bastard and may he rot in hell. But who's the other guy who died in the raid? Yuri something? Sarah mentioned a Yuri during our meeting with Agent Eric, I think—yeah, it was when Henn played that voicemail from her attacker—

I gasp. Holy shitballs. I just got it. *Both*. Henn meant that both men directly responsible for the hit on Sarah died today.

My entire body erupts in goose bumps.

Oh my God.

I don't know how Jonas did it—and what Josh and Henn had to do with it, but those two bad-guys biting the dust today doesn't seem to be a coincidence. It seems I'm not watching a news story unfold on the television screen—I'm watching a PR campaign.

"Josh," I blurt. But before I can say another word, he's standing next to me, pulling me up from my chair, and enfolding me in his muscled arms.

"We did it," he breathes into my lips. "We saved the world." With that, he kisses me with such ferocious intensity, my knees buckle.

When Josh breaks away from kissing me, he moves on to Henn, wrapping him in a massive bear hug. "Thank you," he mumbles into Henn's ear. "You're my brother for life, man."

My heart pangs at the earnest tone of Josh's voice. If I didn't realize it before now, today's victory obviously meant something deeply personal for him.

Josh's phone rings and he pulls away from Henn, rubbing his face. "Yo," he says into the phone. "Yeah, we just saw it." He presses his lips together, obviously containing his emotion. "I'm so proud of you, Jonas. You left no stone unturned." He listens. "I know. We can finally breathe again... No, no, no. Don't second-guess yourself, man. It was the perfect measure of force—like a fucking sniper." He listens for long beat. "Wow. I didn't know if they'd go for that. Fucking fantastic." He beams a smile at Henn and me. "Yeah, they're both standing right here. I'll let you tell them yourself. Hey, guys. Jonas has some exceedingly good news for you."

Josh hands the phone to Henn, a huge smile on his face, and puts his arm around me.

"Hey, big guy—congrats," Henn says into the phone. "You're welcome. I told you, I always wear a white hat." He listens and his eyes go wide. *"Tax free?* Are you kidding me? Oh my God." Henn looks at me, grinning from ear to ear. "Guess what Kitty Kat? We're each getting our million bucks completely *tax-free.*"

"Tax free?" I shriek—and then I promptly burst into gigantic, soggy tears.

Josh embraces me and I wrap my arms around his neck, sobbing like a kid on her first day of kindergarten.

"Looks like you'll be opening that PR firm sooner than you thought," Josh coos into my ear. He kisses my wet cheeks and then my lips. "Ssh," he says gently, stroking my back. "You did so good today, babe. You deserve every penny. You kicked ass."

Clearly, he thinks I'm crying about the money. And I am. That's a shitload of money. Holy shitballs, especially tax-free. But that's not the biggest reason I'm crying, I don't think. Mostly, I think I'm just relieved that the threat of danger to Sarah (and myself) is now, finally, blessedly, over. And I'm also sobbing with relief that I'm almost certainly not gonna get carted off to prison today—which is good, because God help me if I had to call my dad from jail. And, finally, I think I'm crying for no other reason than the fact that I *really, really* need a full eight hours of sleep. Holy Sleep Deprivation, Batman—I can't keep going like this. Even the Party Girl With a Hyphen needs to freaking *sleep* occasionally, for the love of God!

"Aw, babe, ssh," Josh coos, cradling me in his strong arms and kissing my tears. "This is great news—nothing to cry about."

But my body won't stop wracking with sobs. I squeeze Josh tighter and press myself into his broad chest with all my might.

Josh chuckles and squeezes back, kissing every inch of my salty, wet, snotty face, and whispers in my ear. "We did it, babe. It's over now." He puts his lips right against my ear. "Well, this settles it once and for all: you've definitely got a vagina."

I burst out laughing through my sobs, and he laughs with me, holding me close.

After a moment, I feel a tap on my shoulder, and when I pull my nose out of Josh's neck, Henn's holding up the phone to me. "Sarah wants to talk to you for sec."

I wipe my eyes and take the phone from Henn.

"Hi, babycakes," I say. "Congratulations."

"Kitty Kat!" Sarah shrieks. "*You're a mill-i-on-aire!*"

I laugh and wipe my eyes again. "So I've heard," I squeak out, my voice cracking. "I can't believe it."

"Aw, Kat," Sarah says, her voice breaking along with mine. "You were so brave today."

"Oh my God, Sarah, no, I wasn't brave at all," I reply. "I was totally crapping my pants the whole time."

Sarah laughs. "I can't wait to hear all about it."

"I can't wait to hear about D.C.," I reply.

"Ha! Talk about pants-crapping. Jeez. I was in the room with all those men in suits and I was so nervous, I kept imagining myself hopping on the table and tap dancing like a frog in a top hat."

"That makes no sense."

"Exactly. The whole meeting, I was like, 'fleffer fleegan geebah doobah.'"

I laugh.

"But Jonas was masterful." She sighs. "Oh, Kat. He's incredible."

"Things going well with you two?" I ask.

"Amazing-incredible-never-been-happier-best-case-scenario. Gah! I'm so in love, it hurts."

I giggle.

"We're gonna need to do a good-old-fashioned sleepover when I get back so I can tell you all about it."

"Coolio. I'll bring the champagne," I say.

"Hell yeah, you will," Sarah says. "Seeing as how you're now a fancy *mill-i-on-aire*."

"Hey, aren't you a fancy *mill-i-on-aire,* too?" I ask.

Sarah giggles. "Why, yes, as a matter of fact, I am." She squeals. "I keep forgetting about that."

I roll my eyes to myself.

"Okay, I'll bring the champagne," Sarah says. "You bring the chocolate. *If* you can peel yourself away from Josh for a night, that is," she says coyly. "Have you two gone off like a nuclear bomb yet?"

"Um, yeah, pretty much," I say, my eyes drifting to Josh's face. He's watching me intently, his blue eyes sparkling.

"The good kind of nuclear bomb, I hope?" she asks.

"Is there a bad kind?"

"Uh. Yeah. There is."

"Well, it's the good kind, then. The very, very good kind." I sigh. "Oh, Sarah."

"Oh, Kat."

"So when are you coming home?"

"A couple days. We're gonna swing by New York first to visit—oh hang on." She says something obviously not intended for me. "Okay, my sweet love, hang the fuck on. Yes, I know. *Patience,* hunkster." Now she's back to me on the phone. "Jonas wants to talk to Josh again. He's a wee bit amped right now," she whispers. "He's kinda bouncing off the walls. God, he's so cute."

I laugh. "Okay. But—" My voice breaks with emotion again. "I love you, Sarah. Please just know I love you so much. I'm so frickin' relieved you're healthy and safe."

Sarah's voice instantly floods with emotion. "I love you, too, Kitty Kat. And I'm *so* frickin' relieved, too."

I hold out the phone to Josh, wiping my eyes, and he grabs it from me.

"Yo." Josh listens for a beat. "*Tonight?*" He suddenly looks stricken. "Dude, *no way.*" Josh looks at me pointedly as he listens again. "Because I have something *extremely* important to do here in Vegas tonight, that's why." He rubs his face. "Jesus Fucking Christ." He exhales. "*Fine.* But I'll come tomorrow night, not tonight... . Because I can't, that's why, motherfucker... . Because I've got something I need to do here in Vegas tonight... . So what? You head out to see him tonight and I'll come tomorrow—no big deal. *Because I've got something to do, Jonas. Chill the fuck out.*" He listens and then grins broadly. "It's none of your business what it is." He laughs. "Well, I'm not saying yes or no, but if it were that, then I think you'd agree that's something *extremely* important." Josh looks at me lasciviously, like a wolf scoping out a bunny. "Oh, bro, you have no idea."

My clit begins faintly buzzing.

Josh laughs. "It'll be fine, Jonas, trust me. When you're telling Uncle William the news, just hold up a photo of a trout and he won't even notice what you're saying." He belly laughs. "Okay. Bye. You, too. Oh, hey, Jonas?" He pauses. "I'm proud of you, man. Remember the text I sent the other day? Pretend I just sent you another one just like that." He snickers. "Sorry. I know. Fuck me." He slaps his cheek hard, making me jump back with surprise. "Yeah, I did it, cocksucker." He laughs. "Okay. See you tomorrow, bro."

Josh hangs up and looks at me mournfully. "Well, Party Girl, I've got some bad news. I gotta hop a flight to New York tomorrow morning, first thing."

"Oh," I say, the wind completely knocked out of my sails. I was really looking forward to spending a few days (and nights) alone with Josh in Vegas, just the two of us living out our sick-fuck fantasies together before being forced to leave this bizarre bubble and return to real life (and our separate cities). I don't know if this thing with Josh (whatever it is) is going to carry over into the real world or not—and if not, I don't feel ready to find that out. "Why do you have to go to New York?" I ask, trying to keep my voice from sounding too hurt.

"Jonas and I have to talk to our uncle about something important," Josh continues, "and Jonas insists we do it as soon as humanly possible." He twists his mouth. "And, unfortunately, Jonas is one hundred percent right about that. It's not something that should wait."

"I'll be heading off tomorrow, too," Henn says. "Jonas said the feds want me to meet with them in D.C. to help them sort through the database. But, hey, that still leaves us tonight to celebrate, right guys? It's not every day a guy (or girl) saves the world, huh? And especially not with his best friends."

Josh and I exchange a look. What have we been thinking? We went on and on about launching into our sick-fuck fantasy fulfillment the minute our mission was complete—but, clearly, that's a nonstarter. There's no way in hell either of us would ever let our beloved Henny celebrate this incredible victory all by his little, brilliant, quirky self. I make a face at Josh and he smiles wistfully, obviously resigned to our sudden change of plans for tonight.

"*Of course*, we're gonna celebrate, Henny," I say.

"Wouldn't have it any other way," Josh says, fist-bumping him. "And we're gonna do it in style, my man. Leave it all to me—I'm gonna make sure we have the night of our fucking lives."

Henn flashes Josh a look of appreciation and excitement that's so freaking adorable, I want to throw a little rhinestone vest on him and toss him into my brand new Gucci purse.

"Hey, I've got a brilliant idea," I say. "How 'bout we fly Hannah Banana Montana Millikin into Vegas on the next flight to celebrate with us?" I look at my watch. "There's still plenty of time to get her here in time for dinner, isn't there?"

Josh looks at his watch. "There sure is. Great idea. I suddenly feel like we need some additional staffing on that PR campaign." He winks.

"What do you think, Henny?" I ask. "You up for letting Hannah Banana Montana Millikin crash our party?"

Henn grins. "Awesome." He raises one eyebrow. "As long as you tell her to wear her glasses."

"I'll tell her," I say.

"You know," Josh begins, his wheels obviously turning. "As long as Hannah Banana Montana Milliken is gonna come all the way out here, it'd be a crying shame to send her back home tomorrow. How 'bout you two girls hang out for a few days and have some fun? We've still got Jonas and Sarah's penthouse suite—I forgot to check out of it like Jonas asked me to." He makes a face that says, *Yeah, I'm a fuck-up.* "When Henn and I leave, you and Hannah can stay a couple days in the penthouse like a couple of *mill-i-on-aires.* Have yourselves a mini-vacay, on me."

"Really?" I squeal.

"Sure. Book spa appointments, go shopping, see *Thunder from Down Under* or whatever." He laughs. "Order drinks by the pool, dine like queens, get pedicures and massages, do whatever the hell you girls wanna do for however long and I'll pick up the tab. Go crazy, all of it completely on me."

I'm trying to contain myself, but a strange noise erupts from my throat.

Josh laughs. "You've earned it, babe—you kicked ass today. We *literally* couldn't have done it without you. And there's no rush going back to Seattle, right?—you're still on my dime for the PR campaign for another couple weeks."

I'm giddy; I'm not gonna lie. But this seems too much to accept, even for me. "It's too generous," I say. "I'd love to hang out with Hannah for a few days, but I can certainly foot the bill myself, you know. If you haven't heard by now, I'm gonna be a *mill-i-on-aire.*"

Josh swats at the air. "Fuck no. You can't piss away your finder's fee money on debauchery—you're gonna need every dime for Party Girl PR, remember?" He winks. "If anyone's gonna piss away their money on debauchery, it's gonna be me. It's kinda my specialty."

I throw my arms around Josh's neck again, and for a second, I'm in serious danger of bawling again. "Thank you, Josh," I breathe.

Josh kisses my cheek and squeezes me tight. "I'll be counting the days 'til I see you again," he says softly into my ear, his voice low and sexy. "I can't wait to get started on what we talked about."

"I can't wait, either," I say into his neck, inhaling his cologne.

We break apart from our clinch and I move on to Henn, wrapping him in a tight hug. "This is gonna be the best night ever in the history of the world, Henny. You're gonna absolutely adore Hannah."

"Hey, when it comes to celebrating victory over the Evil Empire, the more the merrier, I always say."

"Well, duh," I say. "Isn't that what everyone always says after a long day of saving the world? 'The more the merrier.'"

"It's what they always say," Henn agrees.

"Tell Hannah I'll book the three o'clock flight for her on Alaska," Josh says, looking at something on his phone.

"Okay, I'll call her now. Thank you so much, Josh. She's gonna be thrilled."

Josh pulls me into him and kisses me gently. "It's my pleasure, Kat." He pushes himself into me and his erection juts against my hip. He presses his lips into my ear. "Have fun with your girlfriend—but make no mistake about it: the minute I get back from New York, you're all mine."

Chapter 14
Josh

"Excuse me, fellas," Sarah says, scooting back from the dining room table. "Gonna head to the ladies' room."

When she stands up from the table, Uncle William stands, too, which prompts Jonas and me to do the same.

Sarah smiles shyly. "Wow, so chivalrous, fellas. Golly gosh. Thank you."

The minute Sarah's left the dining room and the three of us have settled back into our chairs, Uncle William leans forward, his blue eyes fixed on Jonas. "You gonna marry this girl?" he asks.

I'm utterly shocked by the question. I mean, I know Uncle William is an old-fashioned kind of guy and all, and Sarah's obviously an incredible girl, and a perfect fit for Jonas, too, but Jonas only just met her, for fuck's sake. There's no way in hell Jonas is even *thinking* about taking a giant leap like *marriage*—

"Absolutely," Jonas answers smoothly. "As soon as humanly possible, in fact."

Uncle William chuckles and leans back in his chair. "Glad to hear it. Congratulations, son. Don't let this one get away. I loved her the minute I met her."

Jonas nods. "Me, too."

I'm in total shock right now. I knew Jonas was head over heels in love with Sarah, but I had no idea he was ready to *marry* her.

"You're sure, Jonas?" I ask.

"Never been more sure of anything in my life."

"That's awesome, bro," I say, my heart racing. "Does she know?"

"No," Jonas says, suddenly looking anxious. "Am I supposed to *ask* her if I can *ask* her?"

I laugh. "No, Jonas, you dumbshit," I say. "That's not what I meant. I'm just saying if you're gonna surprise the girl, then make sure you blow her socks off. This is the story she's gonna be telling her grandkids one day. So don't fuck it up."

Jonas nods, but I've clearly put the fear of God into him.

I lean back in my chair, my mind reeling. I can't believe it. My brother's gonna ask a girl to marry him. And not just any girl. Sarah Fucking Cruz—a badass of epic proportions. A girl who doesn't take any of his shit. A girl with a heart of pure gold.

All of a sudden, I feel an overwhelming surge of relief flooding my body. Jonas is gonna have a *wife*. Holy shit. Someone to love him forever—and someone for him to love in return. He'll finally have someone (besides me) to take care of him, to listen to him, to rein him in when his thoughts start spiraling out of control. And he'll finally have someone besides me to tell him he's a beast every fucking day of his life.

If Sarah says yes, that is.

Oh my God. I clutch my chest. Sarah Cruz had better say yes to my brother. Oh, please, God, let that woman say yes. Let her look past Jonas' fuckeduppedness and stupidity and constant Plato-izing and see what I see—the greatest guy in the whole fucking world.

"You've got to get a huge-ass ring," I blurt. "So big, it sears her fucking corneas."

Jonas nods. "Well, duh."

"You say that but you weren't already planning to do that, were you?"

"Yes, I was. I was already planning to get her a diamond so big she needs a wheelbarrow to carry it around."

Uncle William laughs. "Good boy. He's got it handled, Josh. Now leave the poor boy alone. Jonas loves her. He'll do it right."

"No, Jonas can't be trusted to do this right," I say defiantly. "If this were a business deal, sure, he'd be all over it and I wouldn't say a goddamned thing. But this is a *girl*. Left to his own devices, he'll do some crazy-ass *metaphor* that'll either scare her or bore her to tears."

Uncle William laughs and Jonas scowls at me.

"So what's your big plan for the proposal, Jonas?" I ask, crossing my arms over my chest. "Because it's got to be rock solid, man, I'm telling you—it's got to be a homerun. There's absolutely no room for failure."

Jonas runs his hand through his hair. "Jesus, you're freaking me out. I thought I had the perfect idea, and now you're making me doubt myself."

I'm practically hyperventilating. If Sarah says yes, then she'll *live* with him. In his house. *Forever*. Which means she'll always be there to keep Jonas on track and make him laugh and, most importantly, *I won't have to worry about him anymore*. Or, well, at least, not nearly as much as I currently do.

"Dude, listen to me," I say, my voice spiking with sudden urgency. "We've got to pull out all the stops—trick Sarah into saying yes."

Jonas looks indignant. "Fuck you. I don't need to *trick her*." He looks at Uncle William, apparently hoping for a little backup, but Uncle William doesn't say anything. "Well...I've tricked her pretty well so far, haven't I?" Jonas says, and we all laugh.

Sarah enters the dining room and Jonas' entire face lights up like a bonfire.

"Hi, baby," he says.

"Hi, love," she replies, returning Jonas' goofy smile and taking her seat.

Love? Sarah called my brother 'love'? Oh my fucking God. Sarah Fucking Cruz is gonna say yes. Praise the lord—she's gonna agree to become Mrs. Faraday. If I were capable of shedding a tear, I'd surely shed one of happiness right now.

Chapter 15
Josh

Dessert and coffee are done. And for the past thirty minutes, Uncle William's been telling Sarah stories I've never heard before about his late wife, Sadie, (a raven-haired beauty who died in a car accident about a year before Jonas and I were born).

"Do you have any photos of her?" Sarah asks.

"Of course," he says. "I've got our entire wedding album upstairs."

"Oh my gosh," Sarah breathes, her cheeks flushing. "May I see it?"

"Of course. And I've got a whole bunch of pictures of Jonas and Joshua from when they were little I'll show you, too. You'll get a kick out of those."

Sarah squeals. "And do you have photos of yourself as a little boy, too, Uncle William?"

"Sure, I might be able to dig up one or two," Uncle William says, standing up from the table with Sarah. "Boys? Care to join?"

"Come with us, baby," Sarah says, holding out her hand to Jonas.

"Sure," Jonas says smoothly—shocking me for the billionth time today. He takes her hand.

I never would have predicted Jonas would say yes to voluntarily going down memory lane. As Jonas well knows, almost all of Uncle William's photos of Jonas and me as happy little kids include Dad—and normally, like me, Jonas bends over backwards to avoid seeing a photo of that bastard every bit as much as I do. But, damn, I guess up is down and right is left when my brother's in the presence of little Miss Sarah Cruz.

Uncle William looks pointedly at me and I shake my head.

"I think I'll sit on the veranda and look at the Hudson for a bit," I say.

My reply can't possibly surprise Uncle William. As far as I'm concerned, if I never see Dad's face again, it'll be too soon for me—and Uncle William knows it.

"Okay, son," Uncle William says softly. "Katya's got the blue room in the back all ready for you. Just make yourself at home, as usual."

"Thanks," I say. "I appreciate it."

The trio walks toward the far hallway, Sarah's arm threaded into Uncle William's.

"I bet Jonas and Josh were the cutest little things," Sarah says happily.

"Oh, they were adorable little buggers," Uncle William says, just before they exit the room. "Oh my, did those boys climb every rock and tree and chair and piano. I remember this one time, I found Jonas and Joshua..."

They're gone.

I smile to myself. I so rarely see Uncle William outside of a business context. I'm not used to seeing him acting like this—so relaxed and nostalgic. I can only assume he's acting this way thanks to Sarah. Our crew's fearless leader puts everyone at ease, doesn't she? Especially my high-strung brother. She's like aloe vera on a sunburn for Jonas—a soothing balm for his soul. And anyone can see it. Uncle William obviously has.

I didn't detect even a hint of skepticism about Sarah from Uncle William, not even a whiff he thinks Sarah's a gold digger. His demeanor toward her has been one-hundred-eighty degrees from the cold way he reacted to Amanda when Jonas brought her here that one and only time—and Jonas had been with Amanda almost a year by then, I'm pretty sure. And now he brings Sarah here after a fraction of that time, and Uncle William falls all over himself to make her feel like part of the family? Wonders never cease.

I get up slowly and stretch, groaning, and then amble toward the French doors leading out to the veranda overlooking the river from on top of the world, patting my stomach as I walk. Damn, I've got to start hitting the gym like a madman when I get home. I've been a glutton this whole week in Vegas. Shit, especially now that fitness is gonna be my business, I've got to kick it up a notch, take a page out of Jonas' book. I certainly can't let my stupid brother show me up in the gym. Ha! Oh, fuck, I'm excited. I'm so fucking excited, I feel like a kid on Christmas Eve. My awesome life's about to get a whole lot more awesome. Sayonara, Faraday & Sons, I won't miss you.

I inhale deeply as the cool night air on the veranda hits my face and settle myself into one of the cushioned wicker chairs overlooking the shimmering river in the distance.

I'm just so flabbergasted at today's turn of events, I can't process. Jonas is gonna get engaged to a girl he's basically just met—and Uncle William is thrilled about the idea. Shit, Uncle William just *encouraged* Jonas to do it. I never would have predicted that in a million-trillion years. And that wasn't even the first time Uncle William shocked the hell out of me tonight: he absolutely floored me with his reaction when he found out both Jonas and I are leaving Faraday & Sons, too. I thought for sure he'd try to persuade us to stay—maybe talk about honor and obligation and how much it meant to our father to have his sons carry the mantle of Faraday & Sons. But he didn't say any of it. All he did was look both of us in the eyes and say, "I'm proud of you boys. Always follow your hearts." I swear to God, wonders never cease.

My phone vibrates in my pocket. I grab it and grin at the text message on my screen.

"Hi, Playboy!" Kat's message says. "Wanted to give you a little update on what your generous donation to the Kat and Hannah Hedonism Fund has bought you!" She adds a string of emojis: red hearts, clapping hands, a champagne bottle, a donkey and handcuffs. I laugh out loud. "We're having SO MUCH FUN!!! Thank you, thank you, thank you, my dearest, darlingest Playboy!!!! You are the most generous man in the whole wide world! And the sexiest, too!!!!!!! MEOW!" She adds a dog emoji. I don't know what the fuck that's supposed to mean, especially in light of her "meow," but I laugh anyway.

A second message comes in right on the heels of the first one. "Oops. I meant..." She adds a cat emoji. "The dog and cat were right next to each other on the emoji menu and I pressed the wrong one. The cat is me! MEOW! I'm Kitty Kat and this is you." She adds a muscled arm emoji. "Because you're so big and strong and sexy!! And together we're..." She adds an emoji of a fireworks display.

I can't wipe the smile off my face. Something tells me Kat is drunk-texting right now. And I love it. I'm about to write a reply when I get another message from her.

"And now—dooh-dooh-dooh!!!" Kat writes, followed by a trumpet emoji. "It's time for a slideshow created especially for you, my dearest, darlingest Playboy with the Heart of Gold! Here you go!"

A photo of Kat and Hannah by the pool, toasting the camera with fruity-looking drinks, hits my screen. Kat's holding up a white napkin with the message, "THANK YOU, JOSH!" scrawled across it in black ink.

There's no time to reply. Another photo lands on my screen: Kat and Hannah in fluffy white bathrobes, sitting on an overstuffed white couch, toasting the camera with what looks like ice water. They look like they're in a spa waiting room. Again, Kat's got a napkin with a message written across it: "YOU ROCK, JOSHUA WILLIAM FARADAY!"

Another photo. Kat and Hannah draped around a shirtless, greased-up, tanning-bed-muscle guy, all three of them standing under a neon sign that says "Thunder from Down Under." I laugh out loud at the expressions on the girls' faces in this shot. They're both making "O" faces. The writing on Kat's napkin this time is too lengthy and small to read, so I touch my screen and zoom in on the napkin 'til it's legible. "This man just impregnated both of us, Josh!" the napkin says. "Your money hard at work!" I burst out laughing.

If the glistening guy in the photo didn't look so completely gay, I might blanche at this note. But, what am I thinking? Probably not, actually. Kat's fucking hysterical, no matter what she does. She just kills me. And I must say, Hannah seems to be quite the sidekick for my adorable little terrorist—a great girl through and through. Henn sure thought so when the four of us had a three-hour dinner and then went dancing last night. Talk about instant chemistry—Henn and Hannah clicked like they'd known each other for years. Same sense of humor; same quirky-hipster-cool dorkiness; and, oh my God, what a comedy duo on the dance floor those two turned out to be.

Yet another photo lands on my screen. This time it's Kat and Hannah sitting at a table in what appears to be a high-end restaurant, holding up wine goblets and a napkin that says, "To Josh Faraday, our generous benefactor!"

I can't help smiling. I can't believe this is the same girl who didn't chase me even *once* during my last trip to Manhattan a couple weeks ago. She played it so fucking cool that whole week, didn't she? Doing nothing but replying to my few, brief douchebag-texts to her, always making sure not to say a damned thing to reveal her interest in me. I knew her game, of course—since it was the same game I was playing with her—but, still, it surprised the hell out of me she could hold out so long without revealing a single crack in her hard-to-get armor.

This time, though, the woman's got no game whatsoever. And I love it. She's been peppering my inbox with adorable and affectionate texts almost nonstop since even before I boarded my flight for NYC. And I've been doing the same to her, pretty much nonstop. I can't help myself—I haven't been able to stop thinking about Kat since I kissed her goodbye early this morning and headed to the airport. Man, that was one bed I was sorry to leave.

Another photo lands on my screen. This time, the photo is Kat all by herself, alone in the same bed I left her in this morning. She's wearing her barely there white tank top and G-string—the same clothes she was wearing this morning when I kissed her goodbye. Her hair's tousled. Her eyes are half-mast and full of arousal. Man, that's the look that makes my cock tingle—the same look she gets right after she comes. I'd bet anything she took this photo right after getting herself off—and, hopefully, thinking of me while she did it.

But that's not even the best part of the photo. The best part, the thing that's making my heart pound painfully in my chest, is what Kat's napkin says this time: "Wish you were here."

"Me, too," I say aloud into the darkness of the night. In fact, there's no place I'd rather be than in bed next to Katherine Ulla Morgan. I take a deep breath, my mind smelling her phantom scent all around me. Damn. I miss her.

I touch the button on my phone to call her, my skin buzzing, my heart panging—but before the call connects, the French door behind me opens and Jonas walks onto the veranda. I quickly disconnect the call.

Chapter 16
Josh

"Hey, bro," I say to Jonas, glancing behind him to see if he's alone. He is. Good. I'm eager to talk to my brother man-to-man for a bit, just the two of us.

Jonas hands me a bottle of beer and takes the wicker chair next to mine, overlooking the moonlit river. "Uncle William's moved on to showing Sarah photos of his fly-fishing trips," Jonas says.

"Aaaah! Run away!" I say.

"As fast as my legs would carry me."

I take a sip of my beer. "That man sure can talk about fish."

"He sure can."

"Even a fish would get sick of Uncle William's stories about fish," I say. "They'd be like, 'Dude. Talk about *humans* occasionally. *Please*. You're hurting my fish-ears.'"

Jonas chuckles. "The man loves his fish."

"Do fish have ears?" I ask.

"Sort of," Jonas says. "Fish don't have *traditional* ears, but they have ear parts inside their heads that pick up sounds in the water. Functionally, they're ears, even if not technically so."

I laugh. "You're a fount of useless knowledge, Jonas Patrick Faraday."

He swigs his beer, smiling. "I really am."

There's a long beat as we both drink our beers and look out at the spectacular view of the river.

"Uncle William sure handled the news of our double-departure awfully well," I say. "He shocked the fuck out of me."

"I know. I thought it'd be like jumping off a cliff to tell him, and it was more like stepping off a curb."

117

"It almost seemed like he was expecting it, didn't it?"

"Totally," Jonas agrees. "I had that exact same thought."

We gaze out at the lights on the Hudson forty floors below for another long moment, drinking our beers.

"I can't wait to get started building our baby," Jonas finally says. "I have so many ideas for Climb & Conquer, my head's been going a mile a minute."

"As opposed to when?"

Jonas laughs.

"I'm pumped, too," I say, laughing. "Telling Uncle William felt like getting freed from a lifelong cage."

"That's *exactly* how I felt," Jonas says. "I feel like I'm floating."

"Me, too. *Exactly*. To Climb & Conquer," I say, holding up my beer. "And to the Faraday twins—two fucking beasts among men."

"Hear, hear," Jonas says, clinking my beer with his. "Fuck yeah."

"Fuck yeah," I agree.

"I'll finalize the press release on my flight home. We can release it on Monday."

"Awesome," I say.

"Fuck yeah," Jonas says.

"Fuck yeah."

We look out at the river for a moment, drinking our beers, each of us apparently lost in our excited thoughts.

"So Uncle William sure took to Sarah right off the bat," I say.

"Oh my God. You should have seen him when we first got here last night," Jonas says. "I kept warning Sarah before we arrived not to take it personally if Uncle William was kinda standoffish or super formal, you know?—but he acted like she was his long-lost daughter the minute he laid eyes on her. Just fell totally and completely in love with her."

I chuckle. "Just like you," I say.

Jonas grins. "Just like me."

"Congrats, by the way," I say. "She's perfect for you. I don't know how you managed to find her. She's a needle in a haystack."

Jonas beams a smile at me but doesn't reply.

"So you told her?"

Jonas looks at me funny, obviously not catching my meaning.

"The three little words?" I clarify.

"Oh." Jonas' grin broadens. "Yeah. I told her." I can tell he's blushing, even in the moonlight.

"First time ever saying it?"

"Yeah." His smile broadens yet again.

"Did it freak you out to say it?"

"Not in the slightest. It just felt good—really, *really* good."

I ponder that for a minute. "You were never tempted to say it before Sarah?"

Jonas crinkles his nose like I've said something distasteful. "No."

"Not even to Amanda?"

Jonas shrugs. "Well, I knew I was 'supposed' to say it to Amanda based on the passage of time—I knew she *wanted* me to say it to her. But, no, I was never even tempted. Did you ever say it to Emma?"

I nod. "It took me three years, but yeah."

"Three years? Wow, and here I thought I was the emotionally stunted asshole of the two of us."

I shrug and sip my beer. "Not something to say lightly."

Jonas makes a sound that tells me he agrees with my statement. "Emma's the only girl you've ever said it to?" he asks.

I nod.

"Damn. She hung in there for three fucking years, waiting for you to say it?"

I shrug. "Yeah. But we had the whole long-distance thing, you know—three years wasn't really three years if you add up the time we were actually in the same room."

"How'd it feel when you said it to her?" Jonas asks. "Did it feel good or did it freak you out?"

"Both."

"Did she say it back?"

"Yeah, she said it back—and for a brief moment in time, I felt kind of like, 'Phew. That's a relief. I'm normal.'" I shake my head. "But in retrospect, exchanging those words just lulled me into a false sense of security. Once I said them, I started thinking it was safe to say some other shit too—and, as I found out pretty damned quick, it wasn't."

I can feel Jonas' eyes on me, but he doesn't speak.

"As it turns out, saying the words doesn't make the feelings real." I pause. "It was like Emma was signing a software licensing agreement—she just scrolled to the bottom and pressed 'I agree.'"

Jonas makes a sympathetic sound.

"In fact, come to think of it, Emma didn't actually say the words back to me. She just said, 'Me, too.'"

"Ooph."

"Yeah." I pause. "Ooph."

There's a beat.

"I thought I loved her—I really did," I say. "But now that I'm watching you and Sarah, I realize I probably didn't. I mean can you really love someone if they don't love you back?"

My question is rhetorical, but Jonas answers me, anyway. "I like to think I'd love Sarah even if she didn't love me back. And yet I can't imagine I would have been *able* to love her like I do if she didn't love me. The way Sarah loves me makes me feel like it's safe to love her all the way."

There's another beat during which we both look out at the sprawling view of the river. This has to be the most unexpected conversation of my entire life.

"Emma never looked at me the way Sarah looks at you, bro," I say softly. "Not once." My heart squeezes painfully in my chest at the admission. "Seeing you and Sarah together makes me realize Emma never loved me."

Jonas makes a sympathetic noise. "Then she wasn't The One."

I swallow hard, swig my beer, and look out at the Hudson again. A light from some sort of boat is skimming slowly across the black water in the distance.

"Josh, you're better off," Jonas says. "If a woman doesn't look at you the way Sarah looks at me, then she's not worthy of you."

I nod, but I don't say anything. When the fuck did Jonas become the wise and powerful brother in this duo? The guy falls in love with the greatest girl in the world, and suddenly he's some kind of love guru?

"So, on a related topic," Jonas says, "how's it going with Kat?"

A huge smile involuntarily bursts across my face at the mere mention of Kat's name. "Good."

"You like her?"

I bite my lip, but I can't control the goofy grin that's taken over my face. "Yeah, I like her. She's a handful, though. Kinda crazy."

"Oh, well, that's good, right?—you like crazy."

"I sure do."

Jonas chuckles.

"Which is a good thing," I say, "because she's batshit crazy. And stubborn as shit. But she's also super cool and sweet and funny and smoking hot, too. A handful, like I say."

"Sounds fun."

"She's the most fun I've ever had, if you know what I mean. Oh my God, the woman's like a dude in the best possible way." I snicker despite myself. "She doesn't... hold back."

"*Excellent.*"

"I didn't even know a woman like Kat existed. She's like a whole new species of freaky-ass fish that washes to shore after a nuclear disaster."

Jonas laughs.

"That's what I told her, actually. I told her she's a freaky-ass fish."

"No, you didn't."

"Yeah, I did."

Jonas bursts out laughing. "Now there's some Valentine's Day bullshit if I ever heard it." Oh, man, he's laughing his ass off, which, in turn, makes me laugh, too. "You told her that? And here I thought *I* was the dumb Faraday twin," Jonas says, still laughing.

We laugh our asses off together for quite some time. Finally, Jonas wipes his eyes and takes a sip of his beer. "That's hilarious, Josh."

"I'm a charming son of a bitch, what can I say?"

Jonas shakes his head. "A woman like that, you better make sure you deliver what she expects—don't fuck it up."

I shoot him a look that says he's a moron. "I *can't* fuck it up—I just told you, she's like a dude. She's a slam-dunk, every time. She's amazing—a unicorn."

"Oh, ho, ho. That's what you might *think* with a girl like that. Just be careful—a unicorn will lull you into a false sense of confidence. Don't start getting lazy."

"What the fuck are you talking about?"

"If you don't know then I can't explain it to you."

"Try."

He sighs. "She's *really* good at getting herself off, right?"

I don't reply. I'm a gentleman, after all.

"So that means she doesn't actually *need* you," he continues. "You're nothing but a luxury item to her—a Lamborghini, if you will. And as you of all people should know, no one buys a Lamborghini for basic transportation. They get the Lamborghini because they want all the stupid bells and whistles (and because they're an idiot with their money)."

"What the fuck are you talking about?"

Jonas shrugs. "I'm just sayin' a girl can get dissatisfied pretty damn quick with her ridiculously expensive Lamborghini if it doesn't deliver everything that's been promised in the brochure."

My heart is racing. I don't know how it's possible, but my idiot brother is actually making a shit-ton of sense.

"*So* as your girl's designated Lamborghini," Jonas says, "you need to make it your sacred mission to give her everything she expects from a two-hundred-thousand-dollar car." He swigs his beer. "You gotta convince that woman she actually *needs* a goddamned Lamborghini."

Shit. He's right. "So what do I need to do?" I ask.

"You gotta be able to do stuff for her she can't do for herself. Make her come so hard, she's literally addicted to you."

"Oh, well, *that* I can do. Believe me, I know how to make a woman come hard."

"One way? Two ways?"

"All ways. Fuck off."

"Mmm hmm."

"Fuck you. I'm good."

"But are you *great*? Do you aspire to excellence every single time?"

"What the *fuck* are you talking about? Do I *aspire...*? Just to be clear, we *are* talking about fucking, right? Or is this conversation about something completely different and I've been totally confused the whole time?"

"Ah, grasshopper. Fucking is never just fucking."

I roll my eyes.

"You said she's a unicorn. I'm just saying you gotta bring your 'A' game every time with a unicorn. There are no free passes. You gotta study up—continuously improve your skills—keep ratcheting it up for her. You can never, *ever* just 'wet your dick.'"

I cringe. "*Jonas.*"

He shrugs.

There's a beat.

"Study up?" I finally ask.

"A man catches himself a unicorn, then he best study up so he can feed her the right kind of unicorn-food."

"*What the fuck are you talking about?*"

Jonas rolls his eyes, pulls out his phone, and taps something out on it.

I lean over, trying to get a glimpse of his screen. "What are you doing?"

"I'm ordering some books for you. They'll be at your house when you get home. Read 'em before you see Kat again. You're welcome."

"Fuck you," I say.

"No, fuck *her*—with supreme devotion and expertly calibrated skill." The light from his phone illuminates the huge grin on his face. "I know you think you're the wise and powerful Faraday twin—and you *are* about most things—but about this one thing, I'm nothing short of godly. Just trust me."

"Whatever, bro," I mumble. Of course, I'm beyond excited to read whatever books Jonas just sent to my house, but I'd never tell him that. "Hey, bro, can I ask you something?"

"It's called a G-spot," Jonas says. "And it's the key to the kingdom."

"Fuck you," I say. "I know about the G-spot, fucktard. I'm not a moron."

"Of course, you do. Sorry to insult you. What's your question?"

"What I'm about to say has nothing to do with me *doubting* your connection with Sarah, okay? So don't flip out on me. Just remain calm."

"I would never, ever flip out on you, Josh. I'm nothing if not an endless reservoir of calm contemplation."

We both laugh.

"I'm just wondering..." I say. "Everything's just been so fast for you two—"

"A lot's happened in a short amount of time—we've already lived through a lifetime's worth of shit together."

"Oh, totally. I get that. I'm just wondering, you know..." I clear my throat. "How do you *know*?"

"How do I know what? How to make her come? Read the books I sent you, dumbshit." He laughs, but I don't. He tilts his head, obviously realizing I'm asking him something in earnest. "How do I know I *love* her?" he asks.

"No, not exactly. What I'm asking is different than that—bigger than that." I bite my lip, thinking. "How do you know Sarah's *The One*? How do you know she's the last woman you ever wanna be with—the last woman you ever wanna *sleep* with for the rest of your whole fucking life? How do you know you can promise Sarah *forever* and one hundred percent *mean it*?"

Jonas shrugs. "I just know. I've never been more sure of anything in my whole life."

"But *how* are you so sure? What *exactly* do you feel about Sarah that makes you so sure you don't just *love* her—because I totally get *that*—but that you *also* wanna spend the rest of your life with this *one* girl and not keep searching for some other girl who might be a teeny-tiny bit more perfect?"

Jonas sips his beer slowly, apparently pondering the question. "When you find what you're looking for, you know," he finally says. "We're the greatest love story ever told—our love is the wonder of the wise, the joy of the good, the amazement of the gods."

There's an exceptionally long pause during which I have to keep myself from rolling my eyes. "Oh, well," I say evenly. "That explains everything. Thanks." I take a long swig of my beer and look out at the river. "That reminds me, I like your new ink. In English, I notice. That's something new for you."

Jonas looks down at the tattoo newly inscribed on the outside of his left forearm and his platinum bracelet glints in the moonlight. "Thanks. Yeah, I wanted the whole world to be able to read my words and understand their meaning. It's my declaration of love for Sarah. I'm shouting about my love for her from the top of the highest mountain."

I chuckle to myself. Oh man, Kat's list of "prohibited" tattoos is the gift that just keeps on giving. "So you got a *girlfriend* tattoo, huh?" I say, trying to stifle my laughter. "So, so awesome, bro."

"Soon to be a *wife* tattoo," Jonas says proudly, his excitement palpable. "Why are you laughing, motherfucker? What's so funny?"

"I'm not laughing at you, I swear to God. Kat's got this stupid list of tattoos that she says are uncool or whatever. And girlfriend tattoos are on the list."

Jonas shrugs. "Like I've ever given two shits about being cool?" He swigs his beer, still looking out at the river. "And, anyway, it won't be a *girlfriend* tattoo for much longer." He's obviously bursting with excitement about that last statement.

"Hey, don't feel bad about having a tattoo on Kat's list—dragons and YOLO are on the list, too—both supremely uncool, it turns out," I say.

Jonas chuckles. "Well, I could have told you that."

"No, but get this: Kat came up with her list *before* she saw any of my tattoos."

Jonas bursts out laughing. "Really? Oh my God. That's pretty funny."

"Yeah, Reed and I raked her over the coals pretty good the other night at dinner, along with this hip-hop guy signed to Reed's label. Cool dude. You'd like him. He's a deep thinker, just like you. Anyway, this rapper-dude had an ex-girlfriend tattoo and a dragon." I laugh at the memory. "Kat looked like she was gonna hurl the whole dinner. So fucking funny. I think we made her pay for her sins pretty well."

"Wow, you should see your face when you're talking about Kat," Jonas says. "You *really* like her, huh?"

I can't hide my huge smile. "Yeah, bro, I like her a lot." The image of Kat in her skimpy white tank top and G-string, her eyes drunk with arousal, and her hair tousled pops into my head. "So back to my question, bro," I say. "Do you think you could, maybe, explain things in a way that's not"—I grab his forearm roughly and read his brand new tattoo—"our 'love is the joy of the good, the wonder of the wise, the amazement of the gods'? I know it's hard for you, Jonas, but can you just *try* to talk like a normal person, just once?"

Jonas swigs his beer, apparently thinking. "Okay, how about

this: Sarah's holding my hand and leading me outside a dark cave toward the light that is the divine original form of myself."

I roll my eyes. "Oh, gee, thanks. That's *so* much better."

Jonas laughs. "I was just fucking with you—although that's all true, just to be clear." He laughs to himself for a good long minute. "Okay. The bottom line is that I'd rather be with Sarah than anywhere else in the world. I'd go to fucking IKEA with her if it meant being with her."

My skin suddenly erupts with goose bumps. *"Wish you were here,"* Kat's napkin said—and what thought popped into my head when I saw it? *"So do I."*

Jonas exhales loudly. "It's just so easy with Sarah. I'm *completely* myself with her, you know? I never have to worry I'm saying the wrong thing. I've shown her everything—good, bad, ugly, silly, crazy, creepy—and she accepts it all. And she's *kind.* And nonjudgmental." He sighs happily. "And so *smart.*"

"So you told her everything?" I ask.

"Everything. Absolutely nothing left out. And, hey, that's reason enough right there to marry the girl. I only wanna do that shit once, man. Baring your entire soul to another person is fucking exhausting."

All of a sudden, I'm thinking about how Kat led me into her bed after reading my application and then fell asleep in my arms.

"I dunno, Josh—I just *know,"* Jonas continues. "It's really not all that complicated. For once in my life, it's not about what I think—it's about what I feel. I'll never want anyone besides Sarah, ever, 'til the end of time, and I'm sure of it. It's literally impossible for me to want someone else. Sarah's the divine original form of woman-ness. She's the ideal form of beauty—the pinnacle of perfection that all other women aspire to—the goddess and the muse—so what the fuck else could I possibly want?"

"Shit, I was totally with you until that last bit. 'The goddess and muse,' Jonas? Come on, man. What does that shit even mean?"

He shrugs. "If you don't understand it, then I can't explain it to you."

"Jonas," I say, "I'm serious, man. Please, just break it down for me. If you had to pick one thing that makes you know for sure Sarah's The One, what would it be? Not 'goddess and muse' shit, but, like, something tangible? Something concrete?"

"I can't pick only one thing. It'd be impossible."

I continue to look at him earnestly.

"But, okay, I'll try my best to dumb it down for you, Josh-Faraday style."

"Thank you. Not everyone's a fucking genius about relationships like the wise and powerful Jonas Faraday."

Jonas smiles and his eyes sparkle in the moonlight. "Sarah Cruz, *the goddess and the muse*"—he flashes me a snarky look—"makes me laugh like no other woman ever has—like no other *person* ever has, even *you*. She laughs at almost all of my jokes, even the really lame ones—and she's being totally sincere when she does." He smiles and his white teeth gleam in the moonlight. "Looking at that woman gives me a boner the size of the Space Needle, even when she's just sitting there reading one of her law books and scrunching up her nose." I can see his face suddenly light up, even in the dim light. "And on top of all that, sex with her is akin to a religious experience." He lets out a happy sigh. "If a guy needs more than all that to be eternally happy with one woman, then he's either crazier than me or just a greedy-ass motherfucker."

As if on cue, the door behind us opens and Sarah appears.

"Hey, boys," Sarah says.

"Hi, baby."

"Hi, Sarah Cruz," I say.

"*Hola*, Josh Faraday."

She sits on Jonas' lap and throws her arms around his neck. "I had to come find you." She kisses his cheek. "I started to feel lonely."

"Oh no. You were feeling lonely, baby?"

"Mmm hmm." She kisses his lips.

Jonas puts down his beer and stands, holding Sarah in his arms like he's about to cross a threshold with his bride. "Well, I know exactly what to do to cure my baby's loneliness. See you in the morning, Josh. Nice chatting with you."

With that, Jonas is gone, taking the woman of his dreams with him.

I return my gaze to the slow-moving lights on the dark river in the distance, a certain loneliness I'm well acquainted with descending upon me. Almost immediately, my thoughts turn to Kat. To the awesome photos she sent me from Las Vegas. To the way she fell asleep in my arms after reading my application. To the way she laughs like a dude—and fucks like one, too. To the long list of porno-fantasies she shared with me last night after we got back from our night out with Henn and Hannah. To the way she stomped down that hallway, soaking wet in her G-string, after Reed's party. To the way she kicked ass in each and every one of those banks. To the way she called me "babe" in front of Henn after he woke us up.

I take a long swig of my beer and stare at the dark river, Jonas' words echoing in my head: *If a guy needs more than all that to be eternally happy with one woman, then he's either crazier than me or just a greedy-ass motherfucker.*

Chapter 17
Kat

I look out the window of the taxi at the driving rain pelting the car window. My phone buzzes with an incoming text and I look at the screen.

"Hey, PG," Josh's text says. "I'm about to board a flight from JFK to LAX. Just wanted to say hi real quick."

I smile at my phone. I can't believe how attentive Josh has been these past few days during his trip to New York. What a stark difference from his prior trip to New York right before Las Vegas, when he sent me crap messages all week long like, "Hey, Party Girl!" and "What's up?" Looks like Josh is ready to move past The Game Where We Pretend We Don't Give a Shit. And that's a damned good thing, because I stopped playing that game a long time ago.

"Hey there, Playboy," I type. "I was just thinking about you. I just landed at SEA from... Dang it. What's the airport code for Las Vegas? LVS?"

"LAS," Josh writes.

"Well, aren't you the airport-code guru."

"Yeah, I know them all," he writes. "My life is one giant airport code."

"LOL. (That's not an airport code, btw—that's just me laughing.)"

"Thanks for the clarification," he writes. "For a second, I thought you were flying in from Derby Field in Lovelock, Nevada."

"Wow, you really DO know your airport codes. Why have you been to Lovelock, Nevada?"

"I haven't. I only know LOL because I once read an article about funny airport codes. Other sidesplitting entries include SUX in Sioux City and OMG in Namibia."

129

"LOL."

"Derby Field!" he writes.

"Hey, it's an airport-code version of 'Who's on First?'" I write.

"Totally. OMG."

"Namibia!" I write.

"LOL."

"Derby Field!" I write.

"Gah!" he writes. "Make it stop."

I laugh out loud and the taxi driver's eyes in the rear view mirror glance back at me.

"Can you talk?" Josh writes. "I've got a few minutes before boarding."

"Yes, sir. Call me now."

When his call comes in, I pick up immediately, smiling broadly.

"Hi, Playboy," I coo.

"Hi, Party Girl with a Hyphen," he says. "How are you, beautiful?"

Wow, he sounds incredibly chipper. "I'm great. I'm sitting in a taxi on my way home. How are you?"

"Well, I'm bright-eyed and bushy-tailed and feeling fine as wine, thank you for asking. The world is my oyster."

"Wow. You sound extremely perky today."

"I am. Jonas and I told my uncle we're leaving Faraday & Sons the other night, and yesterday we mapped out the transition with the board of directors. I'm so excited, I'm bouncing off the walls."

"Congratulations. Does this mean you can finally tell me about what you and Jonas are planning?"

"Yeah, but I'd rather tell you in person in between kissing every inch of your naked body. It's too awesome to explain in a brief phone call." He makes a celebratory grunt. "I'm so *pumped.*"

Holy shitballs. He's acting like that "kissing-every-inch-of-your-naked-body" comment was a total throwaway, but it took my breath away. "I'm so excited for you, Josh," I breathe.

"Thanks. Can't wait to tell you about it when I see you, which *by the way,* is the reason I wanted to talk to you. When are you gonna come see me?"

"As soon as possible," I say, though the words catch in my throat. Josh and I were together in Las Vegas for only a week, after all, though it certainly felt a whole lot longer than that, and, now that I'm back in Seattle and returning to my real life, I feel unsure of where things stand between us. "So, hey, thank you so much for flying Hannah and me first class, by the way—we geeked out the whole time. It was awesome, but totally unnecessary."

"Kat, please, you can't fly *coach.*" He makes a sound like he's shuddering.

I laugh, but I'm not entirely sure he's kidding.

"It was my first time, actually," I say. "Wow, the seats are so cushy and the flight attendants are so damned *nice.*"

"That was your *first* time out of steerage? Oh, the humanity."

"Yeah. Hannah's too. She kept asking for extra peanuts just to see if they'd bring 'em."

"Well, get used to the idea of unlimited peanuts, babe—I see lots and lots of peanuts in your future."

My heart stops. What does that mean? Is he saying that, since I'm about to become a *mill-i-on-aire*, I'll be able to book first-class tickets any time I please on my own—or is he implying he'll regularly be flying me first class... *to visit him*?

"Oh, hey, guess what?" Josh says. "Henn has some 'work' in Seattle next week. What a coincidence, huh?"

"Yeah, Hannah told me. They've already got dinner plans. We're invited to join, if we can."

"Next week? Nope. If I get my way, you'll be here in L.A. next week, acting like my paid whore." He snickers.

Holy hell. Josh is positively on fire right now. This is as relaxed and easygoing as he's ever been with me.

"Speaking of which," Josh continues, "I've been thinking about how to pull off all your mini-pornos, and I think I'm gonna hit 'em out of the park."

I giggle. On our last night in Vegas, after coming back from our night-on-the-town with Henn and Hannah, and after having some freaking awesome sex, Josh and I lay in bed together and I told him chapter and verse about each and every one of the mini-pornos that regularly play inside my head. The man was so enthusiastic he even pulled out his laptop and started taking notes.

"Some of that shit's gonna be like putting on a fucking Broadway show," Josh continues, chuckling, "but I'm up for the challenge."

I cup my hand over my mouth to keep my voice from traveling to my driver.

"You don't have to enact *every* fantasy I told you about—" I begin, but Josh cuts me off.

"Oh, I'm doin' em all, PG—and I'm doing 'em *right*. Fuck yeah, I am. I've got a few things I gotta pound out at work for the next week or so," Josh continues, "but then I'm all yours, baby. So what's your calendar look like for a visit some time next week?"

"Um, I dunno," I say, heat rising in my cheeks. This conversation is overwhelming me in the best possible way. "I'll need to look at what's waiting for me on the work calendar and let you know."

"Cool. Don't keep me hanging though, or I'm gonna go all Jonas Faraday on your ass." He laughs to himself. "Oh my fucking God. I can't wait to see you and get started on our little fantasy-fulfillment exchange. It's gonna be *epic*." He lowers his voice. "Kat, I can't stop thinking about—" He abruptly stops. There's a ridiculously long pause. "It."

It? There's a long pause. That felt like a weird choice of words.

"I can't stop thinking about... *it,* either," I say slowly, but I'm not completely sure what we're talking about. Are we saying we can't stop thinking about our upcoming fantasy-fulfillment exchange? Is that the "it"?

"Oh, they're boarding my flight," Josh says quickly. "Be sure to send me a note telling me when you can come to L.A. I've still got you on the clock for my 'PR campaign,' so if it'll make it easier for you to get away from work, I'd be happy to throw some more money onto the 'campaign' and—"

"Oh, gosh, no, don't pay anything more to my firm, Josh. Once I get my finder's fee money, I'll probably be quitting, anyway, to start my own thing."

"Awesome, Kat. Wow. Just think—we'll both be birthin' babies at the exact same time. My new company with Jonas and Party Girl PR will grow up together."

"Ha! Well, our babies might be *born* at the same time, but they're definitely not gonna *grow up* together. Your baby's gonna be in a slightly different tax bracket than mine. Yours will be attending private pre-school and learning to play cello and speak Mandarin while Party Girl PR will be eating paste in the corner at the McDonald's Play Land."

Josh hoots with laughter. "God, you're funny. But, no, Kat, seriously—the size of your business doesn't matter—you'll still be an *entrepreneur*. And in my book, that makes you a fucking *beast*." He makes an exaggerated roar like a T-Rex.

I laugh. "Wow."

"Try it."

I mimic his roar.

"There you go. Feels good, doesn't it?"

"Um... Well, actually, I think my roar is a bit premature. I've got a crap-ton to figure out before I decide if I'm actually gonna do it or not."

"Why wouldn't you do it?"

"Because I don't know what the heck I'm doing. I know PR, but I don't know anything about running a business. I'm only twenty-four, for crying out loud. I'm a wee little baybay, Joshua. Waaah."

He scoffs. "I started the L.A. office of Faraday & Sons at twenty-four and I didn't know a goddamned thing. But I kicked fucking ass and took names, anyway—like the wise and powerful man I am. I learned on the job and so will you."

"Yeah, but I don't have a brother and uncle working with me in case I don't know something—it's just me, and I don't know the first thing about a million things."

"Like what?"

"Well, like whether my company should be an LLC or S-Corp or which billing software I should use. Plus, I've got to figure out a logo and website design and—oh *crap*—what if I wanna hire an actual *employee*? I don't have the first idea how to set up payroll or—"

"Whoa, slow down, High-Speed," Josh soothes. "You're stressing me the fuck out." He chuckles. "I'll help you with all that stuff. Piece of chocolate cake, little baybay."

"Josh, no, you can't help me with that stuff—I have to learn it, that's the whole point of starting my own thing."

"No, doing everything by yourself is most definitely *not* the whole point, you fool." He makes yet another scoffing noise. "The point of owning your own business is being your own boss and getting to do the thing that makes you a fucking beast—which in your case is being a PR phenom—it's definitely not setting up billing software and payroll. And, realistically, you'll probably be a one-woman operation for a while, so getting you up and running will be easy-peasy. Don't stress it, babe. I got you."

"Yeah, but I still don't know how—"

"Ssh. I tell you what I'm gonna do, baby," Josh says smoothly. "I'll line up whatever you're gonna need to get your business off the ground—an accountant, bookkeeper, IT guy, website designer, whatever. I've got all those folks sitting on my contacts list already, so just a couple of quick phone calls and, *boom*, you'll be all set."

I'm positively swooning right now. "You'd do that for me?"

"Of course, I would. I'd do anything for you, Kat."

Holy shitballs. Josh tossed out that last sentence like he was simply stating the obvious, but I'm floored. "I really didn't mean to imply I was expecting you to—"

"Oh, I know. I never thought that. I just wanna help."

"Are you sure?"

"Positive."

"You know you don't have to—"

"*Dude.* You're pissing me off. Just say 'thank you.'"

I smile into the phone. "*Thank you.* Very much."

"My pleasure."

I feel light-headed. "So does that mean you're gonna be, like, an investor?"

"No," he says quickly. "I don't want an ownership stake—I'm not making a long-term commitment here. I'm just offering to help you get your baby off the ground, that's all—no strings attached."

There's an awkward pause. He said all that a lot more emphatically than was necessary, I do believe.

"Okay," I say slowly, my heart beating wildly. Did he just tell me in code he doesn't want a long-term relationship with me?

There's a long pause.

"But, I mean, don't get me wrong," he stammers. "I'm super excited for you and I wanna help you out."

I pause, trying to decide what we're really talking about here. I feel like he just kissed me and slapped me. "Maybe I'd better figure everything out on my own, after all," I say tentatively. "But thanks for your offer, anyway."

He makes a sound of frustration. "What the fuck just happened?"

"What do you mean?"

"You were all happy and grateful and excited and then you suddenly became a chick. What suddenly crawled up your ass?"

I'm shocked. *"What crawled up my ass?"*

"Oh, Jesus. Vagina!" he shouts. "Sometimes I forget you're not just a hot-lookin' dude."

"What the hell...?" I say, bristling. *"What crawled up my ass?"*

"Bad choice of words. Sorry. It's what I'd say to a dude. Forget I said it. Listen, Kat. Here's the deal. I'm gonna help you because you're my Party Girl with a Hyphen—not because I want a stake in your company, that's all I'm saying. Okay? Don't get all freaked out and start overanalyzing everything and start looking for secret codes."

Whoa. It's like he can read my damned mind.

"I'm being above-board with you: I wanna help you. That's how I feel right now. How will I feel a few months from now? I have no idea. All I know is that right now, I wanna help you. And I wanna see you. And be with you and touch you and fuck you and lick you and fucking bite you, and I can't stop thinking about you, no matter what the fuck I do—" He abruptly stops talking.

Suddenly, there's complete silence on the line.

Wow, that was quite the rambling speech from Mr. Joshua William Faraday.

I pause a really long time, collecting myself, my hand on my heart.

He doesn't say another word.

"Okay," I finally say. "Well, then, thank you for your *short-term* and completely *uncommitted* help. I appreciate and accept it."

There's another really long beat.

Josh swallows hard on his end of the line and clears his throat. "Great. You're welcome. So what do you think about calling the company 'Party Girl with a Hyphen PR'?" he asks, clearly changing the topic of conversation. "Is that too long?" he asks.

"Is what too long?"

"The name 'Party Girl with a Hyphen PR.'"

"Oh. Yeah, definitely," I manage to reply. "And also too weird." I clear my throat. "Actually, I was thinking of calling my company 'PG PR'? Is that too boring? I'm thinking 'Party Girl PR' kinda sounds like an event planner."

"Yeah, you're totally right. Good call, PG. That's why they pay you the big bucks. 'PG PR.' I like it. Oh fuck, they're boarding my flight."

"Okay. Thanks for everything, Josh."

"My pleasure."

My pulse is pounding in my ears. "Fly safely."

"That's always the plan, babe. Oh, hey, PG. One more thing. Real quick. I sent you a little present. It should be waiting for you when you get home."

"A *present*? Oh my God, Josh, no. I still haven't thanked you enough for everything you've already done for me."

"It's just a small gift. You'll see."

"But, no, Josh, you've already done too much."

"Hey, you've done a lot for me, too. By my count, we're pretty even."

"If you're talking about all the amazing sex we've had, we're not close to even—that was all for *my* benefit, I assure you."

"Dude. I'm not paying you for sex—though sex with you is so damned good, I gladly would—especially since I know you have a raging call-girl fantasy and all." He snickers. "But no, you big dummy, I'm talking about evening the score for everything you did in Las Vegas. We all owe you big, Oksana, especially me."

"Especially *you*? How's that?"

"Because if something were to happen to Sarah, then Jonas would fall apart—which means my life would suck. So I need to guard Sarah like the crown jewels. Plus, on a personal note, I'd strongly prefer my application never get into the wrong hands, so I'm pretty relieved about the way things worked out."

Oh, I never thought about that.

He takes a deep breath. "*So,* like I said, I'd say we're pretty much even—in fact, I might very well still owe you—oh shit. Gotta run, PG. Hey, there'll be wifi on my flight, so be sure to email me when you get my gift."

"Okay, I will. Thank you again. Fly safely."

He sounds like he's running. "Oh, and don't forget to tell me when you can make it to L.A. so I can book your flight—whoa, whoa, hang on!" He's obviously shouting to someone on his end of the line. "Yeah, I'm on this flight. Thanks." He addresses me again. "Okay, PG? Email me."

"You better go, Josh—don't miss your flight."

"Yeah, I'm walking on board now. Talk to you later, Party Girl with a Hyphen. See you soon."

My stomach bursts with butterflies and my heart squeezes. "Bye-bye, Playboy with a Heart of Gold. Can't wait."

He sighs cartoonishly, like he's Lucy watching Schroeder playing piano. "Bye, Kat."

I can feel his wide smile through the phone line. I hope he can feel mine in return.

"Bye, Josh."

I hang up my phone, my mouth hanging open, my eyes as wide as freakin' saucers. For a long moment, I look out the window of the cab in a daze, staring at the rain pounding insistently on the glass. Holy crappola, as Sarah always says, that entire conversation shocked the living hell out of me. Josh acted like... I can't even finish the thought without possibly making my heart explode.

And *I* acted the exact same way toward him.

We *both* acted like...

Oh my God, both of us did, right? I wasn't imagining it, was I?

I clutch my chest. Holy My Heart's Gonna Burst Out of my Chest, Batman. I'm having trouble breathing. I take a deep, steadying breath. That conversation threw me for a loop. It was just so effing... *affectionate*. And *comfortable*. And *sweet*. (Well, except when he asked what crawled up my ass—that wasn't so sweet.) There was none of our usual cat-and-mouse thing going on—it felt like the cat had already caught its coveted mouse, long ago, and was now pinning it down and licking it from nose to tail.

I stash my phone in my purse—the Gucci bag Josh bought me during our Oksana-inspired shopping spree—and stare at the rain out the taxicab window. Holy hell, Josh's generosity knows no bounds. He's already done so much for me, and now he's gonna help me get my little company off the ground, too? I thought I'd be at least forty before I even attempted to make that particular dream come true.

The windshield wipers are going back and forth at full speed, lulling me into a kind of trance.

I don't care what Josh says—we're definitely not *even* when it comes to the two of us bestowing gifts and favors on each other. I joined our *Ocean's Eleven* crew to protect Sarah and possibly myself, too—not to mention to get a free trip to Las Vegas with my best friend. Yes, everything wound up blowing up and becoming way, way bigger than any of us had ever imagined, but still... Josh keeps doing stuff for me, *personally*, and I most definitely didn't save the world for him specifically. There's no way around it: all I've done is take, take, take from Josh, letting him give, give, give to me 'til he's blue in his ridiculously gorgeous face. And I've done absolutely nothing to deserve his generosity or express my gratitude. In fact, I'm getting perilously close to becoming a total user-abuser, if I'm not already there. But what gift can I possibly give to Josh that would come even close to everything he's already given to me?

My heart is throbbing in my ears. My chest is tight.

I already know the answer, of course. It's not a big mystery: his deepest, darkest sexual fantasies served up on a silver platter.

And that's exactly what I'm going to give him. Right down the line.

Of course, giving Josh complete sexual satisfaction, no matter what form that comes in, isn't some sort of noble or charitable pursuit on my part—ha! It will be my sublime pleasure to give Josh exactly what he desires in the bedroom, a gift to myself as much as him. Hell yeah, it will.

And it's not all the gifts and money Josh has given me that's making me feel this way, either. Nate used to shower me with gifts, too (though on a much smaller scale), and I never once physically ached for him the way I'm aching for Josh right now. I never once daydreamed about feeling Nate pushing himself deep inside me, or closed my eyes and imagined his warm tongue on my clit, or fantasized about waking up in Nate's arms and wordlessly taking his morning wood into my mouth.

I breathe deeply, arousal suddenly seeping into my panties.

I never once felt a near-desperate urge to fuck Nate any which way he likes it, literally, *any which way*, no matter how dirty or naughty it might be, or felt the urge to make his desires my own, or fantasized about sitting on his face or riding his cock 'til I'm screaming his name. And I certainly never once imagined Nate sitting at the dinner table with my family on Thanksgiving, or on the couch with my brothers, watching the Seahawks and eating my mom's famous chili.

I gasp and jerk forward in my seat, clutching my throat like I'm choking on a chicken bone. Oh my fucking shit. What am I thinking? I want to take Josh home to meet my family? I haven't taken anyone home since Garrett.

I stare at the rain battering the window of the taxicab, still clutching my throat, trying desperately to think of some logical reason why I'm feeling like a tortured, lovesick puppy that doesn't involve falling for the world's most eligible bachelor (who, in case I missed it, just told me in not-so-secret code he's not at all interested in a long-term commitment). But I can't come up with a damned thing.

I'm falling for the world's most eligible bachelor.

Oh God.

No. I need to stop feeling this way right now and get a handle on my emotions. I press both of my palms on my cheeks, willing myself to stop feeling this all-consuming ache. Infatuation is fine. Sexual attraction is fine. We'll-see-where-this-goes is perfectly fine. Really liking someone a whole lot is perfectly fine. But risking inevitable, shattering heartbreak is emphatically *not*.

Dude, I need to think rationally, with my brain, and not my lady-parts.

I'm in lust, and nothing more. Well, that and very strong like. Very, very strong like. But once I get back to work and the routine of my real life, once the neon lights and excitement of our spy-caper-porno in Las Vegas have faded for both of us and reality sets in and we remember that Josh and I live not just in different states but in different *worlds*—because I'm not a supermodel and my mom isn't a movie star with houses in the Hamptons and Aspen, for crying out loud—I'm sure my fairytale-delusions will crash down to reality without a parachute.

Indubitably.

Chapter 18
Kat

When I enter my apartment, my youngest brother, Dax, is on the couch, playing his guitar and singing a song I've never heard before. When he sees me, he sets down his guitar and lopes over to me, his lean muscles taut in his tight-fitting T-shirt.

"Jizz," he says warmly, wrapping me in a big hug. "Welcome to my humble abode."

I kiss his cheek. "Hey, baby brother," I say. "Thanks for keeping my apartment safe and sound."

"It was hard work, but somebody had to do it. Was Vegas a blast?"

"Yeah, it was amazing."

"How much money did you lose?"

"Oh, not too much," I say coyly. "So, hey, was that a new song you were just playing?"

"Yeah, I was just fine-tuning it. It's not done yet."

"Play me what you've got." I lead him to the couch and we sit.

"Naw, I'll play it for you when I've got it finished."

"I won't criticize it. Just play me what you got."

His face lights up. "Well, if you insist."

I laugh. "I do."

Dax picks up his guitar and plays an up-tempo song about looking for love in the anonymous faces he passes on a busy city street—and his expressive voice and vulnerable lyrics transport me with every word and note.

"Wistful, hopeful, funny, romantic, and lonely all at the same time," I say when he's done. "I absolutely love it."

"Yeah, but you love everything I write."

"True. But that doesn't mean I'm not sincere."

He grins. "So, hey, I got your mail for you." He slides a stack of mail on the coffee table toward me.

"Oh, thanks. I never thought I'd be gone so long." I start rifling through the stack. "Bills, bills, bills. Credit card offers. Coupons. Catalogs. Doesn't look like I missed—" I look up. Oh. I'm talking to myself. Dax isn't in the room. I look back down at the stack of mail and continue sorting it.

I hear a thudding noise in the center of the room and look up just in time to see Dax straightening up from putting down a heavy-looking box. "This bad boy got delivered a couple hours ago," he says. "From someone named J.W. Faraday."

My skin pricks with goose bumps. "Oh, okay, thanks," I say, trying to sound casual—but, oh my God, the size of that box sure looks familiar. I pop up off the couch, intending to shoo Dax away, because, oh my God, if that box contains what I think it does, there'd better not be any markings on the outside to give it away.

"And, of course, I already opened the box for you, sis," Dax continues, "just to be super-duper helpful."

A weird screech of anxiety escapes my throat.

Dax chuckles. "Whoever this J.W. Faraday guy is, he's *awfully* generous—and somewhat of a perv, too, it seems."

"You *opened* it?" I blurt angrily.

"Of course, I did. I'd never make my sister open a big ol' *box* all by herself with her own two fragile hands. I'm a *gentleman*." He opens the already-cut flaps of the box with a wide smile and pulls out a humongous assortment of dildo-attachments, all packaged together in a clear plastic bag. "So many dicks to choose from, Jizz. I don't know how you'll decide." He places the dildos on my coffee table with a wide smile.

"Oh my God," I say, my cheeks burning. I can't breathe. I've never been so embarrassed in all my life. But Dax isn't done with me. He reaches inside the box, pulls out the main event, and places it carefully on the floor.

At the sight of my brand new Sybian, my face explodes with instant heat, both from excitement and embarrassment, but I force myself to remain calm. Dax might have no idea what a Sybian is, I tell myself—I'd certainly never heard of one before last week when Josh rented one for me.

"This is the first time I'm seeing a Sybian in person," Dax says, standing over it with his hands on his hips.

I throw my hands over my face, completely mortified. I can't believe my baby brother's here to witness this gift from Josh. Nightmare.

"It's really quite the feat of modern engineering," he says.

I don't reply.

Dax laughs. "So who the fuck is this guy, Jizz?"

I still don't reply.

"Aw, come on. It's just me."

As I often do, I decide my best defense is a good offense. "I can't believe you opened my personal stuff, Dax!" I yell, throwing my hands up in outrage.

But Dax completely ignores my outburst—a tactic I've seen him employ too many times to count (and a tactic I've copied and used to great success myself). In fact, he's smiling serenely at me. "I think Sybians cost like fifteen hundred bucks," he says. "Gosh, you must have done something awfully nice to J.W. Faraday to make him wanna send you such an expensive gift."

I open my mouth to yell at him, but nothing comes out. I'm so freaking embarrassed, I can't speak.

Dax bursts out laughing. "Oh, looks like I hit the nail on the head, huh? Well, whatever you did to the guy, you apparently did it very, very well." He buckles over laughing.

"You're so gross, Dax. Stop it."

But he won't stop laughing.

"Stop it."

Nope. He's thoroughly amused.

"You had absolutely no business opening that box." I march over to him in a huff and punch him in the shoulder. "Did the label on the package say 'David Jackson Morgan'? *No*, it didn't."

He scoffs. "Close enough—it was stamped 'Personal & Confidential.' Hell, the damn thing might as well have said, 'Open me, Dax.'"

I can't help but smile broadly, even through my pissiness. That's my line, of course. Dax and I have always shared a brain.

Dax shrugs. "Seriously, a guy can't see a big ol' box sent to his *sister*, addressed to 'Katherine *Ulla* Morgan,' no less, *and* marked

'*Personal & Confidential*' and not open it, for crying out loud. Gimme a break, Jizz—I'm but a man, not a saint."

My irritation is softening. Goddamn my baby brother, I can never stay mad at him for long. "Just don't tell everybody about this, okay? It's really personal."

He scoffs. "Of course not. I'd never tell any of our brothers about any of this."

I laugh. "You tell them everything, Dax, especially Keane."

"I don't tell Peen *everything*. I only tell him about my music and girls—"

"Like I said, 'everything.'"

"But I never tell him your stuff. Seriously, Jizz, I never do." His eyes are earnest. "I swear." He flashes me an adorable puppy-dog smile. "You aren't really pissed at me for opening your box, are you?"

I roll my eyes. "No," I say begrudgingly. "But never do it again."

He crosses his heart. "The next time a guy with a lord-of-the-manor name sends a big box marked 'personal & confidential' to Katherine Ulla Morgan at your apartment, and I'm here all alone when the delivery comes, I swear to God I will not open it before you get home. So who is this 'J.W. Faraday' chap?" he asks, saying Josh's name with a Queen-Elizabeth-British accent. "Sounds like a guy with a butler."

I plop down on the couch and Dax follows suit, settling himself right next to me. I grab his hand (something I've been doing ever since Mom brought him home from the hospital for the first time when I was four), and I lean my cheek against his strong shoulder.

"Joshua William Faraday," I breathe, my heart skipping a beat as I say the words.

"So you know each other's middle names, huh? Sounds serious, brah."

I don't reply. Dax is being flippant, I think—but his comment hits on the exact thing I can't stop wondering: Is this thing with Josh something serious or are we having some sort of extended fling?

"Hey, by the way," Dax says, "you'll probably wanna read this." He holds up a small sealed envelope. "It was inside the box."

I snatch the envelope from him, hyperventilating. Oh, thank God, it's still sealed.

"It pained me not to read it," Dax says. "It really did. But I figure there are some lines even I shouldn't cross, seeing as how you're my sister and all."

I tear open the envelope, pull out a typewritten note (taking great care to keep it out of Dax's line of sight), and read as fast as my eyes can manage:

"My Dearest Party Girl with a Hyphen," Josh's note says. "I hope you get lots and lots of enjoyment from your new toy. Please make use of it every day when I can't be there personally to make you scream. While you use it, I want you to imagine it's me who's fucking you, nice and slow, and whispering into your ear as I do about how amazing you feel, how dripping wet you are for me, and how much you turn me on."

Holy shitballs.

My breathing has suddenly become labored.

"Until we meet again," Josh continues in his note, "I want you to use your new toy every time you feel even the slightest bit horny or lonely. (Because even when I can't be with you in person, I'm determined to keep my hot-wired Party Girl with a Hyphen completely satisfied—wouldn't want her feeling even remotely tempted to fuck Cameron Schulz again, now would I?)

"I'm looking forward to seeing you again very soon and making each and every one of your (highly detailed) sexual fantasies come true. *Exclusively* yours, Playboy."

"Oh. My. God," I say breathlessly. My crotch is exploding with arousal in my panties and I'm panting like a Pekingese running a hundred-yard dash.

"What does it say?" Dax asks.

I press the note against my chest. "It says, 'It's none of your frickin' business, Dax Morgan.'"

"Aw, come on."

"No way."

He makes a wry face. "So what's the status with you two—are you in a relationship or... ?"

"I have no freaking idea what our status is. Whatever we're doing defies standard labeling."

"The guy sends you a fifteen-hundred-dollar gift and you don't know the status? That's a lot of money to spend on a gift for some chick you're just hanging out with."

I shrug. "It's hard to explain."

"Are you at least dating?"

I sigh. "Yeah. I think so. I mean we've both made it clear we're really into each other. But I don't know where things are headed—he gets really skittish the minute he feels like he's being penned in. But on the other hand we agreed to be exclusive."

"You're exclusive? Well, then it's way beyond dating."

I sigh. "One would think. But we're exclusive only temporarily. It's hard to explain."

"*Temporarily* exclusive? That's a new one. I gotta steal that."

"It was me who suggested it."

He flashes me a look that says, "You're an idiot."

I rub my face. "This week was just a unique set of circumstances. We were together day and night, doing this crazy thing to help Sarah, and it was this incredible, fairytale existence. It's like we were in the fantasy suite on *The Bachelor* for an entire week—and my feelings for him were so freaking intense and surreal—and now it's like the show is over and the cameras are off and it's back-to-reality time."

Dax nods.

I shake my head. "I just don't know if what we felt in Vegas will translate to real life. Plus, he lives in L.A. and travels a ton and I'm here, obviously. So, I dunno, it might be kinda tough to keep the fantasy alive."

Dax motions to the Sybian. "Looks like he's giving it the ol' college try."

I bite my lip to suppress a huge smile.

"I must say, giving you a Sybian as a gift is an interesting choice—he could have gone with shoes or a purse."

"Oh, he did. Both."

"And you still don't know if he's serious about you? I think you might be overanalyzing things here. The guy's making his feelings pretty clear."

I sigh. "I don't wanna get my hopes up."

"This is so unlike you. Why are you being so...?"

"Analytical?"

"Annoying."

I make a face. "I don't know. Josh and I are just so incredibly..." I was about to say *sexual*, but then I remember I'm talking to my little brother, not to Sarah. "*Physical*," I say, opting for a tamer word to finish my sentence. "The physical chemistry is so off the charts, it makes me wonder if I'm just in some sort of hormone-induced coma and not seeing things clearly."

"Just because you have incredible physical chemistry with the guy doesn't mean it's not serious, too," he says.

"So I've heard. But from what I've seen personally, at least as an adult, it's one or the other."

He pulls back and looks at me, stupefied. "Are you serious?" he asks.

I nod.

"Jizz, that's fucked up. How'd you get so fucked up?"

I shrug.

"You can have off-the-charts physical chemistry without it being 'serious,' for sure—and thank God for that." He snickers. "But it doesn't work the other way around: you absolutely *cannot* have something serious if you don't have physical chemistry. The fact that you think it's one or the other is so fucked up, it's pathetic. It's like you've got a... what's the word I'm looking for... that complex thing?"

I make a face. "A Madonna-whore complex?"

"Exactly. Only in reverse. What's it called when a woman thinks that about a guy?"

"A Jesus-manwhore complex?"

We both laugh.

"Yeah, I don't think society has a cute little phrase for when it's a guy."

"What about that Nate guy?" Dax asks. "You guys were pretty serious, right?"

"Serious, yes, but we were sort of blah in the physical department," I say. "At least it was blah for me."

"Ooph. I think maybe you *do* have a Madonna-whore complex when it comes to guys, sis, whatever it's called—like you somehow think the guys who turn you on the most can't possibly be boyfriend material."

I make a face. He might have a point there. Hmm.

"But that's the whole point of this grand experiment we call life—finding the serious stuff *and* the physical stuff all rolled up together into one fucking awesome person.

"How'd you get so deep at such a tender age?" I ask.

Dax grabs my hand and kisses it, a move that instantly makes me think of Josh.

"That's not even a remotely deep thing to say, sis," Dax says. "It's pretty fucking basic. I think maybe you're just particularly stupid when it comes to relationships."

I know Dax is kidding, sort of, but I think he might be on to something here—I think I might very well be particularly stupid when it comes to relationships involving me. "I think when the sex is crazy-good-off-the-charts with a guy, it makes me kinda skittish in a twisted way," I say. "Like I think things are too good to be true—and then I start shutting down emotionally to protect myself and the whole thing becomes a self-fulfilling prophecy."

Dax squeezes my hand but doesn't reply.

"The thing is, with this guy Josh, the physical part is so freaking good, he could be Jeffrey Dahmer and I'd be like, 'Oh, em, gee, Jeff, you're such a sweetheart!'"

Dax laughs.

"And that scares me. I feel like I might have a huge blind spot. But on top of that, horror of horrors, he's funny and sweet and generous, too, and he makes me feel really special." I shake my head. "I guess I'm just trying to figure out if he's really as perfect as he seems? Or if this is just too good to be true."

"Well, have you seen any chopped up body parts in his freezer?"

"No, but I haven't been to his house yet. Stay tuned."

"He lives in L.A.?"

I nod.

"What does he do?"

"He runs some sort of investment company with his brother and uncle. Other than that, he climbs rocks with his brother and parties with rock stars and supermodels. Get this: he used to date Gabrielle LeMonde's daughter."

"Seriously?"

"Yeah, and that model that's on all the Victoria's Secret commercials—Bridgette something—the blonde with the perfect body? Her, too."

"Bridgette *Schmidt*," Dax says reverently. "Oh my God. She's my top desert-island pick. Your guy dated *her*? Wow."

"Well, actually, come to think of it, I don't know if he *dated* her, but he certainly *did* her."

"Damn, who the fuck is this guy? Jesus. I guess he's a major playah-playah, huh? Maybe that's the 'not-so-perfect' thing you're afraid is lurking in the shadows of his tormented soul."

I sigh. "He's not as big a playah-playah as he sounds. I mean, don't get me wrong, he definitely likes having sex with gorgeous women—when Josh Faraday is single, he's apparently *very* single— but I don't think he's as much of a playboy as I initially thought. He had this long-term girlfriend he was really devoted to... " I shrug. "But, then again, he had a heart attack on the phone just now when he thought I was trying to pin him down to something beyond next week." I roll my eyes and lean my head back onto the back of the couch. "Aw, shit, I dunno, Dax. I need to just chill the fuck out and stop overanalyzing things. I'm acting like a chick."

"You totally are. I've never seen you act like this. You know what you need to do?" Dax says. "Tap into your inner Peen. That'll cure your chickiness right up."

"Nobody should ever tap into their inner Peen," I say. "Even Peen should stop tapping into his inner Peen."

We both have a good laugh about that.

"So why did this Faraday guy send you a fucking Sybian?" Dax asks. "Did you lose a bunch of money to him in a high-stakes poker game and now you've gotta do porn to pay off your debt?"

"He's not a porn king, Dax. Gimme some credit. He's this—I don't even know what he does, actually. Google him. His company is called Faraday & Sons—Joshua Faraday."

Dax pulls out his phone and Googles while I talk.

"It's some sort of investment thing. He travels all the time, looking at potential companies to buy—I don't even know what he does. He never talks about it."

"Oh, wow," Dax says. He's found the homepage of Faraday & Sons. "Were these guys genetically engineered by Monsanto or what? Which one is your guy?"

"The one with the dark hair. The other guy's his fraternal twin brother, Jonas—Sarah's new boyfriend, actually."

"Whoa, Sarah's dating Thor?"

"Yeah. And he adores her. I've never seen two people more into each other in all my life."

"Aw, good for her." He scrutinizes the photo for a long beat. "Well, now I can see why you're feeling a tad bit confused. I'm completely straight and *I'd* do him, especially if he bought me a dress and shoes and a Sybian."

I laugh.

Dax continues scrutinizing the photo. "He's exactly your type, only the best-looking version of it I've ever seen. He looks a lot like that football-player dude you dated in high school."

I shrug. "Yeah, I know. I guess I've got a type."

"What was his name again?"

"Kade."

"That's right. He looks like he could be Kade's older, better-looking brother." Dax looks up from the phone and appraises me with sympathetic eyes. "Poor, Jizz. I don't know how any woman could figure out if she had actual feelings around this guy. He must leave a wake of exploded ovaries wherever he goes."

"Exactly," I say. "I told you—the dude could keep a severed head in his fridge and I'd totally reach behind it to get myself a Diet Coke while giggling at something he just said."

Dax laughs and looks at his phone again. "Yeah, both of 'em are just stupid-good-looking. It's like God fell asleep at the 'good looking' switch and didn't move on to the next guy on the conveyor belt like he was supposed to."

"And I just spent a week with him in freaking *Las Vegas* of all places—and all expenses paid, too. No wonder I can't distinguish fantasy from reality. The whole thing was like a fairytale."

"Snow White and the Seven Sybians."

"How the hell do you even know what a Sybian is, by the way?"

He scoffs. "Dude, I'm twenty and I'm a guy," he says, as if this answers my question.

I shrug.

"Every twenty-something-year-old male in America knows what a Sybian is—it's a porn staple. Howard Stern even has one in his studio for female guests to ride. It's, like, Porn 101."

"Really? I had no idea. I'd never even heard of one 'til last week."

"Well, are you a twenty-something-year-old male?"

"Not the last time I checked."

"And do you watch a shit-ton of porn?"

"Never."

"Well, there you go. Now you know why you discovered the Sybian for the first time while watching porn with Sir J.W. Faraday."

I bite my lip. Dax has obviously misunderstood the circumstances under which Josh first acquainted me with my new toy—and, as far as I'm concerned, that's a very good thing. No one ever needs to know I rode that thing for Josh's pleasure—least of all my brother. "So, hey, that concludes the 'What Happens In Vegas Stays In Vegas' portion of our program," I say. "There's something that happened in Vegas I actually *want* to tell you about." I take a deep breath, a huge smile bursting across my face. "Guess who I partied with one crazy night while I was there?"

"Who?"

"All four members of Red Card Riot." I can barely keep from squealing.

"What?" he bellows, his face the picture of pure astonishment. "How the *fuck* did that happen?"

I tell him about that night at Reed's party, omitting certain key elements such as Jen's attendance at the party and my near-naked tantrum in the hallway (because I'm a big believer that editing one's life stories in the retelling is a girl's prerogative).

"Damn, I wish I could have been there," Dax says wistfully, shaking his head. "I would have *loved* to hang with those guys. Can you imagine what it would feel like to play for an entire *arena* of people, all of them singing along to a song you wrote?"

I shake my head, awed by the thought. "When I met them, they'd just performed on *Saturday Night Live* the prior week, and the lead-singer guy, Dean, started talking about it with this rapper guy and all I could think was, 'God, I wish Dax could hear this.'"

The look on Dax's face is so cute right now, I wanna throw him into a papoose and wear him on my back.

"You lucky bitch," he mumbles.

"It ain't no luck, son. I *make* my luck."

He laughs. "Yes, you do. Always."

"If RCR comes to Seattle, I'll totally ask Josh if his friend Reed might get us backstage—well, if Josh and I are still doing our 'temporarily-exclusive' thing by then, that is."

"Who's Reed? And why would he be able to get us backstage at a Red Card Riot concert?"

I smile. This is exactly the piece of the story I've been *dying* to tell Dax for days. "Reed's the guy who threw the party in Vegas where I met Red Card Riot."

"How does he know them?"

It's as if we choreographed this conversation in advance. "Well, let me see if I remember how he knows them," I say. "Hmm." I look up at the ceiling like I'm deep in thought. "I think Reed knows Red Card Riot because... *they're signed to his record label*!"

Dax tilts his head like he's not sure he heard me correctly.

I giggle. "Reed *owns* a record label, Dax. Like, he literally *owns* it—*and RCR is one of his bands.*"

Dax is looking at me like I've just proved time travel is real. "And you partied with him?" he asks, incredulous. "You partied with the owner of a record label?"

I nod, grinning from ear to ear. "*Twice.*" I hold up two fingers for emphasis.

Dax's thoughts are clearly racing. "So... oh my God. Does this Reed guy know your name or did you just sort of, you know, shake hands in a crowded bar?"

"No, we totally hung out. Had real conversations. He called me Stubborn Kat."

Dax makes a face of total confusion.

"They were all joking that Stubborn Kat is like some kind of *Garfield* rip-off. 'Oh no, Stubborn Kat ate all the curly fries and now she won't get off the couch!'" I say by way of explanation, but he still looks nonplussed. "Never mind. I just mean we totally hung out and became friends. I went to his party the first night and then out to dinner with him and his friends a second night."

Dax runs his hands through his hair, totally freaking out. "Listen to me, Jizz." His eyes are blazing. "This could be a really lucky break for me. *Fuck.* Oh my God." He bites his lip. "Do you think you could send this Reed guy my demo? Or would that make Sir J.W. Faraday feel like you're just using him to get to Reed?"

I laugh. "Um, there's no way in hell Josh would ever think I'm using him to get to Reed."

Dax's face lights up. "So you'll send him my demo?"

I sigh and shake my head solemnly. "Sorry, Dax. No. I don't feel comfortable sending Reed your demo. I'm sorry."

Dax is obviously crestfallen but trying to hide it. "It's okay," he says evenly. "Yeah, no problem. I totally understand. Sorry, I didn't mean to—"

"But only because that demo doesn't show how totally *awesome* you are!" I add brightly. "Only because we've got this one amazing chance to make an *awesome* first impression with the guy who owns Red Card Riot's record label and we're totally gonna blow him outta the water!"

He looks like I've punched him and kissed him all at once. "Yeah, but that demo's all I've got—at least for now. I'm working on it, but it's gonna be a while."

"How much do you still need?" I ask.

For as long as I can remember, Dax and his band (but mostly Dax) have been saving their pennies to record a full-length studio album of his songs with full instrumentation. But saving that kind of money—fifteen thousand bucks, he estimates, to record and produce the album exactly the way he wants it—is an awfully tall order for a group of twenty-something musicians living hand-to-mouth by playing bars and festivals.

"I had almost three thousand saved, but then my bike totally crapped out on me so I'm basically back to square one."

"So you still need about fifteen grand or so?"

"Well, we could certainly record an album for less if we cut some corners on production value. Or I guess we could just do a few songs instead of a full album—or maybe another basic demo." He puffs out his cheeks like a puffer fish, thinking. "But I really didn't wanna do another demo—been there done that—I wanted to put together a full album that showcases who we are and what we can do." He runs his hand through his hair. "Shit. Maybe I should just record a quick demo with my acoustic guitar on my iPad, just so you have something current to send to the guy before he forgets who you are—"

"Nope. We're not gonna send Reed a demo, Dax." I pull a thick envelope out of my purse and plop it onto the coffee table with a thud. "Because you're recording a full album."

"What's that?"

"Open it."

Dax opens the envelope and peeks inside. "Oh my... What the fuck is this? Did you rob a bank?"

I smirk. Oh, if only Dax knew how spot-on that comment is. I'd originally planned to use this wad of cash to pay off my credit cards and car, of course, but that was before I found out I'm gonna be a *mill-i-on-aire*.

"Where the fuck did you get this kind of cash?" Dax asks, his eyes wide.

"Playing craps," I say matter-of-factly. "That's almost twenty grand there, baby. Enough for whatever album you've been dreaming of making plus a bit extra for bells and whistles: strings, horns, a freaking choir—whatever. Or maybe PR for the album when you release it or a down payment on a new bike. *Whatever*. It's yours. Go forth and prosper."

"How the fuck did you win twenty grand playing *craps*?" Dax asks. "How is that even possible? You must have been betting, like, hundreds of bucks per roll—maybe even thousands."

"Yeah, well, Josh spotted me some gambling money and then his brother walked away from the table and gave me all his chips. So, actually, I didn't win any of this money fair and square. But Josh insisted I keep it, so whaddayagonnado?" I shrug. "And now it's yours."

"Wait a minute. The dude *gave* you *twenty* grand and you're not sure if he's *serious* about you? Are you mentally deficient?"

I wave him off. "No, trust me. You don't know Josh. Just because he's crazy-generous and he gave me an insane amount of money doesn't necessarily mean he wants a serious relationship with me. He has a warped sense of reality when it comes to money. The guy wears two-thousand-dollar shoes (which, true story, I barfed on one night). *He drives a frickin' Lamborghini, Dax.* The guy's not normal."

"Dude, I don't care how rich he is or what shoes he wears or what car he drives. If a guy gives a woman, especially a woman he's sleeping with, twenty grand, then he thinks she's one of two things: a *very* high-priced hooker or the woman of his dreams."

My heart skips a beat. Damn, my brother has a knack for hitting the nail right on the head sometimes.

Dax picks up the envelope and begins counting the hundred-dollar bills inside, shaking his head with awe as he does. When he's finally done counting, he looks up at me, his eyes glistening. "Thank you so much, Kat," he says. "I'll repay you one day, I swear to God, every last penny." His voice breaks adorably. "I'm gonna do everything in my power to make you proud of me, Kat."

I grin from ear-to-ear. It's so rare that Dax calls me Kat. With him, I'm always Jizz or sis (or Splooge or Protein Shake if he's feeling particularly silly). He must feel uniquely overcome right now to be addressing me by my real name.

"You never need to pay me back," I say. "It was never my money in the first place. And I'm already proud of you. All I want is for you to make the exact album you wanna make—no holding back."

He lurches at me and wraps me in a fervent hug. "I love you, Kat. You're my all-time favorite sister."

I laugh and kiss his cheek, my eyes stinging. "I love you, too. You're my all-time favorite baby brother."

We hold each other for a long beat.

"Now get the fuck out of my house, you mooch," I say, pulling away from our embrace and wiping my eyes. "I've got a thank-you email to write to our mutual benefactor, and then I've got a hot date with a certain piece of motorized machinery."

Dax laughs. "No shit, you do." He rubs his eyes. "Thanks so much, Kat. I'll never forget this as long as I live."

"I didn't do it so you'd owe me something. I did it because watching you make your dreams come true will be the same thing as making my own dream come true."

He wipes his eyes again. "I'll make you proud, sis."

"You already have."

There's a beat. We're smiling at each other like simpletons. I think this is one of the best moments of my life. Way better than if I'd received something amazing for myself.

"Now get the fuck out," I say. "You're cramping my style."

He kisses me on the cheek again, shoves his guitar into its case, scoops up his envelope full of cash, and strides toward my front door. But a few feet from the door, he stops short and looks down for a very long beat, his back still to me.

When Dax finally whirls around to face me, I'm expecting him to thank me again, or maybe say something deep and poignant—but that's not what happens.

"*You slept with Cameron Schulz?*" he blurts. "*The baseball player?*"

My eyes dart to the coffee table, searching frantically for Josh's note—but it's not where I left it. Goddammit!

Dax holds up Josh's card between his two fingers like he's holding a cigarette, a wicked smirk on his face.

"Get the fuck out of my house," I say evenly, pointing to the door.

Dax tosses the card onto my kitchen counter. "Wow, Jizz," he says smoothly. "You're my fucking hero, dude."

Chapter 19
Kat

The minute the door closes behind Dax's back, I pull out my laptop from my carry-on bag, log in remotely to my firm's network, and check the shared calendar, trying to figure out when I can realistically commit to a trip to L.A. to see Josh.

Based on the workload I'm seeing on the firm's calendar, I seriously shouldn't go for at least a month. I was in Las Vegas way longer than I ever expected to be, and, based on what I'm seeing on my firm's calendar, my absence has quite obviously been felt. Dang it. If I'm gonna stay at this job, I really should take a chill pill on skipping town for a while. But am I gonna stay at this job or open my own firm in the near future? That's the million-dollar question. And if I *am* gonna start my own thing, then I suppose in good conscience I really shouldn't sit for too much longer on my company's payroll while I'm getting my own ducks in a row. Shoot. I've got some big-girl decisions to make.

I flip into my personal calendar, just to see if there's something requiring my attention here at home next week. Whoa. Today's the *eighteenth*? All this time, I've been thinking it was the seventeenth. I look up sharply from my screen. Wait. Did I miss taking a birth control pill somewhere along the line this past week?

I quickly rummage into my bag and pull out my pills. Oh crap. Yeah, I missed a day. Well, it's no wonder with the crazy hours Josh and I kept in Vegas. Who could keep track of day and night the way we were going?

Quickly, I pop one of my pills to make up for my lapse. It really shouldn't make that big a difference, right? It's just one day. In fact, I'm pretty sure the pill I missed was yesterday.

Okay, back to the calendar. It looks like I can head down to L.A. on Thursday of next week. But should I give notice at my job before I leave? Gah. I just don't know. It'd be a huge leap of faith. I'm conflicted.

I take a deep breath and click into my email account, poised to send Josh a quick email giving him my proposed dates and thanking him for his latest gift, when I think, "Hey, I should attach a photo of the Sybian to my thank-you email so Josh can see that it arrived."

I pull out my phone to snap a quick photo of the machine sitting in the middle of the room, but then I get an even better idea: "Hey, I should take a photo of *me* sitting on the Sybian, smiling happily for the camera."

One side of my mouth hitches up with an even better idea: "I should pose on the machine buck naked."

My smile widens. I'll send Josh a naked photo of myself as if I were one of the hookers in The Club.

Yes.

Surprisingly, I've never sent a man a naked-selfie before (mainly because my mom always put the fear of God into me that any naked photo I'd send, no matter how much I might trust the guy at the time, would eventually wind up on hotgirls.com after things went south in the relationship). But when it comes to Josh, I don't think for one minute he'd betray me, ever, come what may. Hey, if one of the world's top models trusts Josh with a photo of herself sticking her hand up her cooch, then surely, a non-celebrity like me can trust him, too.

I peel off my clothes, situate myself suggestively on the saddle of my new machine, raise my phone above my head, and snap a photo, giggling to myself as I do—and when I survey the resulting photo, I laugh out loud. Well, if I'm going for "treat me like one of the whores in The Club," then I've definitely succeeded with this shot.

I grab my laptop and sit on my couch, still completely nude, and begin writing an email with the photo attached:

"Dear Mr. Faraday," I write. "Thank you for your application to The Katherine Ulla Morgan Club, also known as the KUM Club, also known as the Fantasy Fulfillment Club. We have reviewed the sexual preferences you described in your application and have determined that you are, indeed, one helluva sick fuck, Mr. Faraday. But do not

157

fret because, as it turns out, we absolutely adore sick fucks here at The KUM Club. In fact, lucky for you, our most sought-after girl at The KUM Club strongly prefers sick fucks above all other freaks and perverts—and guess what, you lucky bastard? She's a blonde!

"The fantasy-provider to whom I refer goes by many code names, including The Jealous Bitch and Madame Terrorist to name a few, but the code name she strongly prefers the most is Party Girl with a Hyphen (abbreviated herein as 'PGWH').

"As mentioned, PGWH is *by far* our most popular and coveted fantasy-provider. Wise and powerful men the world over, including sheiks, kings, politicians, and professional athletes (including Cameron Schulz, the shortstop for the Seattle Mariners!!!) clamor for this woman's valuable services. And it's no wonder: it is said PGWH can give a man a blowjob that will make him weep with joy like a newborn lamb.

"PGWH is very selective of her clients, but she has viewed your photos and determined she would be willing to bestow her remarkable talents upon you. If you desire this talented and coveted blonde woman's services (as every other wise and powerful man from around the globe does), then PGWH would be *very* excited to make your every fantasy come true. In fact, she'd like nothing better (as long as you pay her eminently reasonable fee, addressed below).

"Mr. Faraday, PGWH is the top fantasy-provider in the world. As I'm sure you can understand, a woman like that doesn't come cheap. Indeed, you'll have to pay handsomely to experience PGWH's charms: one *million* dollars per night.

"Perhaps you're thinking this price seems a tad high for one night of mind-blowing pleasure with the most sought-after call girl in the entire world (even for a *mill-i-on-aire* many times over such as yourself), but please rest assured PGWH is well worth this fee. In fact, we *guarantee* that by the end of your night with this woman, you'll declare, without the slightest reservation, 'You're worth every fucking penny, baby.'

"Considering your very specific requirements stated in your application, we've attached a photo of PGWH for your approval. We hope you'll find her to be a genuine Gucci bag among counterfeits sold on the sidewalks of New York—the 'divine original' of your blonde-girl fantasies.

"Assuming PGWH meets your approval, she's available to meet you in Los Angeles on Thursday the twenty-fifth for a long weekend. Please reply with details about your *rendezvous*, including the location of the hotel you've arranged, when and under what name she should pick up her room key, etc. (whatever types of details you supplied when arranging trysts during your month-long membership in the far inferior Mickey Mouse Roller Coaster Club).

"We cannot emphasize enough that PGWH wishes to experience what you've outlined in your application, exactly the way you've described it (because she's a high-end call girl, you might recall, and not just a woman who works at a PR firm going on a date with the hottest guy ever).

"So let's talk logistics. In your application, you requested fulfillment of two different fantasies. We are happy to inform you that, with just a few minor tweaks to your requests, PGWH is willing (and quite excited) to deliver both to you, on two separate nights of her stay in Los Angeles (which means, yes, this high-end call girl's gonna cost you a grand total of *two* million bucks). So let's talk about those minor tweaks:

"Regarding your first scenario, PGWH agrees to be part of the two-woman scenario you've requested, but she's not game for both women to be naked when you first arrive to the hotel room. She might need a little coaxing to get the show on the road, so to speak, but she's confident a little alcohol and the sight of your gorgeous, turned-on face will be all that's necessary to give her a little nudge in the right direction. In the end, your fantasies are all that matter—she very much wants to deliver them to you.

"Also regarding your two-woman scenario, as previously agreed, you may touch yourself and PGWH, but you absolutely may not touch the 'other' woman. *Breach of this rule will be deemed unforgivable by PGWH and will result in her leaving the rendezvous immediately.* (If this amounts to 'sexual extortion' we're very sorry-not-sorry. It's just super-duper important to PGWH that you honor this request and never make PGWH feel like a third wheel. She wishes to be your window, not your window dressing. This is non-negotiable. Have we mentioned one of her code names is The Jealous Bitch?)

"If the foregoing revisions to the first scenario are agreeable to you, then our next step is to identify the 'window dressing' who'll be joining you and PGWH. Since you've graciously offered that PGWH may select whomever she chooses, we're happy to inform you of PGWH's selection: supermodel Bridgette Schmidt."

I take my hands off my keyboard and stare at the screen for a long moment.

Up 'til now, this email to Josh has poured out of me in a torrent of excitement—but now, my fingers have paused without my brain telling them to do it.

Am I really up for this? It's pretty kinky. Am I really gonna like kinky as much as I think I will—or am I merely turned on by the *idea* of kinky? And, besides that, when Josh and I first started "negotiating" this particular adventure, I made a big ol' stink that the woman we selected couldn't be someone either of us knows. But now that I've had a chance to think this through, I think Bridgette the Supermodel is the ideal candidate for the job.

First off, she's gorgeous. And since I'm the one who's gonna be making out with her, that's not a small point. Second, Bridgette is bisexual, at least according to Josh, which means the odds are good this won't be her first time making out with a girl—and, hopefully, she'll be more enthusiastic about fooling around with me than my straight friend in college (because that was kind of lame in retrospect). Third—and this is a biggie—Bridgette's a huge celebrity, which means she's not gonna take secret photos and sell them to TMZ.

All these reasons are pretty persuasive to me—and yet there's an even bigger reason to select Bridgette as my co-star in this particular mini-porno: Josh said Bridgette's got "battery acid in her heart."

Well, winner, winner, chicken dinner. Give that girl a salami. Because if I'm gonna voluntarily bring a beautiful, naked, blonde woman into the bedroom with a man I want for my very own—a man I've been fantasizing about taking home to meet my family—a man who makes my claws come out and jealousy rise up from my darkest bowels when I even *think* about him with another woman—then I'm sure as hell gonna make double-damn-sure that woman's not gonna have a snowball's chance in hell of stealing my man out from under me.

I take a long, deep breath and close my eyes.

Oh my, I seem to be feeling a tad bit psychotic right now.

I take a deep breath and shake it off.

And there's another reason to select Bridgette too—a very, very good reason that might be a tad bit self-sabotaging (but, oh well, that simply can't be helped): I want to see if Josh is full of shit or not. He says I'm more beautiful than Bridgette Effing Schmidt, one of the world's most beautiful women? Well, let's see if Josh is able to walk the walk of that particular smooth-talk. Will he be able to keep his hands off Bridgette when push comes to shove? Or will he find her jaw-dropping physical beauty too powerful to resist, no matter how much he feels for me?

Obviously, I might be making a huge mistake by doing this—setting myself up for epic heartbreak. Actually, come to think of it, this might be the stupidest idea I've ever had in my entire life, possibly even dumber than the idea of surprising Garrett at his apartment wearing nothing but a trench coat. But, hey, I've got to look at the big picture here: if Josh is ultimately gonna shatter my heart, I'd rather know it now than when my heart is totally on the line.

I place my hands on my keyboard again and continue typing:

"After explaining the firm no-touch rule to Bridgette, please invite her to join us during one of the nights of PGWH's stay in Los Angeles (whichever night she can make it—we'll work around her schedule).

"And now regarding the second scenario detailed in your application, which we'll call 'Saving the Girl.' Do you think it'd be possible to combine this fantasy of yours with one of PGWH's biggest fantasies, already detailed at length for you, in which she's held captive by a dangerous man? Just let us know. During this trip, fulfillment of *your* fantasies is paramount, so if simultaneously fulfilling PGWH's fantasy would somehow lessen your pleasure, we'll be very happy to fulfill PGWH's fantasy a different time.

"Well, that's about it. We look forward to serving you, Mr. Faraday. Why? Because we here at The KUM Club sure do love a good sick fuck!"

My heart stops. Oh my God, I absolutely cannot phrase that last sentence that way. Jesus God, am I mad? Quickly, I delete the last sentence and rephrase it:

161

"Why? Because we here at The KUM Club sure do enjoy ourselves a good sick fuck!"

Damn. That was a close call. I'm careening out of control here. Jeez. I can't drop the 'L' word like that, even as a snarky figure of speech.

"Exclusively yours," I continue writing, "The KUM Club.

"P.S. PGWH wishes to thank you profusely for your latest extremely generous gift (in a long line of generous gifts)—even though it will surely prevent PGWH from ever leaving her house again (unless it's to see you, of course). Whenever PGWH uses your gift, rest assured she'll imagine she's getting splendidly fucked by you. Certainly, with every orgasm (and there will surely be many), she'll moan your name."

My fingers leave my keyboard. I stare at the screen, my skin electrified, my crotch burning, my heart aching. Try as I might, I simply can't keep myself from falling head-over-heels for this man. The only question now is whether he wants me the way I want him. I know Josh wants me sexually, but does he want the rest of me, too? I'm simultaneously excited and nervous to find out.

I read my email once through, take a deep breath, and press send.

Chapter 20
Josh

I slam my laptop shut.

Holy fuck.

Madame Terrorist strikes again.

I glance furtively at the guy seated next to me on the plane. He's working on his laptop, completely oblivious to the naked photo of Kat that just melted my motherfucking screen. For a long moment, I look around at the other passengers in my immediate vicinity, my heart raging, my cheeks burning, my cock twitching in my pants.

I've seen my share of naked-blonde-woman-photos before now, of course, but my body's never reacted quite like this to any of them. Holy fuck, I feel like I just mainlined a cocktail of Ecstasy and Viagra. You'd think I was thirteen and sneaking my dad's stash of porno-mags the way my body's reacting to this photo of Kat.

But it's not just Kat's tits and ass making my dick so hard—it's how much of Kat's personality comes through in the shot. There's a devilish smile on her lips that tells me she was as turned on snapping this photo as I am looking at it, and, shit, there's a glint in her eye that says, "I got you right where I want you, chump," too. The woman slays me.

I can't believe Kat gave this photo to me, no coaxing required. I had to *beg* Emma to let me snap one measly naked shot of her for my birthday last year, and now Kat's sending me this for no other reason than she likes getting me hard? She's incredible.

What did Kat say after Sarah sent that naked photo of herself to Max and Oksana? *"No matter how smart or powerful a guy might be, he's got the same Kryptonite as every other man throughout history— naked boobs."* I close my eyes for a long beat, shaking my head. God,

163

I hate proving Kat right, I really do, just on principle—but there's no way around it: Kat's naked boobs just flat-out stripped me of whatever superpowers I might have had.

And yet her naked boobs didn't come close to slaying me the way her naked words did. I already knew she was a terrorist, but now I know she's a fucking ninja with words, too.

I made fun of Jonas pretty relentlessly for the way he went ballistic over Sarah's anonymous email, sight unseen, but now I get it. Shit, I might even owe Jonas an apology for the way I gave him shit about that. If Sarah's note was even half as clever and sexy and hot as Kat's, then it's no wonder Jonas fell so hard for—

I jerk my head up from my screen, my heart suddenly rising into my throat. Did I just compare Kat and me to Jonas and Sarah? My chest tightens. I hear my pulse in my ears.

Yeah, I did.

I close my laptop, unlatch my seatbelt, and walk quickly into the bathroom, my head reeling. Once there, I latch the door with shaking hands, splash cold water on my face and rock-hard dick (because the idea of wacking off in an airplane bathroom is too gross even for me) and then I stare at myself in the mirror.

"Just breathe," I say to myself out loud. Shit, I look like Jonas right now. "Don't overthink it, bro. Just stay in the moment. Chill the fuck out."

But the blue eyes staring back at me won't be soothed.

How do you know? I asked Jonas.

I just know, he said.

I look at myself in the mirror for another long beat, water dripping down my cheeks and off the tip of my nose.

"She's your Kryptonite, man," I finally say to my reflection. "You're totally fucked, Superman."

Chapter 21
Josh

"Checking in, sir?" the valet attendant asks as he opens my car door.

"Yeah."

"Need assistance with any bags?"

"Nope." I hold up my car keys and a one-hundred-dollar bill. "No cars parked on either side of it."

"Yes, sir." The attendant grabs my keys and the C-note out of my hand. "I'll make sure of it."

"Bring it back with no dings in the doors and I've got another hundred for you."

"Thank you, sir. You got it."

I grab the small duffel bag on my passenger seat, straighten my tie, and stride toward the front of the hotel. Holy fuck, I can't remember the last time I was this eager to see a woman. Okay, fine, I'm full of shit—I've never been this eager to see a woman, ever, and I know it.

This whole past week, even though I've been absolutely swamped with work hammering out the transition strategy for Jonas and me from Faraday & Sons, I've nonetheless managed to continuously count the minutes to seeing Kat again. When I haven't been working, the only way I've been able to prevent my mind from spiraling into some sort of Jonas-style obsession, has been to keep myself constantly busy. I've gone to the gym and worked out like a motherfucker every night this week, followed by going home to my empty house and distracting myself with one of four go-to activities (all of which I performed while lying naked in my bed): 1) strategizing about how I'm gonna deliver on Kat's crazy-ass (but awesome) fantasies; 2) reading one of the sex-books Jonas sent me (fantastic reading, I must say—I owe my brother a huge 'thank you'); 3) chatting with Kat on the phone (or on FaceTime); and 4) jerking off, an activity which, quite frequently, overlapped with activities one, two and three (but mostly activity three).

A doorman holds open the heavy glass doors of the hotel and tips his hat to me as I enter the building. "Good evening, sir. Welcome to The Four Seasons Beverly Hills."

"Thanks," I say, gliding into the expansive lobby.

Yeah, Kat and I had some pretty fucking amazing phone- and video-chat-sex this past week, that's for sure, including two separate times when she let me watch her turn herself inside-out with pleasure while riding her new toy. But we also just *talked* a whole lot, too, about anything and everything, for hours and hours every single night—and it was *awesome*.

In one conversation, Kat told me a thousand hilarious stories about her family, and I laughed 'til my stomach hurt. Damn, she's got a fierce and funny family—and, man, do they look out for each other. When I found out Kat gave her craps winnings to her little brother so he could record an album with his band, I instantly felt this weird sense of *relief* more than anything else—relief that I'll never have to explain or defend my bond with Jonas. Clearly, the girl already completely understands what it means to put someone else's needs above your own.

I reach the check-in counter in the lobby and stand in line behind an old white guy accompanied by a much younger (and absolutely beautiful) Asian woman.

"I'll be right with you," the clerk says to the couple standing in front of me in line, looking up from assisting a family of five with their check-in. I nod curtly, just in case she was directing her comment to me, too, and then let my thoughts quickly drift to Kat again.

"Michelangelo was the coolest one," Kat insisted during one of our many conversations this past week.

"How can you use the word 'cool' in reference to the Teenage Mutant Ninja Turtles?" I asked.

"Oh, come on. You know you watched them," she chided me.

"Yeah, I *watched* them," I said, laughing. "But I never thought they were *cool*."

"Honesty-game," she said.

166

I exhaled. "Damn, that fucking game. Okay, yes. I thought Raphael was dope."

I smile to myself at the memory and look at my watch. The woman working behind the check-in counter is still helping that goddamned family of five and the couple's three young children are bouncing off the walls.

"Jeremy?" the clerk yells over her shoulder toward an open door behind the front desk. "Are you available to assist, please? *Jeremy?*"

But Jeremy must be off smoking a bowl because no one walks through that open door. It's just the one poor clerk behind the counter, and the line is growing behind me.

As I wait, my mind drifts to Kat again, the way it has all week long. *Kat.* She's upstairs right now, soaking her panties at the thought of being treated like Julia Roberts in *Pretty Woman. Kat.* What the fuck? *Kat, Kat, Kat.* That's all my brain is capable of thinking about anymore. I smile to myself. *Kat.*

I broke down and told Kat every little thing about our plans for Climb & Conquer this week, even though I'd planned to tell her about it in person. I was naked in my bed, listening to her sexy voice and feeling particularly relaxed after some pretty damned good phone sex, and everything just spilled out of me. Well, not *everything.* I didn't tell her about the fact that, since Climb & Conquer will be headquartered in Seattle, I'll finally be moving back home in a couple months. I was tempted to mention it several times, but I stopped myself. I mean, shit, God only knows where things will stand between Kat and me in a couple days, let alone a couple months. Why set her up for some kind of disappointment if things don't work out? All I can do is take it a day at a time and see where things lead, right?

The family of five bounces away from the front desk and the old-guy-Asian-woman-couple in front of me steps up to the desk.

"I'm so sorry for the wait, sir," the hotel clerk says to the old guy, and then her eyes drift apologetically to me. "I'll be with you shortly, sir."

I put my hand up to signal it's all good and the clerk smiles gratefully. The minute she looks away, though, I look at my watch impatiently. Kat's in this building *right now,* wetting herself at the thought of me treating her like my whore tonight, and I'm standing here, growing gray hair. Fuck, fuck, fuck. I seriously can't wait to see Kat.

Kat.

During another conversation this week—and God only knows how we got on the topic—Kat and I talked about what we believe happens to a person's soul after death—which led to a discussion about spirituality versus religion—a topic I'd normally avoid like the plague with anyone but Jonas (that's what years of Catholic school will do to a guy). But with Kat, the whole conversation flowed easily and naturally.

"What the hell is wrong with you, Josh?" Kat blurted at one point during our discussion about spirituality, shocking the hell out of me.

"What?" I asked, worried I'd offended her with my frank honesty on the topic.

"You're not supposed to be the deep-thinking Faraday brother. Pull yourself together, Playboy—you've got a shallow rep to live up to."

"Sorry," I replied, laughing. "It won't happen again."

The old-guy-Asian-girlfriend-couple in front of me *finally* steps away from the front desk, and I step forward.

"Checking in?" the hotel clerk asks. She looks totally frazzled.

"Yes. Joshua Faraday. My guests should have already checked into the room." I hand her my identification and credit card. "I arranged in advance for my guests to access the room before my check-in."

The woman clicks her keyboard for a brief moment. "Oh, yes, *of course*, Mr. Faraday." She suddenly looks stricken. "I'm *so* sorry to have kept you waiting in line. Oh my gosh. *Please* forgive me."

"No problem," I say smoothly, flashing her a smile.

"Let me send you a complimentary bottle of champagne to your suite to make up for the delay."

"Thank you, but, no, I'd prefer no interruptions tonight."

She blushes. "Oh. Of course." She clears her throat. "Uh, looks like your guests have already checked into the suite with no problem—it's the penthouse, as you know—and all catering and amenities requested have already been sent up."

"Excellent," I say, my heart clanging with anticipation. "The bar is stocked with Gran Patron, right?"

"Um, actually, it looks like they brought *Roca* Patron to the suite. Is that acceptable to you?"

"Yes, fabulous. Either one. Thank you."

The desk clerk smiles at me and, suddenly, I'm overwhelmed with a crazy feeling of *déjà fucking vu*. How many times have I checked into a hotel while my "guests" awaited me upstairs, an odd mixture of sexual anticipation and self-loathing coursing through my veins? And yet, today feels totally different than all those other times in The Club. Today, for the first time ever, I feel only sexual *anticipation* pumping through me, not tainted whatsoever by rampant self-loathing. Because today, unlike all the times that have come before, the hottest woman alive is waiting for me upstairs, not some random hooker I don't know or give a shit about—and not only is she hot, she's sweet and funny and smart, too. *And* in a twist of awesomeness I never could have predicted (or even hoped for), the hottest woman alive doesn't give a shit if I'm a sick fuck. In fact, she actually *likes* my sick-fuckedness. It's an incredible feeling.

The clerk hands me my key-card. "Do you know how to get to the penthouse suite, Mr. Faraday?"

"I sure do," I say. "Thanks."

I head toward the elevator bank at the far end of the lobby. My heart's beating wildly. Holy shit, I'm gonna see Kat in a matter of minutes.

Kat.

I would have preferred to personally pick Kat up from the airport this afternoon and bring her to my house for our first night together, rather than meeting her here at the hotel—I hate that I haven't even had a chance to hug her and say hello to her yet, just me and her—and I told Kat as much on the phone last night. But my little terrorist insisted we jump right into fantasy-fulfillment, first thing, before seeing each other in "real life."

"First off, we don't have a choice in the matter," she said. "Bridgette's only gonna be in L.A. Thursday night, right?"

"Yeah, but we don't have to do the Bridgette thing this trip," I said. "We can do it during your next trip."

"No, we gotta do it," Kat insisted. "We're kicking off our fantasy-fulfillment extravaganza with the stuff in your application, no ifs, ands, or buts about it. So that means whenever Bridgette can fit us in, that's when we gotta do it. Plus," she continued, "I wouldn't want to come to your house the first night, anyway, babe. That wouldn't be very call-girlish, now would it?" I could practically hear her licking her lips at that last statement. "Not seeing you beforehand will make me feel even more like a call girl. It's perfect."

The elevator reaches the top floor and I practically sprint down the long hallway toward the room, grinning from ear to ear. Kat talked a good game about wanting to fulfill *my* fantasies during this trip, but it wasn't hard to figure out she was actually chomping at the bit to fulfill her own high-priced-call-girl fantasy. When I texted Kat this afternoon to find out if she'd landed safely and connected with the driver I'd sent, she sent me a reply that made me laugh out loud:

"How the heck did you get my phone number, sir? My name isn't Kat, it's Heidi Kumquat (though, in light of my profession, I never reveal my real name). I'm a world-class call girl, sir, sought after by sheiks, kings, and presidents, working under the code name Party Girl with the Hyphen. I've just landed (safely) in Los Angeles to meet a very sexy but incredibly demanding client (whom I'd very much like to thank for flying me first-class, by the way), and, yes, his driver picked me up exactly according to plan (thank you!), and now I'm headed to my client's ritzy hotel.

"Please don't text me again, sir. My client has paid a pretty penny to have my undivided attention for the whole night, starting RIGHT THIS VERY MINUTE, and he'd be positively enraged if he found out I was texting with another man during *his* purchased time. I've been bought and paid for tonight, mind, body, and soul—which means I'm duty-bound to think of absolutely nothing but fulfilling my client's sexual desires all night long, LITERALLY NO MATTER WHAT THEY ARE, and that's exactly what I'm going to do."

I must say, that was a sexy goddamned text. If there's one thing Kat Morgan knows how to do, it's turn a man on.

I've reached the door to the penthouse suite.

Oh my God, I've got so much adrenaline coursing through me, I'm shaking.

I take a deep breath and rap twice on the door to signal I'm here and coming in, exactly the way I did before entering each new hotel room during my month in The Club—and just like I said I'd do when I replied to Kat's awesome email from "The KUM Club." And then I swipe the key and open the door.

Chapter 22
Josh

When I enter the suite, I stop just inside the door, paralyzed by the incomprehensible sight of Kat and Bridgette in the same room together. Talk about two worlds colliding. My brain can't process what I'm seeing—though, apparently, my body sure can. Hello, instant hard-on.

The women are sitting in side-by-side armchairs, sipping what looks like cranberry-vodkas, giggling happily like they're longtime friends. Kat looks like a million bucks (appropriately) in the Prada dress and heels I bought her in Las Vegas, her long, toned legs crossed demurely, while Bridgette's wearing a simple black tank top, jeans, and flip-flops, her blonde hair tied into a knot on top of her gorgeous head, her legs spread like she's a dude talking football in a sports bar. Talk about two women monopolizing the entire planet's supply of physical perfection all at once. Holy motherfucking shit. Seeing these two women together would almost certainly make a weaker man stroke-out.

"Kat," I blurt, my heart leaping out of my chest. I begin crossing the room to greet her, to take her into my arms and kiss the holy motherfucking shit out of her—has it only been a week since I last saw her, because it feels like a year?—but Kat puts up her hand sharply and shoots me a smoldering look that stops me dead in my tracks.

"So nice to finally meet you, Mr. Faraday," she says smoothly.

Oh, so it's gonna be like that, huh? I come to a complete halt.

"You're even handsomer than in your photos," she purrs. She sits up straight, arches her back, and folds her hands primly in her lap.

"So are you," I say. My heart is pounding in my ears.

171

One side of Kat's mouth hitches up into a devious smirk, and, suddenly, I feel like a fly in a spider's web. I thought we were here to fulfill *my* sick-fuck fantasy—so why do I suddenly feel like I'm merely a pawn in fulfilling hers?

"Let me introduce you to my friend, Frieda Fucks-A-Lot," Kat says. She motions to Bridgette who takes that as her cue to pop up and waltz toward me.

Frieda Fucks-A-Lot?

"Hey there, Mr. Faraday," Bridgette coos in her clipped English, outstretching her arms to me as she approaches.

I take a step back, but Bridgette continues advancing on me. She lays her hand on my shoulder and leans forward as if to kiss my cheek and I jerk back like Bridgette's hair is on fire. I promised Kat I wouldn't lay a finger on the "window dressing" of our threesome, whoever that turned out to be, and there's no way in hell I'm gonna risk making my temperamental "window" beeline out of yet another hotel suite and stomp down yet another hallway in a jealous huff.

But my anxiety about Bridgette touching me and bringing out the terrorist in Kat is all in vain, apparently: Kat's all charm and ease on the far side of the room, throwing her head back and giggling. "Oh, come on, Mr. Faraday," she says. "You can give Frieda a little kiss on her cheek in greeting. *Of course* that's allowed."

Bridgette turns around to look at Kat and the two women break into peals of laughter.

What the hell? How'd these two become besties so fucking fast? And why the hell is Kat acting like Bridgette's in on our game? Bridgette's not a *player* in our fantasy—she's nothing but a fucking pawn.

Bridgette hugs me and kisses me on both cheeks, but when she does, I recoil at her touch. I want absolutely nothing to do with her. The only person I wanna touch right now is Kat; specifically, I wanna rip Kat's clothes off and fuck the shit out of her—it's what I've been fantasizing about doing night and day all week long—not sitting in a chair in a corner, jerking off while watching someone else touch and kiss and lick my girl. In fact, the thought of Bridgette—or *anyone*— laying a fucking finger on my Party Girl with a Hyphen makes my stomach turn over.

"Hey, asshole," Bridgette says, swatting my shoulder. "You

didn't tell me your girlfriend was *this* gorgeous." She motions to Kat. "I was just telling Kat—*Heidi Kumquat*"—she giggles and Kat joins her—"if she ever wants to try modeling, she could make an absolute *killing*. Look at that bone structure! Those legs! That skin! Oh my God, she's to die for. I can't wait to take a juicy bite out of her." She licks her lips.

Kat told Bridgette she's "Heidi Kumquat" for the night? So does that mean Kat's told Bridgette *everything* about our little game? Because when I called Bridgette and invited her to our little party, I certainly didn't. I merely asked Bridgette if she'd come hang out with me and this gorgeous girl I'm seeing, maybe make out with the girl while I watched and wacked off if things were to go in that direction (something I knew would be right up Bridgette's alley)—but I certainly didn't mention Kat being my high-priced call girl. What have these two been talking about for the last few hours before my arrival?

Kat's looking at me with hard eyes, though her mouth is smiling. Jesus. She looks like she's plotting my murder. Literally.

"No, seriously, hon," Bridgette continues, sounding remarkably sincere, "I'll hook you up with a photographer-friend of mine so you can get a kick-ass portfolio together. My agent will crap her pants when she sees you—I'm sure she could get you booked solid, if that's something you're interested in."

"Aw, thanks," Kat purrs, her smoldering gaze still fixed on me. "You're a doll, Bridgette." Her eyes flash. "I mean *Frieda*." She smirks. "I've got your number—I'll definitely give you a call. Thanks so much."

What the fuck? Why did Kat and Bridgette exchange numbers? What could possibly be the point in that?

"Why aren't you sitting, Mr. Faraday?" Kat says, motioning to a chair in the corner. "Please, make yourself comfortable. Frieda and I are both excited to *entertain* you."

I don't move. My brain and body are at odds. I know my role and what I'm supposed to do—what I should be *wanting* to do—but all my body yearns to do is kiss Kat. I haven't seen her in a week and I'm physically aching for her.

Bridgette claps her hands together. "Okay, *lieblinge*, let's start the fun, hmm? You want a drink, Faraday?" She glides toward the bar. "A shot of Patron, I presume?"

Kat levels me with a smoldering stare as she speaks to Bridgette. "Great idea. Would you be a doll and pour me a shot, too? I could use a little liquid courage."

"Aw, of course, *häschen*. Don't be nervous. I'll be gentle." She flashes Kat a brazenly sexual look. "I won't bite you *too* hard." She grabs a bottle behind the bar and begins pouring.

I still haven't moved from my spot just inside the door. I'm leaping out of my skin. Why do I feel like Kat's doing this to make me jealous, rather than to turn me on? And why the fuck is it working?

"Why don't you make those shots doubles?" Kat says to Bridgette. She winks at me and begins gliding toward a couch across the room from my assigned chair, unbuttoning her dress slowly as she goes.

"You got it," Bridgette coos.

Oh shit. I feel like I'm gonna explode. I'm shaking.

I want her.

I look at Bridgette behind the bar. I have no desire to touch any part of her—and certainly no desire to watch her kiss and stroke and lick my girl, either. If anyone's gonna do any of that stuff to Kat right now, it's sure as hell gonna be me.

Fuck this shit.

I march across the room to Kat, thwarting her progress toward the couch, and before she can say or do another goddamned thing, take her into my arms and maul her. My lips are on hers, my hands in her hair, my hard-on pressed into her crotch. Without hesitation, she presses herself into me, throws her arms around my neck, and returns my kiss voraciously.

"Aw, come on—party foul," Bridgette shouts from the bar. "It took all my restraint not to make a move on your girl 'til you got here, Josh. Kat said we had to wait and I've been—"

"We'll be back," I bark, grabbing Kat's hand and pulling her forcefully toward the bedroom. "Come on, babe. Fuck this shit."

The second Kat and I are alone in the bedroom with the door closed behind us, I fucking attack her. "Oh my God," I murmur into her lips. Jesus God, I'm drowning in her—losing my equilibrium. The smell of her. The taste of her lips. I'd forgotten how addicting she is. My dick hurts. My heart is racing. I want her so bad, I'm in pain. I'm dying to taste her pussy on my tongue, feel her tight wetness surrounding my cock, hear her make the sound like I've pricked her ass with a long needle. "Oh my God, Kat. I've missed you, babe."

"I'm not Kat—I'm a hooker from The Club," she breathes into my lips, but it's clear she's so turned on, she can barely stand.

I begin unbuttoning her dress, but my fingers aren't functioning. "I'll call you whatever you want, just as long as I'm saying it while fucking you."

"What about Bridgette?"

"Fuck Bridgette. I don't want her. I want you."

"No, I mean—"

But I devour her lips and she shuts the fuck up.

I've finally got her dress unbuttoned, thank God, and I pull it down past her hips to the floor, sliding my palms along her bare skin as I push the fabric down—and the sexy sight that unexpectedly greets me makes my cock jolt: Kat's wearing a full get-up of centerfold-worthy, sheer lingerie—a push-up bra, crotchless panties, and a garter belt that skims her flat belly just below her belly ring— all of it the shade of the ocean in Tahiti.

"Incredible," I murmur, assessing the fantastical vision in front of me. "Now *that's* a high-priced call-girl, baby."

She squeals with excitement and snaps her garter belt against her hip. "You like?"

"Fuck yeah, I do—I..." I clamp my lips together. I was about to say, "Fuck yeah, I *love* it." But using that four-letter word in any context, even regarding something as harmless as Kat's lingerie, suddenly feels clunky in my mouth. "It's incredible," I say.

I unlatch Kat's stockings from her garter belt and kneel before her, slowly peeling them down her legs, kissing each inch of newly revealed flesh as I go, swirling my tongue around the smooth skin of her thighs and then working my way up to her hips, her belly, her piercing, each flicker of my tongue and kiss of my lips eliciting moans of pleasure and knee-buckles from her.

After several minutes, I brush my fingertips over the gap in her crotchless panties, and my fingers come back slick with her wetness.

"You're so wet for me," I breathe.

"I've been wet for you all week," she whispers. "I've been dying for you."

I lean in and suck on her clit and her knees buckle sharply. She grips my hair to steady herself, and I take that as my cue to penetrate her deeply with my tongue.

"Oh my God," she breathes, running her fingers through my hair. "You're so *really* good at this."

Her knees buckle again and then again, until she loses complete balance—so I rise, take her by the hand, lead her to the bed, and lay her down on her back. She's trembling with desire, physically twitching with yearning. Her blues eyes are on fire.

Slowly, I take off my jacket.

"Oh God," she breathes. She reaches down to touch herself for a brief moment but quickly pulls her hand away, her body visibly shaking.

"Don't stop," I order. "Keep touching yourself."

"But I'm gonna make myself come. I'm almost there."

"Do it."

She complies, her eyes like hot coals as her fingers work her clit.

I slowly remove my tie, watching her.

"Oh my God," she breathes, her hand between her legs.

I peel off my shirt and she gasps at the sight of me.

"I forgot how hot you are," she says. "Oh my *God*."

I rip off my briefs, letting my cock spring free, and crawl onto the bed next to her.

I press my skin against hers, jutting my hard-on into her hip. "Make yourself come while I watch you."

She closes her eyes, exhales, and begins moving her hand more rapidly.

As she works herself, I kiss her shoulder and neck slowly. Goose bumps rise up on her skin. I tilt her head to the side and kiss the long nape of her neck.

She moans.

I continue laying kisses all over her neck, shoulders, and torso while slowly removing her pesky bra, and the minute her breasts bounce free, I take them greedily into my mouth.

She shudders.

I stroke my fingers up and down her arm several times and then let my fingers trail all the way down to hers, until my fingers are lying directly on top of hers, joining hers in pleasuring her pussy. She moans and continues working herself, my fingers fused with hers, my lips and tongue swirling over her nipples, neck, and ear.

"You been thinking about me this past week?" I mumble into her skin, working her pussy along with her.

"Every minute of every day," she chokes out.

Our fingers work her clit together as our tongues slowly dance and swirl together.

I can't take it anymore. I gently push her hand away and begin working her clit and wetness together with my fingers, using one of the fingering techniques I recently read about in one of Jonas' books, and Kat's soft moans instantly transform into full-throated groans. I gotta admit: I thought I knew it all before reading that damn book (twice), but I'll be damned if it didn't teach me a thing or two. I shift my fingers again, giving her something I've never done before, and she begins convulsing with pleasure.

She makes a tortured sound, and I slide my finger up into her ass, right against her anus, just in time to feel her body release with rhythmic waves against my fingertip.

Oh God, I'm so aroused, my cock physically hurts. I've never enjoyed giving a woman pleasure quite this much. "You know what I thought about all week long? Eating my whore's magic pussy."

Her eyes light up.

I wouldn't say I'm a man who normally obsesses about going downtown, though I've always enjoyed it (with the right woman, of course). And yet, for some reason, when it comes to Kat, I've been literally *craving* the taste of her warm pussy day and night.

I spread her legs open and her breath catches with anticipation.

"Are you ready to earn your million bucks, baby? Because this is gonna turn me on."

She nods vigorously, her eyes blazing.

I pull the fabric of Kat's crotchless undies aside and swirl my tongue around and around, but the fabric keeps getting in my way. With a loud grunt, I pull down her undies and garter belt, throw them across the room, and then resume my assault on her with even more enthusiasm, licking and kissing and sucking every inch of her pussy until she's smashing herself into my face, clutching the sheets, gripping my hair, and screaming at the top of her lungs.

"You taste so good," I say, eating her voraciously. "So fucking good."

She releases with a loud shriek, and as she does, the sensation of her flesh rippling against my mouth gets me off so hard, I lose my fucking shit. Without thinking about it, I crawl over her, place a knee on either side of her head, grip her hair (a lot harder than I should), and wordlessly plunge my cock deep into her mouth.

"Time to earn your fee, baby," I growl.

Her response is immediate and through the roof. Either she's a better actress than Gabrielle LeMonde or she's *really* getting off on getting face-fucked. Either way, she's moaning like a sheep at slaughter as her throat receives the full length of me. I respond to her enthusiasm by thrusting even harder and deeper into her warm, wet mouth, almost all the way.

She reaches up and yanks on me, pulling me into her, signaling me to go even deeper, fuck her even harder, so I do. Oh my God, she's going insane with pleasure right now and I'm hurtling toward an epic orgasm myself on a bullet train—which means, motherfucker, I truly have to stop. Yes, I agreed to treat her like my whore—and, as it turns out, I'm quite happy to do it. But I didn't jack off for an entire week on FaceTime, just to blow my load into the woman's goddamned mouth.

I grip the top of Kat's hair firmly and pull out of her mouth—and when she looks up at me, she's in a stupor.

"You're good at sucking cock, baby," I say, rubbing the tip of my cock against the cleft in her chin. "It's no wonder sheiks, kings, and presidents want you so bad."

Her eyes light up. "I like sucking your cock, baby," she says. "Let me do it again and make you come." She lowers her mouth and licks my tip, making me shudder.

"No, babe," I say. "I want my paid whore's magic pussy."

"Yes, sir."

"Say, 'Whatever you wish.'"

"Whatever you wish," she purrs.

Wordlessly, I guide her on top of me—moaning with pleasure as my cock enters her. The minute she's on my saddle, I grip her hips and guide her pelvis into enthusiastic movement.

"Josh," she cries, her tits bouncing wildly as she fucks me. "Oh my God, *yes*."

She's turning me on so much, I can't even think. "You feel so good," I growl, grasping her rocking hips. "Oh my God, Kat, you feel *so* fucking good."

I slide my fingers up her ass—a move that's pushed her over the edge in the past—and this time, as before, it sends her directly into an orgasm. Her entire body stiffens. Her eyes roll back into her head. Her moans and whimpers morph into shrieks.

Note to self: Kat likes ass-play.

When Kat's climax subsides, I throw her onto the bed and guide her onto her hands and knees—and then, without hesitation, spank the shit out of her 'til she's squealing and moaning and twitching, and then I grip her hips and fuck her again from this new position. I've positioned Kat this way for my benefit—doggy-style happens to be one of my favorite ways to fuck—plus, after the orgasm Kat just had, I'm figuring she's all done and it's my turn now. But after only a handful of deep thrusts, it's clear my little whore is ramping up to go off again.

Jesus, she's supernatural.

I slow down my thrusts, trying my damnedest to hang on, and she makes that sharp-intake-of-breath sound that seems to signal an impending orgasm. I'm pretty sure that particular sound means two things: one, my girl's hanging on by the barest of threads, and, two, it's time for me to yank that motherfucking thread and watch her unravel.

I reach underneath her and grope her breasts and pinch her nipples and she jerks underneath my thrusting body like a bucking bronco. Nice. I increase the speed and depth of my thrusts and she begins whimpering. Good. I reach around and massage her clit, using one of the techniques described in my handy-dandy new book, and she wails with pleasure.

"I'm addicted to you, baby," I say, sweat dripping off my brow. "Fucking *addicted.*"

"Oh my fuck," she responds. "Jesus Christ Superstar. Motherfucker."

Clearly, she likes what I'm doing (either that or she took acid before we started fucking), but, still, she doesn't release.

I bite her shoulder. Rub her back. Kiss her neck. Grab her hair roughly. All while thrusting and groping and licking and fingering her.

"Oh my—oh jeeeeeeeeezus," she moans. "*Yes.*"

She sounds like she's possessed. Why isn't she climaxing? Women are impossible to figure out, I swear to God.

Shit. I can't hang on much longer. This is too fucking good.

Oh. I suddenly know exactly what to do.

I drape myself over her back, my fingers still working her clit, my cock thrusting deep inside her, sweat dripping off my brow and onto her slick skin, and press my lips into her ear. "You're worth every fucking penny, baby," I whisper. "Every fucking penny."

Boom. She comes like I flipped on a flashlight, screaming my name as she does. Ah, my little terrorist and her imaginary pornos. They're the key to her soul. Her entire body is clenching and rippling violently around my cock. Holy fuck, I love getting this woman off. It's my new favorite game.

I grab her hips and ram myself into her as far as my cock can go, making her scream with agony or pleasure—I don't really know which (or care)—and blow my load into her like a fucking fire hose blasting a burning building.

When I finish, she collapses onto the bed in a sweaty heap, gasping, and I lie on top of her, my body covering hers, my chest heaving, sweat pouring out of me.

"Holy shitballs," she chokes out.

"Damn."

Once I've caught my breath, I sweep her hair away from the back of her sweaty neck and kiss her hidden Scorpio tattoo. "You're my new favorite hobby, babe," I say.

She giggles. "I like being your hobby."

"You're a beast." I lick the back of her neck. And then bite it. And then I run my hands all over her sweaty body, making her moan with pleasure. Jesus Christ Almighty, I just fucked the living hell out of this woman not two minutes ago and I'm already electrified at the thought of doing it again. I can't get enough of her. I've never felt addicted like this before. I bite her shoulder and she squeals.

I crawl off Kat's back and lie alongside her, pulling her close to me on the bed.

"You're a beast," I say softly, hugging her to me. "So amazing."

"So are you," she replies softly into my chest, her voice quavering.

I tip her chin up and kiss her gently. "You're the most fun I've ever had in bed, Katherine Ulla Morgan."

Her face bursts with pleasure. "Really?"

"Not even a contest. You're in a league all by yourself. The tippy-top."

She grins.

"Worth every fucking penny," I say softly.

"But you didn't get your fantasy. We were supposed to be doing your fantasies first." She runs her hand over my chest, right over my "Grace" tattoo. "You wanna regroup and do the thing with Bridgette? I'm totally willing... now." Her eyes glint with something wicked.

"Fuck Bridgette," I say. "I'm sure she already left, anyway."

"You think?"

"If not, I'll tell her to go."

She smiles broadly. "But you seemed so turned on by the idea in Vegas."

"Eh, things change. Life is fluid. You gotta roll with it. I guess it's time to scratch that motherfucker off my bucket list—at least when it comes to you."

Her blue eyes narrow sharply.

Clearly, I've said something wrong. "What are you thinking?" I ask. "You suddenly look like a chick."

She assesses me with two chickified chips of blue granite for a moment. "I'm just trying to figure out why the change of heart—*at least when it comes to me.*"

I pause. She said that last part like she was gonna bomb my embassy—but I'd said those words to her as a compliment. What the fuck am I missing?

"Just what I said," I say slowly. "When it comes to you, all bets are off. You're a game-changer."

"Oh," she says. Apparently, she likes that answer. "After what you wrote about in your application—and how turned-on you were in Vegas when we talked about you watching me—I'm surprised. What's changed?"

Kat's right. I've done a one-eighty on the subject, at least when it comes to her. I can't honestly say I'd never wanna watch two women again—but not if one of them is Kat. At least not now. But the truth is I felt literally sick about the whole arrangement the minute

181

I walked into the hotel room tonight and saw Kat and Bridgette sitting together. I felt like I was taking a shit right where I eat. No *bueno.*

"Yeah, I was crazy-turned-on when we talked about it in Las Vegas," I admit. "But that was *before.*" I trace her lips with my fingertip.

"Before *what?*"

Damn, she's persistent. "You know," I say.

"I actually don't."

"Before this past week."

She grins from ear to ear. "What happened this past week?"

"I thought about you nonstop."

"Oh." She grins. "Well, I thought about you, too."

"And not once did I fantasize about you fucking around with another woman. The only thing I thought about on an endless loop was doing what I just did to you."

She bites her lip, but she can't hide her smile.

"The thought of sharing you with anyone makes me wanna punch a wall or break a face."

Her face lights up. "Well, gosh, that's an unexpected development. Who would have thought?"

I lean back, narrowing my eyes at her. "You really are evil."

"What?"

I shake my head at her.

"What?"

"I thought I was coming here tonight to play out my fantasy, but we were doing yours all along, weren't we? Right from the start."

She doesn't reply, but her slow blink tells me I'm right—and that I played my part perfectly.

"Evil genius," I whisper.

She grins wickedly. "I was totally prepared to do it for you, I really was—and I still will, if that's what you want. But, yeah, I do admit I like that you couldn't stand watching me with someone else—that you wanted me all to yourself."

There's a very long beat. I don't know what the fuck to say or do, so I kiss her. And then I kiss her again, my heart racing. When we part lips, I touch her face again. She's so fucking beautiful. And so fucking evil. She's perfect.

"So, hey," I say, trying to sound casual. "I think I've had enough of hotels for a while. I can count on one hand the number of times I've slept in my own bed this past month. If it's cool with you, I'd prefer to ditch this ramshackle motel and take you to my house. I wanna kiss every inch of the great Katherine Ulla Morgan in my own bed tonight."

She presses her body into mine. "Awesome. Yeah, I didn't wanna say anything, but this place really is a dump."

I laugh.

"You're sure you don't feel like you're missing out if I don't lesbo-out with Bridgette?" she asks. "Maybe we could do it on my next trip if you're still—"

"*Babe.*" I touch the cleft in her chin and she abruptly stops talking. "*No.*" I exhale a long, shaky breath. "The thought of seeing you with someone else makes me wanna break a face." Her face lights up. "And if I break a face, it's quite possible I could get punched in return. And if I get punched, I might get a mark on my pretty face." I shake my head, chastising her. "We wouldn't want that, now would we?"

She shakes her head in mimicry of my movement. "No way. Your face is much too pretty to get marked up."

"Exactly. So that means from here on out, no one touches my Party Girl With a Hyphen but *me*."

Chapter 23
Kat

"Wow, you really like black leather, huh?" I say, looking around Josh's sleek and spacious living room.

"Yeah. Makes life simple."

"Your house is spectacular. If my mom were here, she'd fall to the floor, weeping."

He looks at me funny.

"She's an interior decorator."

"Oh." He chuckles. "Yeah, I had a top designer helping me." He grabs my hand and pulls me toward floor-to-ceiling glass on the other side of the room. "Lemme show you the view. It's gonna make you say 'Holy shitballs.'"

He pulls me outside into the night air and we're met with a view of what might as well be heaven on earth.

"Holy shitballs," I say.

Josh grins. "Amazing, right?" He motions to the infinite expanse of twinkling lights and rugged hills spanning before us into the night. "This right here is why people pay an arm and a leg for houses in the Hollywood Hills. Okay, so, over there, between those two hills? The Hollywood sign is right through there—you can't really see it right now, but I'll give you binoculars in the daylight. And if you look that way, that's downtown L.A. over there."

"Amazing. No wonder you love it here."

"Oh, I don't love L.A. I love Seattle. I just *tolerate* L.A."

"Really?" I'm floored. I thought Josh loved living in La La Land with all his flashy friends. "I thought you loved living here," I say.

Josh shrugs. "Nah, L.A. definitely gets old, other than the weather—the weather never gets old." He points in a new direction. "See that house down there? That's Chris Pratt's house... "

But I can barely process what he's saying. Josh doesn't love Los Angeles? Does that mean he might be open to moving back home one day? But, whoa, whoa, whoa, what the hell is my brain doing? Josh has made it abundantly clear he's not thinking about a long-term commitment. For crying out loud, only an hour ago the dude said he was scratching the two-woman scenario off his bucket list *"at least when it comes to me"*— which means it's still on his agenda with other women, whenever (if ever?) this crazy whatever-it-is between us has run its course.

"Wow," I stammer, even though I don't know what the hell Josh was just saying. I think it was something about Joaquin Phoenix's house?

"Let me give you the rest of the tour," Josh says.

He leads me back inside and straight past his gleaming kitchen.

"Hang on," I say. "Can I see your kitchen? It looks pretty fancy-schmancy."

"Oh, it is. My designer redid the entire thing top to bottom when I moved in four years ago—we installed professional-grade everything." He flashes me a crooked grin. "But since I don't cook, it's basically just for show."

"You have a kitchen like *this* and you don't cook?"

"Yup. I'm super-smart that way."

"You don't cook *at all*?"

"Not even a little bit. I can count on one hand the number of times I've turned on this stove in four years—and at least two of those times, I was lighting a doobie."

I laugh. "Josh, this is a frickin' gourmet kitchen. Wolfgang Puck would kill for a kitchen like this."

"Yeah, I figured a gourmet kitchen would add value on resale, and I was right." He shifts his weight. "I mean, it... *will*. Add. Value. Whenever the time comes."

Josh suddenly looks like he feels sick. I don't understand the expression on his face. He's grimacing like he's in pain.

"Well, if you don't cook at all, then how do you feed yourself?"

"Um," he says. "I... uh... I go out with friends or get food delivered. Sometimes, if I'm exhausted, I just make myself a peanut butter and jelly sandwich. Speaking of which, are you hungry? I can make you a peanut butter and jelly sandwich that's so good, it'll make you come."

"Wow. That sounds like quite a PB&J."

"Oh, it is."

"I'll definitely have to take a rain check. Every girl should try an orgasm-inducing PB&J at least once. But I'm still pretty stuffed from all the food we had at the hotel. Those crab cakes really hit the spot."

"Especially after we'd worked up such an appetite." He snickers. "Good times were had by all at the ol' Four Seasons, eh?"

"Well, good times were had by two out of three of us, anyway." I join him in snickering.

Ah, that was delicious. Just as Josh predicted, Bridgette was long gone when we emerged from the bedroom, *and* she'd left a delightful text for Josh as a parting gift, too: *"Fuck you, Faraday,"* Bridgette's angry text said—and I'm purring even now remembering the gleeful expression on Josh's face when he showed it to me. *"Lose my number, motherfucker. But tell your hot girlfriend I'll happily comfort her after you've dumped her ass and broken her heart. Auf wiedersehen, arschloch. P.S. I hope she gives you herpes."*

Josh and I laughed pretty hard about Bridgette's text.

"Battery acid in her heart, indeed," I said when I read it.

"I told you," Josh said.

The only thing more enjoyable than reading that text from Bridgette was seeing the look on her face when Josh abruptly changed the plan and dragged me into the bedroom, hell-bent on keeping me all to himself. Delicious.

I'm suddenly aware Josh has been talking while I've been lost in my thoughts.

"... and since I've been home from New York," Josh is saying, "a delivery service has been bringing me gourmet meals every few days." He grabs my hand, leads me to his refrigerator, and opens the door to reveal four neatly stacked see-through containers. "Nothing but lean proteins and greens. Everything low in saturated fats; no simple carbs; all calorie counts precisely calibrated for my weight and fitness goals. All courtesy of the one and only Jonas Patrick Faraday."

"Jonas orders your meals?"

Josh rolls his eyes. "He kept giving me shit about my burgers and fries and Doritos and I was like, 'Dude, I travel too much to think about eating right all the time—leave me the fuck alone.' Next thing I knew, these meals started showing up." He chuckles. "The dude's like having a fucking wife, I swear to God—he's such a nag. I haven't eaten any of 'em yet as an act of protest."

"Is that what you think a wife does? She nags her husband about what he eats?"

"Yeah, you know, like that cliché line? 'Take my wife, please.'"

I roll my eyes. "Wives get such a bad rap."

"Well, shit, I dunno. I have no idea what a wife does—I've never actually witnessed one in its natural habitat."

"Are we talking about a human or a water buffalo?"

Josh chuckles. "Cut me some slack. My mom died when I was little; my uncle's wife died before I was born; and my best friends are either single or in what I'd call *non-permanent* relationships."

I make a face. I didn't mean to be insensitive about Josh growing up without a mom or any maternal influences. I didn't even think about that when I made my snarky comment.

"Plus," Josh adds, seemingly unfazed by my comment, "and most importantly: there were no wives on *Full House*."

"I'm sorry, Josh," I say softly. "I didn't think. I keep forgetting."

He waves his hands like I'm totally missing his point. "Forgetting what? It is what it is. Long time ago. No worries. I'm just saying I've never witnessed an actual wife up close, that's all. I don't know what women are really like if you actually *live* with one."

I'm suddenly starkly aware of just how different my childhood was from Josh's. I can't wrap my head around how disconnected and isolating—and *masculine*—his upbringing must have been. No wonder he has no freaking idea about marriage and relationships.

"Lori Loughlin," I say.

"Huh?"

"Lori Loughlin. She played Uncle Jessie's wife in the later seasons of *Full House*."

"Oh yeah," Josh says. "I forgot about her. I kinda stopped watching by then."

"Oh. Well, she didn't nag. She was happy and funny and supportive. That's what a real wife is like."

"Really? Well, I don't remember all that. All I remember is that she was smokin' hot."

"I thought you stopped watching by then?"

"I might have caught a couple episodes." He laughs. "She was hot."

"Still is. Saw a photo of her the other day. But, anyway, that's just TV," I concede. "Uncle Jessie's wife doesn't really count as spotting an actual wife in the wild, so your point is still well taken."

"Well, tell me, then. You've observed the species, right?"

I chuckle. "Yeah, I'm pretty sure I've spotted a genuine wife scurrying in the bushes a time or two."

"Well, enlighten me. Does your mom nag the shit out of your dad or what?"

"No. Never. My mom's the coolest woman who ever lived—super happy and energetic and just sort of like, 'If you're not happy, then get yourself happy, motherfucker, and stop bitching.'"

"Does your mom actually use the words 'motherfucker' and 'bitching'?"

"No, not unless she's *really* mad—usually at Keane." I laugh. "She's much more likely to use words like 'honey' and 'complaining'—but she'd say both in a *really* 'motherfucker' *tone.*"

Josh looks absolutely mesmerized right now. "Did your mom stay home with all you kids when you were little?"

"Yeah. But she always helped decorate people's houses on the side. At first it was just her friends, and then it expanded to her friends' friends. Nowadays, she's got her own little interior decorating business and she absolutely *loves* it. In her spare time she cooks the most incredible food—the best turkey chili you've ever had, oh my God—oh, and her spaghetti sauce is next level, and her lasagna is to die for. I think she wishes her ancestors came from Italy instead of Sweden." I laugh. "Oh, sorry, what was I saying? I get all excited when I talk about my mom's food."

"You were saying your mom doesn't nag your dad."

"Oh, yeah, that's right. She doesn't. She leaves him the hell alone and makes herself happy cooking incredible food and decorating people's houses and going to her exercise classes. You should see my mom with her little five-pound weights, doing her classes at the gym. She's such a little badass."

He chuckles.

"Oh, and she plays Bunco with her friends, too."

"What's Bunco?"

"It's this stupid dice game. It's basically craps with wine. But I think the dice are just an excuse to get drunk. I can't be sure of that, but that's my strong hunch."

Josh laughs. "I love your mom already."

I bite my lip. I know Josh meant that comment as a throwaway—a figure of speech—but it made my heart flutter nonetheless.

"So do you cook like your mom?"

"Not really. She's always wanted to teach me, but I'm too frickin' lazy to learn. Dax is an awesome cook, though—he's the one who always hangs out with Mom in the kitchen. And Colby cooks in the firehouse all the time, so he's pretty good, too—but he only knows how to cook in quantities for ten guys." I laugh. "Ryan's adequate—a little better than me—but he makes the best guacamole. And Keane is freakin' hopeless. The dude can't boil water."

"Well, thank God you're at least better than *Peen*," Josh says. "Or else I would have had to un-friend you."

I grin. In one of our many conversations this past week, I told Josh a bunch of stories about my brothers, including several that showcased Keane (also known as "Peen" in our family) as the beloved fuck-up of our family.

"Hey, can I get you something to drink?" Josh asks.

"Thanks. Do you have sparkling water?"

"Club soda okay?"

"Yep, same-same. Thanks."

Josh moves across his kitchen and pulls a couple glasses out of a cabinet. "Would you care for a little vodka in your club soda, Party Girl? I've got Belvedere and Absolut."

I shrug. "Why the fuck not?"

Josh laughs. "Words to live by. Which one?"

"Surprise me. I feel like living on the edge." I lean my butt against the counter.

"A girl after my own heart." He grabs a bottle of Belvedere from a low cabinet. "So what do you guys call Dax?"

"Dax is actually his nickname, a contraction of David Jackson."

"I didn't realize that. Cool." He fills the glasses with ice. "And Colby?"

"Cheese."

"Well, shit. That's not fair. You're Jizz and Kum Shot and Baby Gravy and Keane is Peen, but Colby gets to be something as G-rated as 'Cheese'?" He pours vodka into the glasses. "Not fair."

189

"Oh, it all evens out in the end," I say, enjoying the view of Josh's ass as he bends over to grab something from his fridge. "No one gets off easy in my family, I assure you. We all get raked over the coals somehow, just in different ways."

Josh closes his fridge, a bottle of something in his hands. "What about Ryan?"

"Ryan is RUM, Bacardi, Captain, Captain Morgan."

"Oh yeah, you said that in your application." He grins. "Ryan *Ulysses* Morgan."

"That's right." I grin. "Sometimes, when he's dressed up to go out—which he is a lot—he's 'Scion' or 'Pretty Boy.' Ry is basically you if he had a *much* bigger budget to work with."

"I like him already."

"You would, trust me. You'd love him. He's perfectly groomed and put together at all times, slays it with the ladies, charm oozing out his pores. The other guys ride him mercilessly for how pretty he is and how much he cares about his appearance. I can only imagine how much shit my brothers would give you if they ever met you."

Josh chuckles. "Well, thanks for the heads up. I'll make sure to dress down when I meet your brothers. I'll take a page out of Jonas' book and go with a T-shirt and jeans."

"Aw, come on now, Josh—don't go changin' to try to please 'em. You just do *you*, baby." I pause. I really shouldn't say what I'm thinking. But I can't help myself. "So are you thinking you might wanna meet my family one of these days?"

Josh's cheeks flush. He swallows hard. "Um. Yeah." He busies himself with our drinks again, his body language suddenly verging on robotic. "Maybe."

I laugh out loud. This man is a raging head case.

"No pressure, Josh," I say, genuinely amused by his suddenly anxious body language. The man is visibly twitching. "I brought it up just to watch you squirm. No worries." I should leave it at that. I really should. But, no. When it comes to Joshua William Faraday, I simply can't help myself. "But, um, actually," I begin, trying really, really hard to sound easy-breezy-Cover-Girl. "Colby's birthday is next weekend. My mom's gonna make her famous spaghetti and Dax is gonna make carrot cake—Colby's favorite meal." I clear my throat. "Super chill. Just the fam. You'd be welcome to join us for dinner, if you... happen to be... in Seattle. But if not, then no pressure, of course." Oh shit. What am I doing? Even as the words tumble out of my mouth, I know they're a horrifically bad idea. I should know by now: Josh is perfectly fine when we're enjoying each other in the here and now, but the minute I start talking about the future, he breaks into a frickin' cold sweat. I quickly wave at the air like what I've just said is the stupidest thing I've ever said. "Actually, pretend I never said any of that," I mumble. "I'm just kidding. Again."

Josh remains focused on the drinks he's making. Notably, he doesn't turn around and say, "Don't be silly, Kat—that's a great idea!" He just continues silently mixing our drinks, his back to me.

Holy hell, this is awkward. Why did I say all that? I really should know by now that pinning Josh down to anything even remotely relating to the future is a nonstarter.

"A twist of lime?" Josh finally says, his back still facing me.

I look down at my hands, heat rising in my cheeks. After everything I just said, *that's* what Josh asks me? If I want a lime in my drink? I really should have known. I'm such an idiot.

"Um. Sure," I say. "A twist of *lime* would be *amazing*." Oh boy, that last bit came out way bitchier than I'd intended.

But Josh seems to be unfazed by my bitchiness (which seems to be par for the course with him, thankfully). He turns to face me and clears his throat. "Colby's birthday dinner sounds great," he says, his jaw muscles tight. "Thanks for the invitation. I'd love to go." He tries to smile. He's not successful, but he's trying.

My heart leaps into my mouth.

Holy I Think I Just Harpooned a Whale, Batman.

"Tell the truth," I say. "The only reason you wanna come is Dax's carrot cake."

Josh laughs. "How did you know? Yeah, I've always had a soft spot for carrot cake."

"And cheesecake," I say, remembering our scarf-out the night we helped Henn in Las Vegas.

"You remember."

"Of course. I remember everything you've told me, Josh."

There's a long beat.

"Actually, Daxy makes a great cheesecake, too. It's just as good as his carrot cake. I'll see if he'll do both."

Josh's blue eyes darken to sapphire. "No, don't. I'll bring one from a bakery. No reason to make him think I'm a pain in the ass right from the get-go." He bites his lip. "So, hey, now that I'm coming up to Seattle next weekend, how about we check off one of your fantasies while I'm there? There's one specifically I think I could pull off better in Seattle than here."

My heart is absolutely racing. "Great," I squeak out, trying not to sound as thrilled as I feel. "Sounds good." I cross my arms over my chest and quickly uncross them. Crap. I suddenly don't know what to do with my hands.

"Cool," Josh says. He turns back around to face the drinks on the counter. "Just let me know the date so I can put it on my calendar."

"Yeah, I will," I say, my heart pounding in my ears. "Colby's birthday is the fourth. Not sure if we're doing it on his actual birthday or another night. I'll let you know."

"Cool. Sounds good. Assuming I don't have a work commitment that night, of course."

"Oh, of course."

Josh lets out a long exhale and then glides across the kitchen and hands me my drink. "Here you go, Party Girl." He flashes a megawatt grin, relieved of his earlier inability to maneuver his mouth into a smile. "I added just a *touch* of cranberry to the soda for you. Hope that's okay."

"Great." I take a sip. "Yummalicious. What else is in there?"

"The tiniest splash of grapefruit juice, just to take the edge off the cranberry."

"Oh, kinda like a Sea Breeze plus soda."

"Exactly."

"I like it. Thank you." I take another sip. "Ooph. That's a strong drink."

"Go big or go home, I always say." He winks. "Come on, PG. Let's go chill out in the living room."

Chapter 24
Kat

We amble out of the kitchen, drinks in hand, into the living room—and I settle myself onto the black leather couch while Josh chooses some music for our listening pleasure.

"So how long have your parents been married?" Josh asks, fiddling with his laptop.

"Thirty years this August."

He looks up from what he's doing, obviously astonished. "Wow. That's crazy."

"Yeah. Pretty crazy."

A song begins playing through Josh's sound system—a male vocalist backed by an acoustic guitar.

"What is this?" I ask, somewhat surprised by Josh's song selection. I'd have pegged him to play us something with a thumping beat.

"James Bay," he says. "'Scars.' Jonas had it on the other day when I was with him in New York and it slayed me. I bought the guy's whole album on the spot and every song is phenomenal." Josh sits down next to me and puts his hand on my thigh. "This James Bay guy sings with his soul."

"That's a great description."

Josh sips his drink and listens to the music for a moment. "So, thirty years, huh? Are your parents happily married?"

I'm shocked he's asking questions about my family. "Definitely," I say, my skin suddenly buzzing.

"Even after *thirty* years?"

"Well, I'm sure they've both wanted to murder each other more than once over the years. But, yeah, they're still totally in love. More

193

so than ever, I think. I like being around them—they're nice to each other. They still laugh at each other's jokes."

"Wow." He looks deep in thought.

I take a deep breath. I shouldn't ask the question rolling around in my head—I really shouldn't. But I can't help myself. "So, are you gonna be like Reed, you think? Are you gonna ride off into the sunset alone and unencumbered by messy human emotion?"

Josh looks taken aback by my question. "Uh, wow." He makes a weird face. "Is that what Reed said? I didn't interpret it quite that way." He makes a face. "But, um, yeah, I don't really envision myself getting married, if that's what you're asking."

I sip my drink. Why did I just ask him that? I really didn't need to hear him say that so starkly, even if I already knew that's what he'd say.

"I don't have anything against marriage, mind you," Josh continues. "I'm totally happy for your parents if it works for them— kind of in awe of them, actually—I just don't see the logical point of marriage as an institution," he continues. "I mean, if you wanna be with someone, be with them. If you don't, then leave. No need to get a piece of paper from the government that forces you to stay if you'd rather go."

I sip my drink quietly, listening to the music, wishing I could rewind time and un-ask the question. If I were my own life coach, I'd be slapping myself across the face right now and shouting, "Fucking idiot!"

"You disagree with me?" he asks, studying my face.

"No," I say. I sip my drink. "I most certainly do *not* disagree." I really, really should leave it at that. Definitely. That would be the wise thing to do.

"But?" he prompts.

"No 'but.' I don't disagree with you *in concept* one little bit." I sip my drink again. Damn, that's a strong drink. And, damn, I wish I hadn't asked Josh about marriage of all things, for crying out loud. I'm truly an idiot, not to mention quite possibly a masochist, too.

"*But*?" he repeats.

"But..." I say, drawing out the word. Oh hell. Keeping a lid on every frickin' thought that flashes into my head isn't my strong suit, especially when it comes to Joshua William Faraday. "*But* watching my parents through the years—the way they've stuck it out through thick and thin and how strong they are because of it—how strong our whole family is because of it—I think there's a bit more to marriage than just, you know, 'I can't leave your sorry ass because that goddamned piece of paper forces me to stay.'" My cheeks burst with color. Why am I saying all this? "*But*," I continue, trying to appease the shrieking voice inside my head telling me to press the eject button, "I definitely hear you—marriage certainly isn't for everyone." I clear my throat. "I'm not sure it's for me, honestly. I was just saying it's worked out well for my parents." Oh God. I wish I could jump into a time machine, go back to three minutes ago, and say, without elaboration or qualification, "Oh, I totally agree. One hundred percent."

Josh makes a face I can't interpret. "Maybe marriage *might* make sense for people who want to have kids."

There's an awkward pause. Did he just backtrack? Are we meeting in the middle? Hmm. I do believe we are. Which therefore means I should leave it at that. But, oh God, I can't. "Well, *actually*," I begin, ignoring the warning bells going off in my head, "if you think about it, marriage makes *less* sense if you've got a kid with someone."

He looks at me like I've just shouted, "Justin Bieber for President!"

"Because," I continue, pissing off my internal life coach even more, "whether or not you've got a piece of paper from the government, once you have a kid with someone, that person's gonna be in your life forever and ever, regardless. I think it's more meaningful to *choose* to be with someone just because you want to make a life with them, not because you plan to make them a vessel for your mighty spawn."

There's an awkward silence.

I seem to have rendered Josh (and myself) speechless. What the *fuck* am I doing? If I were my own life coach, I'd be throwing my hands up in disgust saying, "You're obviously completely un-coachable."

James Bay's voice fills the room for a very long moment.

"That's kind of the flipside of what my dad always used to drill into Jonas and me," Josh finally says. "He was obsessive about it, actually." He puts on a booming, paternal voice, clearly imitating his

195

father: "'Boys, when you've got Faraday money, women will try to trap you into marriage with an 'accidental' pregnancy right and left—every goddamned time you fuck one of 'em. Don't you dare let me catch either of you *ever* making an accidental Faraday with a woman unworthy of our name or I'll get the last laugh on that gold digger's ass and disown you faster than she can demand a paternity test.'"

My jaw drops. What the fuckity fuck?

"That's why I've always been obsessive about wearing condoms," Josh continues softly. "Way before I'd ever even gotten to second base with a girl, I was already freaking out about unwittingly creating an 'accidental Faraday' with some random woman who was 'unworthy' of my name and bank account."

I clutch my stomach. I feel physically sick. What kind of father says all that to his young sons? Preaching safe sex is one thing, sure, I get that—especially when you've got a kajillion dollars to your name, I suppose—but a father conditioning his pubescent sons to think every girl out there is a gold digger and telling them he'd *disown* them if they ever knocked someone up is pretty fucked up, if you ask me. "Your dad sounds like he was a real peach," I mumble.

"Oh, you have no fucking idea," Josh says between gritted teeth.

A sudden panic rises up inside me. "Josh, I'm on the pill—you know that, right? I would never, ever do that to you—"

Josh looks ashen. "Oh, God, I know that. I didn't mean—"

"I'd never, ever try to *trick* you into anything. In fact, we can go back to using condoms, if you want, every single time—"

"Kat, please. Stop. I know you'd never try to trick or trap me. I'm sorry I said—"

"We can use condoms," I persist. I'm totally freaking out.

"Kat, please. Pretend I never said anything. I didn't mean to imply..." He takes a deep breath and shakes his head. "Jesus, my dad is the gift that keeps on giving, isn't he? Listen to me, Kat, I know you'd never do that to me. The only reason I felt comfortable enough to tell you the fucked-up shit my Dad said is because I know you'd never do that."

Oh, jeez. I've never been so relieved not to be pregnant in all my life. Last week, after losing sleep for two nights over that birth control pill I'd missed, I finally traipsed down to the all-night drug store and bought myself a pregnancy test. And when I peed on that little stick and it came back with only one little pink line, I let out the longest exhale of my life.

"I'm definitely not gestating an accidental Faraday," I say, trying to sound light and bright but obviously not succeeding. "I'm a *mill-i-on-aire* now, remember? I don't need to trap you for your stinkin' Faraday money."

Josh runs his hands through his hair. "Kat, please forgive me. I was just telling you what my dad said because... I don't even know why I said it. I certainly wasn't implying you were trying to trap me in some way or that you'd even *think* of doing that. I think I was just trying to reveal one of the many ways I'm fucked up to you—trying to explain why I might be unusually high-strung or weird about certain things." He shakes his head and exhales. "I think I was just trying to... you know... take a stab at... *emotional intimacy*." He makes a face that says, "I guess I still suck at it."

I chuckle. I can't help it. He's so frickin' cute.

Josh exhales. "The truth is I'm actually pretty fucked up, Kat. I'm just really good at hiding it."

I grab his hand. "No you're not, Josh. Not at all." I grin. "You're actually *horrible* at hiding it."

He bursts out laughing and all tension between us instantly evaporates. He grabs the back of my neck and pulls me into him for an enthusiastic kiss. "You're awesome, Kat," he mumbles into my lips. "So fucking awesome." He pulls back and looks into my eyes for a moment, his blue eyes sparkling. "I've never told anyone about all that. My dad was so fucked up, you have no idea—he said the craziest shit all the time. Sometimes, looking back, I can't figure out what shit was normal father-son stuff to say and what shit was just, like, you know, totally out of line. It all jumbles together."

"I'm glad you told me. I really like the Josh who can't hide he's fucked up."

"But your family sounds so normal. You must think I'm a ticking time bomb of crazy."

"Oh, please. My family has its crazy, too. Not necessarily in the same league as your father, but crazy nonetheless. And, hey, why would I care if you've got crazy in your family? Since I have zero desire to make a Faraday with you, I'll never have to worry about passing your crazy-genes on to my offspring."

Josh bristles. Shoot. I shouldn't have said he has crazy-genes. That was pretty insensitive, given what he's been through with his father and brother.

"You have *zero* desire to make a Faraday with me?" Josh says.

I'm astonished. *That's* what offended him?

"Not even a little bit?" he asks, shooting me a charming smile.

"Not even a little bit," I say. And it's the truth.

"Well, shit, Kat," he says, pouting. "I'm genuinely offended."

I throw my hands up. "You're *offended* I don't wanna make a baby with you? What the *fuck*? Do you have a split personality?"

"Quite possibly. I do have crazy-genes, after all." He makes a "crazy" face.

I chuckle. "I thought you'd be thrilled I don't want to make a Faraday with you."

"Well, yeah, sure, from a practical standpoint, I'm elated. But from an evolutionary standpoint, I'm deeply offended. You should be chomping at the bit to snag my fabulous genes, crazy or not. Look at me. I'm an ideal sperm donor."

I laugh. "Oh, really? You've got a pretty high opinion of yourself, huh?"

"I'm saying from an *evolutionary standpoint*. Our only purpose as a species is to reproduce. There's no other reason for existence. You're born. You reproduce. You die. That's the game of life—finding someone to give you hearty spawn so you can live eternally through them."

"Wowza." I'm speechless for a moment. "Well, I think I'm gonna have to disagree with you—it sounds to me like you're *not* as ideal a sperm-donor as you think. I'd prefer my spawn to have a father who wants them, first of all—that's always nice—plus, I'd want my spawn to inherit a little bit of humility along with their chiseled cheeks and rock-hard abs."

"No, no, no. You've got it all wrong. From an *evolutionary* standpoint, humility is completely counterproductive. Does a peacock say, 'Aw, shucks,' about the feathers on his tail? No, he's genetically engineered to *flaunt* his tail. Why? So he can attract the best peahen in the flock."

"Peahen?"

"The female version of peacock. The name for male and females together is actually 'peafowl.'"

"And you know this factoid because?"

"Because I grew up with Jonas. The dude's got so much weird shit trapped in his brain, it's bizarre."

I chuckle. "Well, I'm not a *peahen*, I'm a human. And, either way, I don't wanna make a baby with you—human, peafowl, or otherwise. Not for really reals and not as part of an evolutionary experiment. I'm too selfish. I've seen what it takes from watching my mom, and no thanks—I'm quite happy going to work and yoga classes and doing shitfaced karaoke." I shrug.

Josh squints at me, apparently disbelieving my sincerity.

I shrug. "What can I say? You can add no-baby-no-thank-you to the list of ways I'm like a dude. I'm missing the baby-gene—it's not personal to you. I don't even like going to my friends' baby showers." I shrug. "But, hey, I'm only twenty-four. Still a wee little baybay. Check back with me in ten years when my biological clock is ticking like an atomic bomb—who knows if I'll be chomping at the bit to board the baby-train then? You never know, I guess."

"Hell no," Josh says. He swigs his drink. "I won't give a shit about your ticking clock when you're *thirty-four*. Pfft. Optimal child-bearing-age is twenty-six. You'll be no good to me when you're thirty-fucking-four."

"Why the *fuck* do you know the 'optimal' child-bearing-age for a woman? You're creeping me out."

Josh laughs heartily. "Jonas. I told you, the guy knows everything. Ask him the life span of a blue whale or the average rainfall in the Amazon or how to make a cherry bomb out of paperclips and he'll know it off the top of his head. The dude's a freak." He sips his drink. "And Jonas says twenty-six is the magic number. Past that, you're just a useless sack of ovaries and fallopian tubes, baby."

I burst out laughing. People aren't supposed to talk this way. I absolutely love it.

After we finish laughing at the sheer ridiculousness of our conversation, there's a long, awkward beat. I keep waiting for him to speak, but apparently, he's waiting on me. Well, hell. I might as well call out the pink elephant sitting smack in the middle of the room.

"So does that mean you might want little Faradays one day with some trampy little twenty-six-year-old? Is that what you're saying?" I ask.

Josh clears his throat. "Actually, no. I don't know why I just said all that. I was just trying to be snarky, but it backfired. For some reason, whenever I'm with you, I say crazy shit I'd never normally say. It's like I get some sort of Kat-specific Tourette's Syndrome."

I laugh. "I know the feeling—apparently, it's a two-way syndrome."

"Actually, I've never been able to picture myself having kids—but, then again, I've never been able to picture myself more than two weeks into the future, unless you're talking about something business related, of course. Ask me to draw up a five-year business plan for Climb & Conquer, and I'm your guy; ask for year-to-year projections on a new investment, I'm on it; but try to pin me down to coffee next week, and I freak out."

"Gosh, I hadn't noticed," I say.

He ignores my sarcasm. "But, hey, same as you—check back with me in ten years. Maybe guys have a biological clock, too."

I sip my drink, trying to seem casual, but my heart is about to hurtle out of my chest and splatter against the wall. I can't believe we're having this conversation. "Guys don't have a biological clock," I say. "Men can unleash their super-sperm any ol' time, even after every single one of their ball-hairs has turned gray."

He laughs.

"And, anyway, knowing you, I'd think I should check back with you in *fifty* years, not ten. Given your extreme terror of commitment, I wouldn't want to cause you undue stress."

"Yeah," he says. "Good idea. I'll unleash my super-sperm at eighty. That way, when I go to the drugstore, I'll be able to buy diaper cream and denture cream at the same time. One-stop-shopping."

I laugh. "Awesome. You're gonna win so hard at the game of life, dude."

He laughs. "'Hey there, whippersnapper! I can't find my teeth! Let's make a baby!'"

I laugh again. "Oh, yeah, I'm sure your twenty-six-year-old tramp is gonna go weak in the knees over your eighty-year-old ball sack and wrinkled ass. Talk about a gold-digger—we both know that poor girl's gonna be looking at her watch every five minutes, just waiting for you to die."

"Well, my future gold-digging spawn-carrying twenty-six-year-old might not get weak in the knees over my saggy ball-sack, I'll grant you that, but she's gonna cream her panties over my wrinkled ass, I guarantee it. I mean, seriously, who could resist a wrinkled ass stamped with 'YOLO'?

I burst out laughing. "Oh my God, Josh. Fifty years from now, your twenty-six-year-old spawn-carrier won't even know what YOLO stands for. By then, YOLO will be the equivalent of 'Daddy-o' or 'far out.'"

Josh puts on his "old man" voice again. "Damn kids. Back in my day, YOLO ass-tattoos were the bees' knees."

"That statement will be a bald-faced lie—I don't care how far into the future you make it."

"Aw, come on. Just wait. I'm a trendsetter, baby. Sure, the trend hasn't caught on *yet,* but it's coming, you'll see."

We share a huge smile.

"I really think we're on to something here, Kat. If I wait 'til after I'm diagnosed with dementia to have my first kid, then I can have him and forget he was ever born all in the same day."

"Brilliant. Talk about a surefire way to solve your fear of commitment." I take a long swig of my very strong drink. Wow, the vodka's really hitting me hard.

Josh blanches. "Why do you keep saying I'm afraid of commitment? You said that earlier, too. I'm not."

I don't reply. Oh shit. He looks genuinely offended. "Oh," I begin, at a loss. "I'm sorry. I thought I was saying something that's just a basic fact, like, 'Your eyes are blue.'"

"I had a girlfriend for three years, Kat," he says. "I'm not the least bit afraid of commitment."

I feel the urge to laugh out loud, so I drain my drink.

"I had a girlfriend for *three* years," Josh repeats. "I know how to commit."

Fuck it. The vodka is giving me liquid courage. "Honesty-game?" I ask.

He makes a face like he's just bitten into a lemon. "Yes?"

"You're a commitment-phobe, Josh," I say simply. "Text-book."

"No, I'm not. Absolutely not."

"Yep." I take a swig of my drink. "You are."

"A three-year relationship isn't a commitment? What's the longest relationship you've had?"

"About a year—with Nate."

"Ha! You're one to talk."

I take another swig. "This isn't about me and my horrible relationship skills." Oh wow, Josh put *a lot* of vodka into my drink, didn't he? "We're talking about *you* and yours—and the fact is you're deathly afraid of commitment in any form. Yes, you had a girlfriend for three years—and certainly that meant *something*, I'll grant you that, but it sounds like it was three years of a whole lot of nothing. I'm sorry to break it to you, but you and your girlfriend apparently never *talked* about anything real. You couldn't be yourself around her at all—and the minute you revealed who you really are, what you really want, she shamed you and ran off with Prince Harry. So, yes, you were in a relationship for three years, and, yes, it shows you have character and integrity, but it doesn't prove you're not afraid of commitment. I mean, in a way it proves your fear of commitment even more so."

"More so? Really? How do you figure?"

"Because you must have stayed with a woman like that for a reason. You must have known deep down she was every bit as incapable of emotional intimacy as you are. You liked that she never required you to reveal a goddamned honest thing about yourself in three freakin' years."

He looks shocked.

I press my lips together. Oh shit. I just dropped another one of my atomic bombs, didn't I? Oh fuck. That was harsh. Honest, but harsh.

I just can't help myself. Ever since reading Josh's application (and seeing Emma's beautiful, shy photo in Josh's Sick Fuck folder), I've had somewhat of a fixation on this Emma bitch. On the one hand, I've felt the primal urge to rip her limb from limb for hurting Josh. And, on the other hand, I've honestly been a bit obsessed with trying to figure out why the heck he stayed so long with a woman who was so obviously his total mismatch in every way (other than the fact that she's litcrally the most stunningly beautiful creature I've ever seen).

Josh looks floored. Pissed, I'd even say.

"Damn, that drink you made me was really, really strong," I say, my face turning hot.

Josh's jaw muscles are pulsing like crazy.

Shit. Maybe I've totally misjudged this. Maybe he can commit. Hell, maybe he was on the verge of asking Emma to marry him, for all I know. Oh, jeez, yes. Maybe that's why he now says marriage isn't in the cards for him? Is Josh just a case study of a man with a shattered heart? But, clearly, I can't ask him if he was about to propose. It's too sensitive. I opt for something slightly more innocuous. "So did you and Emma live together?"

Josh makes a face I'm not expecting, like he's embarrassed about what he's about to say. "No. It was a long-distance relationship. She lives in New York."

Oh, Sweet Jesus. Is he frickin' kidding me? "It was a *long-distance relationship*?" I boom, totally shocked.

"Yeah. So?" he says, clearly defensive. "I get out to New York all the time for work. I saw her a lot."

There's a very long silence.

Josh's face is bright red.

I'm sure mine is, too.

James Bay is singing to us about scars.

I feel like I've said way, way, way too much. My inner-bitch just came out full-force. God, I suck sometimes. "So... what's your favorite movie of all time?" I ask brightly. "If you could be anyone from *NSync other than Justin Timberlake, who would you be? Do you have a spirit animal?"

"You're not what I'd call the world's foremost expert on relationships," Josh says, his voice low and intense. "I wouldn't exactly hire you to write the definitive textbook on *How to Have a Healthy, Lasting Relationship*."

I part my lips, speechless.

His jaw is clenched.

I squint at him for a long moment, trying to look like a badass— but then, goddammit, tears prick my eyes. "You're right," I finally say. "I pretty much suck at relationships." I wipe my eyes. "I'm sorry for saying all that stuff. I shouldn't have said it."

He twists his mouth and exhales. "If you hadn't said it, you'd still be thinking it."

I don't correct him. He's right.

He shakes his head. "I must say, you have quite a knack for *not* kissing my ass, Kat."

I smash my lips together.

"I'm not used to it," he says.

"Sorry," I say.

Josh shakes his head like he's chastising me. "No apology required."

I bite my lip.

He grazes his fingertips up the length of my arm and my skin electrifies under his touch.

"You get really sassy when you're buzzed, you know that?" he says.

I nod. My crotch is suddenly burning.

"But you know what?"

I wait.

"I *really* like sassy."

I bite my lip. My heart is racing at his simple touch.

"Did I hurt your feelings?" he asks softly. His fingers move up my arm and drift along my jawline. "When I said you're a flop-dick when it comes to relationships?"

I smile. "Oh, is that what you said? Jeez, that's a whole lot meaner than what I *thought* you said. All I thought you said was you wouldn't hire me to write some textbook."

He chuckles. His fingertips skim the length of my hairline.

"I'm not mad at you," I say softly. "I'm the opposite of mad at you."

He smiles wickedly. "Oh, yeah?"

"Yeah."

Josh touches my chin and my body ignites. He leans in and kisses me gently.

We sit and stare at each other for a moment. A legion of butterflies has unleashed inside my stomach.

His eyes drift to my empty glass. "Would you like another one, Party Girl? The night is still young."

"Yes, thank you. But not nearly as strong this time, Playboy. I wanna be fully conscious for whatever might happen next. Something tells me it's gonna be good."

He smirks. "Good idea." He stands, grabs my glass, and heads toward the kitchen—but before he turns the corner, he turns back around. "Hey, Kat. Thanks for always playing the honesty-game with me. So few people do that with me—most people just kiss my ass."

"Well, you can hardly blame 'most people,' Josh—you've got a truly kissable ass."

He grins. "Thanks to the 'YOLO' stamped on it—which, I'm telling you is gonna be all the rage one of these days, mark my words."

I laugh. "Keep telling yourself that, Playboy, if it helps you look yourself in the eye every day."

His blue eyes are positively sparkling at me right now. "Your drink is coming right up, Party Girl."

"Thanks."

"My extreme pleasure."

Chapter 25
Kat

I feel myself literally swoon as Joshua William Faraday exits the living room to fetch us another round of drinks. That man is so freaking charming, and so freaking hot, and so freaking funny and adorable and sweet and generous and sexy (and I could go on and on), it's just not fair. I feel like I'm playing tennis against Roger Federer armed with nothing but a fly swatter.

I can't remember the last time I felt like this—so gooey and heart-fluttery and fairytale-believe-y and emotional. I've got to get a grip on myself, slow my shit the fuck *down*. Tap into Classic Kat for a while. Jeez. My feelings are moving too effing fast, especially considering whom I'm dealing with here.

Oh my God, I'm losing it. Falling *hard*.

This is so unlike me. I'm never the one *chasing* the guy—I'm always the one being *chased*. I'm the one who says, "I'm not sure I'm feeling it, sorry," and then *he* says, "Well, then, baby, lemme try to *convince* you." Isn't that *exactly* what Cameron said? Yep. After one date, he was ready to chase me to the ends of the earth, God knows why.

And that's the way I like it. I *like* being chased. What the hell did Josh tell Henn when he was being "Hitch" and teaching Henn to "dick it up"? I scoff out loud at the memory, even though I'm sitting here alone in this room. "Women *think* they wanna be chased," Josh said, "that's what all the movies and books tell 'em they want—but they don't. Not really. If you do the equivalent of driving to her house and holding a boom box over your head, you might as well hand her your dick and balls in a Ziplock baggie, too, 'cause you're not gonna need 'em any more."

What a big ol' bunch of bullshit. Of course, we wanna be chased. Idiot.

And, yet, here I am, aching for him, ready to hand him my whole heart and soul, aren't I? And he's the one who always pulls back.

I look up at the ceiling. What the hell have I gotten myself into with this man? Is he even capable of giving his heart to me—at least at some point? If I break down and make the depths of my feelings known to him, would he be thrilled or scared to death?

I lean back on the couch and squeeze my cheeks, pondering the situation.

Oh damn. I can't feel my face.

My gut tells me he'd be scared to fucking death. Maybe thrilled, too—but his fight or flight instinct would surely kick in. It's just too soon. A guy like him needs more time. Heck, a girl like me needs more time. Usually. I truly don't know what the fuck is happening to me. Where the hell is shallow, hedonistic, meaningless-sex-seeker Classic Kat when I need her?

As I glance around the room, lost in my thoughts, a small, framed photo on a table catches my eye. I can't make out the image from this distance, so I get up to take a closer look.

When I pick the photo up, I can see it's a faded shot of a stunningly beautiful blonde woman sitting in a wicker love seat with two tousled little boys—all three of them tanned and windswept and bursting with what appears to be authentic joy. The smiles on their glowing faces aren't canned "say cheese" grins—these people are bursting with genuine down-to-their-bones happiness. I can almost hear their ghostly peals of laughter rising up from the image.

God, it pains me to think what happened to this poor woman shortly after this photo was taken. Oh, and her poor little boys. I scrutinize the boys' faces in the photo, tears welling up in my eyes. I know Josh and Jonas are fraternal twins, but they look virtually identical in this shot. It'd be impossible to tell them apart if it weren't for Josh's slightly darker hair.

Tears blur my vision.

It kills me to think about how devastated those boys must have been when their mommy was so unexpectedly and savagely ripped from their young lives.

I wipe my eyes, but it's no use. I can't seem to stop my emotions from overflowing out of me. I take a deep breath and try to stuff my emotions down. It's suddenly hitting me full-force that the cute little boy in this picture—the one with the slightly darker hair—is standing in the next room, mixing me a drink, trying his earnest best on a daily basis to "overcome" everything he's had to endure.

Ice cubes rattle on the far side of the room and I snap my head up toward the sound.

Josh is standing at the entrance of the living room, his facial expression the same as when I opened my door to him in Las Vegas after reading his application.

His eyes dart to the photo in my hand and then back to my face.

The music swirls around us for a long moment. Finally, I hold up the photo and try to grin. "Your mom was stunning."

Josh doesn't reply.

I walk across the room with the photo and sit on the couch. "Tell me about her." I pat the couch next to me.

He looks torn.

James Bay is serenading us, singing about scars.

"Come on, Josh," I say. I pat the couch again.

He crosses the room and nestles himself onto the couch next to me, his lips pressed tightly together.

"She was beautiful," I say.

"You're her spitting image," he says softly.

I look down at the photo in my hand. Well, I can certainly see that I bear a resemblance to his mother, maybe even a striking one, but calling me her 'spitting image' is pretty far-fetched. For one thing, from what I can see from this photo, Josh's mother radiated pure kindness—a quality I'm certain I don't possess, unfortunately. Plus, her features are literally perfect. It's like she was concocted by mad scientists in some sort of government-sponsored lab. No one would ever say that about me, I don't think.

Josh takes the photo from my hand and looks down at it wistfully.

"Poor Jonas," he says.

"Poor Josh," I add.

Josh sighs like he's got the weight of the world on his shoulders. "No, I got off easy. I was at a football game with my dad when she died. Poor Jonas saw the whole fucking thing." He shakes his head mournfully. "Poor little dude was so traumatized, he didn't say a word for a year afterwards."

"*Nothing*?"

"Nothing. Literally. Not a word."

"For a whole *year*?"

"For a whole year. I did all his talking for him."

"How'd you know what to say?"

"I just knew. Later, after he'd started talking again, he told me I'd always gotten it right. It was like we shared a brain."

"What did Jonas say when he started talking again?"

Josh smiles. "We were sitting in the car with our nanny, listening to the radio, and I was singing along to a song—whatever it was, I can't remember—and after not saying a single fucking word for a *year*, my bizarre, hilarious, crazy brother said, and I quote, 'Shut the fuck up, Josh. You're singing so goddamned loud, I can't hear the fucking music.'"

I burst out laughing and Josh does, too.

"What made him talk again all of a sudden?"

"Not *what*—*who*. Jonas talked again thanks to one very special and extremely attractive woman: our third-grade teacher, Miss Westbrook. If it hadn't been for her, Jonas wouldn't be here right now, I'm sure of it. Which, of course, means neither would I."

My stomach turns over. "What do you mean 'neither would I'?"

Josh pauses a long time before speaking again, apparently choosing his words carefully. "If it weren't for Miss Westbrook, there's no doubt in my mind Jonas would have methodically figured out a way to kill himself before his thirteenth birthday. Granted, fun fact, Jonas actually *did* fling himself off a bridge when he was seventeen, right after my dad shot himself, but that's a whole other story. But if it weren't for Miss Westbrook, he would have done it much more precisely than driving off a bridge, and he would have succeeded." His eyes glisten. "And if Jonas had succeeded in killing himself when I was still a little kid, if he'd left me alone with my dad in that big house for years and years..." He shakes his head. "I wouldn't have been able to overcome it."

The image of Josh's "overcome" tattoo flickers across my mind.

"Do you think that's why you never envision yourself in the future?" I ask.

Josh looks at me blankly.

"At dinner with Reed, you said when you were twenty, you couldn't imagine yourself at thirty—and now that you're thirty, you can't picture yourself at forty. Do you think your brain has trouble imagining the future because you're subconsciously not convinced you'll have one? Because you're not sure what Jonas might... do?"

He shakes his head like I just gave him mental whiplash. "Wow." He makes a face that says "holy fuck." "Well, shit. I guess that's as good a theory as any. Whoa." He smiles. "Deep thoughts by Katherine Ulla Morgan."

I shrug. "Hey, even a broken clock is right twice a day."

"Can't we just talk about *The Teenage Mutant Ninja Turtles*? How 'bout that Raphael?"

I wince. "Sorry."

"No, no, don't apologize. I'm just kidding." He sighs. "I guess I'm just not used to talking about this stuff."

"Sorry. We don't have to."

"No, it's good. It feels good."

"Really?"

"Yeah."

I bite my lip. "So how did Miss Westbrook get Jonas to talk?"

"Well, to tell you about Miss Westbrook, I kinda have to give you a little primer on Jonas first."

"Okay," I say, leaning back. "I'm not going anywhere."

He pulls me close to him and wraps his arm around my shoulder.

"I know Jonas seems like some kind of gorilla-robot, but he's actually really sensitive. Always has been, especially when it comes to women." He shakes his head. "Like, take my mom, for instance. Even when he was little, Jonas didn't just love her, he *worshipped* her. I loved her, too, of course. With all my heart. And yet, even I could see Jonas loved her differently than I did. As far as he was concerned, Mom was *literally* an angel."

I feel the sudden urge to get even closer to him. I slide myself onto his lap and wrap my arms around his neck.

He wraps his arms around my back in reply.

"He was the same way with Mariela, too," Josh continues. "Our housekeeper before my mom died. I used to beg Jonas to come outside to climb a tree with me and he'd be like, 'No, I'm gonna clean pots with Mariela.'" Josh laughs and shakes his head at the memory. "Right after my mom died, it's a long story, but my dad blamed Mariela for my mom's death and sent her away—and Jonas just completely melted down. I guess losing them both was just too much for the little guy." Emotion threatens to overtake Josh's face. He looks down and composes himself.

"You lost them, too," I say softly, touching his arm.

Josh looks back up, his face earnest. "Yeah, but I'm not *Jonas*."

"I don't understand."

He shakes his head. "I'm *Josh*. The fixer. The closer. Life throws shit at me, I just deal with it. I solve problems. I fix things. I'm coated in Teflon, baby—shit slides right off me and doesn't leave a mark. But not Jonas. Even Mariela told me, 'Take care of your brother, Josh. You know he's the sensitive one.'"

"So you thought it was your job to take care of Jonas, even though you were so little, too?"

"It's always been my job to take care of Jonas, and it always will be. I'm sure in the womb Jonas was trying to understand the functionality of the umbilical cord or articulate the meaning of life, and I was like, 'Dude, chill the fuck out—doesn't this amniotic fluid feel *awesome*? It's like a Jacuzzi!'"

I know Josh's words are funny, but the expression on his face isn't. My heart's suddenly aching for him. I push myself even closer into him, run my hands through his hair, and kiss him gently. When we break apart, tears are streaming down my cheeks, but Josh's eyes are bone-dry.

"When was the last time you cried?" I ask softly.

He shrugs. "Probably not since I was about ten. I cried like a baby when my mom died and Mariela got sent away, and I used to cry a ton the first few years whenever Jonas got sent away. But then one day when Jonas was gone, my dad found me sitting on the grass, crying my eyes out, and he reamed me for being a 'fucking cry-baby-pussy-ass.'" He shrugs. "And that was that. I never cried again. I've come very, very close many times since then, but I've never actually shed a tear."

I'm blown away. "Not once?"

He shakes his head. "I think there might be something wrong with me."

I make a sad face.

"So, anyway, I got sidetracked. I was supposed to be telling you how Miss Westbrook got Jonas to talk, right?" He shifts his body underneath me and I'm treated to the unmistakable sensation of his hard-on poking me in the crotch.

"*Oh*," I say. "Hello."

"Hello." He grins.

"What's that for?"

"You're sitting on my lap."

"That's all it takes?"

"Apparently."

I grin at him. "That's all it takes for me, too," I say.

"I'm addicted to you," he whispers.

"I'm addicted to you," I whisper back, my heart racing.

He nuzzles his nose into mine. We kiss gently for a few minutes, listening to the music. My crotch is absolutely burning.

He pulls back. "What were we talking about?"

"Miss Westbrook."

"Oh, yeah." He lays a quick peck on my lips. "Jonas became Miss Westbrook's after-school helper, and to make a long story short, she did this crazy, amazing thing he hadn't experienced in a really long time: she was nice to him." He shrugs. "And that's pretty much it—well, and she was smoking hot, too." He grins.

"But how do you think she convinced him to speak? A year's a long time."

"I don't know exactly what she said or did to him when they were all alone in that classroom, but whatever it was, he adored her. She could have asked Jonas to fly and he would have figured out how to sprout wings." He sighs. "All I can say is it's a good thing Sarah's not some kind of evil madman bent on destroying the universe because if she were, we'd all be screwed. The boy would figure out how to do it for her."

"I think the feeling's mutual."

Josh nuzzles my nose again. "Don't tell Sarah, but Jonas is gonna pop the question."

I'm floored. "*What*?"

Josh grins broadly. "He's been sending me photos of rings this whole past week. Hang on." He rearranges me on his lap so he can grab his phone from his pocket. "See?"

I look at his screen—and sure enough, Jonas has texted Josh countless images of diamond rings, all of them bigger than my head.

"Holy Hope Diamond, Batman," I say.

Josh laughs. "Which one do you think Sarah would like the best? Jonas won't leave me alone about it."

I scroll through the images, shaking my head. "Hell, if I know. They're all freaking spectacular—oh, wait. No. *This one.* Wow." I point to a princess-cut dazzler that, for whatever reason, screams "Sarah" to me. "She's gonna totally freak out."

"Bless you." Josh grabs his phone from me and shoots off a quick text to Jonas. "You just saved me from hours of torture, Kat. Thank you."

"When's he gonna ask her?"

"In two weeks—he's taking her on a surprise trip to Greece right after her final exams."

I gasp. "He's gonna ask her in *Greece*? Oh my God." I clutch my heart. "Oh my shit, Sarah's gonna crap her pants. *Greece*?"

"You ever been there?"

"No, remember? I've only been out of the country to Mexico and on a cruise to the Caribbean. I told you about the cruise and you said the only way to travel by sea is by private yacht."

Josh laughs. "I said that? Oh my God, I'm such a douche sometimes."

I laugh.

He nuzzles my nose. "So get this, babe. Jonas is planning to make poor Sarah hike to the top of *Mount Olympus*—because, he says, she's 'the goddess and the muse'"—he chuckles happily—"and then he's gonna make her jump *off* the mountain and paraglide down to the beach—and *that's* where he's gonna ask her." He laughs heartily. "So fucking Jonas."

"But Sarah's deathly afraid of heights."

He touches my hair. "Well, sucks to be her, then. He wants to create some kind of *metaphor*."

My brain tells me I should smile and laugh, but my eyes unexpectedly fill with tears instead. Oh my God, I'm a hot mess. I cover my face with my hands. What the hell is wrong with me lately?

"Kat? What's wrong?" He looks genuinely concerned. "Why are you crying?"

I shake my head and laugh at myself through my tears. "I'm just so happy for Sarah," I say, but even as I say it, I'm not sure if this completely explains my sudden (bizarre) tears (though, of course, I am insanely happy for Sarah). "I dunno, maybe I'm just so freakin' relieved Sarah's okay—I was so worried about her when she was attacked." Another true statement—but, again, I'm not sure this is the source of my tears. "Or maybe I'm just sloppy-drunk. That was a really strong drink, Josh." I half-smile.

Or maybe finding out Jonas is gonna propose to Sarah made my heart pang for myself, if I'm being brutally honest. Maybe my heart clanged so forcefully inside my chest cavity when Josh said those words, the sensation literally brought tears to my eyes.

Josh looks at me funny for a long beat.

I feel like I've said something wrong. Or, at least something awkward. I didn't just now say my deepest thoughts out loud, did I?

After a moment, Josh grabs my face and kisses me passionately. Whoa. This is quite a kiss.

"You're a good friend," Josh whispers into my lips, his passion obviously surging all of a sudden. "I like that about you."

"Josh," I breathe. His kiss has ignited me.

He rises off the couch, taking my fluttering, swooning, aroused body with him—and I throw my arms around his neck.

"Okay, Party Girl with a Hyphen," Josh says, his eyes blazing. "Time to finish the tour of my house. Next stop: my bedroom."

Chapter 26
Kat

"Wow. Katherine Ulla Morgan's finally gonna be in my bed," Josh says gleefully. "Glory be."

I giggle, peel off my clothes, and crawl into Josh's luxurious bed, my skin on fire. "Hurry up, Joshua William Faraday. Don't keep Katherine Ulla Morgan waiting."

"I'll be right there. Just getting some music cued up." He glances at me from across the room, his blue eyes smoldering. "Another one from James Bay. I can't get enough of this album."

As the song starts playing, Josh joins me in bed, his erection straining as he crawls over me—and in a flash, his warm skin is covering mine.

"Hey, gorgeous," he says softly, his muscles bulging as he rests his forearms on either side of my head. "Welcome to my bed."

"Thank you. It's a pleasure to be here."

The song is swirling around us, filling the room with words that seem to have been written especially for us—especially for this moment. Did Josh select this song as some sort of coded message to me—or is it just coincidental that James Bay is singing to us to "Let It Go" and reveal our truest selves to each other?

"I love it," I murmur as Josh's lips gently press into mine.

He moans his agreement into my mouth. "Me, too."

Goose bumps erupt all over my body. These words are making my heart pang.

Josh raises my arms above my head, pins my wrists together with one of his large palms, and proceeds to slowly kiss and touch his way down my arms all the way down to my mouth, where he sucks my lower lips and teases me mercilessly for a while with tender kisses, until finally

215

leaving my mouth for my breasts. Oh God, I'm already writhing with pleasure and we're just getting started. His lips leave my breasts and trail down to my belly, where he swirls my belly ring in his mouth, and then moves on to laying soft kisses on my hip bone and pelvis.

"You smell so good," he breathes. "I'm rock hard for you."

I'm on fire.

When his lips finally move to the sensitive folds between my legs, I let out a long, low moan, already on the cusp of climax, and when his tongue finds my clit, I grip the sheet and arch my back, my body clenching and releasing forcefully.

"You're amazing, baby," he says, his mouth lapping at me. "I love the way you get off."

When my orgasm subsides, he works his way back up my body, kissing, sucking, caressing, massaging, and licking me into a frenzy.

I'm enraptured.

His face is suddenly in mine. Oh God, I could stare into those blue eyes forever. The room is spinning. He cups my cheek in his palm and presses his warm skin into the full length of my body. "I can't get enough of you, baby," he says.

"I'm addicted, Josh," I reply. "I'm totally addicted to you."

He slides his fingertips between my legs, brushing my wetness gently until I'm squirming and yelping with arousal, and I return the favor, touching him exactly the way he's touching me—*adoringly.* We kiss and kiss, caressing each other gently as we do, until both of us are trembling and making sounds of extreme arousal.

I feel transported. I can't think. I can only *want.* I wrap my legs around him, pressing my body into his. "Please," I breathe. I'm trembling with desire. "Please. I want you, Josh. Please." I'm using a phrase I've used with him before: I want you. But this time I mean it in a new way. This time, I'm telling him the bare truth: I want *him*, not just sexually. I want him to be mine in every way. I've never ached like this before. My heart hurts. "I want you, Josh," I say again. "I want you so much it hurts." Oh my God, I feel like crying, I want him to be mine so, so much.

"I'm all yours," he says. He parts my legs and slides his hardness inside me, burying his shaft deep inside me, kissing me deeply as he does, stroking my hair, sucking on my lower lip again, thrusting his body slowly in and out of mine—and all of it as "Let It Go" continues to swirl around us.

I caress his ass and dig my fingers into him and he responds by thrusting passionately into me. "Why do you always feel so fucking *good*?" he asks, his voice strained.

"Josh," I breathe. But that's all I can manage. I'm feeling too overwhelmed to say more. With each thrust of his body, each time his chest rubs against mine, each touch of his lips, my heart feels like it's physically reaching outside of my chest to join with his.

Sex with Josh has never been like this before. He's fucked my brains out many times, made me literally pass out with pleasure, but this feels different. It doesn't feel so much like he's *fucking* me, it feels more like he's... what was that word he used when he talked about the way Jonas loves? It feels like he's *worshipping* me.

I've no sooner had the thought than I'm jolted with a palpable electric current. Holy hell, it's like someone flipped a switch on our mutual circuit breaker.

"What the fuck?" Josh says softly, his body moving with mine.

Oh my God. He feels it, too?

"What *is* that?" he asks, his voice ragged.

"I don't know," I choke out.

He touches my face and kisses me, his passion spiking. "What the fuck are you doing to me?"

I shake my head and press my palm into his chest, right onto his mother's name. "I don't know."

As the song builds, so does the crazy electricity between us. It feels too big to contain, too pleasurable to bear.

Suddenly, I don't want an inch of separation between us. I want all of him. Every inch. I hitch my legs up higher around his thrusting body, as high as I can manage, trying to coax him into the farthest recesses of my body and he responds by guiding my thighs to his shoulders. And that's all it takes to send my body releasing with an orgasm so pleasurable, it makes my eyes water.

"Yeah, baby," Josh says, his passion obviously on the verge of releasing. "Oh my God. You're amazing, babe."

In one smooth movement, Josh pulls out of me and rearranges us. Suddenly, he's on his back and I'm on top of him, straddling him, riding him. His hands are all over me. His face is intense. I grab his finger off my breast and suck it voraciously.

He moans and thrusts underneath me with increased fervor.

217

I'm vaguely aware the music has moved on to the next song on James Bay's album. He's singing about "craving." Oh God, these words were written for us, too. I've been craving this man since the minute I laid eyes on him.

Our movement becomes heated. Josh is thrusting into me, grabbing at me, groping me, kissing me, groaning, and I'm gyrating my hips wildly on top of him, rubbing myself against his hard shaft as I do. He touches my clit and massages me—and I absolutely explode with pleasure.

"Yeah," he chokes out as my body undulates around his cock, over and over. "Get it, baby."

Right on my heels, Josh jerks underneath me, his body releasing into mine. "Oh God," he groans. "Holy fuck."

As Josh comes, I gaze at him from my perch on top of his body.

I love watching his features contort from pure pleasure. I love seeing every muscle in his body tense and tighten and then relax. My eyes drift across all the swirling ink decorating his skin—to his abs and chest, glistening with sweat.

His body is quiet now. He's all done. His blue eyes are fixed on mine. Oh, those eyes. I trace his eyebrow with my fingertip and he blinks slowly, obviously completely spent. I lean down and kiss his lips gently and then trail gentle kisses along the length of his jaw, to his ear, and then down to his neck. I inhale the scent of him and swoon. Oh my effing God, I cannot get enough of this man.

I kiss and lick his chest tattoo, each and every letter, and then I let my tongue migrate down his torso to his little fishy swimming in the river and then down to the deep ridges in his abs. I kiss every letter of his "overcome" tattoo along his waist and let my tongue explore the sharp "V" cuts above his pelvis as the song swirls around us, giving voice to what I'm feeling deep inside. After a while, my mouth finds his nipples, then his neck, his jawline, his lips. We kiss passionately for a long time until, finally, we pull away from each other and stare into each other's eyes.

My head is reeling. I've never experienced sex like this. This was something new—the perfect alignment of heart, body, mind, and soul. It took my breath away.

Josh wraps a lock of my hair around his finger and sings along softly to the last chorus of "Craving" straight to the end of the song.

Another song on the album starts, and at the first chorus, it becomes clear what this new song must be called—"If You Ever Want To Be In Love."

Josh stops playing with my hair. "Excuse me for a minute, PG." He abruptly guides me off him, hops off the bed, and practically sprints toward his bathroom, leaving me in the bed alone with my mouth hanging open, listening to the rest of the song by myself.

Chapter 27
Josh

I splash cold water on my face and look at myself in the mirror. What the fuck just happened between Kat and me? I wouldn't even call what we just did *sex*. It felt more like a nuclear reaction. *Sexual fusion.* Is that a thing? Well, if not, it is now.

I stare at my reflection in the mirror.

Water is dripping off my brow and down my nose.

Holy motherfucking shit.

How many times has Kat or I said, "Sex doesn't have to be deep and meaningful"? And now, all of a sudden, I feel like going back in a time machine to each and every one of those conversations and shouting, "Yeah, but sometimes it *is*, Kat—*sometimes it is*!"

Jesus Christ. That was epic. The way her body felt around mine. Her eyes. Her lips. That electricity coursing between us. I could *feel* it. *And the music.* Oh my God. What the fuck was James Bay trying to do to me? Turn me into a blubbering pussy? I thought that James Bay album was cool when Jonas played it for me in New York, that's all—I just really liked the guy's voice. "Hey, that's cool," I said when Jonas played one of the songs for me. "Who is that?" I had no idea those songs would later provide the soundtrack of my complete and total undoing.

Holy fucking damn, that was some seriously mind-blowing sex.

Which, by the way, makes no sense at all. Ever since breaking up with Emma, all I've done is fantasize about all the kinky-ass shit I wanna do, all the ways I wanna let my inner sick-fuck run amok— and *that's* what got me off so hard?—the most straight-forward, basic kind of sex a guy can have? But, oh my fucking God, it was incredible. Kat felt so fucking good, and the music was so perfect, and that electricity came out of nowhere and rocked my world... Holy fuck. I literally had to run away from her when that last song started playing or else I was gonna turn into fucking Jonas and start calling her the 'goddess and the muse' or some shit like that.

For Chrissakes, the way I was feeling in that moment, I was on the cusp of pouring my heart out to her, on the verge of telling her a thousand things I'd never normally say. For Chrissakes, I was about to babble about my upcoming move to Seattle! "When I move to Seattle," I was about to say, "I wanna do this every night with you, babe." Those are the exact words I was on the verge of saying to her! They were on the tip of my fucking tongue—even though I'm not moving for three motherfucking months! How could I even *think* of making an implied promise like that? Sure, I'm addicted to Kat right now—*painfully* addicted—Jesus God—I feel like a fucking labradoodle fetching a stick every time I'm in her presence—but who knows how long this white-hot passion's gonna last? This thing with Kat and me is brand new, after all. At this stage in a relationship, three months from now might as well be thirty years. Things might work out—and, shit, I sure hope they do—God, I hope they do—but they might not. Like I always say: under-promise and over-deliver. That's the path to happiness and peace of mind in all things.

But, goddammit, I wanted so badly to tell her about my upcoming move to Seattle, plus a bunch of other stuff, too. I wanted to tell her how excited I am to sit down to dinner with her noisy, chaotic family, to meet her mom and dad and brothers and just sit there, watching everyone interact. I wanted to explain that it's a big fucking deal for someone like me to sit down for a birthday dinner with a real family—a *big* family—even though it's a ho-hum kind of thing for everyone else. In fact, I wanted to tell her, the whole reason I lived in my fraternity house for my first two years in college (even though the place should have been condemned) was because I craved being around noise and chaos and laughter and *people* so badly after growing up my whole goddamned life in a fucking morgue with Joseph Stalin breathing down my neck.

Oh my God, I wanted to take Kat's gorgeous face in my hands and stare into those icy-blue eyes that see right through me and tell her she blows me the fuck away, and not just in bed, but in every conceivable way—that I can't find a goddamned fucking fault with her—that even her stubbornness and jealousy and evil make me want her that much more, more than I've ever wanted any other woman, in fact. That I can't stand it when we're apart. That she's hilarious. And sweet. And honest. A force of nature. That she makes my heart physically *hurt* when she does nothing more than smile at me.

I lean forward and stare at myself in the mirror. I'm trembling. Panting. Freaking out. I need to get a grip.

I wanted to tell her I'm falling so fast and hard for her, I feel like I need a Dramamine. And a parachute. And a fucking last will and testament.

Fuck.

I stare at my blue eyes reflected back at me in the mirror.

"Pull yourself together, man," I say through gritted teeth. "Stop acting like a total puss." I nod in reply to myself, take a deep breath, and slap my cheek *hard*—and then, once I feel like I've regained control of myself, I turn around and head back into my room.

Chapter 28
Josh

When I emerge from my bathroom, there's yet another James Bay song playing—this one, thankfully, in no danger of sending me into a tailspin. Kat's sprawled naked on her stomach across my bed, looking like a wet dream, her long, toned limbs stretched across my mattress, her blonde hair unfurled across my pillow, her tight ass just begging to get spanked or bitten or fucked. Or all of the above. Jesus. I wouldn't mind being greeted with this vision every time I come out of my bathroom.

I crawl onto the bed and drape my body over hers, pressing my naked body into hers. "Hey, babe," I say softly.

She turns her head and rests her cheek on the pillow.

"Hey," she says softly. "Everything okay?"

"Mmm hmm. Everything's great." I push her hair to one side and stroke the Scorpio tattoo on the back of her neck. "How are you?"

"Good."

She squirms underneath me and I lift up, letting her turn onto her back so that we're lying nose to nose, our bodies pressed together.

"You look like you have one eye," she says, pressing her nose into mine. "One very blue and beautiful eye."

"I'm Mike Wazowski," I say.

She laughs. "Why do you know that?"

"Are you kidding me? I love *Monsters, Inc.*"

She laughs. "You never cease to surprise me."

"Mike Wazowski!" I say in the voice of Boo. "Kitty!"

"Admit it—you were stoned out of your mind when you watched that movie, weren't you?"

223

"*No*, as a matter of fact. I was, like, sixteen or something—still a very nice boy."

She laughs. "Sorry. Didn't mean to offend you."

I pause. "I was a very nice boy at one point, Kat—I went to see cartoon-movies in the theatre and everything."

"I'm sure you were."

I pause. "Although, in the interest of the honesty-game, I watched *Monsters, Inc.* stoned out of my mind later on DVD."

She bursts out laughing and I join her. God, I'm fucking addicted to her. I can't resist reaching out and touching her golden hair. It's the color of straw. Spun gold. Sunshine. I stroke her hair for a moment and she purrs like a cat.

"You blow me away, Kat—not just in bed. All the time. With everything you do and say."

She inhales sharply. "You blow me away, too." Her face turns bright red.

I suddenly feel like I'm on the verge of babbling every thought in my head again—all the stuff I was about to say a minute ago, before I escaped into the bathroom. Fuck me, I wanna tell her about Seattle.

"All right, babe," I say, rolling off her. "Enough talking about cartoons—we've got kinky-fuckery to talk about."

She laughs. "Nice transition."

I sit up in bed. "So here's the deal, Heidi Kumquat. When I wrote my application to The Club I was in a totally different state of mind than I am now."

She nods. This is not news to her.

I exhale. "Would you be terribly disappointed if we moved right into doing everything on your fantasy list and skipped the stuff I wrote about in my application to The Club?"

"Why?"

I shrug. "Doing that shit now just feels like trying to relive my junior prom. Now all I wanna do is go to my *senior* prom—with you."

She grins. "Aw. You're asking me to prom?"

"So you're not disappointed?" I ask. "You seemed pretty excited to be on the receiving end of all that shit in my application."

She shrugs. "Hey, if you're not feeling it, then we don't do it.

And, anyway, I got to be a high-end call girl. That's what I was really jonezing for." She makes a checkmark motion in the air. "Plus, I unexpectedly got a bonus mini-porno out of it, too—watching you get all riled up at the thought of anyone but you touching me was utterly delicious." She shoots me a wicked smile.

"*I knew it.*"

She laughs a full-throated laugh.

"Diabolical," I say, smiling. "Okay, cool. It's settled. We're doing your fantasies, baby."

She squeals with pleasure.

"So this is how it's gonna work. You'll just go about your life, okay?—and sometimes shit will just start happening to you. And when it does, you'll just play along. Don't worry, you'll totally know what to do because—" I slap my hands together hard, making her flinch. "Sorry. I just had a brilliant idea. I'll be right back." I leap out of bed and race to my hallway closet, my pulse pounding in my ears. Holy fuck, this is gonna be epic. I quickly find what I'm looking for and sprint back to my bed. "Open your hand, babe." She does, and I place a poker chip in her palm. "Every time a fantasy is starting, you'll get a poker chip just like this one. That way you'll never be confused about whether a role-play is starting. You know, you won't go, 'Are you *really* a fireman? Is my house *really* burning down—or are you here to eat my pussy?'"

She laughs. "I don't have a fireman fantasy—Colby's a fireman. Too weird."

I roll my eyes. "It was just an example, babe. I know all your fantasies, remember? I took copious notes. I'm just saying the poker chip will be our secret signal so I'll never need to say, 'Hey, Kat, I'm doing a fantasy now.' That way you can just relax and enjoy the ride and play along."

"But what if there really *is* a fire—using your example—and it happens *after* you've already given me the poker chip? You'd be like, 'Fire, Kat! Fire!' And I'd be like, 'Oh, yeah, baby. I'm on *fi-yah.*'" She giggles.

"Good point," I say, laughing with her. "We should have a safe word in case we need to stop the role-play for any reason."

"Okay. How about 'overcome'? Wasn't that what you used with the women in The Club?"

I wave my hands in dismissal. I don't even want to think about those women right now. "That was *then*, babe—this is now. Our fantasy-sex-club is all about *fun*—not exorcising my fucking demons."

"Awesome," she says, her eyes blazing. "How about 'sick fuck,' then?"

"*Babe*. Did you not hear a word I just said? I'm over it. Plus, I kinda dig it when you call me a sick fuck. I wanna keep that phrase as fair game. You never know what you might scream when I'm fucking the shit out of you in a dental chair."

"Ooh." She raises an eyebrow. "We're gonna do the dentist thing?"

"Oh my God, you're a terrible listener. What'd I just say? *Yes.* We're gonna do *everything.*"

She squeals. "Oh my God. This is gonna be *redonk.*"

"So what's the safe word? It can be anything. Onomatopoeia."

She giggles. "Who's the idiot who came up with that word? Who needs so many syllables to say '*Bam!*'?"

I laugh.

"Brouhaha?" she asks.

"What the fuck? *No.* Weirdo."

She shrugs.

We sit and think.

"Peanut butter and jelly sandwich?" she offers.

I jut my lip, considering it. "Since that's the only thing I know how to make, in theory, it *could* come up."

"I truly cannot fathom how either of us would say 'peanut butter and jelly sandwich' while fucking, but okay, if you say so. How about 'rainbows and unicorns'? That'll never come out of my mouth, I guarantee you."

"Might come out of mine—you're a total unicorn, babe. I could totally imagine myself blurting that in a moment of weakness. Even if I don't say 'rainbows' along with it, it could still get confusing."

She laughs. "This shouldn't be that hard."

I sit and think for a moment. "Flesh-eating bacteria," I say.

"Hell no. You're demented to even suggest it. Come on. Dinosaur. Doorknob. Dandelion. Dungarees. Deedle-deedle-dee. Pick one."

I laugh. "No, hang on. I'm kinda digging 'flesh-eating bacteria.' I can't imagine any sexual scenario in which those words would ever come up."

"As opposed to 'dungarees' or 'dandelion'?" She rolls her eyes. "Come on, Josh. Spaghetti. Skateboard. Ballerina. Scooby Doo. Multi-vitamin. *From Justin to Kelly.* 'My Little Pony.' Hot tamale."

"Oh my God." I hoot with glee. "*From Justin to Kelly.* Winner-winner-chicken-dinner."

Kat rolls her eyes. "What? *No.* I was totally kidding. Harry Potter. Chili-cheese fries. 'Go big or go home.' Hunky dory."

"Nope. We've got our winner. *From Justin to Kelly* it is."

She twists her mouth. "You're a silly man."

I laugh.

"You totally saw that movie, didn't you?"

"Hell yeah. It was part of initiation in my fraternity. I saw it during hell-week."

She laughs. "You got *hazed* with *From Justin to Kelly?*"

I nod. "It was brutal."

She's laughing her ass off. "Oh my God."

"So, hey, babe, there's something I wanna run past you before we get started."

"Okay."

"In order to pull off some of your crazy-ass stuff, I might need to enlist a little help occasionally from third parties—not for anything sexual, obviously—never anything sexual—just in setting the stage for a scenario."

She makes a face. "Could you be more specific about how you define 'setting the stage'?"

"Not without giving things away."

There's a long beat.

"I promise you won't be embarrassed or compromised in any way," I say. "You'll always be fully dressed. I just wanna make these imaginary-pornos as close as possible to what you described to me—and occasionally I think I might need to cast an extra or two to do it."

She beams a huge smile at me.

"What?" I ask.

"You're adorable."

I scoff.

"You are."

"So is that a yes?"

She nods. "I've got a safe word, right? If I've got a problem with anything at any time, then I'll use it."

"That's right, babe. You can always count on *From Justin to Kelly* to protect you."

She rolls her eyes. "Oh, Joshua. You're a silly, silly man."

I laugh.

"And a very sweet one, too."

Chapter 29
Josh

"Why don't you shower in my bathroom while I use the shower in the guest room?" I suggest as Kat and I walk into my house. We've just come in from an awesome day of hiking and climbing rocks in Malibu and we're both covered in a thick sheen of sweat and dirt. "I'm gonna take a quick shower and answer a few work emails before we head back out."

"Okay," she says. "Sounds good."

"Feel free to use the sauna in my bathroom, if you want." I look at my watch. "We've got just under an hour before we need to leave to make our reservation. This place is impossible to get into, so we can't be late."

"Hey, you probably take longer than I do, Mr. Exfoliate and Moisturize."

"You've only got one skin, Kat," I say.

She laughs.

I show her where the towels are and leave her to get to it and then race out of my room to make a phone call in the guest room.

"Hello?" the woman on the other end of the line says.

My pulse is pounding in my ears. "Hey, Kaitlyn. This is Josh Faraday. Just calling to confirm we're still on for tonight?"

"Yeah." She exhales. "I really can't emphasize enough how much trepidation I have about this. I'm really putting my faith in Reed. He said you're a great guy and that I can trust you completely, so I'm taking a gigantic leap of faith. Please don't make me regret this."

"Oh, I know this is a huge favor—and I'm really grateful. Reed isn't steering you wrong. I'm totally trustworthy. I paid close

229

attention at our walk-through-orientation on Tuesday, and I'll be ridiculously careful and respectful with all your stuff, just like you showed me, I promise. If I break *anything*, no matter how slightly, I'll replace it with a brand new model—and I won't touch any of the stuff you told me is off limits. Like I said, this is more for show than anything—I just wanna set the stage for her—really wow her when she opens her eyes for the first time."

Kaitlyn clicks her tongue. "Just, please. This could go horribly wrong a thousand ways."

I don't like the anxious tone in her voice. God help me if this woman does an about-face and changes her mind. "Hey, how 'bout I throw another ten grand your way, just to say thank you and put your mind at ease?"

"Whoa. Really?"

"Yeah. Maybe the price we originally agreed upon was too low. It's not like there's a market for this kind of rental. I don't want you feeling taken advantage of."

"Wow, thanks." Her voice is noticeably warmer. "Yeah, another ten grand would definitely put me at ease. Thanks. You still want me to burst in on you at ten?"

I laugh. "Hell yeah, I do. That's a critical part of my girl's fantasy. I'll time everything on my end so we'll be ready for you exactly at ten. I'll leave your plastic sword outside the door."

"Your girlfriend's got quite the imagination."

"Yeah, she does," I say, smiling to myself. I like hearing the words "your girlfriend" in reference to Kat.

"You're *sure* you wanna do the whole sword-fight-thing? I still think it's gonna be more comedic than sexy, Josh."

"Yeah, I gotta do it. My girlfriend's gonna love it."

Kaitlyn exhales. "Okay. If you insist."

"My girl's got this bizarre little script in her head. I've gotta stick to it."

"Okay," Kaitlyn says. "To each her own."

"So we're good, then?"

"Yep. We're good."

"What time can we come?"

"Any time. The place is ready for you now. I'll text the door-code to you. Oh, and I bought some brand new feather ticklers for you to use. They're on that rack I showed you to use—the one next to the harness."

"Thanks so much."

"Please don't touch anything but what I showed you."

"I won't. I promise."

She exhales audibly for the hundredth time during this short conversation. "Josh, I know we already talked about this, but it bears repeating: Don't try to push things too far. You don't have a clue what you're doing and she's a total newbie. The shock value of the place is gonna be the main thing, okay? Don't try anything other than what I explained to you or else you're gonna hurt or scare her."

"I promise. Thank you. This is just gonna be about role-play. Nothing hardcore, I promise."

"Please don't make me regret this."

"I won't."

She pauses. "So can you bring the extra money tonight? All cash?"

"Yup. No problem. I'll put it outside the door with your sword."

"Thanks. You're absolutely *sure* about that damned sword?"

"Positive. It's in the script. Gotta do it." I chuckle. "See you in a bit."

"Okay. See you soon."

Chapter 30
Kat

I lean into the mirror to apply a light sheen of gloss to my lips. I scrutinize my eye shadow. Maybe I should add a little more shimmer to my—

The door to the bathroom bursts wide open.

A black-clad figure in a ski mask lunges at me.

I shriek at the top of my lungs.

But before I can move or react beyond screaming in terror, the blackened figure grabs my hand and places something in my palm. I look down, my throat burning and my hand trembling. *A poker chip.* Holy shitballs. Every single drop of blood in my body whooshes into my crotch, all at once. Is it possible to have a heart attack and orgasm at the same time?

I look back up at the menacing figure in the ski mask, but before I can react further, he wraps me into a stifling bear hug, sending the unmistakable scent of Josh's cologne into my nostrils.

"No!" I shout, wiggling and squirming in my deliciously scented attacker's arms. "Let me go!"

But the brute won't be deterred. He grabs my wrists roughly and slaps soft cuffs on them, immobilizing me with his strong arms as he does.

"No!" I shout again, trying desperately to free myself from the dreaded cuffs. "Let me go!" I squirm and writhe with all my might, but, goddammit, I can't free myself from my bindings or my attacker's strong arms. (Yay!)

"No," I choke out, even though every fiber of my body wants to yell, "Yes, yes, yes!"

I feel something slipping over the top my head and then over my eyes (soft satin!) and suddenly everything goes completely black.

"Let me go!" I yell. "Right now!"

But the horrible man—or dare I say, the *horribly* sexy man?—doesn't stop. He lifts me completely off the ground, crushing my body against his, and, in a flash, I feel myself being carried out of the bathroom in long, delicious, cologne-infused strides.

"Please," I whimper. "Let me go."

He doesn't reply. He's carrying me in loping movements. I nuzzle my face into him and breathe in his sexy scent, my clit burning with intense arousal. This is incredible.

"Who are you? Why are you here?" I shout. Oh, God, he smells good. I'm already twitching with desire.

I hear a door opening. The sound of shoes on hard cement. There's the sound of a car door opening followed by the sensation of my body being laid down in an extremely small space. Oh fuck, no—Josh isn't putting me in the trunk of his car, is he? Oh shit.

"*From Justin to Kelly!*" I shriek.

His movement freezes.

"You're not putting me in the trunk of a car, are you?"

"No, babe," Josh's voice says soothingly. "I'm laying you down in the backseat of my Beemer."

I exhale. "Oh, okay. Whew. I get really claustrophobic—I should have mentioned that."

"Babe, I'd never put you in the trunk of a car. You could get hurt."

I exhale. "Okay. Whew."

"*Babe*. Come on. I'll never risk your safety."

I exhale with relief again. "Okay. Good. Thank you. Proceed."

"You okay?"

"Yeah. I'm great." I grin. "This is so awesome, Josh. Oh my God. When you burst into the bathroom, I had a freaking heart attack."

He laughs. "You should have seen the look on your face. Sorry if I scared you."

"No, no, it was a good kind of scared. I loved it. My panties are already soaked—or, then again, maybe that's pee."

He laughs. "Okay, you ready to keep going now?"

"Yeah. Sorry I pulled the safe word so fast. I won't do it again."

"No, no. Use the safe word as much as you need. That's what it's for. I never want you to be scared. This is supposed to be fun."

233

I exhale. "Okay. Thanks."

"Don't hesitate to use it if you need it, babe."

"Okay." I shake it off. "No more breaking character. Go, baby. I'm already totally wet for you."

He makes a sexual sound. "Don't tempt me to fuck you right here—I'm rock hard." His fingertips graze my thigh and slip inside my undies and then right into me. "Oh my God," he says. "You're soaking wet." His fingers massage me for a moment, making me writhe and moan.

I spread my legs, inviting him to fuck me right here and now.

"Oh my God," he says. "What am I doing? I've got a whole thing planned, babe. Stop being evil."

His fingers retreat from me, leaving me aching and wanting more.

I hear the unmistakable sound of him licking his finger vigorously. "You taste like sugar, baby. So sweet."

My clit jolts. "Josh," I breathe. "Take me now."

"Patience, babe," he says, his voice low and sexy. "You're in for a wild ride." The car door shuts and a moment later, I hear a car engine start.

We're unmistakably on the move.

After a few minutes of driving, music suddenly blares in the car—Britney Spears, "I'm a Slave 4 U"—and I burst out laughing.

Josh's laughter joins mine.

"Hilare," I say. "You're so funny, babe."

"Hey, you didn't say *From Justin to Kelly*," Josh says. "You gotta stay in character unless you say it."

"There's no way I can stay in character if you're gonna make 'I'm a Slave 4 U' the soundtrack of my abduction into sexual slavery."

"Just to be clear, there's no other circumstance when I'd ever play this song—this song is a testament to just how far I'll go for a laugh."

"Mission accomplished," I say.

"Okay, back in character now." The song switches to "Fever" by the Black Keys.

I sigh happily. "This is so frickin' awesome."

After what seems like forever, the car stops and the engine turns off. The driver's door opens—and then the car door nearest to me—and then I'm being lifted up by strong arms and carried like a sack of potatoes, my cuffed wrists dangling down.

Josh stops walking and shifts my body weight slightly. There's a beeping sound, and then the sound of a door opening. He walks several paces and it's clear to me we're now indoors.

Josh sets me down gently onto my feet. I wobble slightly—the blackness of my blindfold is disorienting—and he grasps my forearm just above my cuffs to steady me.

"You okay?" he whispers.

I nod.

"Hang on." I sense him moving away briefly and then returning to me. He grasps my forearm again and guides my body down. "Kneel," he commands at full voice, his tone menacing. My knees are met with a soft cushion. "I saw you walking down the sidewalk last week and I had to have you," he continues in his bad-guy voice. "I've brought you to a place far from civilization where no one can hear you scream. Do as I say or else—" He stops for a long beat. "Hey, babe. *From Justin to Kelly*. I can't do this part. It's making me think about my mom. I feel sick."

My stomach drops into my toes. "Oh, I didn't even think about that. I'm so sorry. Take off my blindfold."

"No, I'll be okay as long as we skip this first part. Let's just pretend I said all the shit necessary to get you under control—that I already crushed your spirit like a sex-slave-master would and made you totally submissive to me. Okay?"

"Are you sure? We can stop."

"No, I'm good as long as we skip this first part. I don't wanna threaten you."

"Okay. No problem. But if you decide you wanna stop, just lemme know."

"Okay." He exhales. "God, I wish you could see your nipples under your dress right now. They're like little bullets. So fucking sexy."

I lick my lips.

"Hey, why don't we get some music cranking?" he says. "That'll help loosen things up. Hang on."

I remain on my knees in the blackness, my cuffed arms dangling in front of me, wondering where the hell he's taken me.

After a brief moment, an old-school funk song fills my ears.

I feel Josh's body heat next to me again. "'Thank You For Letting Me Be Myself,'" Josh says. "Sly and the Family Stone—greatest funk band ever."

I've never heard this song before, but it's definitely got a great groove—my body's already involuntarily pulsing to the beat—and I can't imagine a better song to kick off our mutual sick-fuckedness than a tune called, "Thank You For Letting Me Be Myself."

I hear the sound of Josh's fly unzipping. "Open your mouth," he grunts.

I do as I'm told and warm flesh unexpectedly whacks me in the mouth. I flinch out of surprise.

"Lick my balls," he growls softly.

I smile. That was an extremely porno-y thing to say, especially with this awesome bow-chick-a-wow-wow-music blaring around us. And that's exactly what I wanted—to star in my own porno. Hell yeah. I stick out my tongue and do as I'm told—well, as best I can, anyway—I must say, without the use of my eyes or hands to help me with my task, licking and sucking on balls feels a bit like bobbing for dangling apples—but after a few minutes, I get the *hang* of it (snicker) and really start delivering some seriously excellent ball-licking-and-sucking, if I do say so myself.

"Good," Josh says after several minutes, his voice ragged. "Congratulations. You've just earned the right to suck my cock."

My clit flutters. "Thank you, sir," I purr. I open my mouth. It's watering with anticipation. Being Josh's slave is turning me on every bit as much as I fantasized it would.

I feel the sensation of Josh's wet tip resting against the subtle cleft in my chin (surprise!), followed by his shaft sliding into my open mouth, all the way to the back of my throat—so far, my eyes bug out behind my blindfold. Holy motherfucking shitballs. Good lord, that's a lot of dick all at once.

My throat closes up and I gag.

"Relax," Josh coos, running his hands through my hair. "Take a deep breath and relax your throat."

I breathe through my nose and focus on releasing my throat muscles, and sure enough, my throat opens up and Josh's cock slides farther into me. Holy Big Dick, Batman, Josh is so far inside my throat, I can't do a damned thing but sit here like a blowup-doll. This ain't no Katherine Morgan Ultimate Blowjob Experience, folks—this is nothing but Crack Whore Blowjob. I'm just a warm hole, for crying out loud—no skill or finesse required for this job. I can't suck or lick or swirl my tongue or finger or massage or do any of my other tricks. I could be anyone, really. Anything. It's demeaning, I tell you—dehumanizing. *And I love it.*

Josh lets out a particularly sexy sound and my body begins clenching furiously in reply—but my throat is so filled up, I barely make a sound.

He's rippling in my mouth. He's gonna blow. Oh my God. This is so effing sexy.

But, nope. He doesn't come. He pulls out of my mouth, instead.

I cough and sputter, trying to calm my raging throat muscles.

I can hear Josh breathing heavily. "Since you sucked my dick so well," he says, his voice ragged, "I'm gonna reward you by taking off your blindfold now."

"Thank you, sir," I squeak out in a scratchy voice. Oh my God. My throat is throbbing.

Josh's fingers slide into my hair and then, suddenly, the blindfold is off.

"Holy shitballs," I say, looking around and blinking in the soft light. "What the... ?"

"This is my *lair*," Josh says, obviously trying (but failing) to suppress a huge grin.

Oh my effing God, we're in a *bona fide* sex-dungeon—a glittering, gleaming BDSM dungeon like nothing I've ever seen or even imagined. I knew places like this existed, but this place is... well, out of a fantasy.

It's a large, windowless room with black marble floors. The walls are painted a deep chocolate brown. Gold and crystal chandeliers hang from the ceiling, along with an eye-popping assortment of cages, harnesses, whips, chains, pulleys, racks, and other suspended contraptions I couldn't identify if my life depended on it. There's an X-shaped, padded rack in the middle of the room. A system of pulleys in the far corner next to a bunch of studded leather straps. A neatly arranged assortment of leather riding crops and feathered rods sits prominently in the middle of the room. Oh, shit, what's that spherical cage-thing hanging from the ceiling? It looks like a birdcage for a very, very large canary.

"Come with me." Josh pulls me to standing and drags me across the room to a harness-looking-rack-contraption. Wordlessly, he unlatches my soft cuffs, strips off all my clothes, and straps me into bindings, spreading my limbs out into a four-pointed star. Oh my God. I'm completely opened up in this position—his for the taking, any which way he pleases.

My body is jolting with excitement.

"Relax into the bindings," Josh says, his voice full of smooth confidence. "They'll hold your weight."

I try to let myself relax, but I can't seem to do it.

"Take a deep breath," he commands, grazing his fingers across my belly. "And then let it out slowly."

I do as I'm told and allow myself to melt into my bindings—and, I'll be damned, just like he said, my limbs are being fully supported and held into place. I'm like a fly caught in a web. Immovable. Completely at his mercy. A little sound of arousal lurches out of my throat.

Josh peels off his clothes slowly, his blue eyes smoldering at me as he does, and stands in front of me, his erection straining, his muscles tense. "Your body is mine," he says.

"Yes, sir."

He looks me up and down for a moment, smiling wickedly. "Hmm. What shall I do to my slave first?"

I shudder.

He ambles over to a nearby rack and runs his hand along a selection of implements, finally selecting a long, feathered rod from the rack. When he returns to me, he's smiling devilishly.

"I had to have you," he says. "I couldn't go another day."

He lazily drifts the tickler over my breasts, belly, and hips, culling goose bumps out of every square inch it touches. I moan. He does it again. And then again. And then he leans into me and unexpectedly sucks on my hard nipple.

When I cry out with excitement, he reaches down and plunges his fingers inside me, making me jerk and jolt in my bindings.

"Dripping wet," he says softly. "Such a good girl."

At his words, as if right on cue, I feel a glob of wetness ooze out of my crotch like thick molasses and onto my thigh.

"Oh," he says. He brings his fingers to his mouth. "Delicious."

I let out a long, steady exhale.

Josh walks slowly around to my backside and begins tickling the backs of my thighs and ass with his feather.

I let out a little moan. I can't stand this anymore. I've never wanted a man as much as I want Josh right now. I shift my hips, desperate to relieve the pressure building inside me, but it's no use. I'm about to climax. I can feel it. I'm in pain with this ache.

The feather retreats.

A warm, wet tongue licks my ass, and just when I begin melting into the delicious pleasure, I feel a sharp pain on my ass cheek—the unmistakable sensation of being bitten.

I shriek and jerk in my bindings.

He chuckles.

"Jesus," I mutter.

His tongue returns to my backside and begins exploring every inch of my ass as his fingers slide to my clit and wetness and begin working me with astonishing skill. Oh shit. I've never been touched like this before. Where'd he learn to do this? Oh my fuck. His tongue is lapping at me from behind while his fingers are *owning* me. I want to writhe, but I can't. I want to shift to relieve myself of the pressure building inside me, but I'm completely immobile.

"Fuck!" I say through gritted teeth. "Fuck, fuck. Oh my God. *Fuck.*"

My body suddenly wracks with a twisting orgasm and I jerk against my bindings like a fish out of water.

Before my orgasm ends, I feel Josh rising up behind me. There's the unmistakable sound of fluid splooging out of a bottle and then a finger sliding up my asshole. I shudder. Oh my effing God. He wraps his arms around me from behind, cleaves himself to my back, grabs ahold of my breasts with lubed palms, and slides his slick cock up my ass, eliciting a low groan from deep inside me.

"I own you," he growls into my ear, his voice strained.

I'm incapable of replying. I've tried anal before, but not like this—not when I'm completely sober (and therefore feeling every goddamned inch). Not when I'm bound and trussed like a pig on a spit in a goddamned sex dungeon. Not when the dick in question is a freaking donkey-dick, not to mention attached to the sexiest fucking slab of man I've ever seen—who just so happened to abscond with me out of a bathroom while wearing a freaking ski mask.

I moan loudly.

"I'm gonna make you come so hard," he says into my ear. "Harder than you ever have."

I groan. This is too intense. I'm not sure I can handle this. I thought I could, but it might be too much, even for a dirty little freak like me.

"Beg me for more," he whispers into my ear. "I'm not in all the way yet."

There's *more*? Holy fucking hell. This sure feels like all of him.

"Beg me," he grits out.

"More. *Please*," I choke out, even though I'm not sure I can handle it.

He gives me what I've asked for and I inhale sharply in shock—but before I can exhale my breath, something glides inside my vagina and begins vibrating from deep inside me. Oh my fuck. My breathing is shallow. I'm like a pug with heatstroke. Oh my God. There's more. Something begins swiping at my clit like a tongue. Oh Jesus. He's using some kind of rabbit vibe on me. Oh my fuckity fuck. I let out a strangled cry. I've never been filled up like this, stimulated in every conceivable way all at once. I feel like my body's scattering in a thousand directions, all at once, exploding and melting at the same time. Too much. No more. Can't handle. Gah.

Josh pumps his donkey-dick harder inside me while the vibe does its thing.

"Oh fuck," he says, his voice ragged. "*Fuck.*"

Yeah. My thoughts exactly.

One of his hands gropes my breast and pinches my nipple so hard, I shriek, and just like that, my body spasms violently with pleasure so intense, I dry heave. Oh shit, I've never done that before. Oh God. I do it again. I'm losing complete control of my bodily functions. I feel like I'm gonna barf. Or pee. Or crap myself. Or all of the above. I've never felt this much intense pleasure all at once. My body can't handle it. It's going completely haywire. My insides are twisting violently. It's like the pleasure is literally tying me into knots. I make a strangled, gagging sound, followed by a whimper. And then another shriek. But Josh doesn't stop. In fact, he fucks me harder.

I jerk pathetically, trying to escape the clenching pleasure that's brutalizing me, but my bindings hold me firmly in place.

"No more," I yell. "I can't do it. Stop." I have never in the history of my life said these words during sex. But this extreme pleasure—or is it pain?—is just too much for me to endure. I can't function. I can't survive it. "*Stop*," I say. "*Stop*."

But Josh doesn't stop. In fact, his thrusts are becoming even deeper, if that were possible, and even more passionate.

He bites my shoulder so hard, I'm sure he's broken the skin.

I shriek again and convulse like he's electrocuted me.

"You're *mine*," he breathes.

Warm liquid suddenly (and shockingly) gushes out of me in a torrent. I convulse again and again, enraptured and tormented in equal measure, crying out for relief but getting none. I dry heave again. And then finally, mercifully, my body goes completely slack. I hang my head and a drop of sweat—or is that a tear?—falls down the tip of my nose and to the ground. Holy crap.

Josh quickly unties my wrists and I crumple into his arms, shaking and twitching.

His lips press against my ear. "Did I hurt you?"

I shake my head.

"Did it feel good?"

I nod.

He picks me up and carries me into a small bathroom with red walls and gold fixtures. He sets me down gently. "Can you hold onto the counter for a second?" he asks.

I nod.

He turns on the water in the shower and then guides me under the warm stream.

"You're sure I didn't hurt you?" he asks. "I think I got carried away."

I shake my head.

"You told me to stop, but you didn't use the safe word."

"I didn't want you to stop. I'm glad you didn't stop. Only stop if I use the safe word."

He kisses my mouth and pulls me into him gently, letting the warm water rain down on us. "You're sure you're okay?"

"It was amazing."

He washes me from head to toe, and when he's done, guides me out of the shower and dries me off. "Stay here," he commands. "I have something for you."

I nod and wait. I'm shaking like I've just run a marathon.

He's gone quite a while, it seems, and when he returns, he's fully dressed and holding up a white satin nightie. "Lift up your arms," he commands.

I do as I'm told and he slips the nightie over my head and onto my body. I'm confused as to why he's dressing me rather than keeping me naked, but I'm too fried to give it much thought.

"Come." He grabs my hand and pulls me out of the bathroom and back into the dungeon. Everything's been cleaned—there's no sign of my messy orgasm and absolutely nothing out of place. He guides me to a bed in the corner, lays me onto my back, and wordlessly secures bindings around my wrists and ankles.

"You don't have to tie me up anymore," I say, pulling against my bindings. "I won't try to escape."

"No. I can't risk losing you," he says simply.

A wave of glee washes over me. I know he's simply following my script, but those words make my skin buzz, nonetheless.

"I'm not tricking you," I coo. "I didn't run when you left me alone in the bathroom, did I? You can trust me."

He pauses, mulling that over. "No," he finally says. "I can't risk it. You're a *unicorn*." He shoots me a snarky look, obviously proud of himself for deftly inserting that little gem into our scene. "I can't risk it."

"Please."

He sets his jaw. "No. Now that I know what it's like to have you, I don't think I can live without you."

My heart stops. Was that in the script? Or did Josh say that in real life?

"What's your name?" I ask.

He makes a face like I've just asked him to spell *antideluvian.* "Um," he says, apparently pondering the question. "Joshua Faraday," he finally says.

That's not at all what I expected him to say. I thought he'd come up with some exotic sex-slave-master name like Magnusson Carmichael III. For my part, I've certainly planned a sexy name and backstory—I'm an heiress named Chantel Giodissimo—but, jeez, if Josh is going to be himself for our role-plays, then I should do the same. And, in fact, now that I'm thinking about it, it's probably better if we just "be ourselves," just like the song says.

"Hi, Joshua," I say softly. "I'm Katherine Morgan. It's nice to meet you. I sure wish we'd met under different circumstances than you breaking into my house and absconding with me."

Josh smirks. "*Absconding* with you?"

I grin. "Yeah. *Absconding.* And you gave me a freaking heart attack when you did it, by the way. Oh my God."

He flashes an adorable grin. "I'm sorry, Katherine. I didn't mean to scare you when I *absconded* with you. It's just that when I saw you walking down the sidewalk the other day, I had to have you." He glances at the clock and I follow his gaze. It's a few minutes to ten. He trains his beautiful blue eyes back on me. "Please forgive me if I scared you."

"I forgive you. You've given me intense pleasure, Joshua— pleasure I couldn't have imagined."

His beautiful eyes are smoldering at me.

"Will you untie me, Joshua?" I ask softly.

He shakes his head. "I can't. You'll run away. And if I lose you, I'll be wrecked."

My heart lurches into my throat. He sounds so earnest. I can't tell if that was Joshua Faraday the Sex-Slave-Master speaking—or Joshua William Faraday?

I open my mouth to tell him I'd be wrecked if I lost him, too, but before I can say a word, the door to the dungeon swings wide open and a slender figure wearing a ski mask bursts into the room.

I shriek in surprise and pull violently on my bindings.

"I've come to steal her away," a woman's voice says in a lackluster monotone. She holds up a plastic sword. "I saw her and I had to have her."

I look at Josh with wide-eyed astonishment and he bursts out laughing.

The masked intruder lowers her sword and shifts her weight, her body language conveying total annoyance.

"*From Justin to Kelly,*" I say. "Who the heck is this poor woman, Josh?"

Josh wipes his eyes and motions to the masked figure. "Kat, this is Kaitlyn—she owns this place. Kaitlyn's one of the top Dommes in Los Angeles."

"*The* top," Kaitlyn corrects. "If I do say so myself."

"Sorry. *The* top. You can take off your mask, Kaitlyn. Oh my God. This is so fucking hilarious."

Kaitlyn removes her mask to reveal a very attractive woman, with brown hair and dark, piercing eyes, in her early forties or so.

"Hi," Kaitlyn says to me calmly. "I'm here to steal you away and make you my sex slave."

I giggle. "Nice to meet you, Kaitlyn." I jut my chin at my wrist restraint. "Sorry I can't wave hello. So you're here to fight to the death for me, huh?"

Josh is still laughing. "Oh my God, this is so ridiculous. I'm sorry, Kaitlyn, I should have listened to you."

Kaitlyn rolls her eyes.

"I'm so sorry, babe. I didn't think it would be this lame. I thought it would be fun and silly, but not *lame*."

"It's adorable. I love it. You thought of everything."

"I was originally thinking about hiring a stuntman and choreographing a whole big thing with pyrotechnics, but the logistics just seemed crazy. There would have been, like, twenty people involved, and I didn't think you'd like that."

"Good call," I say, laughing. "Embarrassing myself in front of Kaitlyn here is plenty."

Kaitlyn shrugs. "Don't be embarrassed. My whole life is about helping people fulfill their fantasies. This is a first, I admit, but, hey."

"Thank you," I say. "So what do you say we press fast-forward on the sword fight? Pretend you two have already fought and Kaitlyn lost?"

Kaitlyn nods and looks to Josh for confirmation.

"Hell no," Josh says. He reaches down next to the bed and pulls out a plastic sword to match Kaitlyn's. "We gotta have a sword fight, babe—I don't care if it's ridiculous, it's in your script. We gotta follow the script."

Kaitlyn and I exchange a look.

"Okay," she says. She begrudgingly holds up her sword. "I'm here to steal her away and make her my sex-slave."

I giggle. This is utterly ridiculous. A travesty. I absolutely love it.

Josh leaps up from the bed, on the attack. "*En guarde!*" he shouts.

For a few minutes, Josh and Kaitlyn whack each other's swords like pre-schoolers on a playground while Josh shouts lines from *Princess Bride*, until, finally, Kaitlyn falls into a chair with a sword shoved into her armpit and dies.

"Let this be a lesson to any man who tries to *abscond* with what's mine," Josh says, standing over Kaitlyn's body. "Fuck you, all of you. She's mine."

A ripple of pleasure zings through my body. It's ridiculous, yes—but it's freaking hot, too. The boy has put a lot of effort and thought into making my silly fantasy come to life. I can't help but swoon.

Kaitlyn opens her eyes. "So... Is that it, then?"

"Yeah. That'll do it." Josh helps her up. "Thanks again for everything, Kaitlyn. You're a trooper. Now be gone!" He laughs.

Kaitlyn shakes her head. "Have fun, you two. Now that I've seen you in action, I totally get it. You're total goofballs." She smiles for the first time since she stepped foot in the room and turns toward the door. "Be sure to turn out the lights and lock up when you go."

"Will do," Josh says. "Thanks again."

"Thank you!" I call out to Kaitlyn's back just before she slips out the door.

Josh turns to me. "How cool was that? I just had a sword fight with a real-life dominatrix."

"How'd you hook up with her?" I ask, an alarming thought beginning to creep into my head. "Is she a *friend* of yours?"

Josh rolls his eyes. "Cool your jets, Madame Terrorist. Kaitlyn's a friend of Reed's. I've never used her services." He laughs. "And to answer your next question, no, Reed's not a client of hers, either. They're just friends. Reed knows everyone in L.A.—well, anyone who's interesting." He beams a huge smile at me. "So, my sexy little sex-slave, are you ready to keep going with our porno? We've still got the third and final act to perform, you may recall: The Big Reveal."

I smile broadly. "Ooh la la. The Revelation. Yes."

"Any last words before we get back into character?"

I think for a minute. There are definitely words I'm dying to say to Josh, three little words to be exact, but I can't do it. They're magic words a girl simply can't be the first to say in a relationship.

"Nope. I'm good," I say. "Proceed."

"Quiet on the porn set!" Josh yells over his shoulder to an imaginary crew. "And... *action.*" He crawls onto the bed and cups my cheek in his palm. "Are you hungry, Katherine?"

"Yes, Master Joshua. Starving."

Josh reaches down next to the bed, retrieves a small cooler, and pulls out a sandwich in a Ziplock baggie.

"Aw," I say. "*From Justin to Kelly.* You made me an orgasm-inducing peanut butter and jelly sandwich? So sweet."

"Wouldn't want my sex-slave going hungry." He grins. "I've got an apple and some chips for you, too, if you want 'em."

"You're the sweetest sex-slave-master, ever. Thank you. I was ready to eat my hand when we got back from hiking. Now I'm ready to eat both arms."

He breaks off a bite-sized piece of the sandwich and feeds it to me.

"Whoa," I say, chewing the sandwich with gusto. "You told the truth—I just came."

Josh laughs.

"Why is this sandwich so good? Did you lace it with something illegal?"

"Nope. Just organic strawberry jam."

He feeds me another bite.

"This sandwich is so frickin' good," I say, "it's giving me *Munchausen* syndrome."

Josh chuckles. "No, babe. Not *Munchausen* syndrome. That's when you poison someone slowly just so you can keep being their caretaker."

"Oh." I giggle.

He chuckles. "You're so cute."

"So what did I mean, then?"

"*Stockholm* syndrome, I think."

"Is that where someone held captive falls in love with their captor?" I ask.

246

"Yeah," he says.

"Okay, then, yeah. That's what I have for sure."

We both stare at each other for an awkward beat.

Oh shit. I think I just told Josh I'm in love with him.

He feeds me another bite of sandwich but doesn't say anything for a long beat.

"Water?" he finally asks, his voice tight.

"What?" My cheeks feel flushed. I just told him I love him in a clever sort of backhanded-code, didn't I?

Josh holds up the water bottle. "Thirsty?"

"Oh. Yeah. Thank you."

He holds the bottle to my lips and I take a long guzzle, my heart racing. Damn. I wish I'd told him more clearly than that, in a way that would have left no doubt. I shouldn't have been so subtle. I should have said, "This sandwich is so good, *it made me fall deeply in love with you, Joshua William Faraday*." But I didn't. I left it vague. "Yeah, that's what I have," I said—and nothing more. Idiot. And now the moment has passed.

"Chips?" Josh asks.

"What kind?"

"Doritos." He holds up a little red bag. "Original flavor."

"Thank you."

He pops a chip into my mouth and then into his own. "Fuck you, Jonas—I eat what I want—although I must admit I feel kinda bad I'm chowing down on Doritos while gourmet meals are sitting in my fridge."

"How about we eat Jonas' food tomorrow night?" I say. "We can stay in and rent a movie."

"Awesome. Yeah, a quiet night at home with my Party Girl with a Hyphen sounds damned good. More water, babe?"

I shake my head. "I'm good. I'm done."

"You ready to keep going with the porno?"

I nod.

"Cool. I've got my entire speech ready for act three." He stows the remaining food in the cooler. "Give me my cue, babe," he says softly. "I'm gonna slay it."

I clear my throat. "Untie me, Joshua," I whisper. "I don't want to be a prisoner anymore. I need my freedom."

Josh touches my cheek tenderly. "Katherine, when I *absconded* with you, all I cared about was making you mine, through any means necessary. All I cared about was what I wanted. But now, even though I want you more than ever, I care too much about you to keep you as my prisoner anymore. Now the thing I want more than my own happiness is yours." He touches the cleft in my chin.

Holy Exploding Heart, Batman. Not To Mention Ovaries. I know Josh was merely following the loose script I babbled to him in Las Vegas, but he delivered his lines with such breathtaking sincerity, my heart seems to have lost its ability to discern fantasy from reality.

"Hang on," he says. He gets up and walks behind the bed, outside of my field of vision. I strain against my bindings. What's he doing? He's supposed to untie me now and ravage me as a free woman.

A song begins playing over the sound system and my heart stops. Holy shitballs. He's cued up "If You Ever Want To Be In Love" by James Bay—the song that made Josh literally bolt out of his bedroom when it came on last night. Oh my effing God.

Josh returns to the bed. His clothes are off and his hard-on is massive. He sits on the edge of the bed, gazing at me with smoldering eyes, and slowly begins untying me.

Holy shitballs.

The minute I'm free, he pulls my nightie and underwear off my body and guides me onto his lap and straight onto his erection. I take him into me and wrap my thighs around his waist, throw my arms around his neck, and ride him feverishly, spurred on by the song—and especially what it means that he's decided to play it for me in this magical moment.

"Don't leave me," Josh whispers, cradling me in his arms, fucking me, caressing me, kissing my face.

I'm lost in him. I gyrate my hips on top of him and smash my breasts against his muscled chest, desperately trying to press my beating heart against his.

"Josh," I breathe. I can barely push air into my lungs. I'm gasping for air, suddenly overcome by a surge of energy coursing between us.

I want him. I need him. *I love him.*

"Don't go," he says. "Stay with me."

"I'm not going anywhere," I breathe. "Oh, Josh. I'm all yours."

Chapter 31
Kat

For the past kajillion hours, Josh and I have been sitting on his black leather couch, smoking weed and listening to the Black Keys (the current song is "Tighten Up") and semi-watching our favorite scenes from our favorite movies (on mute)—*Twenty-One Jump Street, Zoolander, Happy Gilmore, Anchorman, Harold and Kumar, This is the End,* and selected episodes of *Parks & Recreation,* too. And while we've availed ourselves of the aforementioned samplings of musical and comedic genius, Josh and I have also been voraciously gobbling down every single morsel of the gourmet, healthy meals supplied by Josh's ever-so-thoughtful and fitness-conscious brother.

Oh, and perhaps I should mention we've done all of the above-mentioned activities in our birthday suits.

Oh, and perhaps I should also mention "eating" Jonas' gourmet, healthy meals has actually entailed licking, nibbling, and slurping food off each other's stomachs and thighs, and out of each other's belly buttons, and, yes, okay, if you really must know, off of (or out of) each other's most sensitive places.

I take a long drag on the joint Josh offers me and blow the smoke into his face in a steady, controlled stream. Man, I'm stoned. Stoned out of my mind. Fred-Flintstoned. Emma Stoned. Sharon Stoned. Rolling Stoned. Sly Stalloned. Oh, wait, no. That last one doesn't really work. I think I meant Sly and the Family Stoned? Wasn't that the funk band Josh introduced me to yesterday in the sex dungeon? Well, in any event, let's just say tonight I've definitely become a naturalized citizen of the peaceful and munchie-eating land of Estonia. I burst out laughing.

"What?" Josh asks, his eyes glazed over.

"I dunno. It was funny, though."

"God, you're beautiful," Josh coos, obviously feeling rather Oliver Stoned himself. "I could look at your gorgeous face forever." He leans forward, grabs my face, and kisses me deeply.

"You said *forever*," I say into his lips, smiling.

"What?"

"I didn't know your mouth was capable of uttering that word."

"You must have misheard me. I don't even know that strange word. What I actually said was, '*Florebblaaaah.*'"

I roll my eyes.

Josh flashes me a goofy grin. "Aw, come on, baby. My douchebaggery is my charm."

"Mmm hmm."

He sighs audibly. "Oh, Kat, Kat, *gorgeous* Kat. Are you gonna wait for me or not, Gorgeous, Stubborn Kat?"

"Hmm? Sure, I'll wait." I grab the remote control and pause the movie, freezing Michael Cera grabbing Rihanna's ass in *This Is the End*. "Go ahead." I motion toward the bathroom.

"No, no. I don't mean wait for me to go to the *bathroom*. I wanna know if you're gonna wait for *me*?"

I stare at him for a long beat. "You mean *florebblaaahhhhhh*?"

He doesn't reply.

"Dude, what are you talking about?"

He bristles. "Never mind." He grabs a bottle of Patron from the floor next to him and takes a swig.

My stomach twists. How does this man make me feel so freaking good and so flippin' insecure all at the same time? Last night in the sex dungeon, after he'd untied me, Josh made love to me so passionately, so *urgently,* I felt that crazy electricity coursing between us again—that same supernatural electricity as the prior night in Josh's bed—and I thought my heart was gonna burst with joy. But, afterwards, did we talk about what we were both so obviously feeling toward each other? Nooooope. Of course not. Because, it seems, talking about our 'fucking feelings' is off limits with Joshua William Faraday.

"You mean will I wait for you to pull your head out of your ass?" I ask.

"Yeah," Josh says without hesitation. "Exactly."

"Yeah, I'll wait. You're definitely worth the wait."

He smiles broadly. "Thank you." He hands me the bottle of tequila.

"But I won't wait three fucking years, I'm telling you that right now, motherfucker." I take a swig from the bottle.

"Well, how long will you wait, then?" he asks.

"I dunno. It depends."

"On what?"

"On what happens between now and then," I say.

He nods. "That's a very deep statement, Kitty Katherine." He runs his hand through his hair and I'm assaulted with the words "Welcome to" flashing me from underneath his bicep. "Hand over the tequila, babe."

I hand him the bottle and he takes a swig.

"I've never done this with a woman before," he says.

"Done what?"

Josh motions to the tequila and the half-eaten food and the TV. "Partied with a girl like she's a dude."

"You call eating vegan creamed spinach out of my cooch 'partying like a dude'?"

He bursts out laughing. "You're so fucking funny, Kum Shot. You're as funny as any of my friends. Funnier."

"Yeah, I'm hilare. And don't call me Kum Shot."

"I could do anything with you and have fun. We could go to the fucking dry cleaners and it would be fun."

"Dude, who wouldn't have fun at the dry cleaners? Those motorized racks are rad. Or here's an idea," I say. "We could go to the fish market and sing the 'Fish Heads' song. Now *that* would be fun."

"I don't know the 'Fish Heads' song."

"No? Are you kidding me?"

He shakes his head.

"Well, shit, boy, Google it now. Search 'Fish Head song YouTube.'" I lean back into the leather couch and spread my naked legs wide, surrendering completely to the chemicals coursing through my bloodstream. "You're welcome, motherfucker."

"I like it when you say motherfucker," he says.

"Motherfucker."

"Sexy."

"Come on, Joshua. Google. 'Fish Heads.' Song. YouTube."

Josh grabs his phone off the table and the moment the unmistakable vocals begin, he laughs his ass off—which, of course, makes me laugh, too.

"How did I not know about this?" Josh asks when the song ends. "Best song ever. Oh my God. When I visit you in Seattle next weekend, I'm gonna take you to Pike's Place Market just so we can sing this song at the top of our lungs."

"At the stall at the very end? Where the guys throw the fish?"

"Of course."

"Aw, that sounds like a fun date. You really know how to razzle-dazzle a girl, Playboy."

"I told you that from day one, didn't I? I said, 'Get ready for the Playboy Razzle-Dazzle.' But did you believe me? Noooooo."

"Oh, I believed you. I just *pretended* not to believe you."

"What was the point of doing that, may I ask? You knew how our story was gonna end. Why torture me?"

I shrug. "I had no idea how our story was gonna end—I still don't."

"You don't?"

"No. Do you?"

He pauses. "No, actually. I thought I did. But now I realize I only knew the ending of the first chapter—not the ending of the *story.*"

"What's the ending of the first chapter?" I ask.

"We fuck like rabbits."

"Oh, that's a good ending." I exhale. "Well, if I tortured you in Vegas, then I'm not sorry. You were too frickin' cocky for your own damn good. You had to be taken down a peg."

"Ha! Liar. You were dying to get into my pants from minute one. You were like, 'Gimme your application, Playboy!' And I was like, 'I'm gonna fuck you first and *then* give it to you, Party Girl!' And you were like, 'Yippee! Yes! Please fuck me!'"

"Is that what I sound like? A chipmunk?"

"Yeah, and I sound like Mr. T. 'I pity the fool!'"

"Well, you're delusional. You were the one dying to get into *my* pants. When I kissed Henn, you practically had a stroke."

252

"Ooph. Totally. But the worst was thinking about you with Cameron Fucking Schulz." He grunts. "Even stoned, thinking about him fucking you makes me wanna break that guy's Captain-America-fucking-face. No one touches my Party Girl with a Hyphen but me. Fuckin' A." He swigs from his bottle again.

I bite my lip. "Wow. Sounds pretty serious, dude."

He bites his lip in mimicry of my gesture. "It just might be."

"It *might* be?" I ask coyly.

"Yeah. It *might* be."

"Can't I at least get a *probably* out of you?"

Josh makes a face that says, "Sorry, come back later."

I scrunch up my face. "You suck balls, Josh. You suck big ol' donkcy balls. God, you piss me off." I grunt loudly.

"Whoa! Where'd Stubborn Kat come from all of a sudden? Don't stress me out, Stubborn Kat. This is a stress-free zone. I'm chillaxing."

I glare at him.

He flashes a toothy grin. "I'm a drifter, baby. It's part of my charm." He flexes his arm and kisses his bicep. "You know you can't get enough of me."

"Yeah. Pretty sure I can. Pretty sure I just did."

He laughs. "Aw, why you so mad all of a sudden, Stubborn Kat? What'd I do to piss you off this time?"

I grunt with exasperation. "Why the *fuck* do you even have a calendar-app on your goddamned phone, Josh? That's what I wanna know. You can't keep straight what you've got planned for the next *week*? Hmm?"

"What?" He laughs. "You're making zero sense. I have no idea what you're talking about."

I huff. "It doesn't matter. Blah, blah, blaaaaaaaaaaaaaah."

"What are you ranting about, you nutjob?"

"Never mind. Forget it."

"Okay. Forgetting is something I'm good at." He looks around at the half-eaten trays of food around us. "You hungry again, babe?"

"Hmm. I might be able to eat a little something-something."

"Green beans? Some sort of squash-thing? What's your pleasure, Party Girl?'

"Squash *a la dick*, please," I say.

"Excellent selection." He smears himself with a trail of veggies from his tattooed chest down to his tattooed waistline and then down his dick and balls—and then he lies back, his arms behind his head, his muscles bulging, his douche-y underarm tattoos on full, douche-y-McDouche-y-pants-display, and flashes me a lascivious grin. *"Bon appetit, beau bébé."*

Without hesitation, I lean in and lick up every morsel of food off his pecs and abs and his "Overcome" tattoo and finally work my way downtown—and I'm not even the slightest bit grossed out as I do any of it. In fact, I find the entire experience highly enjoyable. When every crevice, ridge, crease, bulge, wrinkle, and fold of him is clean as a whistle, I continue licking and sucking on his hard-on for quite some time, doing my damnedest to give him the Katherine Morgan Ultimate Blowjob Experience, but although Josh seems to be enjoying himself tremendously, he doesn't seem even close to climaxing.

"Dude. That is some serious stamina," I finally say, sitting up and loosening my jaw. "Are you made of steel?"

"Sorry, babe. I'm too stoned to come. It feels amazing, though. But, yeah, you could stick a Dyson on there and I'm not gonna blow. Sorry." He laughs and pulls me into him for a kiss. "Jesus, Kat. You're so fucking beautiful, you make me wanna punch a professional athlete."

I laugh. "You're so fucking beautiful, you make me wanna roll you in Nutella and lick you from head to toe."

"Will you please remind me to buy a huge jar of Nutella tomorrow?"

"Sure thing. As long as you remind *me* to remind *you* to buy a huge jar of Nutella tomorrow."

We laugh hysterically.

"Shit," Josh says. "I can barely remember my own name right now. I'm so fucking high."

"Your name is Joshua William Faraday and you're the sexiest man alive."

"Thank you, Katherine Ulla Morgan. You're the most gorgeous woman I've ever laid eyes on. And you're smart and sweet and funny, too. Best girl ever, ever, ever. *Florebblaaaaaaaaaaaaah.*"

"Wow. Can you write my eulogy, please?"

"No, because I don't want you to die. People always seem to die around me and I hate it."

I make a sad face. "I'm sorry."

"It's okay. I'm over it. Just please don't die, Kat."

"I'm totally down for that plan—I promise to live florebblaaaaaaah."

"Cool. Let's live florebblaaaah, just you and me. We'll eat healthy, gourmet food sent to us by my dear brother and we'll fulfill each other's sick-fuck-fantasies and we'll be happy, happy, happy florebblaaaaaah."

"Okay. Cool. Where will we live and be happy, happy, happy florebblaaaaaah?"

"Seattle, of course. Where else?"

I sigh wistfully. "That would be amazing. I wish we both lived in Seattle so bad."

"'Twould be amazing," Josh says. "Hey, did I mention you're sweet? Because you are."

"Yep. That's what you said."

"And you're smart, too."

"Yep. That's me. Sweet and smart." I snort. "That's what everyone always says about me."

"You don't think you're sweet and smart?"

I pause. "I think I'm sweet with the people I care about, but you're not gonna hear anyone say, 'Oh, that Kat—she never says an unkind word about anyone.'"

We both laugh at the ridiculousness of anyone saying that about me.

"And I'd say I'm *witty*. Sometimes *clever*. Often *diabolical*. But, no, based on my college transcripts, not particularly *smart*."

"Fuck that shit. You're smart. Which is why your new company's gonna kick ass. Speaking of which, when are you gonna quit your job and stop waffling?"

"I dunno. It's one thing to have a faraway dream about something you *might* wanna do 'one day' and another to all of a sudden be expected to make it happen overnight." I shrug. "Maybe I'm not as *entrepreneurial* as I thought. Damn, that's a big word."

"What are you afraid of?"

I make a "duh" face. "Failure."

"Bah. Fuck failure. It's what happens right before success." He flexes and kisses his arm again. "I should know. I've failed a lot."

I purse my lips, unconvinced.

"Don't be scared. I'll help you. You can't fail with the muscle and charm of Joshua William Faraday behind you." He flexes his other arm and kisses it.

"Yeah, as long as I don't need help in, say, a *month*?"

He makes a face of pure annoyance.

"Seriously, thanks for the offer," I say. "I appreciate it. It's just a huge decision—definitely not one to make while high as a kite." I pause, not remembering what I was just about to say. "This is only the fourth time I've smoked pot in my whole life. Did I tell you that? Last time was in college. I haven't done this in *florebblaaaaaaah*."

"Really? A party girl like you? I'm shocked."

"Well, Sarah's the one who named me 'Party Girl with the Heart of Gold,' don't forget. Everything's relative, I guess—compared to Sarah, I'm Keith Richards."

He laughs.

"So do you smoke a lot, Playboy? You seem much more composed than I am right now—your tolerance must be pretty high."

"Nah, these days hardly ever. I've just got too much shit to do to put my brain on mental lockdown for hours on end. Back in the day, though? Oh my God. I was baked my entire first year at UCLA. I'm shocked I didn't get kicked out of school, I was such a fucking screw-up. I finally cleaned myself up that first summer, thank God—and then I had a bit of a wobble again right after graduation, before I'd figured out what the fuck to do with myself—but then I finally pulled myself together for good at twenty-four. That's when Jonas suggested I open an L.A. office of Faraday & Sons. I followed his advice and it was exactly what I needed—it gave me some purpose in my life."

"How did you pull yourself together that first summer?"

"I went to Jonas Rehab. We backpacked together through Asia and some other places that summer. Funny thing was, Jonas had just gotten out of the psych hospital, and I was supposedly on that trip to help *him*—but he's the one who helped me, by far."

"How? What'd he do?"

"He was just Jonas. There's nothing like being around Jonas Patrick Faraday and his constant 'pursuit of excellence' to make a guy realize he's a total flop-dick."

"Is that when you got your dragon tattoo? You said you got it in Bangkok, 'drunk and high as a kite.'"

"Damn, you've got a good memory."

"I remember everything you've told me."

"Yeah, it was on that trip—about a week in. Remember how in the beginning of *The Karate Kid* he starts off being a little punk? That was me the first week of my trip with Jonas. We'd been climbing all week and I was like, 'I'm sick of this wax-on-wax-off shit, man; I wanna party,' so I flew Reed and some homeys into Bangkok while I left my dorky brother to climb more rocks on his own up north." Josh shakes his head. "I was such a little prick to leave Jonas like that— such a total fucking douchebag. Inexcusable." He sighs. "So, anyway, when Jonas and I met up again a few days later in Cambodia, I knew I'd fucked up, and I just was like, 'Okay, Mr. Miyagi, I'm ready now. Teach me the art of *karate.*'"

I laugh.

"Jonas had just come from climbing all alone for days and he was this savage *beast*—just, like, oh my God, this golden god—and I looked like something the cat barfed up. I took one look at Jonas, and one look at my pitiful self, and realized it was time for me to stop being a total asswipe-douchebag-waste-of-space. And that was that. Jonas and I became this unstoppable duo—two savage beasts crushing it across three continents. The Faraday Twins. The ladies never stood a chance." He laughs.

I snicker. "Oh, I bet. I can only imagine how women across three continents soaked their panties over The Faraday Twins."

"Oh, shit, it was like stealing candy from a baby. Well, actually, not at first because Jonas was the biggest dork in the entire fucking universe." He rolls his eyes. "But, oh my fuck, even when Jonas was a total train wreck, women still practically threw themselves at the guy everywhere we went. Once, this woman was sitting next to Jonas at this bar, and when she got up to leave, she left her room key in front of him. And Jonas stood up and held up the key and shouted to her across the bar, 'Excuse me, ma'am! You forgot your room key!'" Josh buckles over laughing. "Classic Jonas. But then I started coaching him and he got way better. The trick was not letting him talk—making him the 'something shiny.' That was always our best strategy." He winks.

I laugh. "Josh, you're not exactly the 'something dull,' you know."

"Meh, I'm a good-looking guy—I'm not gonna pretend I don't know that. But Jonas is, like, supernatural. People always fall all over themselves when he walks into a room. He's just got this weird magic about him no one can resist. I think it's the fact that he's obviously so fucked up. People love that shit."

"Well, I think you're every bit as magical and fucked-up as your brother and then some."

He laughs.

"I'm serious. I swear to God, if I'd been one of the girls who encountered you and Jonas during your travels, I would have gone for *you*, hands down."

"Really?"

"Heck yeah. You've got that mischief in your eyes I can't resist. Jonas is sweet and crazy, but you're the bad boy—and I can never resist a bad boy."

"Oh yeah? I'm a bad boy, huh?" He runs his fingertips up my bare thigh.

"Oh, yeah," I say.

"Well, guess what? This bad boy's suddenly hungry again, baby. You got any sweet potatoes over there? I'm thinking about macking down on some sweet potatoes *a la pussy*."

"Oooh, sounds delish." I smear the requested food all over my pelvic bone and clit. "*Bon appetit, monsieur.*"

Josh leans down and laps up the mashed potatoes off my pelvis, making me writhe, and then he devours my clit like a starving man on a Snickers bar. It feels insanely awesome, but there's just no way I'm gonna reach orgasm.

After a while, Josh sits up from between my legs and stares at me. "Nothing?"

I shake my head. "Feels fantastic, but I can't get there. Too stoned."

He leans back. "Well, at least we look good, huh, PG?"

"Damn straight, we do, PB." I flex my bicep and kiss it.

Josh laughs. "Okay, it's official," he says. "This sucks. No more weed for you. It's been fun and all, super-duper fun, you're hilarious—but it's now abundantly clear I'm the idiot who turned a Ferrari into a fucking lawnmower. I should be taken into the woods and shot for doing that."

I shrug. "You didn't do it. I'm the one who sucked on the joint."

"No, I'm the one who pulled it out and said, 'Hey, PG, ya wanna?' But I've officially learned my lesson. From here on out, I'll never do anything ever again to keep my beautiful Ferrari from hitting top racing speeds like she was built to do."

I sigh. "Probably for the best. But we had fun, though, didn't we?"

"Fuck yeah, we did. Good times were had by all." He smirks. "So, hey, PG, whaddaya say we take a shower and clean all the spinach and sweet potato out of your cooch and then roll around naked in my bed for a while? I wanna see if I can get my little Ferrari's engine revving to full-throttle again, against all odds."

"Sounds fun."

"Everything's fun with you, babe." He kisses the top of my hand, pulls me up, and leads me toward his bedroom like a rag doll. He lets out a long, happy sigh. "Another fantasy checked off the list," he mutters softly, seemingly to himself. He makes a sloppy checkmark with his finger in the air.

"We just fulfilled a fantasy?"

"Fuck yeah, we did. The very best one."

"What was it?"

Josh beams me a goofy smile. His eyes are droopy and glazed. "Hottest Girl Ever Turns Out To Be *Coolest* Girl Ever." He makes another checkmark in the air with his finger. "And she says we're gonna be happy, happy, happy *florebblaaaaaaaaaaaaaah*."

Chapter 32
Kat

My phone beeps with a text just as I'm walking through the front door of my apartment. I put down a stack of mail on my kitchen counter and check my phone.

"Hey, PG," Josh writes.

My heart explodes the same way it does every time I see the name "Josh Faraday" land on my screen.

"Hey, PB," I write back, grinning broadly.

Oh my God, being away from Josh this past week has been torture—I've literally been counting the hours until he lands in Seattle to visit me and meet my family. Just forty-eight more to go. Gah.

"Are you home from work yet?" Josh writes.

"Just got home this very second."

"Cool. A package is being delivered to your apartment in exactly five minutes. You'll have to sign for it personally. Wanted to make sure you'll be there."

"Five minutes? Lucky I'm here."

"I'm a lucky guy."

"Are you hiding in the bushes outside my apartment watching me?"

"No. But that's a good idea. Note to self."

"Why not bring this package with you when you come on Saturday?"

"Nope. This particular package had to be delivered to you TODAY."

"Ooooooh! Is it youuuuuuuuuuuuuuuuuuuuuuuuu?!!" I write.

"LOL," he writes. "No. Sorry."

"Derby Field," I reply. "Darn."

"I gotta go. Just wanted to make sure you'll be there for my package. T-minus four minutes."

"So mysterious! Gimme a hint, PB."

"Okay, one hint: good things come in very large packages."

"OMG!!!"

"Namibia!!! What?"

"It's youuuuuuuuuuuuuuuuuuuuuuu!!!!!"

"Nope."

"Darn. I thought I was so smart. Waaaaah."

"LOL."

"Derby Field."

"Haha. Bye, PG. See you in two days. Can't wait. Enjoy your package."

My heart melts. "Bye, PB. Can't wait." I add a heart emoji and a kissing emoji.

I stand and stare at my phone for a minute.

Oh my God. I'm a smitten kitten. A fish on a line. Done-zo, as Sarah would say. And the amazing thing is that Josh seems to feel the same way about me. Of course, I still don't know where I stand with the guy beyond next week. There are no labels allowed, no relationship-status updates, no declarations of serious feelings—ha!—nothing ever assumed, planned, or implicitly promised more than ten days out (it's kind of hard to put *florrebblaaaaaah* on the calendar). But still, as long as I stay in the moment and don't wonder what might happen a month from now, everything's fantastic. Better than fantastic.

But damn. Not looking to the future is easier said than done when you've fallen in love with someone as amazing as Josh. In fact, that's all I seem to want to do—fantasize about the future—about one day living in the same city, sleeping every night in the same bed, maybe even planning a trip to Europe for next summer with a little of my finder's fee money. But in what world can a woman be the first one to say "I want you to be mine and only mine forever and ever until the end of time" and not have everything implode after that? And that's especially true when the man you wanna say it to is the raging commitment-phobe, Joshua William Faraday. And so, I've made a pact with myself to keep my big mouth shut and just enjoy the ride.

The doorbell rings. I look at my watch. Damn. Josh's deliveryman is freaking prompt. I lope to the front door and open it—and, lo and behold, The Terminator is standing on my doorstep in a T-shirt and jeans, his hand in his pocket.

"Jonas?" I look past him into the walkway. "What are you doing here? Is Sarah here, too?"

Jonas holds up a poker chip.

"No way!" I shriek, instantly elated. It doesn't matter what specific fantasy Jonas is here to kick off—all that matters is what that poker chip clearly implies about Josh's current geographical location: that boy is here in Seattle!

Jonas hands me the poker chip and rolls his eyes. "Hi, Kat. I'm *Blane*," he says, his tone oozing with complete disdain. "Great to finally meet you. You look even more beautiful than in your online profile."

I throw my hands over my blushing face with embarrassment and glee. Just from these few words, I know exactly what imaginary-porno Josh and I are about to act out and how I'm supposed to play along. Oh my freaking God.

Jonas makes a face like he's being tortured. "Is any of what I'm saying making *any* sense to you? Josh gave me the exact script, but if this isn't making any sense to you—"

"No." I laugh. "It makes perfect sense. I know exactly what this is."

In fact, I've got zero doubt about what's on the fantasy-fulfillment docket for tonight: we're gonna do my "slut who ditches her boring date to have sex with the hot bartender in the bathroom" fantasy—a scenario I explained to Josh in detail during our last night together in Las Vegas (along with my other fantasies, too). "And in *this* fantasy," I explained to Josh that night, "I'm on a first date with some random guy—like, some accountant I met on Match dot com or whatever—and it turns out he's The Most Boring Man in the World. He'd probably be named *Blane*."

"Blane?" Josh said. And then he quoted the exact line from *Pretty in Pink* I was referring to—about Blane being an appliance, rather than a name.

"Oh my God!" I squealed. "I guarantee no other man on the planet could quote Ducky from *Pretty in Pink*."

"I'm wise and powerful, babe," Josh said. "I keep telling you."

I laughed.

"So what happens next in this particular fantasy?" Josh asked. "Something tells me it doesn't end well for poor Blane."

"No, it doesn't. I'm on my date with *Blane* and he's talking my ear off about taxes or politics or whatever, and I keep locking eyes with the hot bartender. So, after a bit, I excuse myself to go to the restroom. And on my way, I slip the bartender a note on a napkin that says, 'Bathroom in five.'"

"Whoa," Josh said. "You little minx.'

"Hot, right?"

"Definitely."

"So then I fuck the bartender in the bathroom and when we're done, I go right back to my sweet but boring date like nothing ever happened. When Blane and I leave the bar, the bartender winks at me as I pass by—but we don't exchange phone numbers or anything like that—we both just know it was a one-time thing. Blane takes me home and I kiss him on the cheek and thank him for a lovely evening like the proper young lady I am. And then I never see him again."

"Where the fuck do you get this shit?" Josh asked.

"Well, this particular fantasy came about as a total 'what if' on a real-life boring date."

Josh laughed.

"But that's the thing, I have these little pornos playing in my head all the time, but I'd never actually *do* them. Believe it or not, I'm actually not as big a slut as I seem."

"I don't think you're a slut," he said earnestly. "Not at all. Well, not any more than I'm a slut. Am I a slut?"

"Yeah, a little bit."

Josh laughed. "No, I'm not. Not nearly as much as I seem."

"Then we're even."

Jonas clears his throat, drawing my attention back to my present-day doorstep. He looks remarkably uncomfortable. "So you ready to head out?" he asks. "I've been given strict instructions to take you for cocktails and to be extremely *boring*." He rolls his eyes again.

"What did Josh tell you about tonight?" I ask, my cheeks suddenly feeling warm. God help me if Josh told Jonas everything about my imaginary-pornos.

"Josh didn't tell me a thing," Jonas says.

I exhale with relief.

"All he said was, 'Kat's got, like, a thousand crazy pornos playing in her head at all times and I need your help setting the stage for one of them so we can act it out tonight.'" He shrugs.

I cover my face. "Gah! Josh said all that? Jonas, that's not exactly 'not a thing.' Oh my God, I'm completely mortified. *Jesus*."

"Aw, don't worry about it, Kat. That's literally all Josh said. He didn't give me any details. He just told me to show up here and be 'super-duper boring'—which, he said 'should be like falling off a log' for me. I told him to go fuck himself, but then he went ballistic on me, screaming about every fucking favor he's ever done for me through the history of time—which is a lot, I must admit—so I was like, 'Fine, motherfucker! Stop acting like me! I'll do it—if only to make you stop screaming at me like a fucking lunatic.' And then he laughed his ass off and was like, 'Ha! Welcome to my world, motherfucker.'"

I laugh. "So you're here to ply me with alcohol and bore me to tears, then?" I ask.

Jonas shrugs. "Yeah, talk about asking two fishies to swim, huh? You get to drink and I get to be boring."

I giggle.

"Wait, you do drink, right?" Jonas asks.

I give him a perplexed look.

"Kat, I'm *Blane*, remember? I don't already know you're a total lush."

I snort. "Oh yeah. Well, yes, Blane, on occasion, I do indeed imbibe."

"Okay, that's fine. I don't drink at all—I hope that's okay. I'm a professional baseball player and I don't drink a drop during the season."

I burst out laughing.

"Okay good. I'm glad that means something to you. Josh gave me explicit instructions to say that exact line, but I have no idea why." Jonas leans forward like he's telling a secret. "But actually I'll totally have a drink with you—you know that, right?" He winks.

"Awesome. Will Sarah be joining us? I bet she could use a break from studying. She seemed really stressed about finals when I talked to her the other day."

264

"Who's Sarah? I told you, my name is *Blane*." He leans forward like he's telling me another secret. "Actually, I tried to pull her away from her books for the night, but she's totally freaking out about her exams next week. She said she can't afford to go out two nights in a row so she'll just see everyone tomorrow night."

"What? We're going out tomorrow night?" I shriek happily. "I had no idea." I clap my hands and jump up and down. "Will it be all four of us?"

Jonas suddenly looks like he's been caught with his hand in the cookie jar. "Uh." His face turns bright red. "Fuck. Josh is gonna kill me. That's supposed to be a surprise." He runs his hand through his hair. "Just pretend I never said anything. My name is Blane. You look even better than your online profile. I don't drink. I'm a professional baseball player. I'm boring."

I squeal. "Josh is so sneaky-freaky-deaky. I thought he was coming into town on *Saturday*, did he tell you that? He's meeting my family." I squeal again, overwhelmed with excitement. "He's such a sneaky little fucker."

"Shit. Kat. Stop it. He's gonna kill me. I'm Blane. I'm boring. You look better than your online profile. Gah."

I put out my hand, laughing. "Nice to meet you, Blane. I'm super-duper excited about our boring date. Let's go." I step outside and lock my door and we begin walking down the pathway toward the front of my building. Well, actually, Jonas is walking—I'm careening down the walkway a good five paces ahead of him, my heart exploding with joy.

"Hey, Kat. Real quick. Hang on."

I stop sprinting.

"Before I'm stuck being Boring Blane for the rest of the night," Jonas says, "can I be Boring Jonas for a minute? There's something I wanna ask you about."

"Sure, Boring Jonas—bore away."

Boring Jonas takes a deep breath and pulls a ring box out of his pocket. "Do you think Sarah's gonna like this?" He opens the ring box and I'm blinded by the most spectacular rock I've ever seen. "Or should I have gotten bigger?" he asks.

My knees literally buckle. "Holy shitballs, Jonas. It's flippin' gorgeous!"

"You think she'll like it?"

"*Like* it? She's gonna sob like a baby with overflowing *love* for it! It's jaw-dropping. Glorious. Fabulous. *Beyond.*"

"But would you go so far as to call it '*magnificent*'?"

I laugh. "Absolutely. That's exactly what it is. *Magnificent.*"

"Phew. It's big enough?"

"Jonas, any bigger and her knuckles would drag on the ground."

He exhales in obvious relief and shuts the box. "Okay. Thank you." He runs his hand through his hair again. "I've been losing my mind lately, thinking about getting this right. Josh says this is the story Sarah will be telling her grandchildren one day so I'd better not fuck it up."

"Josh said that?"

"Yeah."

"Josh said, 'This is the story Sarah will tell her *grandchildren*'?" I ask, my chest tight.

"Yep. That's exactly what he said."

"Wow," I say. "That's an incredibly romantic thing to say." I clutch my chest, trying to get ahold of myself. "I didn't know Josh was capable of saying something so... *epic.*" My heart is suddenly slamming against my chest bone, banging mercilessly, trying to lurch out of its cage. I can't fathom Josh assuming children and grandchildren for Jonas and Sarah. That's so... *futuristic* of him. "Well, yeah, Josh is right," I manage. "Sarah will most definitely be telling your future grandchildren about your proposal one day."

Jonas grimaces.

"But the good news is that you can't fuck it up no matter what you do. As long as you speak from your heart, whatever you say will be grandchildren-worthy, I promise."

We begin walking down the pathway toward the street again.

"God, I hope you're right," Jonas says. "I've been making myself sick, planning this whole elaborate speech in my head, trying to get it exactly right."

I wave my hand in the air. "You're overthinking it. Just tell her how you feel and she'll be thrilled. All that matters at times like these is that you tell the one you love how you feel, straight from your heart. Keep it simple."

We've reached Jonas' car on the street in front of my building. He opens my door for me and I settle myself inside the car.

"Thanks, Kat," Jonas says. "I think you're right. I'll keep it simple and straight from the heart. Nothing too elaborate."

"There you go. That's all any girl could ever hope for in a marriage proposal—a simple declaration of love from the man of her dreams."

Jonas shoots me an adorable look that clearly says, "*Oh my God, I'm really gonna do this.*"

"You'll do great," I say.

He shuts my door and walks around the car to the driver's side.

I think this is the first time I've ever chatted with Jonas alone, just him and me, with no one else around. No, wait. That's not true. This is the *second* time. The first was at Jonas' house the morning after The Club broke into my apartment—the morning after I first laid eyes on Jonas' sexy-as-sin brother. Wow, that feels like a lifetime ago. What did I say to Jonas that morning, standing in his kitchen? "Sarah thinks you're in love with her, Jonas. *Don't crush her.*" I roll my eyes at myself. Yet another whiz-bang example of my amazing ability to sense a man's true intentions.

Jonas settles into his car seat and turns on the engine.

"So, I gotta tell you, *Blane*," I say. "I don't have high hopes for a second date. It's a really bad sign when a guy asks for advice on how to propose to another girl on a first date."

Jonas laughs. "Sorry. From here on out, I promise to focus all my energy on boring you to tears."

"Thank you. I really appreciate that."

Jonas pulls his car into traffic. "In fact, you know what I'll do?" he says, grinning. "*I'll bore the pants off you.*" He snickers.

My stomach clenches. "Josh told you everything, didn't he?" I choke out.

Jonas laughs gleefully. "Nope. Josh gave me absolutely no details, just like I said. But I'm not a complete idiot, Kat, despite appearances. If me showing up at your apartment and handing you a fucking *poker chip* doesn't somehow lead to you and Josh fucking in the bathroom, then I don't know what would be the fucking point."

I cover my face with my hands.

Jonas laughs again. "Aw, come on, Kat. It's just me—and I'm a huge fan of bathroom fuckery, believe me. Besides, what do you care what I think? I'm *Blane*. I'm the boring guy you'll never see again."

I laugh and look out my car window for a long moment, letting the blush in my cheeks subside. "So where are we going, Blane?"

"A bar near my house called The Pine Box. Are you familiar with it?" He's got a wicked grin on his face.

"Yeah, as a matter of fact, I am. My best friend and I once went to The Pine Box to spy on this guy she really liked."

"You *spied* on him, huh? What was he doing?"

"Hitting on another girl."

"Ooph. Sounds like an asshole."

"Yeah, that's what I thought. But I've since learned he's a total sweetheart. Best guy, ever. And a perfect match for my best friend, too. I couldn't be happier for them."

I look over at Jonas and he's absolutely beaming with joy. God, he's such a cutie, I can't stand it. I wanna roll him in glitter and glue and hang him on my fridge.

He looks at me, his face bursting with happiness. "You're definitely way cooler than your online profile, Kat."

Chapter 33
Josh

I don't know what to do with myself, so I pick up a dishrag and wipe off the top of the bar for a long minute. I'm so amped to finally see Kat again, I can barely breathe. A week has never felt so long. Fuck. I look at my watch. Jonas should be here with her any minute now. *Fuck.* I'm leaping out of my skin. *Fuck.* I haven't been able to get that woman out of my head all fucking week, despite how busy I've been with work. The smell of her. The softness of her skin. The way she laughs like a dude. That electricity that courses between us when we have sex, nice and slow. What the fuck *is* that? It's gonna be the death of me.

"Hey, bartender," a guy in a charcoal three-piece suit calls to me.

I nod to the guy. It's been a long time since anyone's called me "bartender" in an actual bar. Sure, I'm always "bartender" at parties with my friends, but there's a special kind of jolt to being the guy who's large and in charge in an actual bar. I'd forgotten how much I love that feeling.

I glance at Tim to my left, the actual bartender at The Pine Box, seeking permission to assist the guy in the suit and Tim motions for me to go right ahead. He's not just being nice, of course—I've paid him and his boss (the owner of the bar) handsomely for the privilege. But, still, I can't help feeling giddy to be doing this again after all these years.

"Hey there, man." I say to the dude in the suit, sauntering to him. "What can I do you for, sir?"

"A Manhattan," the guy says. He motions to a cute brunette standing just behind him. "And a Chardonnay."

"Absolutely. Guess what? Great news. Tonight just so happens

269

to be Dudes In Charcoal Suits Drink For Free Night." I slide two cocktail napkins onto the bar in front of him. "Your drinks are on the house, man."

The guy looks surprised. "Really?"

"Yep. They're on me." I flash him a huge smile. "Tip included."

When I contacted The Pine Box (at Jonas' recommendation) and asked the owner if I might help tend bar for an hour tonight (because, I said, I was trying to decide if I wanted to quit my fancy job and go back to my college job), he wasn't the least bit open to the idea. As usual, though, money made the guy change his mind and decide to help a brother out. "But you can't handle any customers' money," the owner warned. "Leave that to Tim." "No problem," I assured him. "How about this: I'll pay for every single drink in the place, all night long. And I'll serve all premium liquor the whole time I'm there— you'll make a mint, bro."

"Whoa," the guy in the charcoal suit says, stuffing his wallet back into his pocket. "A random act of kindness. Thanks."

"Something like that," I say. "So check this out, bro. I'm gonna make your Manhattan with a little extra kick, okay? I'm gonna use a premium rye whiskey—maybe Overholt?—plus, I'm gonna go off the rails and use orange bitters."

The guy raises his eyebrows. "You're going rogue, huh?"

I laugh. "I know what you're thinking—is he mad? Just roll with it. If you don't absolutely love it, I'll make you one the traditional way. But you'll see. The rye whiskey's gonna really offset the flavor of the bitters nicely."

"Okay. Cool. Thanks, man. Awesome."

I look at the adorable brunette behind the guy. "Are you in the mood to try something besides Chardonnay tonight? I've got a Purple Rain recipe I'm dying to make for a lucky lady tonight. Also completely on me, of course. If you like gin, you'll love it."

"I love gin," she says, her face lighting up. "I'll give it a whirl."

I glance at the door. Jonas should have been here already. Maybe Kat kept him waiting when he came to pick her up. Kat didn't know Jonas was coming, after all. She probably made him sit and wait while she put on makeup or changed her clothes. That girl is never fucking on time for a goddamned thing. I smile broadly. And she's always worth the fucking wait.

270

I push the drinks across the bar to the dude and his date.

"Whoa," the guy says. "Best Manhattan I've ever had."

"Love it," his date says. "What's in it besides gin?"

I tell her and she praises me for being fucking amazing, which, I must admit when it comes to making drinks, I am. "When you're ready for round two, lemme know. I'll keep my tab open for you all night long."

"Thanks. Wow. You're the man."

Damn, I should totally do this once a week, just for kicks. This is fun.

A smoking hot brunette comes into the place alone, sits at the bar, and motions to me that she wants to order something. I glance at Tim on the other end of the bar and he motions to me like, "She's all yours, man."

I saunter down to her. "Hey, beautiful," I say. "What can I do for you?"

She raises her eyebrow. "Answering that question with a drink order seems like such a shame."

Oh. Well. I glance at the door. I'd forgotten about how much women hit on the bartender. That was always one of the best perks of tending bar.

I smile at her. "You here alone, sweetheart?"

"Waiting for a friend. She just texted she's running late." She makes a sad face.

"Well, no one gets lonely when I'm tending bar. That's the rule. What can I get you? It's on me."

Her eyes blaze. "Oh, thank you. That's awfully sweet of you."

I look at the door. No Jonas. No Kat.

"Um," she says. "Do you have a recommendation for me? I feel like going outside my usual tonight. Maybe taking a walk on the wild side." She levels her dark eyes at me.

Oh man. This woman's not fucking around.

"Hmm. Well, would you like a screaming orgasm, perhaps?"

"You read my mind."

"Coming right up." I flash her my most lascivious look.

"And what do you recommend to *drink*?" she adds.

I laugh. "What's your name, beautiful?" I ask.

"Lucy." She puts out her hand and I shake it.

271

"Hi, Lucy. Love the name. I'm Josh. Pleased to meet you."

"You're new here?"

"Yeah. Just on a trial basis. Just for tonight."

"Oh, well, lucky I came in tonight, then. I'd be happy to tell the owner to hire you. You're the best bartender, ever."

"I haven't made your drink yet."

She flashes a flirtatious smile. "It doesn't matter." She licks her lips.

I run my hand through my hair. Shit, have women gotten more aggressive since I used to do this in college? "Well, Lucy. Thanks for the vote of—" I glance down at the other end of the bar and I'm met with two eyes of blue steel boring holes into the back of my skull like a fucking Gamma Ray. *Kat.* In full Jealous Bitch mode. My heart and dick both leap at the sight of her. How is it possible she's even more beautiful than she was last week?

I wink at her and her eyes flicker.

She grits her teeth.

It's all I can do not to burst out laughing. Fuck, I love Jealous Kat. She's never sexier than when she's plotting a murder.

I quickly turn my attention back to my new brunette admirer. My gut tells me letting Jealous Kat simmer for a little while longer will only make this porno hotter in the end. Plus, I'm not one hundred percent sure how this particular porno's supposed to play itself out. I know Kat's on a date with Boring Blane and I'm the hot bartender who catches her eye. That part is clear. But the rest is kind of nebulous. I'm pretty sure she's gonna slip me a note. Yeah, that's it. She's supposed to slip me a napkin with a note scribbled on it. And then we fuck in the bathroom. And then she returns to her date like nothing even happened. Fucking hot.

"Sorry, Lucy," I say. "I got distracted there for a second. Thanks for the vote of confidence. Yeah, if you could tell the owner you want me to get the job, I'd be grateful. Seems like a cool place."

"Sure, Josh. My friends and I come in here about once a week after work. You'd be a sight for sore eyes after a long day, that's for sure."

I flash her my most charming smile. "Thanks. You're a sweetheart."

She throws her head back and laughs. "Oh, my. You're

adorable." She bites her lip. "Absolutely adorable." She leans in. "How late are you working tonight?"

I lean in. "I'm not sure yet."

"Well, let me know when you find out," she whispers.

I grin. "First things first, lemme get you that screaming orgasm."

"If I get my way, that'll be first things first. Second things second. And third things third."

Oh shit. This woman is a fucking carnivore. Were women this savage when I was tending bar at twenty-two? Shit, if they were, I don't remember it quite this way. If I weren't here to deliver a porno-fantasy to the woman of my dreams tonight, I'd no doubt be banging this woman to within an inch of her life an hour from now. Jesus God.

"Just a second, Lucy. I've got a customer flagging me down at the other end of the bar. Your screaming orgasm will be coming right up." I wink.

As I walk the length of the bar toward Kat, I feel like a man walking a gangplank. She looks literally homicidal. Damn, she's gorgeous. Especially when she's in terrorist mode. I have the sudden impulse to leap over the bar and take her into my arms and kiss the hell out of her, but this slow burn is way too hot to fuck with. Kat's got fantasy-pornos playing in her head? Well, I guess it turns out I do, too. She's jealous of the man-eater down at the other end of the bar? Well, good. It'll only make sex in the bathroom that much better.

I come to a halt immediately across the bar from Jonas and Kat. My brother looks like he wants to throttle me and Kat looks like she wants to filet me and cut off my balls.

"Hey, guys," I say. "Welcome to The Pine Box." I push two napkins in front of them, my eyes fixed on Kat. "Hey, beautiful," I whisper. "Man, are you a sight for lonely eyes. I haven't stopped thinking about you all week, babe."

Kat bites her lip. Her chest is rising and falling visibly. (And, damn, what a fine looking chest it is, especially in the cleavage-baring blouse she's got on.)

"Hey, bartender," Kat says, her voice tight. She clenches her jaw. "I've been dying to see you, too." Her cheeks flush. "Surprised to see you working the crowd so well."

I shrug. "It's what bartenders do, babe. Can't keep a fish from swimming."

She practically snarls.

"So, you two on a date tonight? Lemme guess. Did you two kids meet online?"

Jonas rolls his eyes, clearly not willing to play along.

I laugh. "What can I get you? Drinks are on me."

"What are you having, Jonas?" Kat asks.

"I'd like the most complicated and annoying drink you can possibly imagine. Something that literally *pains* you to make because it's so fucking involved. I don't normally drink because I'm a professional baseball player and I'm highly disciplined during the season, mind you, but for some reason now that I'm seeing you here, acting like a total douchebag"—he motions to the other end of the bar—"all I wanna do is cause you maximum *pain.*"

I glance down the bar in the direction Jonas has indicated. Lucy is biting her fingertip, watching me, her eyes burning like hot coals.

I clear my throat. "Hey, bro. No *problemo.* I know exactly what to make you. I've got the perfect drink for you." I look at Kat. "And you, miss? What can I do for you? My wish is your command."

I can almost hear Kat's heart beating from here.

She's so fucking gorgeous, she's causing me pain.

I shouldn't do it—I know I shouldn't—it's obviously not part of the role-play—but I can't resist. I've missed her too much not to feed my addiction right fucking now.

I reach across the bar and touch that hot little cleft in her chin.

At my touch, Kat parts her lips and exhales a shaky breath.

And just like that, I'm rock hard.

"What can I get you?" I breathe. "Name it. It's yours. Anything at all, babe."

She swallows hard. "*I want a douchebag,*" she says.

There's a long beat. I can't decide if that's a drink order or if she's referring to me.

"Crown Royal and a splash of Coke," she clarifies, solving the mystery for me.

"Really? Is that really a thing?"

She nods. "Look it up. It's a real thing. And I want one—I want one bad."

I smirk. "Okay, then. A douchebag it is. With pleasure." I look at Jonas. "And for you, sir, I'll be making something called The Dork.

274

White rum, Pisang Ambon, Licor 43, lemon juice and pineapple juice—served in a highball glass. Hope you enjoy it."

Jonas makes a face of pure disgust.

I laugh and slide a Heineken across the bar.

He grins despite himself.

My eyes flicker back to Kat. "I'll be right back to serve up your douchebag, gorgeous. I gotta go give that brunette down there a screaming orgasm first." I motion to my admirer down at the other end of the bar. "While I'm gone, enjoy your date. This guy seems super interesting. Have fun, you two."

Kat's eyes flash wickedly at me, but I turn my back on her and traipse on down to the other end of the bar, my cock tingling.

"Sorry for the delay, Lucy. Got to chatting with a couple down there. They're on a blind date. Cutest couple ever."

"No problem. Tim came over and offered to give me a screaming orgasm, but I told him I only want one from *you.*"

"Aw, shucks, Lucy. That's awfully sweet of you. That makes me feel so special." I glance at Kat on the other end of the bar. Her eyes are trained on me like a sniper. She looks ready to jump on top of the bar and leap on this woman like a cheetah downing an impala. "Well, then, I guess I'd better get moving, huh? Don't worry, it only takes me a couple minutes to give most women the best screaming orgasm of their life. You're only minutes away from complete satisfaction, sweetheart."

She shifts in her chair and makes a sexual sound.

I steal a quick look at Kat—and she's about to lose her fucking mind.

I turn around and grab the ingredients I need for Lucy's drink, laughing to myself about what a stroke of luck it was to unexpectedly have this hot little tamale on my tip right in front of Kat. I couldn't have planned it better if I'd tried.

I serve up Lucy's drink to her and she takes a greedy sip.

"*Orgasmic.* Thank you. And thank you for buying it for me."

"My pleasure," I say.

"Excuse me," Kat's voice says from behind Lucy's shoulder. She's standing literally right behind Lucy, her hands on her hips, her nostrils flaring. I straighten up to get an unimpeded view and I'm met with Kat's blazing face in full Jealous Bitch mode.

275

"Oh, hey, miss," I say, trying not to grin too broadly. "Your douchebag is coming right up. I'm sorry I'm kinda slow. I'm new. I was just giving Lucy here a screaming orgasm."

"Forget about making me a *drink*," she says. "I want a *douchebag*." She elbows her way to the edge of the bar, right next to Lucy, completely invading the other woman's personal space. Much to my surprise, she turns her head and smiles with full teeth at Lucy, the way a great white shark smiles at a sea lion. Oh shit. I've never seen her look more like a murderer than right now. "I'm on a blind date with that guy down there," she says breezily. She points to Jonas.

Lucy cranes her neck and catches sight of my brother in all his magical glory—and, not unexpectedly, the woman's eyes pop out of her head. "Oh my God, honey. You're on a *blind* date with *him*? Jackpot."

"Yeah. His name is *Blane*." Kat rolls her eyes.

Lucy squints at Jonas and then looks at me. "He looks a lot like you, actually. Are you two related?"

I crane my neck and look at Jonas. "Hey, yeah, he does kinda look like me. Huh." I shake my head. "Nope, never seen that guy before in my life."

"Wow. He's your doppelgänger."

"You think?"

Kat leans in and whispers. "He's so boring I wanna gouge my eyes out. He's a professional baseball player and he keeps talking about *Plato*." Kat makes a sound like she's snoring.

I laugh.

"He's a professional baseball player?" Lucy steals another look. "Honey, if it were me, I'd let that man talk about anything he wanted to, whether it's Plato or Play-Doh. Good lord, girl. You better get back over there. Don't let some other woman swoop in and make a move on him." She cranes her neck to look at Jonas again—a move I've seen women in bars perform more times than I can count. "Holy hot damn. *Go*."

Kat sniffs and trains her eyes on me. Oh man, she's absolutely on fire. "Eh. He's okay, I guess. The problem is, while I was sitting over there with *that* guy, I kept getting distracted by *another* guy—a smoking hot bartender to be exact." Kat leans over the bar, notably edging Lucy out of the pocket (and giving me a fabulous view of her pretty titties in her low-cut blouse). She lowers her voice to barely above a whisper. "This bartender I've been watching all night has so much swagger, I figure it can only mean one thing."

I lean forward, my pulse pounding in my ears. "And what would that be?"

She licks her lips. "I figure it means he's gotta have a *really* big dick."

Lucy's face turns bright red.

Oh my God, she's ruthless. "What's your name, sweetheart?" I ask, leaning into Kat even closer, my dick lurching in my pants.

"Kat."

"Nice to meet you, Kat," I say, putting out my hand. "I'm Josh."

"*Josh*. Sexy name, *Josh*. That's the name of a guy with a really big dick if I've ever heard one." She wets her lower lip slowly like she's licking barbeque sauce off a rack of ribs. "Please believe me, I've never done this before, and I know I'm on a date with *Blane* down there—and I know I'm probably coming off like a world-class slut—but I don't give a crap. You're so hot, I can't stop myself." She lowers her voice again. "If I leave here tonight without knowing if I'm right about what your *swagger* means, I'm gonna regret it for the rest of my life."

Lucy physically jolts on her barstool like she's been stuck with a cattle prod—and I'm right there with her, jerking like Kat just gripped my dick.

I lean into Kat's ear, right next to poor Lucy, like we're having a conversation about how Kat and I are gonna rob a bank, right in front of Lucy the Bank Teller. I feel vaguely guilty Lucy's become an unwitting pawn in our little game, but it can't be helped—having another woman as part of this conversation is turning me on too much to spare the odd-woman-out from discomfort. "Well, gosh, Kat," I say. "What do you propose to do about your date? He seems like a nice enough guy—pretty damned good-looking, too. And a professional baseball player to boot. Maybe you ought to give him a chance."

I crane my neck to look down the length of the bar at Jonas. He flashes me a look that can only be described as utter contempt for making him sit through this.

Kat glances down the bar at Jonas. "Oh, I'm not gonna ditch

him. I'm going home with him and I'm gonna make him fall in love with me—he's a professional ball player, after all. But that doesn't mean I don't wanna know if I'm right about your *swagger*—I won't be able to sleep tonight if I don't find out." She straightens up and winks. "Bathroom in five, bartender."

She leaves.

I look at Lucy. Her mouth is hanging open. Her eyes are wide.

If I weren't so fucking turned on right now, I'd throw my head back and howl with laughter at the expression on Lucy's face. Damn, Kat's the best. Never a dull moment with that woman.

But I don't laugh. No way. This porno is too fucking hot.

I lean across the bar toward Lucy, my dick pulsing in my pants. "Well, that was unexpected, to say the least," I say, smirking. I reach down and shift my hard-on to the side, trying to get relief from the persistent throbbing.

"Wow," Lucy says, obviously at a loss for words.

"Hey, hon!" a female voice calls from behind Lucy's back.

Lucy turns her head—and as she does, I steal a quick look at Kat. She's sitting with Jonas, chatting, flipping her hair as Tim serves them a second round of drinks. Oh my God, she's a fucking sociopath. She really is. How is she looking so light-hearted and happy right now when I'm about ready to blow a fucking gasket, I'm so turned on?

"Josh?" Lucy says.

I hear my name, but I can't peel my eyes off Kat. She's a fucking force of nature, that woman. A tsunami. God help anyone who stands in the way of something she wants. She's a fucking beast.

"Josh?" Lucy says again.

I force my eyes to look at Lucy, though it pains me to do it.

"This is my friend Christine."

"Hi, Christine," I say, my voice lacking its usual charm. I glance down the bar at Kat again. She's throwing her head back, laughing. Diabolical.

"Hi," Lucy's friend says.

I peel my eyes off Kat and look at the new woman. She's a short redhead with freckles and an adorable smile.

"Hi," I say. "What can I get you? It's on me. Whatever you want."

Christine's about to reply, but Lucy hijacks the conversation.

"Hang on, honey. Josh, what the *fuck* are you gonna... do... about her?" She crinkles her nose and tilts her head toward Kat's end of the bar. "Are you actually gonna... meet her?" She makes a face like that's a patently ridiculous notion. "She just said she's gonna do two guys in one night." She grimaces.

I look stealthily to my right and then left, and then I lean over the bar toward Lucy like I'm about to tell her a scandalous secret.

Lucy leans in and licks her lips with anticipation.

"Fuck yeah, I'm gonna meet her," I whisper. "I'm not proud of it, Lucy, I'm really not. But I'm only a man. And I can't resist showing that woman she's *exactly* right about what my swagger means."

Lucy's eyes pop out of her head and roll around on the floor.

I glance down the bar at Kat again and this time, her blue eyes are trained on mine, too. She smiles wickedly and I shoot her a look of pure arousal. "I'm gonna meet that diabolical woman in the bathroom and fuck the living shit out of her with my huge dick and give her a screaming orgasm that has absolutely nothing whatsoever to do with vodka." My eyes shift to Lucy. "And then, don't you worry, beautiful, I'll come right back out here and make you whatever drink you desire."

I've clearly rendered Lucy speechless.

"Hey, Tim," I call to the real bartender, straightening up. "Get these two spectacularly gorgeous women whatever they want, on me. Food, drinks, whatever it may be—a bottle of your finest champagne. They can name it. I'm gonna take a short break."

With that, I throw down the dishrag in my hand, stride to the opposite end of the bar from where Jonas and Kat are sitting, slip around the end, and waltz toward the bathroom, my throbbing hard-on leading the mighty way.

Chapter 34
Josh

I have to wait a couple minutes outside the bathroom door for someone to come out, but once they do, I slip inside, my breathing ragged. Holy shit, I'm so turned on, I can barely breathe.

Kat was supposed to slip me a note on a napkin—that's what she said when she described this particular mini-porno that night in Las Vegas—she wasn't supposed to proposition me right in front of another woman. But my jealous little terrorist went for the fucking jugular, didn't she? There's no controlling that woman when her eyes turn a blazing shade of green.

Fuck, she turns me on.

Damn, that was hot.

Goddamn, I can't wait to fuck her.

There's a soft rap on the bathroom door. I open it slightly and Kat wordlessly slips inside, already breathless with obvious arousal. I've barely locked the door behind her when Kat's mouth is on my lips, her tongue in my mouth, her body pressed into mine.

"Kat," I say, wrapping my arms around her and kissing her deeply. "Oh my God, I've missed you."

Our kiss is instantly blazing with passion. I feel like I'm drinking water after a long slog across Saudi Arabia wearing nothing but a Speedo. How is it possible I'd forgotten how good this woman tastes in one short week? I grind my hard-on into her. How have I lasted seven days without tasting these delicious lips? Touching this soft skin? Smelling this glorious mane of golden hair?

"Are you wet for me?" I ask, furiously unbuttoning her jeans.

"Dripping wet," she breathes.

"That got you going, huh? Watching that brunette make the moves on me?"

"She would have left with you in a heartbeat if you'd asked her."

I kiss Kat's neck while sliding my fingers inside her jeans. "Yeah, she made that clear."

My fingers find Kat's wetness. She moans and so do I.

"You sure didn't discourage her," Kat says.

"All part of the role-play, baby—I'm the hot bartender all the women wanna fuck, right?" I unbutton my jeans and pull down my briefs, freeing my cock.

"You like making me jealous," Kat says, gripping my shaft.

I exhale sharply at her touch. "You know I do. So hot." I maneuver her to the sink, push her belly up against it, and press myself into her back, staring over her shoulder at us in the mirror. "Making you jealous turns me on," I say. I move her hair off her neck and kiss her hidden Scorpio tattoo.

She shudders.

"I like it when you're a terrorist." I yank her jeans down farther and slide my fingers into her wetness from behind. Oh yeah, she's dripping wet. I slide my fingers up to her clit and shudder at the texture of it. It's swollen and hard, slick against my fingertip. I swirl it around and around and she groans with excitement. I lean into her ear. "I like knowing you want me all to yourself."

I bend my knees and slide my cock inside her slowly, ever so slowly, my gaze fixed on hers in the mirror as I enter her, and we both exhale audibly with relief and pleasure at the fucking awesome sensation.

She grips the sink with white knuckles as I begin thrusting in and out of her, my eyes locked onto hers as I do.

"You feel so good," I whisper, fondling her breast under her blouse. "You've got a magic pussy, baby."

Her nipples are rock hard. I pinch them greedily and she yelps.

"Say you want me all to yourself," I command. I trail my hand down from her breast to her clit and she presses herself into my hand. "Tell me you were so fucking jealous you couldn't stand it."

She's staring at me in the mirror with ice-blue eyes.

My hips are rocking with hers. We've found the perfect rhythm. It's slow and sensual.

"I was so fucking jealous I couldn't stand it," she breathes, moving her hips with mine. "You're *mine*."

"Oh, I like that," I whisper in her ear, my eyes still locked on hers in the mirror. "Say it again." I bite her earlobe.

"*Mine,*" she says, gritting her teeth. She reaches her arm up and around my neck.

I suck her earlobe like it's her clit. "You feel so good," I say. "You always feel so fucking good."

"You make me so wet," she whispers. "No one's ever made me wet like this."

"You like the way I fuck you, babe?"

She makes a sound like she just got burned with hot coffee.

"Yeah, baby. Here we go. Give it to me. This is the money right here—what I've been craving all fucking week."

She whimpers. "*Fuck.*"

"Yeah, baby. Come on."

"It's a big one." Her eyes darken.

"Yeah, baby. Let it go." Our bodies have picked up speed. Sweat is beading on her face. Her cheeks are flushed. My fingers are working her hard clit furiously. This is so fucking good, I'm about to blow.

"I missed you so much, babe," I whisper in her ear, my gaze never leaving hers in the mirror. "Had to come see you early, I missed you so fucking bad."

Her eyes flutter and roll back into her head briefly. She lets out a loud groan and I clamp my free hand over her mouth.

"Let it go, baby," I purr into her ear, gyrating into her, fingering her like I own her. I lick her neck, nibble her ear. "Let it go for me."

Her entire body heaves and jolts and spasms. She arches her back, a pained sound pooling in her throat. I clamp my hand over her mouth again, trying to muffle the sounds coming out of her.

"Yeah, baby," I whisper into her ear. "Here we go."

She bites my finger. "*Fuck.* Oh, Josh. Oh my God."

She buckles, almost like she's dry heaving, and then every bit of warm, wet flesh surrounding my cock suddenly squeezes and clenches around me, like a glorious dam breaking. It feels so good, I release into her like a tsunami, slamming myself into her as I do.

The minute I've got my equilibrium back, I turn her around, grab her face and kiss her deeply. "I missed you, baby," I say. "I couldn't wait 'til Saturday to see you."

She kisses my lips, cheeks, neck. "I've been going crazy all week. It's been torture."

I wrap my arms around her, bury my nose in her hair, and inhale. "I wish I could bottle this smell so I could sniff it whenever I'm lonely in L.A."

"Bumble and Bumble Crème de Coco Shampoo and Conditioner," she says. "Seventeen ninety-nine per bottle."

I laugh.

I pull back from our embrace and zip up. "Okay 'slut who ditches her boring date at a bar to fuck the hot bartender in the bathroom.' What happens next? I do believe you're supposed to slip out of the bathroom, rejoin your boring date, and never look back, right?"

Kat shrugs. "Yeah, that's what the script says." She tilts her head. "But there's no fucking way I'm letting you go back in there and serve that bitch another drink."

I laugh. "So I take it we're changing the script?" I say.

"Damn straight we are," she says.

I smirk. "How 'bout this? What if the bartender goes out there and quits his job because he can't stand the thought of you leaving here to fuck that other guy? And what if he does it right in front of the woman who was hitting on him all night?"

Her face lights up. "Oh, I like that ending to the porno a whole lot better."

"Yeah, except now it's not a porno—it's a fucking rom-com."

She smiles. *When Josh Met Kat.*

I return her smile. "So, hey, I should tell you. Jonas and I are waking up at chicken-thirty tomorrow morning to go climbing for the day. I'll take you home, see your place—but then I'm gonna stay at Jonas' tonight since we're heading out before sunrise, okay?"

"That's cool with me. I've got to work tomorrow, anyway."

"When are you gonna quit your job already, you puss? I told you I'll help you."

She makes a face.

"What are you waiting for, PG?"

She considers for a beat and then nods decisively. "You know what? You're right. Fuck it. I'll quit tomorrow."

"Really?"

"Yeah. YOLO, right?"

"Damn straight."

"Starting my own business can't be that hard, right? I'm smart. I can do it. If I fail, I'll just pick myself back up."

"Atta girl."

There's a beat.

Damn, she's gorgeous.

"Hey, Jonas' house is really close, right?" she asks.

"Just a few blocks."

"Yeah, that's what I thought. In that case, it doesn't make sense for you to take me all the way to my apartment when you're staying at Jonas' tonight. I'm sure Sarah will give me a ride home later. Let's walk to Jonas' house from here and—" She gasps. "Oh my God. I just had an idea. You, me, and Jonas should leave the bar together. That'd be so frickin' funny."

I chuckle. "And just like that, our movie's back to being a porno again."

Kat laughs.

"Do you really gotta do that to the poor woman? She already hates you enough to hire a hit on you."

"Hell yeah, I gotta. It's just too freaking hilarious. How much you wanna bet that tiger-woman is out there hitting on Jonas right now?"

"I'm not stupid enough to take that bet. I've been in far too many bars with Jonas over the years."

Kat laughs and throws her arms around my neck. "God, I missed you."

"I missed you, too, babe." I wrap my arms around her and kiss her.

"I'm so glad you came to Seattle early," she says into my chest, squeezing me tight. "This long-distance thing is killing me, Josh. It's brutal."

My chest constricts. If ever there was a cue for me to tell Kat about my upcoming move to Seattle that was just it. But I'm not ready to tell her. I can't. It's definitely happening—I've just made an offer on the perfect place a few miles from Jonas'. But now's not the time. We're in a fucking bathroom, for Chrissakes, and there's probably a line of people waiting outside the door. And, anyway, my move is happening a whole two months from now, maybe even three. I should probably wait another month or so before I tell her and we start making plans.

"Come on, PG," I say. "Let's go see if Lucy's torn Jonas limb from limb yet, or if she's at least left the poor guy with a stump to stand on."

Kat pulls herself together and smooths down her blouse. "Oh my God, I can't wait to see that woman's face when I suggest we three leave together." She does a little shimmy. "This is gonna be the best porno *ever*."

Chapter 35
Kat

"Thanks again for the ride, Sarah," I say, flopping onto my couch. "Sorry if I pulled you away from valuable study time."

"No, I needed a break," Sarah says, plopping herself down next to me. "There's only so much a girl can read about *mens rea* and *caveat emptor* before she starts to go a little cuckoo for Cocoa Puffs."

"Well, thanks. It's awesome to see you. You've been studying like a banshee lately."

"I love how adding 'like a banshee' to anything makes it totally next level," Sarah says, laughing. "I don't even know what a banshee is or what the hell one does in real life."

"Hell if I know. I think they scream?"

"And study for law exams, apparently."

"Well, whatever they do, those damned banshees put their entire heart and soul into it, every time, that's for sure."

We both laugh.

"So when do exams finally start? Seems like you've been studying every minute since Vegas."

"Next week," Sarah says. " I've got exams Monday through Thursday. And then on Friday Jonas is whisking me away to an undisclosed location. He says he's taking me somewhere really special, but he won't tell me where."

My heart swoons vicariously for her. She's gonna flip out.

"So things are good between you two?" I ask.

Sarah absently touches the platinum bracelet around her wrist. "Things couldn't be better. I didn't know I could love someone this much. It physically *hurts*—like I'm literally straining my heart muscle."

286

I bite my lip. "I'm so happy for you."

Sarah smiles sheepishly. "Thank you. I'm happy for me, too. So tell me about you and Josh. You guys were on fire in Las Vegas. Like, kerzoinks. Whenever we were all together, I kept looking around for fire extinguishers, just in case."

I laugh.

"You like him?"

"Yeah, I'm gone—*Gone, Baby, Gone*. I'm Ben *and* Casey Afflecked."

Sarah squeals. "And Josh? Is he *Gone, Baby, Gone*, too?"

"Well, all signs point to yes. Not all *words*, mind you, but all signs. I've definitely gotta read the tea leaves a bit when it comes to Joshua William Faraday."

Sarah rolls her eyes. "Those Faraday boys sure weren't raised to talk about their 'fucking feelings.'"

I sigh wistfully. "You can say that again."

"Aw, sounds like you're a smitten kitten," Sarah says.

I twist my mouth. "Sarah, I'm not smitten. I'm head over heels in love with him."

Sarah's eyes widen. "Holy crappola, girl. I've never heard you say that before."

"I've never said it before. But I am."

"Have you told him?"

I shake my head. "I've told him he's the sexiest man alive. And that I think he's awesome and I'm addicted. But we certainly haven't traded the magic words—we haven't even called each other boyfriend and girlfriend yet." I roll my eyes. "It's the weirdest thing. We're so intimate on the one hand—so close and open and honest and connected—it's insane how connected—and yet we're so closed off in some ways. Like there are these unwritten rules." I shrug. "I don't know how to explain it."

"I get it—believe me—more than you know. Well, have you had the whole 'let's not date other people' conversation, at least?"

"Yeah. But not in the usual way. It came up through this weird back door."

Sarah grimaces.

"Oh, Sarah. You and your fear of anal." I laugh. "I wasn't being literal. I meant it came up because we were talking about doing all sorts of freaky sex-stuff and we decided to be exclusive for that. It wasn't like, 'Oh, darling, my heart simply can't beat without you. I'm ready to take our intimate and budding romance to the next level.'"

Sarah makes a commiserating face. "Same with Jonas. He invited me to be the 'sole member of The Jonas Faraday Club.' He never said, 'Let's be exclusive.' Everything's always in code with that guy. But, really, is there some official way a guy's supposed to ask to be exclusive? It all gets you to the same place in the end, right?"

I shrug. "Yeah, that's true. And he did say he doesn't want anyone touching me. He said it makes him crazy to think of someone else with me."

"Well, see? There you go. He's telling you. And he flew you down to L.A. for a long weekend, and now he's up here to see you the very next weekend. That sure screams 'girlfriend' to me."

"Under normal circumstances, I'd agree. But I don't know for sure."

Sarah grabs my hand. "Kat, you're overthinking it. I saw you two in Vegas. The chemistry is through the roof. He's totally into you."

"I know he is. He's made that clear. I'm not blind. It's just that our relationship is so sexual—which is fan-fucking-tastic, don't get me wrong. But I just can't tell if it's all about the sex and excitement and here-and-now for him or if he wants something more. You know, something a bit more permanent."

"Here's a crazy idea: just ask him. Talk like adults."

"Pfft. Yeah, because that's what *you* did, right? I seem to recall Jonas not saying the three magic words after Belize and you were like, 'I don't need no stinkin' magic words. He told me in a super-secret code and that's just great with me.'"

Sarah makes a face. "That's true. I did say that."

I motion like she's just made my point.

"Okay, I get it," Sarah says. "Well, then. Here's a different approach. How about you get yourself stabbed in a bathroom at U Dub? That'll jumpstart a conversation about your fucking feelings in a New York minute."

"Hey, there's an idea. Why didn't I think of that?"

"God only knows if Jonas ever would have told me he loves me if external forces hadn't intervened."

"Well, I'm gonna pass on getting stabbed, thank you very much. But how about this as an 'intervening external force': Josh is meeting my family on Saturday night."

Sarah squeals. "No way. Really? You're sicking the Morgan clan on the guy? Holy hell, now that's a frickin' 'intervening external force' every bit as powerful as a hitman in a bathroom. Holy hell, the guy doesn't stand a chance coming out of that night all in one piece. By the end of the night, he'll be like, 'Just tell me what you want me to say! Please! I'm sorry!'"

I laugh. "I know, right?"

Sarah looks thoughtful for a minute. "You know, I really wouldn't get too hung up on expecting Josh to say certain words or make conventional promises to you. If Josh is anything like his brother, then he's way more fucked up than you even realize. I think their childhood was just utterly crippling in a way we can't completely understand. I've got my own issues, for sure, as you know, and they *pale* in comparison to what Jonas has had to overcome in his life."

A vision of Josh's "overcome" tattoo suddenly leaps into my mind.

"Even with all my fucked up stuff, I always had my mom, teaching me how to love," Sarah continues. "Who did Jonas and Josh have? I don't think either of them has ever learned the first thing about how to express emotion or love in a healthy way. They literally don't know how to love or be loved."

I process that for a moment. "When we were talking about my mom, he said, 'I've never actually witnessed a wife roaming in its natural habitat.'"

Sarah laughs. "Josh said that?"

I nod.

"Poor Josh." Sarah touches her platinum bracelet again. "Same with Jonas. He doesn't understand conventional, fairytale commitment. We never talk about the future or make any long-term plans. He's just not *capable*. He'll never, you know, ask me to marry him or anything like that—and I totally accept that."

I can barely keep a straight face.

"I just take what I can get in the here and now and that's enough for me. But I trust him with my life and I've learned to just let go and enjoy what we have. Jonas has already promised me forever the way he knows how," Sarah continues. "He gave me this engraved bracelet and he's got a matching one—and he got tattoos in my honor—one in Spanish and one in English." She chokes up. "The most beautiful and poignant words you ever saw." Her eyes are brimming with tears. "And that's enough for me. More than enough." She wipes her eyes and smiles.

I squeeze Sarah's hand, smiling to myself. Of all the tattoos I babbled off-the-cuff about being "lame" and "prohibited" to Josh, the "girlfriend" tattoo is by far the one I regret the most. It's absolutely awesome—whether the relationship winds up working out long-term or not. I was such a fool. "You can't get much more 'forever' than a guy getting a tattoo for you," I say. "Florebblaaaaaah," I add.

"Floreblaaaaaah?" Sarah asks.

"That's as close as Josh comes to saying that word."

Sarah laughs and wipes her tears again. "Maybe you can just decide to 'hear' what Josh is telling you with his actions, and not get too bogged down in needing particular words or assurances?" she suggests. "Maybe he'll never give them to you, Kitty Kat. Maybe he just *can't*." She wipes her eyes again. "I'm a firm believer that actions speak louder than words, anyway. And from what I can see, Josh has been screaming about his feelings for you from the rooftops."

"Thank you, Sarah." I exhale. "You're right. I'll do my best to just be happy about right now and not look forward. Unfortunately, I'm not nearly as patient or kind as you are."

"Well, you might not be as *patient* as me but—"

"I'm not."

Sarah laughs. "But you're every bit as kind. You've got a heart of gold, my sweet. Just tap into that golden heart and cut Josh a bit of slack. He's damaged, you know—just totally fucked up—but he's also a sweetheart. Just listen to his actions and forget about ever hearing the words. He's a freaking Faraday, after all. Normal rules don't apply."

My cheeks flush. "Thanks, Sarah."

We stare at each other for a moment, smiling.

"So, I gotta know," Sarah finally says. "What the *eff* was the dealio with tonight? Jonas left, saying he was taking you for drinks because Josh wanted to act out an imaginary-porno with you? What the fuck?"

I blush. "That's how Jonas described it?"

"Yeah. I was studying so I was like, 'Have fun, dear.' And then after he left, I looked up from my book and I was like, 'Wait. Did I just hear that right?'"

I laugh. "Yeah, Josh and I like to get a little freaky-deaky. But don't worry, Jonas was just our ignorant pawn—an unwitting extra in our movie. No Jonas Faradays were harmed in the making of our imaginary porno."

"So what was the plot of this imaginary porno? And what was Jonas' part in it, if you don't mind me asking? Did he 'come to fix the kitchen sink' wearing a huge tool belt?"

I giggle. "No. Jonas' part was *very* G-rated, I assure you."

"You're making me very intrigued—and very uncomfortable."

"No, I swear. It was harmless." I laugh. "I have this fantasy— well, I *had* this fantasy—I've now officially checked it off the list— that I'm on a date with some boring guy, like, you know, a guy I met online named *Blane* or whatever, and—"

"*Blane?*" Sarah says, aghast. "Blane's not a *name*—that's an appliance!"

"Exactly!"

We share a long laugh.

"I love Ducky," Sarah says.

"So, anyway, *Blane* and I are at a bar, and while poor Blane is babbling about something excruciatingly boring, I catch eyes with the hot bartender and it's like ka-boom."

"It's on like Donkey Kong."

"Exactly. So I excuse myself to go to the restroom and on my way I slip a note to the bartender—you know, total slut move—"

"Total."

"He meets me in the bathroom and fucks the crap out of me and then I return to my date like nothing happened."

"Oh my God. *Hawt.*"

"Isn't it?" I shudder. "So hawt. Gah."

"And extremely freaky-deaky."

"This coming from a girl who processed sex club applications?"

"People weren't nearly that creative in their applications, believe me. You'd be shocked how same-same people are. Most people aren't hankering to star in imaginary-pornos. They just want their dick sucked by a pretty girl."

I laugh. "Sarah," I say. "So unlike you to talk like that."

Sarah bats her eyelashes. "Jonas is bringing out my dirty girl lately. I'm spinning out of control."

"Good. It's about time."

"So my sweet Jonas was Boring *Blane,* huh?" She makes a frownie face. "That's so mean—you guys are such meanies."

"I didn't do it to him. Josh arranged everything. Jonas just showed up on my doorstep and handed me a poker chip."

"A poker chip?"

"Oh. Yeah. That's Josh's code for 'Let the imaginary-porno begin.'"

"Oh my gosh. You guys are crazy."

I shrug. "I told you. We're freaky-deaky."

"Well, I'll have you know Jonas isn't boring," Sarah says, sniffing the air. "He's really funny and smart and very, very interesting. In fact, Jonas is the most interesting person I've ever met."

I laugh. "I believe you. It wasn't me who cast Jonas as Blane—it was his mean brother." I make an apologetic face. "Are you mad?"

"*Mad?* No! I'd much rather you cast my boyfriend as the date you ditch than the hot bartender you screw in a bathroom."

We both laugh.

"Speaking of which, did you snag your hot bartender or what?"

"Of course. He didn't exactly play hard to get."

"Was he actually tending bar or just sort of standing near the bar, pretending?"

My eyes blaze. "Oh, he was actually tending bar, all right."

"Really? Wow."

"I don't know how he arranged it—the guy's a magician—but when Jonas and I got there, Josh was behind the bar serving drinks like effing Tom Cruise in *Cocktail.* In fact, there was one woman who was just about ready to jump his bones."

"Oh. You made mincemeat out of her, I imagine."

"Of course."

"Oh, Kitty Kat."

"Meow."

Sarah giggles. "What bar was it?"

"Oh, you're gonna laugh. *The Pine Box.*"

Sarah throws her hands over her face. "No!"

"*Yes.* The whole time I was having flashbacks to when you and I watched Jonas with that bitch."

Sarah shakes her head. "Why would Jonas take you *there*?"

"Actually, it was really sweet. While we sat there on our date, he gave me a detailed play-by-play of when he first saw you behind that stupid menu."

"He did? Aw." Sarah visibly swoons. "Jonas is so sweet."

"Well, yeah, he might be sweet, but he's a date from hell. What guy goes out on a date and babbles the whole time about falling in love, sight unseen, with another girl? What a jerk. Who could blame me for screwing the hot bartender in the bathroom?"

Sarah makes a truly ridiculous face. "I can't believe you had sex in the bathroom at The Pine Box."

"Aw, come on now. Don't be a Judgy McJudgy-pants, girl. I thought you said Jonas has been helping you find your dirty girl. Trust me, there's nothing wrong with engaging in a little bathroom sex on occasion. You should try it some time, little Miss Goody Two-shoes. You might like it."

She snickers. "Well, gosh, thanks for the tip, Kitty Kat. Maybe I will. One day. If I can muster the courage."

There's a beat. Sarah's the absolute worst at playing it cool. She looks like a cartoon character with a secret.

I smirk. "So I take it from that ridiculous expression on your face you and Jonas have already had some über-hot bathroom-sex, huh?"

Sarah bursts into hearty, snorting laughter and her face turns bright red. "At The Pine Box!"

Chapter 36
Kat

I'm absolutely screaming with laughter.

Henn and Hannah are onstage right now, delivering a straight-up *redonk* karaoke version of "You're the One That I Want" from *Grease*. I knew these two would be magic if I could get them together, I just knew it, but even I couldn't have predicted how truly destined for each other they'd be. John Travolta and Olivia Newton-John have absolutely nothing on these two in the made-for-each-other department. They're utter perfection.

I hear Sarah squeal with laughter to my right and I glance at her. She's dancing in her chair and singing along as she watches Henn and Hannah onstage.

God, this is the best night ever. Better than any fantasy.

Yes, being Josh's million-dollar whore was pretty damned exciting; and, yes, having him pick me over a supermodel felt pretty damned good; and, of course, being bound and fucked in a sex dungeon was freaking hot, too; and yesterday's tryst in the bathroom with that Hottie McHottie-pants bartender was ridiculously scorching, not to mention the look on that woman's face when I emerged from the bathroom and left with two hot guys. But, as titillating and sexy and hilarious as all that stuff has been, none of it is what I thought about while missing Josh and getting down with my battery-operated boyfriend this week. Nope. When I crawled into my empty bed at the end of each long and lonely day this past week, aching for Josh a thousand miles away in Los Angeles, I fantasized about one thing and one thing only: Josh making love to me to that James Bay song.

And today at work, whenever my mind meandered to daydreams of Josh (as it so often did), what did I dream about (besides the way he made love to me last week to that James Bay song)? Sex dungeons? Bartenders? Ski masks? Nope. I thought about how excited I am to introduce him to my family tomorrow night. And to sing the "Fish Heads" song at the fish market—an activity we've planned for tomorrow, perhaps after a leisurely brunch (after we've spent our first night together in *my* bed).

I lean into Josh's shoulder and breathe in his scent and he wraps his arm around me. I look up at him and grin and he beams a heart-stopping smile at me.

When Josh picked me up at my apartment two hours ago, dressed to kill in a trim black Armani suit and sunglasses, I immediately checked out his palms, expecting to see him carrying a poker chip. But, nope.

"No poker chip?" I asked as we waltzed down the walkway hand-in-hand toward his car.

"Not right now. But you never know when a sneaky guy might whip one out, so you better keep on your toes, Party Girl."

I peel my attention off Josh's striking face and watch Henn and Hannah singing the final lines of their song. Man, they're killing it. They're milk and cookies. Bert and Ernie. Macaroni and cheese. *Peanut butter and jelly.* I lean into Josh's shoulder again and squeeze his hand and he squeezes right back.

Maybe Sarah was right. This is enough. I've been overthinking. I don't need promises. All I need is the way I feel right now.

Henn and Hannah traipse happily off the stage toward our table, getting high-fives and cheers from everyone they pass, while a large guy with a bushy beard assumes the stage to belt out "Living on a Prayer."

"Utter brilliance," Josh says when Henn and Hannah plop themselves down.

"You're definitely tied for best of the night with Josh and Kat," Sarah agrees. "You both can actually sing."

"As opposed to *me*, is that what you're saying?" Josh says, laughing.

"No, that's not what I'm saying. Your performance was brilliant, Joshy Woshy. You didn't just *sing* your parts, you told the truth with every goddamned word."

Josh laughs and re-enacts his repeated "turn around" refrain from "Total Eclipse of the Heart," which Josh and I performed together earlier in the night to raucous applause from the entire bar.

"Hey, at least I'm a better singer than Jonas," Josh says.

"Josh," Jonas pipes in. "Don't congratulate yourself on being a better singer than me. I'm literally tone deaf—hence the reason you'll never catch me doing karaoke."

"Love, what you lack in actual singing ability, you make up for with the heart of a lion," Sarah says. "But yeah, the lead singer of our group's boy-band is definitely Henny. I didn't know you could sing, Henn."

"Yeah, I sang in an *a cappella* group at UCLA."

I exchange a smile with Josh. Why am I not surprised about that? That's so damned Henn.

"But I'm chopped liver compared to Hannah," Henn continues. "I sing like a choir boy, but she's got true *soul*. You should hear her singing Beyoncé in the shower. Sexy."

Hannah pushes up her glasses and busts out the chorus of "Say My Name." "Queen Bey better watch her back, that's all I'm sayin'," she says. And then she snorts.

"I love it when you sing," Henn gushes. "You're *amazing*."

I exchange a smiling look with Sarah. Oh man, that boy's in love.

Hannah giggles. "Henn. You think everything I do is *amazing*. I made you buttered toast the other day and you said it was the best toast you'd ever had."

"Well, it was—just the perfect amount of butter. It was even better than amazing—it was *schmamazing*."

We all laugh, though I personally have no idea what the hell that means.

Henn looks at all of us with puppy-dog eyes. "And you should see how well she draws *anime*, too. And she makes the best chocolate chip cookies you've ever had. They melt in your mouth."

Oh my God. It's all I can do not to leap across the table, grab Henn's lapels and shake him like you're not supposed to shake a baby. The boy's *in love*! It makes me feel as gooey as a fresh-baked chocolate chip cookie.

"Chocolate chip cookies, computer coding. Same-same," Hannah says. "Both take equal amounts of genius."

"You can't eat *code*, baby. I'll take the cookies. *Hey*. There's a hacker-pun in there somewhere, I'm sure of it." He snickers. "So, anyhoo, we've already seen Josh and Kat's spectacular rendition of 'Total Eclipse of the Heart,' which was legendary, by the way, guys, and now Banana and I have stopped the earth rotating on its axis for approximately four and a half minutes with what can only be described as sob-inducing spectacularity—so what are you two planning for our delight and entertainment?" Henn says, looking at Jonas and Sarah. "I'll die a happy man if I get to witness you sing karaoke, big guy."

"I don't do karaoke, like I said," Jonas says evenly, swigging his Scotch. "I can't sing for shit. I'm not in the business of embarrassing myself—at least not on purpose."

"Oh, baby," Sarah purrs, stroking his forearm. "You have a beautiful voice." She leans in and whispers something to Jonas and he grins broadly. He looks up and quickly catches the attention of the waitress across the room.

I lean into Josh. "The countdown clock just started on Jonas singing tonight."

Josh leans his lips right into my ear. "What's the over-under on how long it takes Sarah to get him up there?"

Josh's hand is on my bare thigh, making my skin buzz with every touch of his fingertips. His cologne smells divine. His eyes are a scorching blue. I feel intoxicated, though I've barely had a sip of alcohol. I feel drunk on Josh.

"Come on, PG. Give me your prediction."

"I'm not gonna say an amount of time," I say. "I'm gonna go with the number of Scotches, instead."

"Ooh, good call. How many?"

"Two more tops, and then he's gonna be singing like a tone-deaf canary."

"Two *on the outside*, huh? That's pretty ambitious."

I shrug. "That's the over-under. So you're betting *over*, then?"

Josh grins broadly and runs his hand up my thigh, right up to the hem of my mini-dress, making my skin erupt in goose bumps. "I've learned my lesson, babe. I'll never bet against you as long as I live. If you say two Scotches is all it's gonna take to get my brother up there, then that's what it'll take."

The "Living on a Prayer" guy leaves the stage and we're treated to three adorably silly women launching into a heartfelt rendition of Wilson Phillips' "Hold On."

The waitress approaches our table. "Hey, folks," she says. "Another round?"

Josh looks pointedly at everyone, gathering drink orders, and I shake my head, signaling I'm good. For some strange reason, alcohol just isn't hitting the spot tonight.

But Josh doesn't seem to understand my headshake. "Yeah, sure," Josh says absently to the waitress. "Another round. Plus Patron shots for everyone, too, please. With limes."

"And a club soda," I add. "Please."

"And a couple bottles of champagne, too," Jonas adds. "We're celebrating tonight."

"Oh yeah?" the waitress asks. "What are we celebrating?"

"Oh, just, you know," Jonas says, pulling Sarah into him, his face bursting with pure happiness. "*Life.*"

Oh, jeez, those two. I've never seen two people more madly in love. I wish so badly I could watch Jonas pop the question to Sarah next week in Greece. I'd bet dollars to doughnuts she's gonna lose functionality in all four limbs and flop on the ground like a freshly caught trout.

The waitress leaves and Josh leans back in his chair, adjusting his dick in his pants. God, he's a sexy dude. Gotta love a man in a designer suit whose dick is so big, it won't fit comfortably inside his pants.

"Well, Jonas might be celebrating *life,*" Josh says, "but I've actually got a few specific things I'd like to celebrate tonight." He raises his old-fashioned and the rest of us follow suit, holding up our various drinks. "First," Josh begins, "I wanna celebrate Hannah officially joining our *Ocean's Eleven* crew. Welcome, Hannah. You fit right in."

"Thank you," she says, pushing up her glasses.

"We all have our roles to play, Hannah," Josh continues. "So now that you're officially part of the crew, I'd like to christen you our cookie-baking Olivia Newton-John."

Hannah nods. "Wow. Thank you. I accept my role with humble gratitude. What's everyone else's roles?"

"Well, he's the asshole," Josh says breezily, motioning to Jonas. "And also the comic relief, though hardly ever intentionally."

Sarah laughs.

"Sarah's our George Clooney—our fearless leader—and also Jonas' handler. Without Sarah, Jonas becomes very, very cranky—so I'd like to take this moment to expressly thank Sarah Cruz for coming into my brother's life. By doing so, you've made mine immeasurably better." Josh beams a huge smile at his brother, and, much to my surprise, Jonas laughs heartily.

"Thank you," Sarah says, blushing. Jonas kisses her cheek and I swoon.

"Henn's our fucking genius, of course," Josh continues. "I'm sure that's not news to you, Hannah—plus, the guy's heart has a ten-terabyte storage capacity." He flashes Henn an adoring look.

"Yes, I'm well aware of that," Hannah says.

The look on Henn's face is priceless. Oh my effing God. He's adorable.

"And you and Kat?" Hannah asks. "What are your roles in the crew?"

"Well, unfortunately, I'm nothing but a playboy—just coasting on everyone's coattails, pretty much—not particularly useful or smart—just the eye candy of the group."

We all laugh.

"Don't listen to him. He's wise and powerful beyond measure," I say.

"Oh, well that's true," Josh agrees. "Hannah, you might as well learn it now: I'm wise and powerful beyond anything your feeble mind could possibly comprehend. Let me just say, in advance of whatever pearls of wisdom I'll bestow upon you one day in the near future: you're very welcome."

Hannah laughs. "Okay. Thank you, Josh, in advance. Wow, I'm honored to be in your presence."

"As you should be. Thank you. And Kat here—well, the list is too long to say it all right now, but I'll give you the Cliff's Notes version. She's our secret weapon. The Party Girl with a Hyphen who also happens to be The Party Girl with the Heart of Gold. Plus, she's a suicide bomber, a terrorist, and, sometimes, if you really rile her up, a very stubborn cat."

I giggle.

Josh chuckles and squeezes my hand. "And, she's got the best laugh you ever heard, as I'm sure you already know. The girl laughs like a dude."

"I'm well aware."

I giggle again.

"Hey, I have an item for the toast," Jonas says.

"Hang on, bro," Josh says. "I'm not done with Kat." He looks into my eyes. "She's loyal. And honest. A force of nature when she wants something. She loves her family. And her hair smells incredible."

I can't breathe.

Josh holds my gaze for a long beat. "There's more, but we'd be here all night," he says softly. He kisses me tenderly on the lips and my heart bursts out my chest cavity and zings around the bar.

"I wanna salute Sarah for making it through her first year of law school..." Jonas is saying. But I'm only half-listening. I'm caught in an alternate universe with Josh. Yes, Sarah was absolutely right. He's screaming his feelings for me from every mountaintop the best way he knows how. And that's enough for me.

"Well, jeez, don't jinx me. I gotta get through my exams before I'm toast-worthy," Sarah says.

I manage to peel my eyes off Josh's face and look at Jonas and Sarah, clasping Josh's hand.

"But you finished your classes yesterday," Jonas says. "No reason not to celebrate that." He grabs her hand and kisses the top of it and she melts.

"Can I add an item to the toast-list, too?" Sarah asks. "I wanna toast Henn and Kat for officially becoming *mill-i-on-aires* this week. Congrats, guys."

"Didn't you get your finder's fee money this week, too?" Henn asks.

"Yeah." Sarah beams a smile at Jonas. "But I can't even think what to do with it—I want for absolutely nothing these days."

Henn and I shoot a look at each other like that's the stupidest thing either of us has ever heard. I'm glad Sarah's googley-eyed in love and all, but who couldn't use an extra million bucks, for crying out loud?

"Yeah, congrats to all three of you," Josh says. He grabs my hand and kisses it the way Jonas just kissed Sarah's hand, making me swoon, and raises his drink to me. "Which reminds me of a biggie. To Kat. She officially took a leap of faith today and quit her job to start her own PR firm. Congrats, babe. Sky's the limit."

Everyone expresses congratulations and excitement.

"I'm so excited for you," Hannah says. "Even though I'll miss you terribly." She sticks out her lower lip.

Of course, I'm not blindsiding Hannah with this news—I told her about my plans earlier today at lunch, and she was full of congratulations and excitement then, too, but she also cried. "Working with you has been the best part of my job," she said.

"Well, like I said at lunch," I say to Hannah, "the master plan is to bring you on as soon as humanly possible, Hannah Banana Montana Milliken," I say. "As soon as I know what I'm doing, you'll be my right-hand woman."

Hannah raises her drink. "Cheers to that. Just call me and I'll come running, girl. Whatever you touch turns to gold, Kitty Kat—I have no doubt your new company will be golden, too."

"Thank you, honey."

The waitress returns with our new round of drinks, plus the shots and bottles of champagne, and we pour bubbly all around.

"What are you gonna call your new company?" Henn asks.

"PGPR?" I say without confidence—but even as I say it, it sounds pretty lame. "Short for Party Girl PR," I add, hoping that clarification makes the name more palatable.

Sarah scrunches her nose.

"You don't like it?" I ask.

"Kinda stodgy, don't you think? A little boring—and you're anything but boring."

I twist my mouth, considering. She's got a point.

"It's not an accounting firm, right?" Sarah asks. "It's publicity. It's gotta have some pizzazz."

"Yeah, at first I thought maybe Party Girl PR—but that sounds too much like an event planner."

"Yeah, you're right—it kinda does. Hey, but you're the Party Girl *with the Heart of Gold*, right? Hannah just said everything you touch turns to *gold*. Why not Golden PR? You could have a sexy golden-blonde avatar of yourself as your logo. That'd be adorable. Or, hey, better yet, maybe even Golden Kat PR and make your logo a sexy golden cat with long eyelashes."

I look at Josh and he nods enthusiastically. "Either one. Probably have more luck securing Golden Kat for trademark purposes."

"Great idea, Sarah," I say. "I'll look into that."

Sarah smiles. "You bet, baby. I got a million ideas." She taps her temple. "I'm at your service, baby."

"Thank you."

We grin at each other.

"Okay, everyone, get 'em up," Josh says—and we all raise our glasses of champagne. "To Hannah and Henn, and to Sarah for finishing her first year of law school, and to three newly minted *mill-i-on-aires*, and, last but not least, to Kat and her new baby." Josh looks at me, his blue eyes sparkling. "YOLO, Kat—I'm glad you've decided to go for it. May you climb and conquer."

"Hear, hear!" we all shout, bringing our champagne to our lips.

"Wait!" Sarah blurts and we all stop. "*Duh.* We gotta toast Climb & Conquer!" She raises her shot of tequila. "This one we gotta do with Patron, in Joshy-Woshy's honor."

Everyone raises a shot glass.

"To Climb & Conquer," Sarah says. "I can't wait to watch the Faraday twins 'climb and conquer' every peak of their dreamscape."

Jonas and Josh share a look of unmistakable excitement.

"Hear, hear," everyone says, clinking glasses.

"Please hire me soon, Kat," Hannah adds and everyone laughs.

"I'm so proud of you," I whisper to Josh, squeezing his hand.

"Thanks," he says, his blue eyes sparkling. "I've never been so excited about anything in my life."

As everyone throws back his or her shots, I put my glass down, untouched. Just the smell of the tequila is making me kinda queasy. Maybe it's something I ate?

Josh kisses my cheek. "To new beginnings," he says softly into my ear. He grabs my tequila and downs it for me, seemingly unfazed by my disinterest in it. "And to giant leaps of faith." He kisses my lips and rubs my cheek with his thumb. "I missed you this week, PG. I was going out of my mind."

Boom.

That's it.

Put a fork in me.

My body can't physically contain these feelings any longer. This sexy beast of a man's got me hook, line, and sinker. I'm gonna tell him how I feel when we're alone later tonight. I can't take it anymore. I love him and I've got to tell him so, come what may.

Sarah leaps up suddenly, pulling gently on Jonas' muscled arm. "You ready, hunky monkey boyfriend?" she asks. "The alcohol has started to kick in—it's time for you to pay your debt."

Jonas grimaces—but Sarah's persistent. She pulls on his arm again, flashing a seductive smile. "Come on, love," she purrs. "You lost fair and square and you know it." She leans into Jonas' ear again and whispers something, and Jonas begrudgingly stands and lets her lead him toward the stage.

Josh flashes me a look of pure astonishment. "You were right."

"Of course, I was. I'm always right when it comes to two things," I say.

Josh chuckles. "Men and PR, I know, Party Girl." He gazes at his brother for a beat. "Look at him," he says, motioning toward Jonas and Sarah taking the stage. "God, he must really love that girl."

Chapter 37
Josh

This is officially the most entertaining thing I've witnessed in my entire life.

Jonas and Sarah are doing a God-awful rendition of "I Got You Babe" by Sonny and Cher. Sarah's actually pretty good—she really comes alive up there. But Jonas is so fucking terrible, the entire bar is on its feet, cheering him on. But why am I surprised? Even when Jonas sucks at something, people love him for it. In fact, now that I think about it, I'm pretty sure people love Jonas *especially* when he sucks at something, not despite it.

How Sarah gets my brother to do any of the shit she gets him to do is beyond me. But there he is, standing in front of strangers, singing this ridiculous song to her at the top of his off-key lungs. And, by God, he actually looks like he's having fun. Well, fun mixed with pain—utter, tortured, unthinkable pain. But with Jonas, that's just about the best anyone could ever hope for.

I put my hand into my pocket and finger the edges of the poker chip sitting there. Now would be a fantastic time methinks. We're all nice and loose. I look at my watch. We're not due at the laser tag emporium for another hour. All is going perfectly according to plan.

"Excuse me for a second," I say, unclasping my hand from Kat's. She doesn't bat an eyelash—apparently too enthralled with the train wreck unfurling onstage to care about where the heck I'm going.

I move across the room to the karaoke DJ, wading through clapping, screaming, hooting people, all of them hurling love with both arms at Jonas and Sarah, and make my way to the DJ.

"Hey, man," I say. "You ready to do that thing we talked about?"

"Whenever you are, bro."

"Okay. How about you do one song after Sonny and Cher for whoever else and then we launch into my thing?"

The DJ grabs the piece of paper I slipped him earlier (along with a fat tip that ensured there'd be no waiting all night long for anyone in our group). "This still what you want me to say?" he asks, looking at the short script I gave him.

"Yeah. Hey, can you hand me that scarf I stashed earlier?"

"Sure." He grabs the scarf behind him. "Fucking hilarious, man," he says, handing it to me covertly. "You think she's gonna ham it up? Or will she chicken out?"

"Oh, my girlfriend never chickens out about anything—it's not in her DNA. Did you see her doing 'Total Eclipse of the Heart'? She'll ham it up for sure."

"Cool. Okay. One more song after Sonny and Cher and then we'll do it."

"Thanks." I stick the scarf in the waistband of my pants, hidden by my jacket.

The guy looks up at Jonas and Sarah, singing their adorkable hearts out, and chuckles. "Man, this guy's *horrible*—absolutely atrocious. Pretty much the worst I've ever heard and I've been doing this a really long time."

I look at my brother and grin. He's totally outside his comfort zone right now—sweating bullets, moving across the stage like a gorilla with hemorrhoids. God, he's awesome.

Out of nowhere, my stomach clenches vicariously to think about what he's about to do next week. He's taking a huge fucking step— the hugest step known to mankind—but, damn, he sure looks happy. Hard to argue a guy off doing anything that makes him smile that fucking big.

"Yeah, he's terrible, huh?" I say. "Gotta love him."

I head back to our table, my fingertips toying with the poker chip in my pocket, and sit back down next to Kat. She's clutching Henn's forearm, tears of laughter streaming down her cheeks.

Jonas and Sarah reach the slow finale of their song and the entire place erupts into a standing ovation.

When the song is done, Jonas dips Sarah dramatically, kissing her like no one else is in the room, and she comes back up red-faced and giggling.

The waitress pays another visit to our table. "Another round?"

"Yeah," I say absently. "Why the fuck not?"

Jonas and Sarah make their way back toward our table while two young, toker-looking guys get up onstage and start singing "American Pie."

"Awesome, bro," I say to Jonas when they return to our table and plop themselves down. "I can die a happy man now."

"Never again," Jonas says. "That memory's gonna have to last you your whole life long."

"How the fuck did you get him up there, Sarah Cruz?" I ask.

Sarah shrugs. "I'm magic, Josh Faraday."

"Sarah and I had a little bet and I lost," Jonas says. "I'll never bet against her again, I swear to God."

I look at Kat and she flashes me a smart-ass grin, obviously telling me, "See? Never bet against a woman."

"What was the bet?" Kat asks.

"Oh, the details aren't important," Sarah says. "But let's just say I held onto my title in the underwater breath-holding Olympics."

We all look at each other and make a face. Clearly, this is a sexual innuendo of some sort, and God knows we don't wanna know.

"Well, you were awe-inspiring, big guy," Henn says.

"Hey, Kitty Kat, you haven't gone in a while," Hannah says. "What are you gonna sing next?"

"Oh, I dunno. You wanna do another duet, Josh? A little 'Islands in the Stream,' perhaps? Or am I flying solo?"

"Yeah, a duet for sure," I say, the hair on the back of my neck standing up. I can't let Kat go up there again and ruin my little plan. "But let's give it another song or two, okay? I've got drinks coming for us."

Kat leans back. "Sure. So, hey, Henny, how long are you in town? You and Hannah wanna do dinner with Josh and me Sunday night before Josh heads to the airport?"

"Sorry, leaving tomorrow. I've got a job in Munich, actually." He looks at Hannah. "But after that I'll be home in L.A. for a good long stretch. Maybe you and Hannah can come visit Josh and me together and we can all go out in La La Land?"

Kat looks at Hannah for confirmation. "Great," she says.

"Hey, maybe you should think about opening Golden PR in Los

Angeles instead of Seattle," Hannah suggests. "Maybe you could do PR for the entertainment industry."

"Well, that'd be pretty stupid," Jonas pipes in, sipping his Scotch.

"What would be stupid?" Henn asks, clearly feeling defensive on behalf of Hannah. "Sounds like a great idea to me."

"No, I mean, it'd be stupid for Kat to move to L.A.," Jonas clarifies. "What would be the point of Kat moving to L.A. right when Josh is moving back home to Seattle in a couple months?"

Fuck me. My stomach lurches into my throat and my eyes bug out. This isn't the way I'd intended to tell Kat about my upcoming move. Shit. I didn't even think to warn Jonas I hadn't told Kat about the move.

"What?" Kat asks, her eyes blazing with instant excitement. She whips her head to look at me. "Is he serious?" She clutches her chest, obviously overcome. "*You're moving to Seattle?*" She's practically shrieking with joy.

I open my mouth to speak, but nothing comes out.

"For good? You're moving here... for good? To *live*?" Yep, full on shrieking. She's acting like she just won the showcase showdown on *The Price is Right.*

"Yeah. Um. I'm moving home. Just got a place."

She's bouncing happily in her seat. "When? This is *awesome.* A dream come true."

"In a two or three months, probably."

"Really? Oh my God. Why didn't you tell me? Did you just decide today? Why didn't you tell me? This is incredible news. Oh my God. I'm elated."

"You didn't know?" Jonas asks, his face etched with obvious confusion.

Kat takes in the expression on Jonas' face and her entire demeanor changes on a dime. *Boom.* She knows something's up. Just like that. Thanks, Jonas.

"No, he didn't mention it to me," she says slowly, her eyes drifting warily to mine. "Why didn't you mention it to me, Josh?" she asks, her tone edged with obvious apprehension. "Were you planning to... surprise me?"

Oh shit. This isn't good. This is really, really bad. "Uh..." I begin.

"How long have you known?" she asks quietly, understanding dawning on her. "You said you already found a place?"

Shit. I've totally fucked up here. I've really, really fucked up.

"I've known for just a little while," I say. "Let's talk about it later, okay?"

She swallows hard. "How long have you known, Josh?" Her lip trembles.

I look at the group. They're all staring at me.

"Did you know when I said that thing about the long distance thing being brutal? Did you know then?"

Shit. "Let's talk about it later, babe," I say, trying to sound charming and smooth. "Don't get all worked up about it. I was just waiting until it was for sure."

A strange cocktail of emotions flashes across her face in response to that comment—like she's not sure whether to be extremely disappointed or relieved. "Oh, it's not for sure? That's why you didn't tell me?"

"Well, no. Actually." I swallow hard. "It's for sure. I'm moving."

"Oh." She shifts in her seat. Her cheeks flush. "That's great. So you've already made... plans? You've got a place?"

"Let's talk about it later. What's everyone planning to sing next?"

The entire bar is boisterously singing along to the final chorus of "American Pie." But I feel anything but festive. My stomach is churning. My chest is tight.

"Have you put your house on the market yet?" Kat asks, her chin wobbling.

Oh shit. This is a catastrophe. Why didn't I foresee how badly this would go down?

"Uh. Yeah, actually, it sold last week."

"It already *sold*?" Her face turns bright red and her eyes prick with tears. "How long was it on the market?"

"Can we talk about this later. In private?"

"How long was it on the market?" she asks between gritted teeth.

"About three weeks."

The two "American Pie" guys depart the stage to raucous applause.

"And now," the DJ says into his microphone, reading from the piece of paper I gave him earlier. "I have a very special treat for you."

"Kat, we'll talk about it later, okay? Here." I pull the poker chip out of my pocket and plunk it into her palm. "Please. I'll explain everything to you later. Right now, I've got a surprise for you."

She looks down at the poker chip, her eyes filling with tears, and I know I just made matters worse, not better. Much, much worse. Oh Jesus. I'm an idiot.

I stand and motion to the DJ to tell him to stop, but he doesn't see me because he's looking at the fucking piece of paper in his hand—the paper I gave him and asked him to read into his goddamned microphone.

"We unexpectedly have a superstar among us tonight, folks," the DJ says, reading from my script. "The one and only *Rachel Marron*."

People at nearby tables are looking at each other quizzically, clearly not recognizing the name.

"Poor Rachel's endured some death threats recently, so she's here with her devoted and stoic *bodyguard* Frank Farmer—former Secret Services detail for the President of the United States."

There's a tittering in the crowd. People are starting to get it.

I look at Kat and my heart squeezes. "Babe," I say. "Please don't leap to conclusions. It's not what you think. Just enjoy the poker chip."

"Under Frank's watchful eye, Rachel's agreed to sing her signature song for us. A heartfelt rendition that's sure to make you weep."

The place is going crazy all around us.

"I don't understand why you didn't tell me. You already sold your house. You didn't want me to know you were moving here?"

"So let's hear it for Rachel Marron everyone!"

Everyone in the bar hoots and screams.

"You're not excited to live in the same city with me? To see each other every day? You don't wanna go to the dry cleaners and the fish market?"

"Looks like she's feeling shy, folks. Let's get her up here, huh? To perform her classic hit, 'I Will Always Love You!'"

The place explodes with excitement.

But Kat looks like a wounded deer in headlights right now.

My heart is breaking. What have I done?

"Babe, you're totally misunderstanding the situation," I say. "I'll tell you all about it later. Right now it's poker chip time. Enjoy it. This is your biggest fantasy."

"Come on, Rachel!" the DJ calls. "Come on up here with your bodyguard!"

Kat looks down at the poker chip in her palm, a pained look in her eyes, and it's abundantly clear acting out her bodyguard fantasy is the last thing on her mind.

I pull the scarf out of my pants and hold it up, trying to make her smile. My heart is beating a mile a minute. I've fucked up. Oh, fuck me, I've royally fucked up. I've got to get control of the situation. Make it better. I've got to charm her back to being Happy Kat.

"Remember the last scene of the movie—when Whitney wears the scarf on her head?" I coo. "I brought the scarf for you, babe. So you could look just like her."

Kat's dumbstruck. She looks at the poker chip in her hand again, tears filling her eyes.

"Kat, come on—be my Whitney, baby. I've got it all planned. We're doing the song here and then I rented an entire laser tag place for the six of us. It'll be everyone else against you and me, baby, all night long—I'll protect you. *I'll be your bodyguard.*"

"Rachel?" the DJ says. "Are you coming or not? Your fans are waiting. Last chance."

"Sing here, then laser tag, and then I'll take you home and let my feelings override my stoic sense of duty." I smile, trying my damnedest to charm her.

"Rachel? Last call."

She abruptly snatches the scarf out of my hand, wraps it around her head a la Whitney, and marches in a huff toward the stage, determined.

Thank God. She's playing along. This is gonna be okay. That's my girl. She'll understand when I explain it to her. She'll totally understand. I let out a huge sigh of relief, slide my sunglasses on, and follow my beautiful Whitney to the stage, my heart pounding in my ears.

Chapter 38
Kat

Everyone in the place is cheering and banging on their tables. But I'm in a daze. I can't think straight. Josh is moving to Seattle? That's incredibly awesome news. I'm ecstatic about it. *But why didn't he tell me about it?* Was he planning to surprise me—the way he burst into his bathroom wearing a ski mask?

Josh places a chair at center stage for me—and I position myself onto it exactly the way Whitney sits on a chair in the snow in the music video—and then Josh fusses with the scarf around my head, making it Whitney-with-a-broken-heart-on-the-private-airplane-perfect, and everyone in the place laughs and hoots, totally loving the set-up. When he's done with me, Josh turns to the audience and makes a big point of sweeping the crowd for snipers and wackjobs—and everyone slurps him up like a tray of Jell-O shots.

The music starts.

I'm in automatic pilot. I've heard this song ten million times. I don't even need to think to sing it.

There's got to be a logical explanation why Josh didn't tell me about his move that has nothing to do with him intending to break up with me when he moves here. He had to have his reasons. Good reasons. The fact that he didn't tell me doesn't mean he doesn't want to be with me. There's got to be another logical reason. But I can't think what it could be. What other reason could there possibly be except that Josh doesn't want to be with me when he moves to Seattle?

Tears fill my eyes. Why doesn't he want to be with me? I want to be with him more than anything. More than I want literally anything else. I think it's fair to say I want to be with Josh more than I want to breathe.

I pick up the microphone.

Maybe he was just gonna surprise me with the news—and Jonas let the cat out of the bag? But, no. I saw Josh's face when Jonas spilled the beans. He didn't look like a guy whose happy surprise got unwittingly spilled by his brother. He looked like a guy who just got busted on something—a guy whose cover just got blown.

The teleprompter begins scrolling the words to the song, and, even though I have no desire to sing it right now, my mouth begins half-heartedly mumble-singing the first lines. But the words are slaying me. They're too close to home. They're about Whitney having no choice but to leave her lover. She loves him, but she's got to go. It's just the way it is.

Everyone's cheering uproariously. As far as they're concerned, I'm giving the performance of a lifetime—an emotion-packed Whitney-tribute.

I yank the scarf off my head. Fucking scarf. Why the fuck am I doing this? I don't want to role-play a freakin' fantasy right now. I wanna talk to Josh in real-life. I wanna know why he didn't tell me.

The teleprompter reaches the words of the chorus—the words I've been singing at the top of my lungs in the shower since I was ten years old.

I look at Josh. He's standing stock-still, no longer playing his part. He's looking at me with the same expression he had when I opened my door to him in Las Vegas after reading his application.

My eyes drift to the teleprompter again, though I certainly don't need it to know the lyrics.

I can't sing these words to Josh. Not like this. These are sacred words—magic words. The words I'd planned to say to Josh later tonight when we were all alone in my bed.

The words I'd planned to say when I thought Josh loved me, too, but just didn't know how to say it. And now, suddenly, I realize he doesn't feel the way I do.

Without conscious thought, I toss the scarf into the air, letting it flutter to the ground, bolt out of my chair, and sprint out the front doors of the bar, ugly tears streaming down my face.

Chapter 39
Josh

"Kat!" I yell. She doesn't turn around. The night air is chilly, but my skin is blazing hot. This is a fucking catastrophe. "Kat!" I yell again, my voice strained.

She whips around to face me, heat wafting off her skin. "Why didn't you tell me?" she blurts, tears streaming down her cheeks.

My heart is physically pained at the sight of her. I grab her shoulders, desperate to make her understand. "You're blowing this way out of proportion. Just listen to me, okay?"

"You put your house on the market three weeks ago—you've obviously known for a while."

I exhale. "I only decided for sure about a month ago."

She throws up her hands.

"But I'm not moving for two or three months," I say. "I can't move until I've got everything squared away with Faraday & Sons."

Her expression is a wicked combination of devastation and fury.

"I didn't wanna say anything until it was closer," I say soothingly. "That's all. I was gonna tell you. Just *later*."

She clenches her jaw. "Why?"

"Why what?"

"Why wait 'til later to tell me?"

"Because I didn't want you to get your hopes up if..." I stop. I can already tell this isn't gonna go over well. Oh shit. I'm fucked.

"If what?"

I pause.

"If *what*?"

"If things didn't work out. Between. Us."

There's an excruciating silence.

"Let me see if I understand this," she says. "Standing here right now you're not one hundred percent sure you wanna be with me *two months* from now?"

I throw up my hands. "Well, shit. When you say it like that, it sounds horrible. But, yeah, I just wanted to wait until I was sure I wasn't gonna get your hopes up and then somehow, you know, disappoint you."

She blinks and huge, fat tears streak out her eyes and down her beautiful cheeks.

"Kat, please," I say, my voice quavering. My eyes are burning. I close them and compose myself for a beat. "It's no reflection on how I feel about you. I think you're amazing. And gorgeous. Funny. Smart. Sweet. I think about you night and day—that's why I came to Seattle early. I've never had so much fun in my life as I have with you."

Oh shit. Something I just said lit her fuse—and not in a good way.

"*Fun?*" she spits out, utterly enraged.

I roll my eyes. "Did you hear anything else I said? *Fun* was the very last thing I said—*after* saying a bunch of other really awesome things. And, by the way, saying you're fun is a huge compliment."

"Oh, thanks for the compliment. Makes me feel *great*. You can always count on Kat for a little *fun*." She wipes her eyes, but it's pointless—tears are streaming out.

I look up to the night sky and roll my entire head in frustration. This is so fucking horrific. I can't believe she's overreacting like this. She's so fucking temperamental, I swear to God. "This is spiraling way out of control," I say. "How much have you had to drink? Are you drunk?"

"No, I'm not drunk. I've hardly had a drop."

"Well, you're acting drunk."

"I'm not drunk. I'm pissed. And hurt. Deeply hurt."

"Why the fuck are you 'deeply hurt'? I'm sorry I didn't tell you I'm moving, but I'm not gonna apologize for saying I'm having *fun* with you—because I am."

"I was gonna bring you home to meet my family, Josh," she says, her eyes watering and her voice cracking. "I obviously can't do that if all we're doing is having *fun*."

"What the fuck? You're not gonna let me come meet your family now? You're *uninviting* me from the birthday party?" Now I'm pissed. That goddamned party is the whole reason I flew the fuck up to Seattle in the first place.

She's in full terrorist mode. "I've brought a grand total of three guys home to meet my family, Josh. *Three.* And the last one didn't work out so well. Colby sniffed Garrett out like a St. Bernard tracking a lost skier. Colby knew Garrett was with me for nothing but *fun* while I was in it for a whole lot more. I'm not gonna subject myself to that ever again."

I'm speechless. She's comparing me to Garrett Bennett? She thinks I'm *using* her? Could she possibly believe that, after everything we've been through together? After everything I've said and done to make my feelings clear?

"That was such a low blow," I say between gritted teeth.

"Why is that a low blow? You can't imagine dating me eight measly weeks from now," she seethes. "Fifty-two *days*. My family would know you're not in it for the long-haul—especially Colby—and they'd eat you for breakfast."

"Shit, Kat. Motherfucker. I fucked up, okay?" My voice cracks. I press my lips together, regaining my composure. I wait. My eyes are stinging. I take a deep breath and push everything down. "I should have told you, okay? I'm sorry. But you're reading way too much into this. I'm not Garrett-Bennetting you. You can't seriously believe that."

She shrugs.

"What did that fucker say to you, again?"

"He said I'm *fun*."

"No, the other thing."

"He basically called me a slut."

"But what were his exact words?"

She shifts her weight. "He said I'm not 'marriage material.'"

I close my eyes and shake my head. I'm an idiot. This is Kat's Achilles' heel—her Kryptonite—and I've served it up to her on a silver platter.

"Listen to me, babe." I grab her shoulders and look into her eyes. "I never said I don't wanna be with you eight weeks from now. All I said was I can't make promises about the future. But that's only

315

because nothing's for sure *in life*—it has nothing to do with you, personally. That's a factual statement. Anything can happen. But right now do I *want* to be with you? Yes. So bad it hurts—that's why I came to Seattle early."

Yet another battery of tears springs into her beautiful blue eyes.

"Kat, please, trust me. I'm crazy about you. It's just that, except when it comes to business, I take things a day at a time. It's all I can handle—" I have to stop. If I say anymore, I'm gonna lose it. My eyes are burning.

"I don't wanna be some kind of glorified booty call," she says softly.

"*What?* Did you hear a word I said? I think maybe you're clinically insane. Or maybe you're PMSing or something because that's the furthest thing—"

She makes a sound that can only be described as prehistoric, making me stop dead in my tracks.

"I'm *not* PMSing! I'm crying because you hurt my frickin' *feelings*—not because I have ovaries. You're the one who can't imagine dating me fifty-two freakin' days from now, so don't try to worm out of your assholery by playing the PMS card!"

Her nostrils are flaring. Her eyes are wild. She looks like a fucking dragon.

"Oh my fucking God," I say. "You're overreacting. Again."

"No, I'm not overreacting. You didn't tell the girl you're supposedly 'addicted to' you're moving to her frickin' city in eight weeks! How'd you expect me to find out? By bumping into you at Whole Foods?"

I look up to the sky, biting my lip. She's pissing me off. I should have told her, yes, but she's making mountains out of molehills. "Yes, Kat. You guessed it," I say. "I was gonna wait to tell you until after we'd bumped into each other at Whole Foods."

She abruptly turns around and marches away from me. "I'm going home," she says.

I roll my eyes at her backside. Her purse and phone are inside the bar and I'm the one who drove her here. How the fuck does she plan to go home? *Déjà fucking vu.* We might as well be in another hotel hallway right now. For a split second, the image of her dripping wet ass cheeks stomping down the hallway after Reed's party flashes across my mind and I smile. She's a handful, this one—never a dull moment.

"Wait," I command.

She doesn't wait.

"*Wait.*"

"Enjoy living in Seattle," she tosses back to me over her shoulder. "Hope you have *fun.*"

"Oh my God. The drama," I say. In five easy strides, I've caught up to her. I grab her shoulders and turn her around and kiss her. Without hesitation, she presses herself into me, throws her arms around my neck, and surrenders to me.

I always say, when it comes to women, especially angry ones, there's very little that can't be fixed with a fucking awesome kiss.

We stand together, kissing like crazy for several minutes, both of us bursting with desire and emotion and arousal.

"I just don't understand why you didn't tell me," she whispers, abruptly pulling away from me. "I would have been bursting at the seams to tell you if the situation were reversed. You would have been the first person I would have called."

My heart drops into my toes. When she puts it like that, I suddenly understand why she's so upset. "Babe," I say. "I'm just not wired to make promises about the future, that's all. My brain doesn't work like a normal person's."

"I'm not asking for promises about the *future*—you think eight weeks from now is 'the future'?" Kat shakes her head and steps back from our embrace. "I'm not thinking clearly. You kiss me and I lose my mind. That's always been my problem around you. I'm so physically attracted to you, I can't think." She rubs her forehead. "I think we need to take a step back. Slow things down. I think we need to find out if we actually like each other in real life. Obviously, you're scared shitless this thing between us won't translate to living in the same city—and maybe you're right." She swallows hard. "Maybe we should trust your gut."

"*What?*"

"We've been living in a weird sort of fantasy from day one," she continues. "First we were in Las Vegas doing our *Ocean's Eleven* thing and now we fly to see each other on weekends so we can role-play imaginary-pornos and get stoned. Everything with us is nonstop excitement—*fantasy*. We never do normal, real-life stuff like play a board game or go to the freakin' grocery store." She shrugs. "Maybe you're just addicted to excitement, and not to me, specifically. Maybe none of this is real."

My blood is pulsing in my ears. "Kat, no. Everything I've ever said or done when I'm with you is real. Always. Even our fantasies are real—that's what's so awesome about us—real life is a fantasy when it comes to you and me."

"Your move to Seattle is for sure?" she asks softly.

"Yeah. I made a cash offer on a place yesterday. It's ten minutes away from Jonas' place."

Kat's face contorts. "I just can't believe you didn't mention that to me—especially after how many times I've said the long distance thing is killing me or I wish we lived in the same city."

"I'm sorry. I was just... " I don't finish my sentence. There's really no adequate way to explain why I didn't tell her. I'm suddenly realizing I'm a complete idiot.

She sniffles. "I get it. Sarah told me to listen to your actions and not your words. Well, I guess I just heard you loud and clear. From here on out, I'll expect nothing from you. We'll continue to have *fun* with no expectations and no promise of a future. We can date other people, whatever. We'll start from scratch. Get to know each other outside all the excitement and fantasy."

"You wanna date other people?" I blurt, my heart exploding with panic.

"No," she says quickly. "Not at all. I don't want anyone but you." Tears flood her eyes. "That's what I've been trying to tell you."

"Well, I don't want anyone but you, either," I say. I clutch her to me, relief flooding me. If she'd said she wanted anyone but me, I would have lost my shit. "Kat, we both feel exactly the same way." I kiss her temple. "Please don't read into me not telling you. It doesn't mean anything—we feel the same way."

"I don't think we do, Josh. I don't think you realize how much... " Her words catch in her throat. Tears spill out of her eyes. "If I'd bought a house in L.A.," she says, "I would have been *thrilled* to tell you about it. I would have talked your ear off about it."

"Kat," I choke out. "You're breaking my heart. I feel the way you do. I'm just not good at... saying certain things. I'm not good at committing to certain things. But that doesn't mean I don't *feel*. Please, Kat. I just need time, that's all."

Kat wipes her eyes again. "I get it. Take as much time as you need. You're not ready for a commitment of any kind. Good for me to know—better I learned it now than later." She wipes her eyes and sets her jaw. "Obviously, I can't take you home to meet my family tomorrow. I'm sure you understand."

"No, I don't understand. I really wanna meet your family—I'm *dying* to meet your family."

"I'm sorry. It's not possible—not when my heart is on the line like this."

A little voice inside my head is screaming at me to tell her my heart is on the line, too, but the words don't come. I swallow hard, forcing down the lump in my throat again.

There's an awkward silence.

Her eyes are glistening with obvious hurt.

"Kat," I finally say. "Maybe I should have mentioned it. I just... Please believe me—you're my fantasy sprung to life."

Her jaw tightens. "Yeah, I'm the fantasy you don't want 'tainting' your real life when you move back home."

Shit. That was a not-so-subtle reference to my application to The Club, wasn't it? Yeah, it was. *Because I don't want this shit to taint my real life,* I wrote in my application. Oh, God, this is a complete disaster.

"Kat, no," I say. "You're not a Mickey Mouse Rollercoaster. Now you're just being crazy. Please don't do this. You're spinning out of control."

"I'm not doing anything but agreeing with you. From here on out, we're gonna do things Josh-Faraday-style. The future doesn't exist. There are no expectations, no commitments. All we have is right now. *YOLO.*" Her lip is trembling. "If I wanna stay, I'll stay. If I wanna go, I'll go. There'll be nothing to keep us tied to each other but however the wind blows on any given day. *Just the way you like it.*"

Chapter 40
Josh

I flip on the TV in my hotel room and quickly turn it off again.

What's wrong with me? Am I really *this* fucked up?

I told Emma the magic words, didn't I? Which means I'm capable of saying them. But Emma gave me a lot more time than this—ten times more time than this.

But what am I thinking? There's no comparison between Kat and Emma. I never felt this white-hot passion with Emma—this *electricity*. How the hell does Kat expect me not to fuck up when I constantly feel like I'm gripping a goddamned electric fence around her?

I get up and look out the window of my hotel room, a glass of Jack Daniels from the mini-bar in my hand. I've got a perfect view of the Space Needle from my room. It's lit up like a Roman candle at night.

I could have stayed at Jonas' house tonight, of course, but I was too embarrassed not to be staying with Kat to ask him. Plus, Jonas looked so happy tonight, I didn't have the heart to bring him down with my pathetic sob story. Jonas is the one who's supposed to cry like a big fat baby to *me*—our relationship doesn't work the other way around.

"Let's take a break for a couple days—see how we're feeling then," Kat said when I walked her to her door earlier tonight. "Maybe I'll realize I'm overreacting; maybe not. I'm just too hurt to think straight right now. I think I need some time to regroup and figure out what I'm feeling."

I take a swig of my whiskey, shaking my head. How did things go so wrong? I was on top of the world when I picked Kat up tonight.

I couldn't wait to see her—the same way I always feel when I'm away from her. I couldn't wait to take her to the fish market tomorrow morning to sing the "Fish Heads" song with her like a couple of dorks. And I was losing my mind about meeting her family tomorrow night, too. And, most of all, I was chomping at the bit to fuck her on her Hello Kitty sheets.

And now it's all gone. *Poof.* And here I am, yet again, where I always am, sitting in yet another hotel room, another drink in my hand, looking out at yet another lonely cityscape.

I turn on the TV and flip the channels. Sports. Local news. I flip around and around and finally land on a music station. Lenny Kravitz is singing "Fly Away." Hey, at least something's going right for me tonight.

I sit down in an armchair in the corner, lean back with my whiskey, and listen to the song. Yeah, Lenny, I agree: let's fly away to anywhere but here—you and me, bro—to a place without stress and responsibility and worry. A place where I won't have this thousand-pound weight on my chest at all times—a place where I won't feel so fucking *lonely* all the time. And so fucking *guilty.* To a place where I'm not constantly being crushed by shit I can't control and feelings I can't express and memories that haunt me.

I run my hands through my hair. I've never thought of this song as sad before, but, motherfucker, it's making me wanna cry. Fuck this shit. I turn the channel to the next music station, only to run smack into "Little Lion Man" by Mumford & Sons. They're in the midst of singing the chorus and it's like they've written the words for me. Kat told me her heart is on the line tonight, didn't she?—and I really, *really* fucked it up.

Jesus.

I take another huge guzzle of my whiskey and stare at the Space Needle.

The torturous song ends, thank God—but there ain't no rest for the wicked: the next song is Adele. She's wailing her heart out in "Someone Like You." And kicking me square in the balls.

I take a gigantic gulp of my whiskey.

No, Adele, I'll never find another woman like Kat. Fuck you. She's a fucking unicorn, Adele. One of a kind.

I rub my forehead and look out the window with burning eyes.

Goddammit, I fucked up—maybe even irreversibly. I didn't realize it at the time, but tonight was a fork in the road for Kat and me and I took the wrong path. I should have told Kat about my move to Seattle in the first place, for sure, but even more than that, I should have handled things differently tonight when the shit hit the fan. I should have said all the right things—the things Kat was dying to hear.

But I didn't.

I imagine myself saying, "My heart's on the line, too, Kat." Damn, I should have said that to her. Or, at the very least, "Mine, too."

But who am I kidding? Kat didn't want to hear me say my heart's on the line—she wanted more than that. She wanted the magic words—the whole nine yards. And I let her down.

I drain the rest of my drink and pour myself another tall one.

Jesus. Adele's voice is cutting me like a thousand razors dragged across my heart.

Kat wanted a promise of forever from me tonight. It was written all over her face. But what she doesn't understand is there's no such thing as forever—I mean, shit, there's no such thing as *next week.* Anything could happen. Nothing's guaranteed. A guys' life can change in a single afternoon. I mean, hell, a guy might go out to a football game with his dad in the morning and come back later that day to find out no one will ever sing "You Are My Sunshine" to him again. Or call him Little Fishy. Or, worst of all, say the words, "I love you."

I take a long swig of my drink.

"No, son, they don't let kids go to the morgue," my father said. "You'll just have to say goodbye to her in your prayers, son."

"But I wanna say goodbye to her face and kiss her lips and tell her I love her. Not like in a prayer. For real."

"You can't do it to her face—you have to do it in a prayer."

"But I wanna see her face when I say it. Not like talking on the phone."

"Fine. Shit. I dunno. Then say it to her photo, then."

"But I don't have a photo of her."

"Well, Jesus Fucking Christ, Joshua William. Fine... Take this one. Your mother always loved this photo of the three of you. Say everything to her face in the photo and stop talking about it. I've got my own goodbyes to say, son—we're all hurting, not just you. I'm sorry but I can't talk about this anymore."

My eyes are stinging. I rub them and take another long gulp of my whiskey.

Kat wants me to promise her fifty-two days? Shit. I can't even promise her tomorrow.

Because a guy might go to school one morning and then return home that afternoon to find out his dad had shipped his brother off to a "treatment center" without even letting him say goodbye. And just to add insult to injury, the guy's dad might even say his brother will "never come home again" because "that boy's fucking crazy" and "we're better off without him" and "you need to stop crying about him like a little fucking baby."

Motherfucker.

I drain the last of my drink, refill my glass, and settle into my chair again.

What's the point in putting anything on the calendar at all when a guy could get called at a football game because his dad's brains have unexpectedly exploded all over the carpet in the study? And not only that, his brother's lying in a hospital bed, not talking or responding to anyone, after driving himself off a fucking bridge? When a guy could sit in his big, empty house in the dark, right after the cleaning crew's finished scraping his dad's brains off the ceiling, and fight tooth and nail to convince himself that marching into his father's bathroom and taking every fucking pill in the medicine cabinet is a terrible idea rather than the best fucking idea he's ever had?

I swallow hard, keeping my emotions at bay, and take another long sip of my whiskey.

Kat wanted to hear those three little words tonight—I know she did. But those are words I simply can't deliver to her. Not yet, anyway. If only she'd give me more time. If only she'd understand. I said those loaded words to Emma and look what happened—the relief of saying them for the first time lulled me into saying other things, too—things I shouldn't have said—and only a month after I'd first said the magic words, Emma was long gone. *I love you,* I told her. *Please don't leave me. Please.*

But she left.

I bought myself a fucking Lamborghini after Emma left me—so what am I gonna buy myself this time when the girl doing the leaving is my fantasy sprung to life? A jumbo jet?

Fuck me.

I look down at the glass of whiskey in my hand and, suddenly, a rage wells up inside me like a fucking tsunami. Fuck *overcoming*. Fuck this shit.

Fuck me.

Without a conscious thought in my head, I hurl my glass against the wall, shattering it into a million tiny pieces and spraying glass and whiskey all over the white fluffy bed.

My chest is heaving. My eyes are stinging. I rub them and force down my emotion. Fuck you, Adele, you fucking bitch. No, I won't find someone like Kat. I'll never find someone like her again as long as I fucking live. I'll be alone and lonely and fucked up and worthless—just like I've always been. Just like I'll always be.

Forever.

Chapter 41
Kat

Whitney's sitting in her private jet, a scarf wrapped demurely around her head, looking out the airplane window at Kevin standing out on the tarmac, his arm in a sling.

Why is Kevin's arm in a sling? Because he took a bullet for Whitney. *Because he loves her.* And she loves him, too. But the horrible tragedy is that, despite their love, even though he took a freaking bullet for her, they simply can't be together. And they both know it. Because they're from different worlds, after all. And life isn't always fair, motherfucker. But the injustice of it all only makes their love more intense—harder to give up.

Whitney yells to the pilot to stop.

The jet engines abruptly stop and the airplane-steps come down. Whitney runs out of the private plane to Kevin and throws her arms around him. They kiss passionately.

And the most gigantic ugly cry ever released in the history of ugly cries leaves my mouth. "Josh!" I sob, throwing my head back onto the throw pillow on my couch. "Jooooosssssshhhhhh!"

Oh, I talked such a good game in front of the karaoke bar, didn't I? "From here on out," I said, "we're gonna do things Josh-Faraday-style. The future doesn't exist. There are no expectations, no commitments."

But I was full of shit.

I love him. With all my heart and soul. I don't want anyone but him.

I know he's 'crazy about me.' And that he's done a million amazing things for me, just like Richard did for Julia in *Pretty Woman.* Yes, just like Julia, I've been showered with gifts and money and offers to help me in countless ways—and, I suppose, for most women, all of that would be more than enough. But I'm not most women. I'm just like Julia—I want it all. I want a commitment. I want true love. I want a knight in shining armor on a white horse. Goddammit, I want more than *florebblaaaaah.* And I simply can't pretend I don't.

I clutch my stomach and put the pint of Ben & Jerry's I've been scarfing down onto the coffee table. I'm so worked up about all this, I feel physically ill. Queasy. And my nipples are sore, too, by the way, which is really weird. I know Josh pinched my nipples pretty hard yesterday when he fucked me in the bathroom at The Pine Box, but did he really pinch them *that* hard? Jeez. They still hurt.

Whitney's glowing face appears onscreen in close-up, her teeth a spectacular shade of computer-paper-white, her mocha skin flawless.

She begins singing The Song—the most famous song in the world.

Oh, God, she's an angel. My beautiful Whitney.

And I'm a sobbing mess. *Again.*

This song was written for Josh and me and no one else. I love him and he doesn't love me back. He's crazy about me, sure—addicted to me. But he can't promise me tomorrow, he says. Which is a telltale sign he's not in love with me. Because when you love someone, you're willing to promise forever, even though you intellectually know you can't make that promise. You don't *not* promise forever to the one you love simply because we're objectively mortal—you promise it, regardless, and hope forever turns out to be more than fifty-two days.

No one knows what life might bring or what might happen two months from now, I get that, but the point is that when you're in love, you're stupid enough to think you can promise forever. You wanna believe it so badly, you're willing to tell that little white lie. And if you're not willing to tell it, well then, that's the surest way to know you're not really in love, after all.

Whitney's done singing.

I grab the remote control, and just that sudden movement makes my stomach flip over violently, almost like I'm gonna barf. But that's ridiculous. I hardly drank a drop tonight.

Out of nowhere, my body dry heaves.

What the hell? I cock my head to the side, totally perplexed. What the heck was that? My body heaves again—only this time, holy shit, fluid has gushed into my mouth.

I sprint off the couch into the bathroom, my palm clamped over my mouth, and only semi-make it to the toilet before another, violent heave makes me vomit up every drop of fluid and Cherry Garcia in my stomach, not to mention the chicken wings and guacamole I ate at the bar.

Oh, jeez. Not pretty. Not pretty at all.

What the hell? I barely drank tonight.

I barf again.

Damn, I feel horrible.

Were the chicken wings bad? I wonder if anyone else is feeling sick, too?

I rinse out my mouth and clean the barf off the toilet seat and floor and shuffle back to my couch.

Damn, my nipples are hurting.

I can't imagine bad chicken wings would make my nipples extra sensitive.

I begin to nestle back onto the couch and grab the remote, but then all of a sudden, I sit up, tilting my head like a cockatiel. An alarming thought just skittered across my brain like a cockroach after the kitchen lights have been turned on.

No.

It couldn't be *that*.

I took a pregnancy test ten days ago and it was negative—and I haven't missed any pills since then. Have I? I don't think so. I didn't take them at the exact same time every day like you're supposed to, granted, but close enough.

I sprint back into my bathroom. The box of pregnancy tests I bought the other day had three pee-sticks in it, and I've only used one.

I pull out one of the unused pee-sticks, sit on the toilet, and pee on it, my heart racing. There's no effing way. That would be ridiculous. Unthinkable. I just quit my job with medical benefits *today*. Ha! No. God doesn't have that mean a sense of humor.

I sit and stare at the stick, waiting. One line means I'm in the clear. Two lines means I'm fucked six ways from Sunday.

I sit and wait.

I thought it was weird I almost barfed in the sex dungeon, but when I Googled "vomiting from intense orgasm," the Internet was littered with countless women who'd experienced the exact same thing. So I didn't sweat it.

"Don't you dare let me catch either of you *ever* making an accidental Faraday with a woman unworthy of our name or I'll get the last laugh on that gold digger's ass and disown the fuck out of you faster than she can demand a paternity test." That's what Josh said his father told him when he was barely a teenager.

The faintest second pink line begins to appear on the pee stick and my eyes pop out of my head.

"No," I say out loud. "Go away. Go away!"

The line is getting darker.

"No," I say, pulling at my hair. "Please, God, no."

This has to be a mistake. A false positive. Yes, that's what it is. A false positive. Of course. I run into the living room and grab my laptop. I Google "false positive pregnancy test" and it turns out there's no such thing, basically—except in cases of certain medication (no), defective test (maybe?), or, rarely, certain kinds of cancer. Is it wrong to be wishing I have cancer right now?

Okay, maybe the test was defective. That's my only hope.

I drink a couple glasses of water and sit on the couch, Googling like a madwoman for at least thirty minutes, trying to find a reasonable explanation for those two pink lines that doesn't involve a little Faraday growing inside me, and when I feel the tiniest hint of pee in my bladder, I run back into the bathroom and pee on the third pee-stick.

I would never try to trap you, I assured Josh. *I'm a millionaire now, Josh—I don't need your stinkin' Faraday money.*

Oh, I know you'd never do that to me, he assured me. *Of course, not.*

I look up at the ceiling, another massive wave of nausea slamming into me.

Within a minute, a second pink line appears on the new pee-stick. I stare at the two positive pregnancy tests lined up on my counter, my eyes bugging out of my head, my recent conversation with Josh echoing in my head. Oh God, Josh is gonna shit. He's gonna kill me, and then he's gonna shit.

And then he's gonna call me a gold digger.

And then he's gonna run away, his arms flailing.

And then he's gonna shit again.

My heart is aching.

This is a complete disaster.

Worst-case scenario.

"Shit," I say out loud.

I amble into my living room in a daze, clutching the two positive pregnancy tests.

I sit down on my couch, my eyes wide, my head spinning.

"Shit," I say again.

From the minute I laid eyes on Josh, I felt like I'd hopped aboard a bullet train.

Well, it looks like our train just jumped the tracks.

And now there's only one possible outcome.

Crash.

Acknowledgments

This book is for The Love Monkeys, my devoted and wonderful readers. Thank you for loving my characters as much as I do—and, therefore, loving me.

Author Biography

USA Today bestselling author Lauren Rowe lives in San Diego, California, where, in addition to writing books, she performs with her dance/party band at events all over Southern California, writes songs, takes embarrassing snapshots of her ever-patient Boston terrier, Buster, spends time with her family, and narrates audiobooks. To find out about Lauren's upcoming releases and giveaways, sign up for Lauren's emails at www.LaurenRoweBooks.com. Lauren loves to hear from readers! Send Lauren an email from her website, follow her on Twitter @laurenrowebooks, and/or come by her Facebook page by searching Facebook for "Lauren Rowe author." (The actual Facebook link is:

https://www.facebook.com/pages/Lauren-Rowe/1498285267074016).

Additional Books by Lauren Rowe

All books by Lauren Rowe are available in ebook, paperback, and audiobook formats.

The Club Series (The Faraday Brothers Books)

The Club Series is seven books about two brothers, Jonas and Josh Faraday, and the feisty, fierce, smart, funny women who eventually take complete ownership of their hearts: Sarah Cruz and Kat Morgan. *The Club Series* books are to be read in order*, as follows:

-*The Club* #1 (Jonas and Sarah)

-*The Reclamation* #2 (Jonas and Sarah)

-*The Redemption* #3 (Jonas and Sarah)

-*The Culmination* #4 (Jonas and Sarah with Josh and Kat)*
　　*Note Lauren intended *The Club Series* to be read in order, 1-7. However, some readers have preferred skipping over book four and heading straight to Josh and Kat's story in *The Infatuation* (Book #5) and then looping back around after Book 7 to read Book 4. This is perfectly fine because *The Culmination* is set three years after the end of the series. It's up to individual preference if you prefer chronological storytelling, go for it. If you wish to read the books as Lauren intended, then read in order 1-4.

-*The Infatuation* #5 (Josh and Kat, Part I)

-*The Revelation* #6 (Josh and Kat, Part II)

-*The Consummation* #7 (Josh and Kat, Part III)

In *The Consummation* (The Club #7), we meet Kat Morgan's family, including her four brothers, Colby, Ryan, Keane, and Dax. If you wish to read more about the Morgans, check out The Morgan Brothers Books. A series of complete standalones, they are set in the same universe as *The Club Series* with numerous cross-over scenes and characters. You do *not* need to read *The Club Series* first to enjoy The Morgan Brothers Books. **And all Morgan Brothers books are standalones to be read in *any* order.**

The Morgan Brothers Books:

Enjoy the Morgan Brothers books before or after or alongside *The Club Series,* in any order:

1. *Hero.* Coming March 12, 2018! This is the epic love story of heroic firefighter, **Colby Morgan,** Kat Morgan's oldest brother**.** After the worst catastrophe of Colby Morgan's life, will physical therapist Lydia save him… or will he save her? This story takes place alongside Josh and Kat's love story from books 5 to 7 of *The Club Series* and also parallel to Ryan Morgan's love story in *Captain.*

2. *Captain.* A steamy, funny, heartfelt, heart-palpitating insta-love-to-enemies-to-lovers romance. This is the love story of tattooed sex god, **Ryan Morgan**, and the woman he'd move heaven and earth to claim. Note this story takes place alongside *Hero* and The Josh and Kat books from *The Club Series* (Books 5-7). For fans of *The Club Series,* this book brings back not only Josh Faraday and Kat Morgan and the entire Morgan family, but we also get to see in detail Jonas Faraday and Sarah Cruz, Henn and Hannah, and Josh's friend, the music mogul, Reed Rivers, too.

3. *Ball Peen Hammer.* A steamy, hilarious enemies-to-friends-to-lovers romantic comedy. This is the story of cocky as hell male stripper, **Keane Morgan**, and the sassy, smart young woman who brings him to his knees on a road trip. The story begins after *Hero* and *Captain* in time but is intended to be read as a true standalone in *any* order.

4. *Rock Star.* Do you love rock star romances? Then you'll want to read the love story of the youngest Morgan brother, **Dax Morgan,** and the woman who rocked his world, coming in 2018 (TBA)! Note Dax's story is set in time after *Ball Peen Hammer.* Please sign up for Lauren's newsletter at www.laurenrowebooks.com to make sure you don't miss any news about this release and all other upcoming releases and giveaways and behind the scenes scoops!

5. If you've started Lauren's books with The Morgan Brothers Books and you're intrigued about the Morgan brothers' feisty and fabulous sister, **Kat Morgan** (aka The Party Girl) and the sexy billionaire who falls head over heels for her, then it's time to enter the addicting world of the internationally bestselling series, *The Club Series.* Seven books about two brothers (**Jonas Faraday** and **Josh Faraday**) and the witty, sassy women who bring them to their knees (**Sarah Cruz** and **Kat Morgan**), *The Club Series* has been translated all over the world and hit multiple bestseller lists. Find out why readers call it one of their favorite series of all time, addicting, and unforgettable! The series begins with the story of Jonas and Sarah and ends with the story of Josh and Kat.

Does Lauren have standalone books outside the Faraday-Morgan universe? Yes! They are:

1. *Countdown to Killing Kurtis* – This is a sexy psychological thriller with twists and turns, dark humor, and an unconventional love story (not a traditional romance). When a seemingly naive Marilyn-Monroe-wanna-be from Texas discovers her porno-king husband has thwarted her lifelong Hollywood dreams, she hatches a surefire plan to kill him in exactly one year, in order to fulfill what she swears is her sacred destiny.

2. *Misadventures on the Night Shift* – a sexy, funny, scorching bad-boy-rock-star romance with a hint of angst. This is a quick read and Lauren's steamiest book by far, but filled with

Lauren's trademark heart, wit, and depth of emotion and character development. Part of Waterhouse Press's Misadventures series featuring standalone works by a roster of kick-ass authors. Look for the first round of Misadventures books, including Lauren's, in fall 2017. For more, visit misadventures.com.

3. *Misadventures of a College Girl* – a sexy, funny romance with tons of heart, wit, steam, and truly unforgettable characters. Part of Waterhouse Press's Misadventures series featuring standalone works by a roster of kick-ass authors. Look for the first second of Misadventures books, including Lauren's, in spring 2018. For more visit misadventures.com.

4. Look for Lauren's third *Misadventures* title, coming in 2018.

Be sure to sign up for Lauren's newsletter at www.laurenrowe books.com to make sure you don't miss any news about releases and giveaways. Also, join Lauren on Facebook on her page and in her group, Lauren Rowe Books! And if you're an audiobook lover, all of Lauren's books are available in that format, too, narrated or co-narrated by Lauren Rowe, so check them out!

Lightning Source UK Ltd.
Milton Keynes UK
UKHW040626150319
339203UK00001B/148/P